The Soldier's Girl

The Soldier's Girl

Jean Chapman

PIATKUS

Copyright © 1997 by Jean Chapman

First published in Great Britain in 1997 by
Judy Piatkus (Publishers) Ltd of
5 Windmill Street, London W1

**The moral right of the author
has been asserted**

*A catalogue record for this book is available
from the British Library*

ISBN 0–7499–0372–4

Set in 11/12 pt Times by
RefineCatch Limited, Bungay, Suffolk
Printed and bound in Great Britain by
Bookcraft (Bath) Ltd

Acknowledgements

My thanks are due to Redruth library for their patient searching and copying of newspapers, transfer of books, etc. These gave me the official views and attitudes but more particularly I am grateful to Doris Ellis and her brother Sid Scott. Doris and Sid who now both live in St Just-in-Penwith, Cornwall, told me the real stories behind the facts.

Chapter 1

The long oval mirror on the front of her mother's wardrobe door was useless! Standing sideways, pulling her stomach in as hard as she could, the glass was so narrow Vi still could not see her complete outline. She bent her knees and arched her back to bring the profile of her bosoms into the widest part. Straightening slowly, she was forced to admit that beneath the boned bodice of the dance dress which she clasped to her naked chest there was not much to see.

Discreet padding, she decided as she turned and, lifting one shoulder towards her cheek, looked yearningly towards the mirror, the way film stars did on star-studded photographs in cinema foyers.

'Vi! You'll be late for work,' her mother shouted from the kitchen.

'For the office,' Vi corrected to her reflection, changing her pose from yearning to challenging. 'And *Miss Tulley*, if you please.' She bobbed a curtsey at herself, then pulled a face and mimicked the martinet tones of the senior partner's secretary. 'Miss Tulley! Bring the clients' ledger to my desk! Tea, Miss Tulley! You've neglected the ink pots, Miss Tulley. Stand on your head, Miss Tulley, and turn to gold, Miss Tulley.'

'Even that wouldn't please the old battle-axe . . . battleship.' She mentally red-inked the amendment like they did important totals in the ledgers. Miss Swanton was invariably plated in shiny, steel-grey dresses with matching hair marcelled into steep uniform waves. Work at Chase and Fieldman, Chartered Accountants, would have been a lot more congenial if it were not for the crotchety old spinster.

'Oh, Miss Swanton, I sure don't want to be like you. I want to go everywhere, do everything.' She threw her long bare arms out into the chill bedroom as if to reach and embrace all she yearned for. 'Life!' It was the only word that came near to her longing. 'I want to really live!'

Her pa said women like Miss Swanton had probably lost their men and their chances of marriage in the Great War. When she had complained about the 'old slavedriver', he had worked out that in the 1914–18 war Harriet

1

Swanton must have been about the same age as his daughter was now. He made her think. That was her pa.

'You want a fella, that's wot you want!' She adopted the voice and the sentiment of her fellow sufferer at the office. There was Roy. 'An excitin' fella!' She could hear Audrey's comment on the tail end of the thought. Audrey's belief was that 'an excitin' fella' was the answer to all a girl's problems. The way Audrey carried on sometimes, Vi thought it might well be the beginning of her friend's.

'I wouldn't mind a fling,' she murmured and immediately felt guilty about the ever-faithful Roy as she stepped on to the cold linoleum to pull the bedside mat back into place with her foot.

'Violet! It's quarter past eight!'

Downstairs, her young brother Sidney pushed his spoon to make a pathway through the middle of his porridge, then he subdivided it into quarters, revealing the much scratched pattern of bears playing hockey. He was forced to skim and eat a small section of porridge along one of his roadways to stop it closing up again.

Florrie watched the dark curls of her son getting closer and closer to his dish and shook her head slightly. As if aware of her scrutiny, he looked up. 'The Germans are winning,' he said as the porridge nearly reunited. He took two large and sweeping spoonfuls across the dish and grinned at her, mouth oozing oats.

Her heart thumped with an unexpected surge of love and concern for this boy born so unexpectedly ten years after their only other child. She reached to her back and tied the strings of her crossover apron tighter, as if her heart needed girding up against the burdens it carried.

Vi came flying downstairs, still buttoning up her tweed skirt and, in a more vigorous repeat of her mother's action, shook her head at her brother, as his large dark eyes regarded her with such adult solemnity.

'Wonder who got it last night?' he asked, repeating a phrase that was echoed in most East End houses after another night of the London Blitz.

'With my luck it won't be Chase and Fieldman,' Vi said and reached over to tousle Sid's hair, adding, 'give us y' curls!'

'You can 'ave 'em,' he replied darkly and swirled his remaining porridge into a new pattern, murmuring, 'It's the sea now.'

'What'll we do with 'im?'

'Call him Tiny Tim and stick him in the chimney corner,' Vi said dismissively as she pulled her one decent pair of stockings from the clotheshorse and concentrated on getting her seams straight.

Florrie mulled over the unconsidered aside and wanted to protest that Tiny Tim had been a little ailing child and if Dickens hadn't sent ghosts of Christmas to haunt old Scrooge, Tiny Tim would not have survived. Sid was fanciful but not sickly.

2

Violet glanced at her mother and realised from the stricken expression that she had said the wrong thing. 'No, perhaps not,' she said with a laugh at a new idea. 'We'll make *you* Tiny Tim and Sid can be the Christmas goose!'

Florrie made a token glance towards the swinging pendulum of the wall clock and pushed a cup of tea across the table. Vi's skill with figures had, twelve months before, brought her the offer not just to act as a clerk but to study for her accountancy exams and *qualify*. An astounding opportunity to Florrie's mind, certainly not one to be played fast and loose with.

Vi helped herself to one of the thick, uneven slices of toast her mother moved from hob to table. The cosy room was replete with the yeasty smell of crusty bread toasted golden brown before the fire. The gas stove installed in the cold back kitchen was abandoned in wintry weather in favour of the old black-leaded range in the kitchen proper. 'Was Pa on first shift?' she asked, thinking of him already out and about.

It was the early workers in London who braved the new obstacles: the unexploded bombs; unsafe buildings, blasted from being homes and work-places into jagged teetering ruins; pavements and roads holed or buried under huge waves of rubble by a further night of blitzkrieg. To drive the first bus was the Home Front equivalent of a reccy into no-man's-land.

'If we'd gone to the underground as usual, he'd 'ave been nearer the depot.'

Vi heard all the doubts in her mother's voice, all the wavering, the inner cross-questioning. It had been this same uncertainty, this second-guessing the right thing to do, which, two days before the Prime Minister's declaration that 'this country is at war with Germany,' had made Florrie agree to evacuate to Cambridge. Then, as separation from her beloved Harold had been accom-panied by lack of any air activity from the Boche, though definite antagonism and condescension from those they were billeted on, Florrie had found the train fare to bring them back to the East End in time for Christmas 1939.

With another Christmas only some five weeks away, Stepney, Poplar, Ber-mondsey, Southwark, Lambeth, Deptford, Shoreditch, Holborn and their own Bethnal Green had already taken the main weight of the enemy bombing.

'Ma,' she said gently, 'we all decided to take our chance, stay home after . . .'

The two exchanged glances. Flo sighed heavily and Violet glanced at the head bent over the dish, neither of them wishing to put into words Sid's almost miraculous escape.

He had been playing with two of his friends, the Arcott twins, on the way home from school at midday when the air-raid alarm had gone. Sid had begun to run with them to the Anderson shelter in their garden which was nearby. At the last minute he had changed his mind and came scuttling home as the bombs had begun to fall. Ma and he met head-on as they raced to find each other among a bedlam of exploding bombs, the clanging of firebells and

3

ambulances and the incessant hysterical barking of dogs. It had gone on all lunch time and so much shrapnel and debris was coming down in the streets, rattling on the slates, Ma and Sid just stayed in the house.

The all-clear had gone before the lunch hour was over and some of the top class had gone back to the junior school – but not the two brothers. An anxious neighbour, who had seen Sid with the Arcott boys, had come to the house, peered in at the door, and seeing Sid had drawn Florrie outside to tell her that the Arcotts had all been in their Anderson shelter in the garden which had received a direct hit. Ma had not as yet been in a shelter again.

'But are we doing the right thing?' she asked, her head shaking with the difficulty of the problem.

'Come on, Ma, don't worry. You know what they say – if it's got your number on . . .'

'I *do* worry,' Flo said earnestly. 'Not only does your pa have further to go to work but we could all be buried in that . . .' She gestured towards the shallow cellar, really no more than a deep cold pantry down five steps, where they had put mattresses along the wall.

'I know,' Vi said gently, 'but we weren't. We're all right as ninepence.' She put her arm over her mother's shoulders. She had been taller than her mother since she was twelve and at nineteen she was nearly as tall as the dark wavy-haired father she totally adored. Vi always thought their family paired up – mother with son, daughter with father. Harold was practical, decisive and Florrie was full of doubts and fancies like her son. 'Come on,' she repeated, 'you know Pa, he'll always get through.'

'Say that poem!' Sidney suddenly demanded.

'Talk about walls having ears! You're not missing much!'

'Go on, Ma!' he urged, ignoring his sister.

'For goodness sake, what poem?' Florrie asked teasing. 'Anyway it's the wrong time of day for *that* poem.'

He regarded her frowning, calculating. 'When our Pa goes to work early, 'e comes back early. It'd be nearly right. Go on, Ma.'

Florrie drew in a breath, pleased but self-conscious even in front of her children.

'And *do* it!' Sid added.

She let her breath expire in an exasperated gust but moved to the fire, took up the hearth brush and, standing with it poised above her head, began by first pointing to the clock:

> ' "The clock is on the stroke of six,
> And father's work is done,
> Sweep up the hearth and mend the fire,
> And put the kettle on." '

The first verse acted out, Florrie stood erect as if listening to the elements beyond the terraced house.

> ' "The wild night wind is blowing cold,
> Tis weary crossing all the wold.
> He is crossing all the world alone,
> But he is mightier than the storm,
> He does not feel the cold.
> His heart it is so strong." '

The final line was accompanied by a blow on her own skinny chest and the applause of the audience.

'Mightier than the storm,' Sid repeated. 'He is, our Pa, he is mightier than the storm.'

'Nothing stops Pa!' Vi laughingly agreed as she picked up the pigskin shoulder bag she was so proud of, a "starting work" present from Pa over four years ago.

'Last a lifetime,' he had said, 'and *then* make me a good nail bag!'

'Are you going dancing tonight?' her brother asked in his high clear treble.

Vi turned her back on their mother to scowl a warning at him, the frequency of her outings was often linked with a reminder to write to Roy, who was training with REME in the Midlands. 'I might,' she said, then turning added, 'it's only at the Co-op Hall. Audrey's going.'

'Do you like soldiers, or sailors, or airmen the best?' Sid asked, pushing the remaining porridge into islands.

Vi knew her brother well enough not to risk entering into any speculative discussion. 'Soldiers!' she answered decisively.

He nodded deeply as if acknowledging she had made the right choice.

'I'm off. See you teatime.'

'I'd give you my curls if I could,' Sid called after her.

'You're not a bad kid – for a brother!' Vi called back.

Outside, the November morning was bright but hazy. She could smell smoke and brick dust. Londoners, emerging from a night in underground stations, or Anderson shelters in their back gardens, or the metal Morrison 'table' shelters in their homes, sniffed the air to judge not the weather but how far away and how severe the raids had been during the night.

She pulled the yard gate to behind herself, humming the tune of 'The Gay Gordons'. She enjoyed that and the Palais Glide but the Co-op was becoming more up-to-date these days. She supposed it was all the service personnel who worked in the War Departments. They had found the Hall and had demanded the latest hits. Glenn Miller and Tommy Dorsey's numbers were favourite and they *jitterbugged*. She felt a bit breathless just thinking about it.

'Abandoned,' her mother called it. 'Throwing girls around!'

When she had told Audrey this she had said, 'Yeah!' like a Yank and they'd 'cut a rug' in the office until they heard Mr Fieldman coming.

Vi had felt the raids must have been light, but by the time she turned the corner on to the main road she could see columns of smoke coming up from the direction of Holborn and the City. She glanced with some feeling of selfishness and guilt in the direction of the Co-op Hall, but the bombing seemed to have moved a little further west.

A weary-looking woman in green overalls and green turban leaning on the bus stop caught her eye and smiled companionably. 'Night work!' the woman said as if explaining her appearance. 'Wears you as thin as y'old man's socks!'

'Know what you mean,' Vi answered, picturing her mother's ever high-piled darning basket.

'It does me good to hear a young woman laugh. You enjoy yourself when you have the chance.' The woman hailed the approaching bus. 'I'm off to see if my old dad's all in one piece. 'E won't move, sez no Jerry's puttin' 'im out of his 'ome.'

'Good fer 'im! And I *mean* to 'ave a good time,' Vi answered as she climbed aboard after her. As she ran up to the top deck, the quick clacking of her shoes on the stairs reminded her that she meant to improve her jitterbugging so much that by the time Roy came home on leave again he'd be astonished! He liked dancing, wrote about the camp dances and made her laugh when he described some of the ATS personnel, 'big chests and big feet' as he put it. She didn't have either of those problems, she thought ironically.

'Looks as if some poor sods have had a rough night.'

'Westminster I 'eard, poor bleeders.' The expletive from a bent old man behind Violet was full of tender concern.

She looked out over the older, partially cleared bombsites to where fresh rubble steamed in the morning sun like something just brought from the oven. It hadn't been all in the City, this was Stepney. She felt a fearsome thrill of concern run like ice over her spine as they passed a blackened and weary fire crew still rolling up their hoses. Audrey lived in Stepney.

There were some queer sights, a bath hanging suspended in space, only the plumbing holding the fitting against the one remaining wall. The bus turned a corner and against a pile of rubble someone had propped up one end of the sagging road sign with beams. Below that was pinned a Union Jack. In the middle of the rubble a chimney wall had preserved a mantelpiece with green bobbled plush cover, a container of spills and a photograph frame.

Further along the same street, she glimpsed a wrecked pram half buried in the ruins of an entry; a gang of men were labouring under a towering wall from which clumps of bricks hung in ragged threats.

'Somebody still under that lot!' The old man in the seat behind poked Vi in the back. 'D'you reckon?' She nodded dumbly as, at the end of the newly

6

devastated street, a black mongrel lay by a doorstep at the edge of the debris, head sideways on its outstretched leg in that attitude of patient canine waiting – long useless waiting.

The next corner turned and this Vi was finding the strangest thing to come to terms with, the way one moment she felt in the midst of the Blitz with all its horrors, destruction and people's personal disasters visible on all sides, then on the same day, even the same bus ride, around the next corner life looked normal. Children went to school, birds sang in the plane trees. 'A Nightingale Sang in Berkeley Square'. Of course, whether it would be there the next day was another matter.

Perhaps it excused her and Audrey having such a good time. They *could* for a time forget that most of their generation of young men, nearly all their school year, had been whisked away to the war. Once they entered the crowded hall with the subdued lighting of strings of multicoloured bulbs, there was mystery and excitement. They were always quickly swept out on to the dance floor by guys in smooth superior uniforms, 'exciting fellas' who knew new dances and spoke in fascinating transatlantic accents.

She sighed, then grabbed the seat in front as they lurched precariously around a corner on the wrong side of the road to avoid an unexpected pile of rubble. The jolt brought her back to reality, reminded her that their future in London was very unsure. After Sid's near miss, she had overheard her parents again discussing the wisdom of them all staying in London when, as Pa said, they didn't *all* need to.

She thought of the many children they had seen being evacuated from their schools, class groups in long crocodiles. Little top-coated and hatted figures, each with gas mask, one suitcase and the regulation cloth name-tab strung into a buttonhole – tearful children, tearful mothers. She knew there was no chance of her mother allowing Sid to be taken to a 'safe area' on his own. But perhaps even if Ma took Sid, she might be allowed to stay. *I could look after Pa. Pack his sandwiches, cook his dinners, make his bed.*

She brooded over their experience of evacuation to Cambridge. She remembered trees and towers and a river that had looked a bit puny after the Thames. She had felt as out of place as one of the Tower of London ravens might if hurled into the middle of the River Cam and told to swim. She had seen her mother being treated like an extra maid in the house where they were billeted and, worse, had seen her begin to act like one.

No way did she want any of that to happen again. Better they all took their chance together, stayed where they were known. She looked across to the Victoria Park where a rocket battery had been set up. All around were close communities with many meeting points for all ages, Sunday schools, clubs of all kinds from cinema rushes to church and chapel fellowships and the public houses where men and women met and sang on Saturday nights. She and Audrey met their own generation in the Co-op Hall and at the cinema but,

7

more than anything else, she dreaded with a heavy chill in the pit of her stomach the idea of leaving her father again.

She peered hopefully down as the bus slowed at the next bus stop. Sometimes, if Audrey was up early enough, she walked to the Mile End Road and caught the same bus. She anticipated a good gossip, a good giggle. Occasionally, if they became too animated, someone would intervene with the much used reproach, 'You'd never know there was a war on!'

Vi pressed her head to the side window as the bus drew in towards the stop. Audrey's bright red hair was unmistakeable. She raised a fist to knock at the window, but then her fingers flew to her lips in concern.

It *was* Audrey, but the usual bouffant hairstyle was flat and dishevelled – and her clothes? Under the black jacket she usually wore in the evenings, Vi saw her friend's green taffeta dance dress.

Vi was on her feet and clattering noisily down the bus stairs as it jolted to a halt. She jumped from platform to pavement as she saw that, not only was Audrey still in the clothes she would have been out in the night before, but her face, her clothes, were all streaked with dirt, her hands bleeding and dirty.

'You gettin' on or wot?' the rotund conductress came forward, her podgy hand already prodding up towards the bell. Then she gaped, changed her tone. ''Ere, she alright? You'd better both get on, we pass the 'ospital?'

'No,' Audrey moaned, shook her head violently at the suggestion and, feeling the shudders that shook her friend's frame, Vi lifted a hand in acknowledgement of the offer but said, 'She's my friend, I'll look after her.'

She gripped Audrey around the waist as the bus drew away. 'What's happened? Audrey!' She pulled her close, held her tight. The shudders gave way to a kind of rigor, a stiff unresponsiveness that was somehow more frightening.

Vi looked round as if for help, unsure what to do. 'Can you walk?' she asked, calculating they were nearer her own home then Audrey's – and if Audrey was still in the clothes she had worn to go out the night before . . . She sternly told herself that speculation was not going to move any mountains, she had to act. 'Can you walk?' she asked again.

Audrey showed no sign of even having heard but as Vi turned her along the pavement, her legs seemed to move mechanically, reminding Vi forcibly of the little toy dog Sid had. If you put it on a slope and got the angle just so, it stayed upright and 'walked' down. Getting Audrey back to Brierly Street needed as much attention and some strength as she leaned heavily against her.

The two attracted some curious glances – it was the bright emerald green dress beneath the black jacket with the nipped in waist. One woman commented to her uniformed companion, 'Another war casualty,' and both laughed, but those who had the time to look closer showed their concern. One or two asked if Vi needed any help.

When they reached the back yard, the door was locked. Florrie would have taken Sid to school. She reached to the hook behind the drainpipe for the key. Inside, she pushed Audrey into her father's many-cushioned chair by the fire and transferred the kettle from the slow hob to the fiercest jet on the gas stove.

When she came back Audrey had collapsed forward, on her knees. She feared she would fall and tried gently to push her upright again, but Audrey startled her by jumping to her feet, pushing Vi aside. 'Leave me alone! Don't touch me! It's not fair!' she shouted. 'Not bloody fair.'

Vi was startled and shocked by the anger, the action, the shouting, after the tight tense silence. Then she gasped as Audrey began to kick at a newspaper lying by the chair – kicked again and again.

She felt hysteria form in her throat as the newspaper tore and stuck on Audrey's shoe but, just before it bubbled over, Audrey sat down again and burst into tears, not noisy tears just a great flood of streaming grief. Vi knelt before her, grasped her hands as tightly as ever she could, so tight it concentrated her friend's mind on her. 'Now tell me,' she ordered. 'Tell me!'

Audrey certainly opened her mouth but shook her head. The words failed to come, as if there was just too much to tell, or she did not know where to begin.

Vi nodded towards her dress. 'You said you weren't going out last night?' Another thought came to her mind. 'It wasn't one of those fellas?' Vi always found it alarming the way Audrey made a beeline for the poshest-seeming blokes and hung on their every word. Vi felt such officers lived in a different world and were best left alone. She preferred someone she felt at home with. She turned over Audrey's hands, saw the grazes and scratches, then reached up and pushed the hair from a begrimed forehead. 'Audrey! You've not been attacked?'

'No, no. No!' The voice and the face were angry again, full of aggression.

'Where've you been?' Vi made her face as stony hard as she could to force her friend to the brink of explanation, to the release of telling, of sharing the trouble. 'Tell me, Audrey! Tell me! Where did you go last night?'

'To Dorking.'

The answer was so unexpected, Vi felt her stomach quiver with a ludicrous desire to hoot with nervous laughter as she repeated, 'Dorking?'

'Some of those officers we met at the Co-op saw Lizzie and sent her round to see if we'd go to a dance at a pub in Dorking. They'd got one of those buses that take people out of London at night instead of going down the underground to shelter, then they come back in the morning – only we were going to have a good time, not sleep. Audrey paused and for the first time seemed to see her friend properly. 'I'd 'ave come for you but there wasn't time. It was a last minute thing to fill the bus'.

'So what happened?' she asked, wondering if the bus had crashed.

'We got back about a quarter past five this morning.' Audrey stopped, hung her head and murmured that they'd had a great time.

'Then you went 'ome.' Vi said slowly, rubbing her thumbs across Audrey's

9

knuckles but swallowing hard as the grime on her friend's hands reminded her of the similarly grimed and weary firemen on the outskirts of Stepney. 'Your place?' she asked urgently. 'Your folks? They'd be in the underground . . . wouldn't they?'

Audrey drew in a great shuddering breath. 'When I got to the corner of our street,' she said, 'the whole road was sort of broken up. The houses . . . some looked as if they'd slipped into holes. It was like hell.' She ended in a whisper as she looked again into the awful nightmare. 'They were still pulling bodies out. They'd lined them up in a clear space in the middle of the road.' Her voice became almost inaudible. 'It made me think of when our pa took us fishing. You remember he put the fish in a row on the pier.'

'You don't mean . . .' Vi tried to imagine finding her own parents lain out side by side in the street. The thought was violently disturbing – unbearable.

'I ran towards the bodies, they were covered with coats and things, but someone waved me away, a woman . . .' She paused and frowned in a effort to remember more clearly. 'A neighbour, I think. She shouted, "Round the corner." I didn't know what she meant, but I ran to the end of the road and turned.' Audrey paused and looked up. Her eyes were suddenly quite clear, *this* memory was very clear. 'The wall of a building had suddenly collapsed, just as people were coming up from sleeping in the underground. There were people pulling away bricks and rubble and I helped, but then someone told me Ma and Pa had already been found and taken to the 'ospital. I ran there, all the way. I found them, Vi, but it was too late. But . . .' Her face contorted with anguish. 'But their hands were still warm. I held their hands, Vi . . . my ma and pa . . . but, but . . .' She paused, shaking her head at the awfulness of the experience. 'Their fingers, they didn't hold mine.'

'Oh, Audrey!' Vi clasped her tight as the girl sobbed uncontrollably. She patted and stroked her friend's back in instinctive gestures of compassion. It was all she could think to do.

'I've no one and nothing now,' Audrey said as finally they released each other, her voice not just calm but hollow, empty.

'You'll come here to us then.'

Neither of them had been aware of Florrie's return nor of how long she had stood, knuckles white, as she gripped the back of a chair, tears falling unheeded down her cheeks. She came quickly round to hug and hold the girl.

'Oh, Mrs Tulley, why didn't they wait a few more weeks, a few more days? Pa 'ad his calling-up papers yesterday. 'Im and Ma were talking about it just last night. He wanted us to go to the country while he was away.' She paused and shook her head in a torment of disbelief. 'And why aren't I dead?'

'There are some things only God knows,' Florrie answered. Vi heard the quiver in her voice and guessed she was plunged into yet another inner turmoil, the knowledge that after all her heart-searching they had stayed at home and survived while those who had sheltered had perished.

10

'I'll make some tea,' Vi said and saw her mother make that mental and physical move away from her introspection.

'That's right,' Florrie said, 'then we'll clean up those hands of yours.'

'It doesn't matter.' Audrey glanced down at the dirty and torn fingers and nails. 'I don't care.'

'We all have to go on caring, no matter what,' Florrie said with new resolution, then looking at her daughter added, 'and you ought to go and ring your office, let 'em know what's 'appened.'

'Tell 'er about my mother and father!'

'Of course.' Vi was shaken again by the anger and aggression in Audrey's voice.

She went to telephone Miss Swanton, aware this was the first time she had encountered real grief. She knew nothing about this kind of extreme sorrowing. She thought of Mr and Mrs Kingston. She had always felt that the sandy-haired whippet of a man had done very well marrying the plump auburn-haired woman and producing a real coppernob with the energy of a racing dog but the nicely rounded figured of her mother. Gone! Poor Audrey!

To her surprise the rehearsed defiance, the defensiveness for her decision to stay away with Audrey, were not necessary, for Harriet Swanton was full of sympathy, wanting to know if there was any way she could help and telling Vi not to worry, she would manage. Vi felt a twinge of guilt because between them, she and Audrey worked the office switchboard and intercom, flicking the keys up and down to direct the calls to the various offices. Miss Swanton always cut people off if she tried to work the relatively new addition to the office.

As Vi left the telephone box on the main road, she heard her name called. 'Pa!' She turned and ran back towards him, catching his hand. 'What're you doing 'ome at this time?'

'Jerry's bust m'bus! I've got to go back on the late shift instead.' He paused and took in his daughter's flustered appearance. 'And you?'

The story broke from her lips in a flood.

'Steady on, gel.' Harold stopped walking and pulled his daughter close to the boarded-up window of a fishmonger's shop where painted cartoons of grinning fish were topped by the words 'Business as Usual'. He held gently on to her arm as he prompted, 'Now then.'

His face, which Vi always thought was so kind and reassuring, became paler and a nerve flicked along the line of his jaw as he listened.

'And she's with your ma?' When she nodded he added, 'She must stay with us.' He did not interrupt again and after she had finally run out of words he turned his daughter homewards in much the same way she had propelled Audrey earlier. All the way back they walked in complete silence.

Vi opened her mouth to speak once or twice but, glancing up at his face, she knew there was some very serious thinking going on and it didn't take

11

much guessing what about. Only her respect for him kept her quiet. Later there would be time to argue her corner – maybe she *and* Audrey could stay in London and look after him. She noticed too, as she had when they had so nearly lost Sid, that his limp became much worse when he was worried, almost as if he forgot to make the effort to walk like a man who'd never been trampled by a horse, a pain-free man.

When they arrived back, Florrie had bathed Audrey's face and hands, had wrapped her in an eiderdown and had a roaring fire in the grate. Vi was shocked by her appearance. Her friend looked much worse now she was cleaned up. The skin over her cheekbones was like white transparent paper, her eye sockets were black with fatigue and grief. The jacket and dance dress lay discarded on a chair – like good times gone, Vi thought.

Harold dropped his leather workbag on the floor, reached high into the cupboard next to the fireplace and took down the quarter bottle of brandy kept for emergencies. He mixed half brandy and hot water and added a good spoonful of sugar. 'Sip that,' he told Audrey, 'then you're going to bed.'

'I'll run the warming pan around our Vi's bed. We'll sort it out proper later on.' The pan was off the wall, hot cinders shovelled into it, and Florrie was hurrying up to the middle bedroom with it in no time, as if relieved to have the onus of decision-making taken momentarily off her shoulders.

'Vi!' her father suddenly said. 'You should go to work. Two of you away ain't fair and it's not necessary.'

'But . . .'

'Audrey'll rest better on her own, and while she sleeps I'll go to the hospital and find out what needs to be done.' He moved over to Audrey and gripping her shoulder asked, 'Is that what you'd want?'

'Please, Mr Tulley. My mother has a younger brother, Uncle Tom, but 'e's in a submarine somewhere.'

'Leave it to me.' Harold rose and, slipping his arms under Audrey, carried her towards the stairs, pausing as Florrie reappeared. 'Come on, Ma, you bring your mending basket and sit by this gel while she rests. I'll light you a fire in the bedroom.'

Chapter 2

'Don't say it, our Vi,' her father admonished as another 'but' formed on her lips.

'Just let *me* stay with you then, Pa ...'

'Am I likely? Evacuate your ma, Sid and your friend and let you stay.'

Vi clenched her teeth against both anger and tears. In the three days Audrey had been with them, she had felt this moment coming, had read it in his prolonged stares at her ma and the way he had begun to say 'Hmmm!' to himself at intervals, as if stacking evidence, coming to conclusions.

He had risen from the Sunday lunch table to help her clear away. With the funeral of Audrey's parents arranged for the next day it was only as they met in the kitchen that their argument – begun when he made the announcement over breakfast while Audrey was still in bed – continued.

'I knew this would 'appen,' she mumbled, swishing the washing-up water madly with the soap ends in the wire saver. He did not answer but stood shaking out the tea towel ready to dry. She had to restrain herself from pulling it from his hands and stamping on it. Why couldn't he understand she wanted to stay and take her chance with him, not be sent to some God-forsaken place where no one wanted them at any price.

The trouble was she did not know how to reframe the words again, was constrained by all Audrey had to bear, by her mother painstakingly sewing wide black ribbons around coat sleeves, by Sid, eyes as big as saucers, listening to every word, watching every gesture as if he was taking evidence at the Old Bailey.

The trouble was she'd already been through every argument – reasonable or not – and her pa had been through all his patience and some time ago had used that ultimate sanction 'until you're twenty-one you'll do as I say'.

The clink and rattle of the crockery was jarring and loud as the washing-up continued in a tense silence, a pause in the muted hostilities. Vi was in turmoil. She stared fiercely into the bowl, conscious of her father's hands at the edge of her vision as he picked up and dried each item. The air was full of the

13

lingering aroma of the roast beef her mother still managed to cook however impractical, for often these days the joint fell through its wire trivet into the Yorkshire pudding. Ma's efforts apparently meant nothing, Pa would just split the family, sending them away.

The over-full kettle began gently rattling its lid as it began to bubble, then to boil over on the gas stove. *That's how I feel,* she thought, *ready to spit.*

'Need any more?'

'No.'

Her father turned off the gas and led the way into the main kitchen, closing the door behind his stiff-backed daughter, drawing the thick velour curtain and kicking the long draught excluder into place.

Vi glanced at the others: Ma watching Sid draw pictures of planes with huge guns firing up at them; Audrey, eyes glazed with her own thoughts; and Pa who returned her stare, look for meaningful look. He knew all too well that she'd be unable to stay silent for much longer.

There was a knock on the street door and as her father rose to answer it she muttered fiercely, 'You don't know what it was like in Cambridge.'

The knock was repeated and her pa motioned Florrie to stay where she was as he paused on the way to say quietly to his daughter, 'I know there were no bombs.'

'You two!' Florrie remonstrated even more quietly. 'Both want the last word.'

Sid made a booming sound as he pencilled in lines from gun to plane fuselage, then as they heard strange footsteps coming along the narrow red and black tiled passage from the front door asked, 'Who's come?'

'Miss Swanton!' Audrey exclaimed, so surprised that for the first time since that awful Thursday morning her voice sounded momentarily normal.

'Hope you don't think I'm intruding.'

Vi thought she looked bigger than ever as she came into their kitchen in grey Robin Hood style hat and grey overcoat, carrying two large bulging oilcloth bags in addition to her usual black leather handbag shaped like a miniature Gladstone bag.

'Audrey, m'dear, I'm so sorry!' There was an awkward pause then she moved over and bent a little breathlessly to kiss Audrey's cheek. 'So very sorry. My heart aches for you, my dear. Mr Fieldman sends his condolences and wishes to attend . . .' She broke off with a glance towards the black ribbons. 'The office is to be closed.'

'Eleven o'clock tomorrow,' Harold supplied. 'I'll write it all down for you before you go.' He asked if she would take off her coat and sit down. To Vi's continued astonishment she did and accepted the offer of a cup of tea.

'I understand you have lost everything, Audrey, house—'

'They're knocking it all down with a great ball on a chain,' Sid interrupted, adding a decisive swing with his fist and another echoing 'B . . . o . . . o . . . m!'

14

Vi scowled and shook her head at him, half afraid he might repeat something she'd said about Miss Swanton to her face.

Audrey gave a deep shaky sigh. 'We all went with Vi's pa this morning. I wanted to go. They're knocking our house down – and next door.'

'They're unsafe. There's nothing that can be saved,' Vi said, remembering the shock of the burnt-out houses which reminded her of nothing so much as a pair of rotten black teeth.

'We've dugged up the rose tree,' Sid put in.

'Go to the kitchen to help your ma,' Harold ordered, apologising to their visitor.

'At that age they don't really understand.'

'I don't understand either,' Audrey said quietly.

'No.' Harriet Swanton's single word held a wealth of understanding. Vi remembered how appalled she had been when told Audrey's parents had not been killed in their ruined home but as they came from spending the night in the underground. The older woman had added quietly, 'I've always known life was not fair.'

Miss Swanton turned to smile at Violet. 'I thought how noble it was of Violet to come to the office on Thursday.'

Harold raised his eyebrows a fraction at his daughter as he saw her lips begin to frame the truth. 'We agreed it was right,' he said, as if the pair of them were engaged in one of their everyday harmless conspiracies to pull Ma's leg. She might have raised a smile if it were not for the evacuation project and his breakfast talk about having seen 'a mate' who might be able to fix them up. It was her opinion her pa had too many 'fixers' as mates. Over the years there was always someone he knew who could 'fix' his shift for him, turn a new leg for a table, weld a kettle handle – mention the problem and he would know someone!

'It's so unfair,' Miss Swanton was saying, 'here's my mother been a poor bedridden creature for years while your parents had each other and were so young.'

Vi had not thought of Audrey's parents as particularly young. Neither had she ever suspected that Miss Swanton went home to nurse a sick mother! Not only had she probably lost her fiancé in the first war, she was tied to the caring of a parent. It was expected of unmarried daughters, of course, but Vi didn't suppose that made it any easier. She wondered if the young Harriet had ever had a real good time – danced at the Co-op? She hoped so as it didn't look as if there was going to be much more fun for anybody while the war was on. Only grief for those such as Audrey. Her pa was telling Miss Swanton that he was sending them all away from London.

'I think it's a very wise decision, Mr Tulley.'

Vi felt her new sympathy for the office manageress evaporate.

'Young people . . .' Harriet paused and glanced at Audrey but her face had

15

assumed that closed stunned look of one newly bereaved. 'Young people need our extra care.' In an effort to re-engage her, she hauled one of the huge bags she had brought onto her knee and began to pull out coats and dresses. 'Now I know these won't fit and I know they're not the style for a young girl – but the material's good. One thing my mother did teach me was always to buy the best you could afford. So there's lots of wear in the fabrics and the woollens could be pulled out and reknitted.'

Vi had never seen such a wealth of woollen coats and skirts, dresses and cardigans. Her mother leaned forward appreciatively. 'My goodness we can make these over.' Then, as Harriet Swanton piled them onto her knee, Ma looked across at Audrey. 'We'll be able to make you a real good wardrobe! You'll be dressed up to the nines! My goodness it's very kind of you.'

'It is kind,' Vi echoed, 'and we can both help, can't we, Aud?' She picked up what she thought was the nicest green and heather plaid skirt and spread it across Audrey's knee. 'Isn't that lovely?'

Audrey nodded at the skirt, then smiled briefly at Miss Swanton. 'Thank you.'

There was an awkward moment but Flo was soon picking over the clothes again. 'I can't wait to get started,' she said, 'such lovely expensive clothes. Your ma knew a bit of good stuff when she saw it.'

'I always thought it was a nuisance that things never wore out when I was a girl. You 'ad everything for so long!'

The atmosphere in the kitchen was suddenly easier for the Tulleys with the dropped aitch and the sincerity of the confession. 'My mother always had things made, 'ad delusions of grandeur I think – still 'as, come to that.'

Harold and Flo laughed, their glances going briefly and almost guiltily to Audrey. 'We're never satisfied, are we?' her pa stated, but Vi was still finding this relaxed homely Miss Swanton difficult to come to terms with. She still found it hard to think that the person who drank a second cup of tea and kissed them both before she left was the same taskmaster who ruled their days at the office.

When she'd gone they busied themselves with some serious sorting out, with much trying against and thoughts of how they could undo some of the skirt side seams, cut out pieces big enough to do something else with and leave the pleats untouched. The coats and jackets would have to be carefully unpicked and remade.

'If we can get 'em undone quickly I could get Mr Rubenstein to recut the coats, don't suppose he'd charge much. They're worth it!' Flo hugged a soft warm jacket appreciatively.

'Quickly?' Vi picked the word out of her mother's enthusiastic sewing plans. 'We're not rushing off that quick – or are we? Pa!'

'I don't know for certain, I told m'mate it couldn't be Monday,' he said without compromise.

16

Vi stared at him, trying to divine the truth. How long did she still have in her home? He held her gaze and added, 'I told your good lady from the office that she should regard you as on notice to leave.'

'Pa!' she exclaimed. 'You can't 'ave! You can't!'

He shook his head at her outburst, gesturing towards the others. 'You're not the only one to consider.'

No, she wanted to shout at him, *Audrey's parents can't send her away, but you – you can't wait to get rid of us*. She turned and ran from the kitchen, along the passage, snatching her coat and beret and slamming the front door after herself.

She raced along, past front doors echoing entries towards the main road, pulling her hat and coat on as she went, just running, getting away, not sure where she was going, not caring.

There were very few people about to hinder her flight. Sunday school was over and the late November day held the smoky warning of chill and fog clamping down later. She slowed to a walk as she saw Victoria Park across the road. Without thought she had come to what had once been her idea of heaven. A place of swings, seesaws, of bread-and-dripping picnics with Audrey and their dolls. There had always seemed to be sunshine, green grass, bright flowers and beautiful swans gliding across the lakes. To her it had always been the place the hymn 'All Things Bright and Beautiful' was about.

Audrey, best friend since first schooldays, had often helped when Sid had arrived and had to be pushed out in his pram. Her friend, obsessed even then with attaching herself to the upper classes, always wanted to go to the park and once there pretended to be a nursemaid from a big house, making Vi call her baby brother 'Mr Sidney'. Vi reacted by playing the fool – they had often fallen out about it.

They had once tried to take the pram over one of the two bridges to an island in the middle of the lake, an island made glamorous for them by being prohibited to unaccompanied children under the age of fourteen. They had been chased off by a vigilant park keeper and in the haste to escape had tipped Sid out of his pram as they reached the far end of the bridge. She had scooped up the screaming baby and Audrey had belted after her with the empty pram.

The island was still unconquered territory as far as Vi was concerned, it seemed a waste to walk there by yourself. A place of winding paths and alcoves, with seats in every one, and a grand red pagoda in the centre, it was a place much frequented by young couples. Audrey had longed to be asked to walk there and *before* they left school there had been one exciting skirmish with a young guardsman.

Vi's only chance had been with a youth they called 'Spotty' Foster. She had not considered him a serious proposition for a walk anywhere, certainly not on the special island. It now seemed her most vivid memory of Viccy Park island would be of being chased off by a morose old park keeper.

Everything was being spoilt. She went slowly along, not wanting to cross and see the trenches dug in the park as shelter for many hundreds of East Enders. This great green area was a precious part of her life. Her pa had told her how the place had been a bishop's deer park, preserved for the enjoyment of Londoners. She remembered all the facts he had related, word perfect. On June 6th 1892, which was a late hot Whitsun, three hundred thousand visitors visited Victoria Park. There had been historic rallies. She recalled names like Eleanor Marx, Sylvia Pankhurst, Oswald Mosley.

Three hundred thousand people in one day had enjoyed her park, while she'd never even shelter from Jerry there. She was certainly never going to have the chance of a proper 'chap' walking her there.

'Vi!'

The voice close by made her jump. She turned, then started to walk quickly away, but her father caught her arm.

'Why 'ave you come after me?'

'You're just making it 'arder for all of us.' His pressure on her arm was not enough to stop her progress, only hinder it as she walked on with him gripping a handful of her coat at the elbow. 'Tell me before you go any further, 'ow many nights bombing we've 'ad this month? 'Ow many we 'ad last month?'

'It was quiet again last night!' she retorted, though she slowed down a little as she realised he was not going to let her go. 'It's not *all* the time.'

'August 24th.'

She stopped suddenly, as if wearied with this particular game he was insisting on. 'Wot about it? No one's birthday is it?' She heard and inwardly flinched at the hard insolence in her own voice.

'No, no one's birthday, Vi,' he replied with monotone patience. 'It was the day the first bombs fell on Stepney and Bethnal Green. The East End, the docks, 'ave been *the* target for the Luftwaffe ever since.' He stood looking across the road towards the great open space where there were no buildings to fall, injure and kill. '*That* was the day I should 'ave sent you all off out of it agen.'

'Even though you know we'll 'ate it. You didn't see 'ow they treated our ma – like a servant! I'd sooner be killed.'

'Stupid talk, that is.' Harold took his daughter's arm. 'Let's have a walk in the park before it's dark, start again. We can't go on arguing and upsetting Audrey. The gel's had enough and she's got tomorrow to get through yet.'

Miserably, she shook her head. Then, as they waited to cross the road, she added, 'But you don't understand 'ow I feel.'

'Violet, *you* don't know the 'undredth part of what I feel.' He put his hand under her elbow more gently as they waited for two horse-drawn drays to pass. The open drays were laden with furniture – someone else bombed out, or lucky enough to be moving out of the City to somewhere safe.

'Sometimes,' he said, 'it's the things one loves best that 'urt one the most.'

She looked at him questioningly and he nodded towards the horses.

'You mean like your accident?'

'Yes – a bit . . .' He paused and laughed. 'Though I'm not goin' to knock you down and trample all over you!'

She refused to walk on now even though the road was clear, instead she stepped back from the edge of the kerb. 'What 'as your mate arranged?'

He looked at her for a moment, then looked quickly away, taking a deep breath before he went on. 'There's a family should 'ave gone but they've got a child down with pneumonia.'

'Gone where?'

He leaned forward confidentially. 'Cornwall probably, though some may stay in Devon.'

'Pa!' She snatched her arm out of his hand, a feeling of utter panic flooding her mind. 'Pa! There's thousands still 'ere in the East End, kids going to school and everything. Cornwall's . . .' She couldn't find words to express where Cornwall was, how far away – it was just like a strange foreign land as far as a Cockney kid was concerned.

He took her arm again and firmly propelled her over to the park. 'Yes and every time there's a raid, there's more injured and killed. 'Ow do you think I'd feel if I let you all get 'urt or killed, when I could've sent you to safety? Answer me that!'

'I only know I'd sooner you knocked me down and trampled me,' she whispered.

'M'dear old gel!'

She looked at him sharply, it was a phrase he usually used when he was pulling her leg.

'Even that old 'oss didn't really mean to 'urt me. There's no way I ever want to 'urt you. It'd be like running a knife through myself.' He was shaking his head sadly as he went on. 'But sometimes we 'ave to take our medicine, do things we 'ate and detest. This is one of those times. I 'ave to stay to do my war work, keep the buses running, that's duty to King and Country and I 'ave to send you away to be safe, that's my duty as 'usband and father.' He paused for a moment then added, 'I have to be able to live with myself, Vi – and by myself.'

More than any argument, the falling tone of the last three whispered words gave her pause, made her walk at a more amenable pace. She heard and realised both her father's struggle with his conscience about the prospect of this second separation – and the anguish of that parting.

She turned to look up into his eyes and saw her own suffering mirrored there. 'Oh, Pa! I'm sorry.' She suddenly saw how his life would be, how the

19

house would be without them, the emptiness, the cold grate, no meal pre-pared when he returned from work. They at least would have each other – or she supposed they would. Her pa would be alone. 'I don't want to go though.'

He smiled briefly at the sting in the tail of her capitulation. 'They'll need you, our Vi, you're the one with the head on your shoulders.'

She hadn't thought of that either, but as her mother, her brother and her friend came into her mind like a formal group posed for a photographer, she saw it was true. She knew how the eyes of such a picture could follow you wherever you went!

'Come on,' he said patting her hand, 'now we're 'ere let me walk my gel across to the island in the Viccy Park. We've just about time.'

She sniffed and blinked back tears. He couldn't surely know how she felt about the island? Then, as he crooked his elbow for her, she wondered if he'd ever walked her ma there when they were courting – and was suddenly quite convinced he knew about *everything*. With an exaggerated gesture to match his pretended bravado, she threaded her arm through his and the two of them fair strutted across the park.

It was a walk she felt she would always remember. It was like the history of this park, part of London's story, part of her story. She was aware of every-thing as if she was already packing to leave, storing a precious memory to take with her. The wooden bridge beneath their feet, the slight suspicion of fog rising from the surface of the lake, in the distance a pair of swans floating, it seemed, already misted in memory.

Then, coming to the winding paths with the alcoves in every secluded spot, she thought there might not be may people abroad, but every one of the seats was occupied. All the young men were in uniform, in some booths both girl and boy were in khaki or blue, private in their whispering worlds of hopes and promises, though the trees held no more than old brown rags of their leaves and the air was so thin and chill.

She was aware her father walked proudly, hardly limping at all. She won-dered if he regretted not being in uniform – there was glamour and glory in a uniform proudly worn. He had once told her how in the First World War he had volunteered for the Flying Corps, but Gran Tulley had found out and had him sent home because he was only sixteen. Then between the wars he had been trampled by one of the horses he worshipped where he worked in hackney carriage stables. There must have been a lot of disappointments in his life, opportunities that had slipped out of his grasp – yet no one would ever guess. She wondered if she was a disappointment to him?

'I think it's important war work driving a bus,' she told him and he fol-lowed her glance towards yet another uniformed couple.

'Keeping the country on the move,' he agreed. 'I suppose so.'

'Getting the workers to their offices and factories – keeping things going.'

'Giving 'em a cheery greeting and a smile!'

20

She glanced up at him and he winked, then tipped his Sunday cap to a rakish angle and pretended to swing a cane with his free hand.

Her heart was full and she silently told him, *I love you, Pa! I won't ever let you down again.*

It was almost as if he heard for he nodded back to her.

They reached the big red pagoda in the middle of the island and Pa invited her to take a seat for a few moments. She thought Ma had been lucky to find Harold Tulley. Any fella had to be pretty special to compare with her pa.

Chapter 3

Paddington station was a noisy mass of people smelling of damp worsted clothes. Voices had to be raised to be heard above the teeming rain outside and the excess steam the waiting train discharged inside.

Vi kept firm hold of the collar of Sid's navy gabardine mac as, instead of looking where they were going, he continually gazed upwards, fascinated by the steam as it rose, billowed and thundered beneath the high-vaulted roof.

Her father had gone to find out which part of the train they should board, many carriages were clearly reserved for the school parties. 'Organised chaos,' Vi muttered, watching out for some sign of Pa's return over the throng of small overcoated and hatted figures.

'Look at 'em, poor mites,' Flo said to no one in particular, though she had her arm firmly linked into Audrey's. 'Like little soldiers going to war with all their kit.'

'All their worldly possessions' was the phrase that sprang to Vi's mind. Each child was burdened with the 'essentials' their mothers thought they would need. Many had several layers of clothing, scrappy brown paper bundles, little cases, rolls of comics. All had gas masks. One or two stood out from the crowd: a brother and sister in brilliantly shiny new Wellington boots standing silent, bewildered, holding hands; a dark lanky twitchy girl ramming sandwiches into her mouth was losing others from the bottom of a soggy paper bag; a boy clutching a black cat with one white paw; a woman with a wicker basket opening the lid.

'They shouldn't be eating already,' Flo added, catching sight of more children already making inroads into their supplies. 'They'll not last the journey.'

'They'll be sick!' was Vi's down to earth verdict. 'I just hope we're not near any of them when they are.'

She felt if she allowed herself to indulge in sentimentality she would not be able to cope either with this departure or the lingering trauma of the day before.

The funeral had been in the morning. A few of the Kingstons' friends and neighbours had come back to Brierly Street but, once they were gone, tired and emotionally exhausted as they had all been, the preparations for the evacuation were forced to be completed.

Audrey had been remarkably controlled but so quiet, then towards the end of the afternoon had surprised them all with the announcement that she needed to go back to the cemetery. 'It might be a long time before I'll be able to see . . . the place again. I can go by myself.'

'No, of course you can't,' Vi had said with certainty, but saw her ma sag a little with sheer weariness. She looked to her pa for guidance.

'Let's see what we think over another cuppa. We're all of us done in.'

In the end, Vi and Audrey had made the return journey to the City of London Cemetery. Vi had thought the request almost unreasonable given there was so much to do, until she saw that it did give Audrey some comfort to see the grave already so carefully tidied, the displaced sods of turf neatly piled over the soil and their flowers arranged on the top. Her friend stood silent for a long time, then spent a while rearranging the wreaths and the bunches of flowers.

When they returned, her father had obviously given Audrey's feeling more thought. He said if Audrey wished, he knew someone who would arrange for a temporary polished wooden cross with her parents' names on to be planted. Then, when the war was over, Audrey could come back and see a proper headstone put into place. Audrey's face had lit up with such a smile of thanks it had moved Vi more than any tears.

Vi sighed and hoped *all* Pa's arrangements would go smoothly.

Many were being ushered aboard the train now and still there was no sign of her pa coming back. There was also a sense of competitiveness growing among those still left on the platform – and to her mind there seemed far too many people for the number of carriages. There was also a rumour being overheard, and passed rapidly around, that the first four coaches had no corridor. The rumour was growing to the status of a certainty as Vi saw her pa beckoning urgently over the heads of the crowd.

'Come on,' she said hastily, grabbing Sid's sleeve and urging Audrey and her ma along with the bags and parcels she carried.

Pa had an elderly railway porter guarding one long seat in a compartment facing five women all with babies. 'Better than no toilet and unaccompanied children,' he whispered to Ma as she boarded, at the same time brushing her cheek with a kiss.

Vi saw him swallow hard then force a smile as he playfully cuffed Sid's chin, hugged him then urged him aboard to his mother. Audrey he hugged and kissed. 'I won't neglect anything,' he told her. Then he turned to Vi – not intentionally last but at the end of the line because of the bulk of the baggage she had used to shepherd the party towards him. He began to unburden her, passing the luggage aboard to Audrey. When all were on the train, he put his hands on her shoulders and she saw in his eyes all the agony of parting she was going through. 'I'm relying on you,' he said in no more than a whisper, 'look after them all.'

'I'll do my best, Pa.' Gritting her teeth against the sharp pain behind her eyes heralding tears, she leaned forward to his chest. He took her tenderly into his arms. 'Goodbye, m'gel,' he breathed close to her ear.

'Pa.' It seemed so much was acknowledged in that one word, his instructions, his stand about their going, his love for them all – but above all his daughter's concern for him. Quickly then, she turned and climbed into the compartment, blinded by the tears she could no longer restrain.

Almost immediately there came the final slamming of doors, shouts of 'Stand clear!' 'Mind the doors!' Then the long warning blast of the guard's whistle. Pa stepped back, raised his arm, and behind him the guard brandished his green flag.

The train jerked into motion, taking up the slack couplings between the carriages with a noise like a chain gang of giants stirred to action. A series of raucous belligerent-sounding chuffs from the engine, and they began to inch away. Slowly, those remaining to face out the Blitz in their London homes began to fall behind and were partially obscured by the steam and smoke from the engine.

Like the swans in Victoria Park. Like a misty memory. *I can't bear it*, Vi thought glancing at her stricken Ma. Then, as if fired by the same emotion, Sid flew from the carriage to the still open corridor window and leaned out dangerously as far as he could. Vi instinctively rushed to hold on to him. The next moment Ma and Audrey were there too, all waving, their cries and tears dragged away by the wind and the rain as the train left the shelter of the station. They stayed and waved a full minute after they could see Pa no longer, as if reluctant to admit he was truly out of their sight.

Just as Flo drew Sid back from the window and Vi heaved on the leather strap to close it, he cried out that he had something in his eye.

'We shouldn't have looked out of the window, you always get bits of soot in your eyes,' Vi said.

'You did it,' he accused, his eyes streaming and wrenching his mac belt straight where his sister had again gripped a handful of his coat.

'I know,' she appeased and took her handkerchief from her sleeve and found a clean corner. 'Let's see if I can get it out.'

The tiny hard smut removed, they made their way slowly back to the compartment. It was a sad anticlimax to resettle themselves and begin to make the acquaintance of their fellow evacuees. They were not the only ones in tears.

One young woman, looking little more than a child herself, began to cry copiously as the baby in her arms woke and began screaming. She seemed at a loss what to do.

'It's my sister's,' she told them. 'My family was all dun for except me and 'er. So I've brought 'er out of it. But . . .' The gesture was eloquent of her ignorance of the baby's needs.

'You poor gel,' Florrie murmured. Then there was an immediate flurry of help and advice. It seemed to give the whole carriage a focal point from which they could work.

Stories began to be told and, as the young mothers had spent much of the last few months sleeping in the underground stations, they had become adept at making do and fixing up everything they had to be used to the best advantage. They reorganised the carriage so that two of the mums who were breast-feeding could be screened off near the window and the blinds pulled down if need be. Dirty nappies were dealt with in the toilet, then rinsed and stored in the papier-mâché baby bath that one mother had packed her baby things in.

It was debatable whether Sid fell into the charge of Audrey, or the other way round. Flo and Vi helped with the babies, but Sid, after holding his nose as the babies were changed, persuaded Audrey to go out into the corridor with him. From Sid's ever tipped back head and pointing finger, he was plaguing her with endless questions about the passing countryside.

'D'you think Audrey's fed up with our Sid?' Ma asked.

'Probably – but it's taking her mind off things. Let 'em stay together out there,' Vi replied.

'I wish we could all stay together,' Mary said over the head of her young sleeping niece.

'You ought to be with one of the other mums, give you a lot of 'elp, that would,' Florrie agreed.

'D'you think you'll 'ave 'er adopted?' one of the others asked.

Mary gazed down at two-month-old Wendy and, with trembling fingers, gently brushed the down-soft hair. 'We're the only relations each other 'ave in the whole world.'

'You stick to 'er and we'll stick out to be together,' another promised.

'I mean us to,' Vi said, without giving any thought to an alternative, but she saw her mother's expression change as she reviewed the possibility.

'You and Audrey must be together,' Florrie said a little later.

Vi glanced at her friend leaning on the window rail, listening to Sid. Her face was a thin pale shadow of the fun-loving Audrey of so short a time ago. She wondered how near the edge of endurance Audrey was? Vi reached over and held her ma's hand for a moment. 'Don't worry. I'll make sure we're all right.' Her words sounded far more confident than she felt. Listening to the others tell how they had come to be evacuated, she was rather fearful that their unofficial status would not be well received when it came to the end of their journey.

It was early afternoon when the train slowed, then was shunted backwards in what appeared at first to be a totally deserted siding. Somewhere nearby a

25

Cockney woman's voice mimicked the usual nasal tones of a station announcer: 'Destination Unknown! Destination Unknown!' They were all beginning to feel the effects of the journey that had begun over seven hours ago, the strains of the inconvenient, crowded train were taking their toll – but it made them smile.

'There's a man coming down the corridor with some papers,' Vi announced to her compartment. A few moments later an elderly man, grey hair sticking up distractedly either side of a smooth brown pate, looked in on them. Seeing the babies he came in, consulting his papers.

'Mothers, the WVS will have a special van in the sidings with everything you might need, clean nappies, dried milk. I'll send one of the ladies to help you. Then there will be hot soup and sandwiches for everyone. There are steps being brought to help you down because we're not near a platform, so mind how you go.' He turned and smiled in their direction. 'And you will be?'

'We're with the family parties,' Vi said.

'Yes, my dad arranged it,' Sid spoke up, though a moment ago he had been nowhere in sight.

The organiser peered over his half-glasses for a moment, then began shuffling through his papers.

Along the corridor they all clearly heard someone say, 'Shall we get out? It looks like a long drop.'

'Oh dear!' He was clearly in a dilemma as to which to do first.

'You could do with some help,' Vi said.

'My sister's going to be an accountant,' Sid volunteered.

Vi was tempted to flatten him but she saw that she was being reassessed in light of the information and she added, 'I'd be very willing . . .'

Further along the train came the sound of a door being opened and banging back on the side of the carriage. 'I have another group of mothers with young babies to contact – but if you would find and mark yourself and all the other family parties off on these pages . . .'

Vi was taking over the papers and the indelible pencil as someone called, 'Somebody better go and sort out these deserters.'

'Won't be long,' Vi told her mother.

It was some fifteen minutes later that, locked in the toilet compartment, she thought of her father as she carefully copied the printed capitals of the rest of the sheets to add the Tulley family name on a spare line at the top of the fourth page. *The Lord helps them*, she thought, *as 'elps themselves*.

Returning the papers to the grateful official, she asked where they were. 'In Cornwall, I think – or Devon anyway. After this stop there'll be several places of disembarkation. Everyone will be told when it is their turn – and everyone should be in their new homes tonight.'

As evening came, Vi began to wonder if she'd made an awful mistake, had put their names on the wrong page. Two of the mothers with young babies left at the first stop after the refreshments. Then they began to travel along by the very edge of the sea. It seemed to them a high wild tide and they watched the waves breaking over a narrow beach and rocks only yards from the track. Sid watched, reinforcing each wave with a long drawn out 'C...r...a...s...h!' Audrey, released from his constant chatter, fell asleep but Florrie, while fascinated, wondered about high tides and was glad when that stretch of the journey was over.

By night Vi wondered just how many there were still on the train? She had walked the length of their compartment and there were only four other boys aged about nine or ten in the charge of one elderly schoolmaster.

She calculated they had been travelling over thirteen hours when finally the train slowed and stopped. They waited a moment, listening, then Vi went and opened the blacked-out window in the corridor. They had drawn under a huge shed-like construction and, leaning out, she could see they were at the end of the track, only a set of buffers stood in front of their engine.

Opening the door, she stepped down onto the platform, only to find that after so long a journey the ground still seemed to rock about. She held on to the door to steady herself.

'All right, m'andsome?' A tiny bow-legged porter called as he came forward to help.

'Where are we?'

'You'm in Penzance, m'lovely.'

'Penzance.' She climbed back aboard to help the others in a weary state of bemusement. The only time she had heard of Penzance was when the local amateurs had sung 'Pirates of Penzance'. She wasn't even sure she'd realised it was a real place.

Sid was so exhausted and so deeply asleep now, she heaved him up on to her shoulder, leaving Audrey and her ma to carry the bulk of the bags. At the end of the platform they could see a bus with the elderly teacher and his papers standing by the steps. There were also buxom, green-uniformed WVS workers, one or two elderly couples and a sprinkling of younger women, waiting and watching the approaching Londoners with rapt attention and some apprehension.

The little crowd were halted at the end of the platform.

The schoolmaster had borrowed a chair from the station office and climbed up to address them. 'We're in Penzance, Cornwall.' He waited while a little buzz of interest rose and quickly died in the weary group. 'Some of you will be finding billets here in the town, while those whose names I shall call out still have a short bus journey to go. The bus will stop at various houses and farms and those who have volunteered to offer you homes will come aboard to meet you.'

Vi felt a slight churn of unease. Did he mean come on to the bus to pick who they fancied?

'I think I've met most of you, but in case I forgot to tell anyone, my name is Albert Finch. I'm travelling on the bus to see everyone settled but I shall be coming back to lodge in Penzance. As soon as I know my address I will let you all have it, so if any problems arise you can contact me. I shall also try and come to you all in turn. So now the bus passengers . . .'

When their names were called to go on the bus with many of the older children, boys and girls from about nine to twelve, Sid finally roused sufficiently to ask, ''Ow much further?'

'Don't worry, boy,' the bus driver said, 'you can't go much further, you'm nearly at Land's End.'

'Land's End.' Sid repeated the words like they meant the end of the world but was too tired to launch his usual question list.

'Don't worry,' Vi told him, 'I won't let you fall off.'

The driver laughed as they struggled aboard, Vi leading the way right to the back so that the little party could sit on the two rear seats. She heard her ma make some remarks about 'this'll do,' halfway along the aisle, but she ignored it. It seemed important to her to ensure they were all together, a compact group, and to be as far removed as possible when those who were 'offering homes' came aboard. It might just give more thinking time, more time to manoeuvre. Common sense told her it was going to be difficult to find one household willing to take two young women, a mother and a boy.

Possessions were piled haphazardly on the spare seats. Many of the children fell asleep again before they drew away from the railway station. Peering from the dark interior out into the night, Penzance seemed not a large place; within yards they were again alongside the sea, then a huge wall and beyond she could see very little, though a pale moon came from behind cloud to light the water, which looked vast, stretching away to the horizon and sea wall, though it was calmer here.

Then the bus turned inland and Vi shivered, everything was so cold and grey in the fitful moonlight as now they passed granite walls, granite houses, deeper grey shadows between. She leaned back in her seat, rocked and thrown about by every twist and turn of the rickety old vehicle. Vi felt a sheen of icy perspiration on her face and wasn't sure whether she felt travel-sick, hungry or just plain ill.

They had travelled only a couple of miles when the bus stopped and the driver took a shaded hurricane lamp, lit it and climbed out. The whole bus was hushed, listening to the sound of the driver's departure, then a knock on a door, a delay, then some conversation and the approach of several lots of footsteps.

'Mr and Mrs Ellis'll take two boys,' the driver announced from the top step. Then, before Mr Finch could rise, a man who appeared to be dressed in several rough jumpers and cord trousers took the light and made his way along the aisle, lifting the lamp to look first one side and then the other.

Vi saw several boys sink lower in their seats. He stopped a couple of rows in front of them and addressed two boys. Neither answered. He repeated what was obviously a question.

'The boys do not understand your accent,' Mr Finch said, coming up behind the farmer, 'and neither do I.'

'He wants to know if they're brothers?' the driver said.

'That's my brother.' One ten year old pointed to a much smaller boy in the seat in front. 'This is my mate.'

The man stood and looked at the two boys seated together, said something else to the driver and, nodding to Mr Finch, pushed by him and climbed out of the bus.

Cutting the atmosphere on the bus was probably not possible, Vi thought, as they all listened to the man talking to his wife in what sounded to them like some foreign language. She remembered indignities they had already suffered – the pathetic scramble to help the children without toilet facilities every time their train had stopped. There had obviously been some pretty desperate remedies resorted to. She wondered if they were all treated like cattle being taken to market for long enough, they would begin to feel like animals.

The conversation outside the bus stopped and the man climbed onto the bottom step and mumbled something to the driver. He in turn nodded to Mr Finch and smiled. 'They'll take all three,' he said.

The tension that had built up ebbed with the news of this unexpected kindness enabling both brothers and friends to stay together, though Vi still felt appalled that such a selection system was going to operate. Everyone would want good, strong, healthy-looking children they could order about without trouble and certainly without the interference of older sisters and mothers!

It was strange too, she thought, to off-load three young boys into a dark strange land, to people they could not even understand. They called, 'Good luck!' and 'Keep y'peckers up!'

'See yer!' the eldest called back with an attempt at a smile. The others, heads down, stumbled reluctantly from the bus.

Vi peered out into the gloom and as they passed could just make out that the man and his wife were insisting on carrying the heaviest items. It relieved her mind no end.

'The trouble is,' Flo commented wryly as they drew away, 'me and Sid don't look up to much.'

'Is somebody coming for us?' Sid asked. 'I don't want—'

'We're staying together,' Vi interrupted with quiet determination.

Another stop brought two spinster ladies onto the bus, and saw the departure of two young girls, struggling under the weight of their own baggage.

Vi wished she could rid herself of the thought that the men were choosing cheap labour for their land and the women for their houses. Memories of Cambridge still coloured this second evacuation.

A short distance more and Mr Finch rose to announce that this was the final stop. 'We shall all disembark here and go inside the chapel where officials and local people are waiting to greet the rest of you.'

'To share us out,' Vi silently mouthed as they once more manhandled all their clumsy bags and parcels off the bus.

When they first entered the chapel there was a gap, a divide, as the small wave of heavily laden, travel-crumpled evacuees filtered in, forming a line facing the reception committee.

Coming in last from the back of the bus, Vi found herself and Sid in the middle of her group. Sid turned back and leaned heavily on her, making her stagger. Chalk and cheese, she thought. Jellied eels and Cornish pasties.

''Ere come on, m'ol'mate.' A man, squat-square and tanned, lifted Sid effortlessly away from her side and sat him in a pew. Sid seemed too fascinated by the height of the lift to protest.

'Come'n sit down, there's tea and sandwiches.'

'I'll soon look like a bleedin' sandwich,' a weary boy murmured.

The remark brought a noticeable pause, like a trip in a dance step, as the residents prepared to take the floor.

'We're always glad of a cuppa though,' Vi stated loudly, defiantly emphasising the London accent.

By her side Florrie murmured to Audrey flagging on her arm, 'Bear up, gel.'

The quiet concern of Florrie seemed to break the awkward spell. People moved forward, questions about how long they had been travelling were followed by exclamations of dismay. Mr Finch was soon consulting with a lady who was obviously an officer in the WVS – she had two lines of medal ribbons on her green uniform. Together they were consulting and comparing lists.

Vi turned away, trying to warm herself on her teacup, though it felt as if her very organs were turning to ice. The moment of truth this was called – though truth had very little to do with it. What would happen if someone spotted that their names were a fraudulent addition?

It began to seem more and more likely as names were ticked off and children were taken away by various people. But it became apparent their names were not the only ones still on the list – and there had obviously been some confusion about the children already dropped off or left behind in Penzance.

'I suppose it will all clear itself up in a day or two,' Albert Finch said wearily.

At that moment a woman with a weather-beaten face, dressed in several layers of clothing, brown tweed coat and beret overlaid with headscarf and shawl, came into the hall to claim the two remaining boys. 'I'm sorry, Mrs St

30

John Trewellan,' she said to the WVS officer, 'we got held up. Our animals got out on that dratted road.'

Mrs St John Trewellan! Vi made a quick reappraisal of the officer, but shook her head as she glimpsed her mother's expression of awe and noticed that the second cup of tea she had just received at that lady's hands Florrie now reverently put down. Ma would never change, always overwhelmed by those she saw as superior, be it vicar, school teacher, doctor, nurse, or this WVS lady, always a worrier – always needing support. No wonder Pa went over the top the other way – every man equal, his offspring as good as any!

It seemed that Mrs St John Trewellan too saw how the Tulley family hierarchy worked, for after some further consultation of lists, while she smiled and talked to Flo, it was to Vi that her eyes continually wandered.

'I'm so sorry, but we have obviously not made sufficient provision,' she said. 'We have no one else expected to collect people tonight.'

Vi felt that while her manner was dignified, her face was friendly, her blue eyes really concerned. She sensed too that this was the time they had to stand firm or they would be split up willy-nilly – and once separated it would be next to impossible to demand a place where they could all be together.

'Nobody wants us, do they, Vi?' Sid questioned.

'Seems not,' she replied uncompromisingly.

'Don't worry, we'll find you all beds – somewhere.'

'We're staying together,' Vi warned.

'For tonight it may not be possible.' She paused, then added gently but frankly, 'And it will be difficult anyway to house three grown-ups and your . . .'

'Brother,' Vi supplied.

'. . . all under one roof.'

'Vi, don't you think –' Ma began.

'Then we'll stay 'ere.' Vi sat down defiantly. 'Once you lot separate us we'll never get back together, *ever*.'

The WVS lady compressed her lips and turned to Mr Finch and the bus driver, who was now impatient to drive back to Penzance and his own bed. Receiving no help in that direction, she turned back to Florrie.

'For tonight?' she queried.

'No, Ma!' Vi interrupted. 'I promised Pa!'

'No!' Sid echoed. 'I wish we 'ad stayed with Pa.'

Audrey slumped down on the chapel pew by her side and leaned her head on Vi's shoulder, leaving only Florrie standing. 'I'm sorry, ma'am,' she whispered and, with a move that was half a kind of bob curtsey, she sat down by Audrey.

31

Chapter 4

Vi woke stiff with cold and cramp and for a second, as her eyes focused up and up to what looked like the huge polished beams of an inverted boat, she did not recall where she was. She moved and the wooden and canvas camp bed creaked alarmingly. Then she remembered the collapsible beds and blankets that had eventually been brought to the chapel.

Her back ached with lying on the taut canvas. Like a hammock with no give, she thought, and wondered that any of them had slept at all. She turned her head. The mound under her mother's blankets looked no larger than Sid. Audrey lay sleeping like the other two but what she could see of all their faces was so pale, so battle-weary already. She felt terribly responsible for them all.

Slowly, and as quietly as the bed would allow, she swung her legs to the ground and got to her feet, suppressing the urge to groan as she straightened and stretched. She shivered as her toes curled against the impact of the stone floor and picking up her shoes and coat she moved away from the little row of beds.

Mrs St John Trewellan had shown her the chapel kitchen where they could make tea. She tiptoed that way but, as she reached the front door, curiosity to view where and what they had come to in the light of morning overcame her. Slipping her feet into her shoes and wrapping her coat tight round herself, she opened the heavy oak door with infinite care, pulling it to behind herself.

If she had shivered inside, she shuddered now. She was appalled by the greyness of *everything*. The early morning light barely pierced the grey veils of mist which appeared to hang like giant predatory cobwebs over the whole scene. She had not realised they were on top of a steep hill. Terraces of tiny-windowed, grey-stone houses fell away either side of the chapel. Their squat appearance, after the three-storied Victorian and Georgian terraces she was used to, made her think they looked more poverty-stricken than anything she'd seen in the so-called slums of London. On the other side of the road there was a stone wall, a gateway and fields.

There was no colour anywhere. She walked quietly a few paces along the

32

street, peering ever closer at the windows for signs of life – but these had deep stone sills, some both inside and out. Grey granite, cold grey granite. She shivered and turned back towards the chapel, slowly climbed the steps. What was she going to tell the others when they woke? Was there *anything* cheerful? Perhaps when the next train left for Paddington, she thought.

Then, turning round to view the scene again, she realised that far over the top of the grey village she could see a long line as if ruler-drawn straight across between sky and land. 'Oh! It's the sea.' A slither of bright excitement pierced her heart as she remembered a day trip to Southend, a day when her father had whistled all day long. 'Pa,' she breathed, 'wish you were 'ere!'

As she gazed at the blue horizon, she realised she could also see ships in the distance, no more than dark dots of differing sizes on the broad expanse of water, while behind her far over the land it was becoming lighter, the mists lifting away. Dark grey was becoming lighter grey. The sun might even break through! Perhaps it might not be all bad.

She heard her mother coughing as she crept back to the chapel kitchen to pump up the tiny oil stove. She wondered where they would spend their second night? There was her mother's health – and Audrey's. Everyone knew you were vulnerable after a shock such as her friend – all of them, really – had suffered.

Sid was outside, watching the ships, when a pony and trap came smartly up the hill towards the chapel and stopped outside. ''Ere's that lady,' Sid called. Then, as Mrs St John Trewellan tied the reins to the trap and dismounted, he pointed out to sea and asked, 'Are they Jerries?'

She shaded her eyes. 'No, I'm sure they are ours. Part of our brave navy.'

''Ow d'ye know?' Vi heard him ask as she came out to join them.

'Well . . .' Mrs St John Trewellan shaded her eyes with both hands this time. 'I think because they are in an ordered formation, a convoy, and they are sailing in near to our shore, *that* makes me think they are ours.'

'Hmmm!' Sidney shaded his eyes in exactly the same way, then looked up and asked, 'Is that your 'orse?'

'Yes, his name's Double Life.'

'Go and tell Ma and Audrey the WVS lady's 'ere,' Vi said as she saw the next question coming. She stood inwardly uncertain before this member of the local upper crust she had defied the night before, but she stood erect and raised her chin. There was a moment when their eyes met, held – and each made appraisal.

'Yes,' the older woman said, as if endorsing a former opinion. 'Apt to ask awkward questions, is he?'

'You might say that,' Vi admitted but returned the smile.

'I hope you've not been too uncomfortable?'

'We've all slept at least some of the time.' Vi felt her colour rise as in the

33

back of her mind she heard her father's oft-repeated words, 'A few manners never 'urt anyone.'

'Thank you,' she added, 'thank you very much for all you did last night. We 'ave to be together you see . . .' She stopped herself, feeling in danger of babbling on, of sounding like someone likely to *beg* for favours.

'Yes.' The interruption was quiet, understanding. 'I believe I do. And this morning?'

'Two ladies from the village brought us porridge to warm up and eggs to boil. It's the best meal we've 'ad since Sunday dinner at 'ome!'

'Good! Well done!' she approved, then asked, 'Has no one else been?' When Vi shook her head she added, 'I'm expecting Mr Spurrier. He's our local butcher and, more importantly, a tenant on one of the Trewellan farms. I . . .' She stopped and indicated down towards the village where a van was labouring up towards them.

One of our farms – Vi registered the information as they waited.

'Yes, this looks like him now. Mr Spurrier owes me a favour and we are about to take it up.'

For the second time that morning Vi thought of her pa. It seemed this lady might be a fixer too! They certainly needed one right now.

'I do have hopes of keeping you all together . . .' She paused to watch the butcher's van which, to her obvious surprise, stopped some thirty or so yards short of where they stood. 'If my Mr Spurrier comes up trumps . . .'

The stocky man who alighted from the van had the air of doing anything but 'coming up trumps'. His movements were abrupt, sharp. He banged the door of his van belligerently, approached with short heel banging steps and, while he acknowledged Mrs St John Trewellan with a snatched removal of his cap and a brief and brusque nod of balding head, he looked at no one else. 'Can I 'ave a word?' He nodded again back towards the van.

Vi watched, folding her arms as she saw the negative and agitated slicing actions of hand and arm while Mrs Trewellan stood perfectly still looking fixedly at a point above the shorter man's head. The others, summoned by Sid, came to join her.

'Looks like we might as well leave the beds up,' Audrey said by her side.

'It's Sunday tomorrow,' Ma commented, 'they won't want us 'ere then.'

'No,' Vi agreed, and as Sid leaned back against his mother, she put an arm around her friend's shoulders as they all stood drawing their own conclusions about the strange confrontation.

Mrs Trewellan's tactics seemed to be to allow Mr Spurrier to run himself out of steam as she stood silently impassive. Then, as the man's arms finally dropped to his sides, she turned her head slightly in his direction and seemed to say about two words.

Her riposte was certainly short, but obviously devastating, for the butcher gave one last enormous shrug of his shoulders, followed by throwing his arms up in a gesture of capitulation, before he turned back to his vehicle, climbed in and drove away.

'I wonder what she said?' Audrey pondered.

'I wonder what she's got on him?' Vi added more meaningfully, as Mrs Trewellan came towards them – grinning, Vi thought – if ladies did grin? 'She looks,' Vi whispered, 'as smug as the cat who's caught her fish without wetting her feet.'

'It's all arranged,' she told them. 'There's a farmhouse at your disposal at Gerrard's Head. It's been unoccupied for a time. The last tenant has left a few things behind and if you take the camp beds and bedding from here . . .'

'A farmhouse?' Ma queried with disbelief.

'Mr Spurrier assures me it is perfectly weatherproof and can be made comfortable. I *don't think* he would say that unless it was true!'

'A farmhouse?' Ma repeated.

'It's been empty some years . . .'

'But our own place? On our own?' Florrie looked up at Mrs Trewellan with hands clasped as if in prayer.

'It's primitive, m'dear, don't expect too much.'

'It's *more* than we could've expected, ma'am.'

'You can thank your daughter for insisting you stay together!'

In the next few minutes they learned their new home was some three miles away, within sight of the sea, and that Mrs Trewellan would contact Mr Spurrier's man to come and take their belongings over there as soon as possible. 'If I were you, I should buy some groceries to take with you.'

'We'll manage!' Vi countered the look Mrs Trewellan cast at their bags. 'Don't worry about us. Once we're settled . . .'

They gathered outside to watch the pony depart at a spanking trot with Mrs Trewellan's tweed-suited figure keeling the trap slightly to one side.

'What do you think?' Audrey asked.

'I think she carries a lot of weight!' Vi replied, and the others drew in their breaths then gave relief to a lot of pent-up feelings by rushing into the chapel, closing the door and laughing raucously, outrageously – out of control.

'Vi!' her mother remonstrated at last. 'That's not very grateful. You're as bad as Sid with his remarks.'

'She is fat,' Sid added, having at last understood the joke. 'Fatter than Audrey.'

'Thanks very much!' Audrey said.

Vi felt she was ungrateful but really meant no disrespect to the lady, in fact quite the opposite, and seeing Audrey forget and smile for a moment was worth almost anything.

'Come on,' she said, 'let's get these camp beds folded up.' She picked up three long green canvas bags. 'They came in these.'

35

There was little more they could do once the camp beds were stowed away, the blankets folded and everything piled near the door.

'Shall we buy some groceries?' Vi asked.

'I'll stay 'ere with the things in case this chap comes,' Audrey volunteered.

'Yes,' Ma agreed without any degree of certainty in her voice. 'The thing is we must be careful. We don't know 'ow much rent we'll be charged for this . . . farmhouse . . .'

'Surely not much!' Vi was outraged at the idea. 'And if it was empty anyway, perhaps they won't charge us at all.'

'I didn't much like the look of Mr Spurrier, and if he's our landlord . . .' Florrie said, opening her handbag and taking out her purse. 'We won't spend more than five shillings.'

It was something that had not occurred to Vi. The thought of that local butcher as their reluctant landlord was not comforting. 'We could get heavy things like spuds, flour, bread – if we're getting a lift, and we'll 'ave a look at the grocery shops and see which one it'll be best to register with.'

The main square of the village had a free-standing clock tower, a perimeter of shops with a church spire behind. Overhead, great gulls, bigger than anything they had seen before, circled, screamed and swooped as if they too had an interest in the shopping centre.

Ma gave Vi a nudge to draw her attention to 'Spurrier's Family Butchers'. There was more fresh meat displayed in the window than either had seen for a long time and a white-overalled woman and a youth were busy serving. There was no sign of the van or the owner.

'Looks like he's doing all right without taking rent from us,' Vi commented.

'Ah!' Ma tempered disgust with a worldly-wise laugh in the back of her throat. 'And much usually wants more.'

The little shopping area was busy and, as well as the shopping, a good deal of gossiping was going on. Men and women hailed each other, stood laughing and talking, catching up with each other's lives. They also took stock of the passing newcomers. In their city-black coats and close-fitting hats, Vi knew they must stand out like cats among Trafalgar Square pigeons.

They walked over to where a greengrocery shop had a good display of root vegetables, apples and potatoes. 'Get a stone of potatoes, I can carry those,' Vi said.

'Thar's no need to carry anything,' the brisk shopkeeper, her hair a bush of rusty grey and her cheeks as red as her Cox's apples, said. 'I've a young tacker 'ere with nothing to do. Where y'want 'em delivering?'

They bought potatoes, turnips and carrots, bags of dried lentils, butter beans and peas, in return for which they parted with two and eight pence halfpenny and a lot of information.

36

'Not much she don't know about us now,' Florrie commented as they left the shop.

'Worse than bloody Londoners!' Sid added.

'You watch your language!' Ma admonished. Vi did her best to keep her face straight but it was something she'd tell Pa in her first letter from Cornwall – make him laugh.

'Baker's across the way.' She pointed to where a small crowd of shoppers were going in and out.

'Smells nice – like Mr Popp's old shop,' Sid cried, dancing along in front of them. '*Where* did Mr Popps go?'

'Into an internment camp for the duration of the war,' Vi reminded him, knowing it was the fascination of the idea and the words that intrigued him.

'An internment camp for the duration,' Sid declared as they entered the shop – where all other conversations died on their feet and all gazes focused on the three strangers.

Sid dropped behind his mother, but Vi, compensating for his retreat, stepped smartly forward into the shop. Someone behind her murmured, 'There is a queue.'

Vi felt her colour rise but Ma caught her arm and they stepped to the side where a line of people had indeed formed, waiting to reach the counter. The humiliation was not over.

'Shouldn't think they get bread in internment camps,' the same thin impatient voice commented.

Vi swung out of line again, took the middle of the shop floor. 'I don't know what you 'ave got in your petty little minds, but just to put you straight, my Pa is driving buses in London in the Blitz.'

'Real war work! While you're here trying to buy up our food! All the bread's ordered here. There's none to spare.'

This time the speaker was identified. Vi focused on the sour-faced woman tied around with sacking over her clothes. 'So you're the biddy!' The idea of her father being unjustly put down by *anyone*, let alone this malicious ragamuffin old harridan, made her seethe.

'Well, well!' Vi strode by the woman and back again. 'I can see you're another one of the local nobility!' She stopped, arms akimbo. 'Let me tell you, we'd rather eat where we came from than 'ere! We'd *rather* be where we came from than 'ere! Even though my best friend's parents 'ave been killed and her 'ome levelled to the ground, I'd sooner be there!'

'Vi! Leave it, Vi!' Ma was moving away from the queue but several women immediately in front of her motioned for her to stay, though her daughter was still way out of control and Sid stood chewing hard at his bottom lip.

'You know what?' Vi pushed her face towards the woman, who stood her ground, lips curled in disdain. 'I'd sooner 'ave them Jerry bombs. They're more friendly than you lot.'

'Don't judge us all by one, m'andsome.' A younger woman put her hand on Vi's arm, but she pulled away, her anger still too great for sympathy to do more than add fuel.

'I was going to cancel one of my loaves,' the woman called to the girl behind the counter, 'let the lady have one of mine.'

'And mine,' another offered.

'We don't want your bleedin' charity!' Sid's voice was overwrought. 'Do we, Vi?' He rushed to clasp his sister's hand and pulled her towards the door. 'Come on, Ma!'

'You'll want tea, though,' Ma said, opening her purse.

It was a very sober party that returned to the chapel. Vi and Sid held hands while Ma carried the loaves. Vi was torn between a feeling that Ma had somehow let her down and yet she had done what she always did – look after the interest of her family. Matters of pride did not seem to enter into that.

They had plenty of time to come to terms with each other again for their promised transport did not come until after Ma had again gone to the shops. Surprisingly Sid insisted on going too. They had come back with fish from a fisherman's cart and they fried the most delicious mackerel they had ever tasted and cleaned their plates with slices of the bread.

'It doesn't even smell like fish,' Ma said, sniffing as they again washed and stacked away the chapel crockery. 'I was worried about that!'

'The man said "caught this morning, m'andsome",' Sid supplied. 'What is "m'andsome"?'

The conversation was stopped as another voice hailed from the body of the chapel. 'Anyone thar?'

They all emerged to find the daylight from the open chapel door partly blocked by a figure in black outline.

'Come to take you to Gerrard's Head,' the man announced.

Chapter 5

Vi saw the man pull himself up from where he lounged against the doorpost as they went towards him. Then, half scowling, half grinning, he pulled off his cap. He was dark haired, powerful, stocky, but younger than she had first thought. She wondered why he was not in the army?

'*You're* going to Gerrard's Head?' he asked.

'Yes! Why? Some reason we shouldn't?' Vi questioned the disbelief in his voice.

He shrugged. 'All the same to me, but – just women and a boy? It's a bit—'

'We're used to managing,' Vi cut in finally as he span his cap between his fingers and just what Gerrard's Head was seemed to elude him. It was more the way his eyes became bolder and lingered on the two of them that made her feel they might be vulnerable. She remembered from the days in Cambridge that some people thought all London girls were fast, game for anything.

'I can give you a 'and from time to time,' he answered, ignoring Ma struggling with the ungainly camp beds and reaching across to take the paper carrier of bread from Audrey.

'Thanks!' Vi forestalled his intention by sweeping the carrier into her own hand and nodding meaningfully to the bulky beds. 'Not on light work, are you?'

For two seconds their glances held, then he grinned, flapped his cap back on his head and turned to Sid. 'Right, soldier! Let's get you onto the cart first.'

Vi knew he could not have hit on a better moniker to captivate Sid and, when her brother was sat on the front of the cart and given the reins to hold, there was one member of the Tulley family completely won over.

'Keep him steady.'

'Wot's 'is name?' Sid asked without moving a muscle from the task of holding the reins.

'Major.'

'Steady boy, steady Major!' Sid solemnly ordered the motionless old shire horse. 'Wot's your name?'

The second question brought a pause in the loading of the cart as they all introduced themselves. They learned his name was Paul Kerrow and that he had an exemption from the forces because he worked on Mr Spurrier's land.

'Where d'you live?' Sid asked.

'Oh! 'Ere and there,' Paul answered.

'That's right! Don't you tell him. He's got to learn not to ask so many questions,' Vi approved, but, glancing at the young man, it seemed it was she who had misinterpreted the truth. Could he really live ''ere and there' in different places, she wondered? Perhaps he was a sort of gipsy?

An early dusk was already beginning to fall by the time everything was loaded on to the none too clean farm cart. The only protection for the women as they sat in the back were a few cleanish sacks. Vi elected to perch uncomfortably on the bags containing the camp beds. They did not talk much as they travelled, for while it was bumpy enough down into the town, as the road climbed very steeply out the far side it became even rougher. It looked as if some attempt had been made to spread tarmacadam, but for long stretches it appeared the roadmakers had given up.

Some ten minutes later they topped the hill and saw they were on a road running along the cliff tops. Today the sea was spread large, rough and wild over to their left as they travelled away from the small town. Mist obscured the horizon but it all smelled so different – no lingering aftermath of smoke or soot in this fog. No cosiness reminiscent of friends and firesides either. It reminded Vi of the bleak prints of Victorian sea storms her grandmother used to have hanging in her parlour.

Jolting along in this solitary cart, Vi felt as if they had gone back into history, like the tumbrils on the way to Madame Guillotine. She wondered if Pa was home in Bethnal Green, if the fire was lit in the middle kitchen? Then, dismally watching the road extend behind the cart, she realised that while the road had turned inland they were going the opposite way, as if straight for the sea. The jolting became a lurching as the cart's wheels fell into deep worn ruts.

They passed through two rough hewn granite gateposts shortly afterwards and the cart stopped in a square yard edged with stone outplaces and what was obviously the back of the old farmhouse.

'Is there a key?' Vi asked, down from the cart first and approaching the back door, once painted brown but flaked off to its raw grey wood in most places.

'It's not locked,' Paul answered.

'You've been here before, then?' she questioned.

'I . . .'

He stood as if transfixed by her question, as if there was much he should say but could not, she gave him a little sharp nod of encouragement.

40

'We . . . we . . . came to clear up a bit this morning.'

'Mr Spurrier?'

He nodded and Vi turned to grasp the handle, pressed the thumbpiece to lift the latch. The door swung open easily to reveal a bare room with a stone sink and a filthy iron cooking range. The floor appeared to be just compacted soil and there was an underlying suety smell, as if the butcher, or one of his dirty aprons, might still be lingering around somewhere. She heard Ma make some remark about San Izal.

Vi went ahead into a longer room where two windows looked out towards the sea – not that this was visible. The mist was rolling in quickly and now obscured anything beyond the cliff edge.

'This is a bit better,' she called, making a real effort to lift her voice and the others' spirits. 'At least there's furniture in 'ere.'

'Looks as if it's all in 'ere,' Ma commented, looking at the selection of tables and odd chairs, a wardrobe at one end, old brass bed-ends and a miscellaneous jumble of rusted cooking pans and farm tools.

'Everything's been dumped in one room.' Vi turned as if to accuse their transporter.

'I'll help you put the kitchen things back,' he said and no sooner had he spoken than he lifted the heavy old deal table. Twisting it on its side, he manoeuvred the legs around the doorframe and soon had it standing in the middle of the room with the sink. Next he took the old kitchen chairs.

Vi realised that he knew exactly where each piece had been before. He was no stranger to this place. Had he been living here, she wondered? She didn't find the thought comforting, or the fact that his physical strength was obviously so prodigious. He was not, she sensed, someone it was going to be easy either to get to know properly or to be comfortable with, though she noticed Audrey's eyes followed him all the time.

'Is there anything to light a fire with?' Ma asked.

'I'd best run a bush down the chimney first. There'll be a right heap of old nests up there.'

'You did say "a bush" *down* the chimney?' Vi queried.

He laughed. 'Proper job!'

'Proper job?' Vi repeated when he was outside. 'Whatever that means I shouldn't unpack anything, Ma,' she added ironically as she prepared to follow him to see just what he did intend.

Outside, Sid was attempting to lift a full bucket of water up to the horse's nose.

'I expect he can bend his head if you put it down.'

'I want to hold it,' Sid panted, adding as if in justification, 'we've got a well!'

'Oh cheers! Just what we need!' she groaned, then added firmly, '*You* stay away from it!'

41

She followed the path she had seen Paul take towards the front of the house. She stopped once out of sight of Sid, wondering how far away the sea was. She could hear it pounding subdued yet powerful, just like she remembered hearing it in a shell she and Audrey had listened to in Petticoat Lane market, a distant but positive dream. The mist too moved at the limitation it made on her vision, seeming to rise, swirl, then fall back on itself, but in doing so becoming thicker and pushing nearer to the house.

The steady low, deep roar of the waves seemed only to emphasise the silence and made her feel as if suddenly she was the only person in the world. She had been lost once in a smog in London, but this fog was not hemmed in by buildings. This fog felt as if it stretched away forever with untold mysteries and perils in its folds.

The next moment her heart was in her mouth, as well as most of her fists, as a noise like nothing she'd ever heard before seemed to be closing on her. It sounded like the approach of some mythological beast, claws scraping and scratching at the stone and gravel path. 'Come from the deep', was the unfortunate phrase that entered her head.

She was about to turn and run when common sense told her it had to be Paul returning with his bush, though it sounded more as if he was dragging a whole park-load of trees.

She forced herself to stand still and seconds later a man's figure emerged from the fog dragging a large and biblical looking thorn bush. Twisted and gnarled, it caught and dragged at everything it passed.

This ungainly, huge bush could not be what he intended to put down the chimney!

'Better tell 'em to clear things away from the fireplace inside,' he told her, as with an agility she had only ever seen before in an alley cat, he put one foot on a water butt, from where he leapt onto the concreted tiles of the roof and walked up to the chimney, pulling his rope and bush behind with a rapidity and ease which made her again feel a chill of unease about this man, his strengths – and his peculiar talents.

Before she could move to go inside, Paul was scooping out and throwing down great handfuls of straw and grass from the low square chimney top. Then he held up a dead bird's skeleton by its leg and swung it in Sid's direction before finally tossing it to earth.

Vi and Sid exchanged a look. 'I like the 'orse,' Sid reaffirmed darkly.

By the time Vi was inside, the end of the rope was looping down the chimney to the hearth, and Paul walked in after her. As he passed Audrey he pulled something from his pocket and gave it to her. 'For luck,' he said. 'It grows on the cliffs here at Gerrard's Head.' It was a sprig of deep purple autumn heather.

'Oh! Thank you.' Surprise put a depth of added meaning to Audrey's tone as she held it up for the others to see.

'Stand clear,' he ordered with an air of proprietorship as he knelt in the fireplace and began to haul in the rope. The noise the bush had made being dragged along the path was nothing compared with the screeching protest it made as it was broken and scraped down through the confines of the chimney. It brought down with it a fair lot more straw, feathers and another dead bird entangled in the broken carcass of the bush.

'That's going to take some clearing out!' Vi stated.

'What with?' Ma asked in a small desolate voice as the enormity of all they faced became ever more obvious.

'No need for that.' Paul kicked the stray pieces back into the fireplace and reached into his pocket for matches. In seconds, straw, bush, all but the rope which he retrieved, were roaring back up the chimney in a sheet of flames. 'Got a good draught!' he grinned.

The flames, outrageous and out of control as they were, cheered them and they stood around with stupefied grins on their faces. Then, before the flames could subside, Paul ran outside to fetch more kindling, then repeated the journey calling to Sid, 'Put more furze on.'

'Furze?' Vi queried, pulling a face as he left and watching Audrey as she tucked the heather into her blouse.

'As long as it burns and gives out 'eat, I don't care what 'e calls it,' Ma said as she returned from a foray upstairs. 'We'll 'ave a clear up in here and all sleep where there's a fire tonight. My lord! It's going to take some getting right!'

'It's so cold,' Audrey said, running her hands up and down her arms as she stooped before the fireplace.

Crouching next to her, pushing bits of wood into the flames, Sid informed them, 'You can see right up the chimney to the sky.'

Vi took one of the blankets and placed it round Audrey's shoulders. The thing they could not afford at the moment was for one of them to be ill, and she was desperately worried about her friend, so enervated, so stricken.

'So what 'ave we got?' She clapped her hands together and began a kind of review. 'Four camp beds and blankets and an open fire.'

'And what we've bought,' Ma added.

They had an impromptu meeting around their belongings. 'Glad we went shoppin',' Ma said. 'Now if we could clean just one pan, boil it up a few times . . .'

'It's a well,' Vi remembered, 'the water comes from a well and I don't even know where it is – and you're not showing me,' she told Sid, who showed signs of explanation, 'it's practically dark out there.'

''As Paul gone, then?' Audrey asked.

'Surely he would have said,' Vi commented, but without conviction, mentally labelling him what Pa would call a 'real odd bod'.

At that moment a light shone from outside one of the windows. They watched it move across the second window and out of sight. Then it spilled into the kitchen and Paul came in carrying a lighted storm lantern and a kettle. They greeted him almost as if he were the second coming.

'Are they for us?' Ma asked as he knelt by the hearth and carefully balanced the kettle in the flames. 'It's full,' he said, 'be careful.'

'Ooh! You're a good boy!' Ma exclaimed, resting a hand lightly on his shoulder as he knelt. 'A good boy!'

Paul turned with the flames of the fire warming his cheeks. There was a sense of some wonder on his face – almost, Vi thought, as if he had never been called a 'good boy' before and was savouring the strange feeling.

The light of the lamp suddenly made Vi aware of how dark it was. 'You'll not find your way back . . .' She stopped before she reached the word home, beginning to be unsure whether he had one.

'Major'll take me,' he answered. 'I'll fetch you another load of wood, then I'll go. I've brought in another bucket of water, too – it's under the sink. I wouldn't go out tonight if I were you, with this fog coming in.'

'I don't know what we'd 'ave done without you,' Ma exclaimed.

Paul shrugged and looked over to the two girls.

'No, that's right,' Vi felt his glance prompted her to say. 'You've been . . .'

'Lucky for us,' Audrey added, touching the heather in her buttonhole. 'Lucky you came.'

'See you tomorrow, then.'

Vi bit her lip – and her tongue – against the uncharitable reservations she felt. She just hoped they were not going to need too much of his help and, glancing at Audrey, she just hoped he was not going to be around very often, either. Amorous complications they did not need, and Audrey was just ripe to fall into a pair of sympathetic arms.

'You 'ave to feed your 'orse, first,' Sid put in. 'My pa says a good man looks after his animal first.'

' 'E'll take me 'ome and I'll feed 'ee,' Paul agreed.

Once they were alone, Ma came into her own. As soon as the kettle boiled, she carefully brewed tea in the cups they had brought with them on the journey. Then she sliced bread and they made toast before the fire. Onto this Ma thinly sliced up the cheese ration they had also brought with them.

The food and warmth gave them the energy to make some final efforts to make themselves comfortable for the night.

Vi gingerly picked up all the rusted kitchen utensils and made a new pile of these in one corner of the kitchen. Underneath them she found a small pile of clean hemp sacks. 'Reckon these come as standard issue down 'ere,' she quipped, 'you sit on 'em, wear 'em . . .'

'Walk on 'em.' Ma pointed to the floor by the beds they had set up in a rectangle, with the fireplace on the fourth side. 'Waste not, want not, they'll do for mats.'

Ma had one more thing she said she wanted to do before Sid said his prayers. She carefully unwrapped two objects from the cloth bag she had carried so carefully on the journey and, with the air of a triumphant conjurer, placed on the stone mantelpiece her beloved cream and pink rose vases from the parlour in Bethnal Green.

'Aah! Ma!' Vi exclaimed. 'Not those awful vases! You haven't brought those all this way?' She could hardly believe that between them they had helped carry what she firmly regarded as just old-fashioned junk.

'They were your grandmother's!' Ma said defiantly. 'And I don't feel at home anywhere without them.'

'Put this in one,' Audrey said, reaching over with the sprig of heather, 'give us all some luck.'

Again Vi wanted to express the unjustified sentiment that she did not feel Paul Kerrow would bring anybody luck, but a movement as Audrey lay back on her pillow caught Vi's eye. She saw her friend put her hand over the locket her mother had worn the night she was killed. It was the only possession she had which had been her mother's.

'Well, I suppose I prefer even those vases to the cross and candlesticks in the chapel,' Vi capitulated, 'but I can't really believe we've toted those things from eleven Brierly Street to here.'

'Can I say my prayers in bed tonight?' Sid asked, yawning.

'I should think so, for once. You say on and we'll all listen and say ours quietly with you,' Ma agreed.

It was a routine Violet too had learned as a child. Before being tucked in, she would kneel by the bed, hands together, eyes closed and recite first the Lord's Prayer – then a string of personal pleas was allowed. Sid's consisted of a comprehensive list of people to 'God Bless'. Vi knew this was because there was a dread of missing anyone out. If you did, and anything happened to that person, it would be your personal fault. Vi could still vouch for the same feeling, her list too tended to grow.

Tonight Sid's roll call had two extra names. 'And God Bless Paul and Major!'

The prayers over and the lamp put out, the camp beds creaked as each tried to find the most comfortable position. The fire crackled gently and, watching the flames, Vi made another kind of inventory: warm, fed, together. *So far, Pa, so good.*

She was sure her eyes had only just closed when she was brought bolt upright by a shattering explosion.

A bomb? Gunfire? Sirens?

'What is it?'

'An air raid!'

'I thought we'd left the Blitz in London?' Audrey gasped.

The guns roared out again.

'Ma!' Sid appealed. Soon all four were clasped together in terror. Then another thought occurred to Vi and Ma at the same moment.

'I bet they've seen our fire! We've no curtains!'

'And Sid said he could see straight up the chimney.'

'We must put the fire out,' Ma decided. 'Quick, Vi!'

Vi pulled some of the logs from the blaze, then, feeling one of the sacks beneath her feet, she rushed to the kitchen and doused it in the water bucket.

'Stand back,' she called as she dropped the wet hessian over the flames. Sparks, ash and wood flew and sizzled, but the sack was thick and wet enough to damp down the glow.

There was more gunfire.

'They must be overhead,' she said.

'Let's get under the stairs,' Ma said. 'That's always supposed to be a strong place in a building.'

They dragged all the blankets under the stairs and huddled together. The noise of this unexpected battle echoed and thundered, it seemed, all around the house.

'Perhaps I'll have to wet another sack and put it over the fire, make sure it's properly out. I don't want that one drying out and bursting into flames.' Vi wondered what Pa would say if she got them all killed the first night they were evacuated?

The thought had hardly formed when, softly at first, Audrey began to cry. Soon they were all trying to comfort her as her shoulders heaved and she cried fit to break her heart.

'I can't bear it,' she sobbed. 'I can't bear it. I can't bear it!'

All the control she had managed during the funeral, the journey, coming to Gerrard's Head, evaporated under the strain of the guns and sirens.

'Don't give in now, Aud!' Vi begged. 'What you've been through was worse than this.'

'I know! I know! I don't care about this! I don't care!' she shouted, as if to drown out the explosions outside. 'It's Ma and Pa . . . and London . . . and everything! I just want to die!'

'We're not are we, Ma?' Sid was suddenly alarmed at the word. 'Not like the Arcott twins?'

'No, no,' Ma reassured him, 'and we're all together.'

'Not Pa!' he protested as the guns boomed out again, the sound rolling out and all around the house like the fog or the sea. 'Not Pa!'

Vi, arms around as many shoulders she could encompass, wondered what she would write to Pa if she survived the night. It was not going to be easy to make light of this place, this Gerrard's Head. This place, she reminded herself, she had brought them to by her insistence that they stay together.

46

Chapter 6

It was nearly seven o'clock when Vi woke from a short, exhausted sleep to a pale light, and – she lifted her head from the crook of her arm to be sure – yes, silence. As she stirred she saw Ma was also beginning to rouse and listen. 'It's over,' Ma mouthed.

'At last!' she whispered back, glancing at Sid and Audrey who lay at awkward angles on the blankets, but both were deeply asleep. Audrey had cried until Vi had wondered whether a heart really could break, until she had feared for her friend's sanity, until Sid too had sobbed in sympathy and cried for Pa. For a time she had been fearful Ma too might give way when, like a flash of inspiration, she had remembered what Pa had said about a panicking runaway horse. 'Best thing is to ride the beast, urge it on! That makes 'em think!'

With no more than an instinctive feeling it might work, she had encouraged Audrey to have her cry out, 'get it out of your system'. Miraculously, it had stemmed the worst of the sobbing and control came. Audrey and Sid had fallen asleep regardless of the raid, while she and Ma had kept the long vigil.

Now the two of them carefully and painfully extracted themselves from the huddle and crept out into the main room.

'What 'ave we come to?' Ma muttered, questioning more than the sprawl of their abandoned beds, more than the flakes of grey ash that had settled everywhere from Vi's efforts to keep the fire damped down.

'At least all this wood's dry . . .' Vi felt she could not afford the emotional energy necessary for another review of their miserable state. She began to collect small pieces of kindling from the stock of wood she had expected they might use up through the night. Without too much trouble, she had relit the fire while Ma redressed, complete with two great cardigans and a woolly hat. She sniffed deprecatingly at the arms of her woolly. 'Begin to smell like a gipsy already.'

'I'll see if I can find the well,' Vi said with equal regret as she smoothed down the good tweed skirt she had pulled on during the night to try to keep warm. 'Reckon trousers'll be the best thing to wear in this place. It's going to be like being in an army camp.'

'Not if I can 'elp it,' Ma retorted, handing her the kettle.

Vi picked up the bucket from the kitchen, thinking this room looked and smelt more like a cow shed than part of a house. She pushed her toe down at the floor. How could anybody live with just an earth floor in this day and age? Then she frowned as where she had scored the soil there appeared to be some kind of pattern underneath – something to investigate later.

She carried the kettle and the bucket outside through the back door into the yard where Sid had watered the horse. She looked all around the farmyard but could find no trace of the well. Eventually she retraced her steps of the night before towards the front of the house where she had encountered Paul coming back with the bush.

There, at the far end of the house front, was what she had previously taken for a divergence of a boundary wall. She could now see it was a separate circular granite wall with a wooden cover. But before she investigated the well further, she was completely captivated by the view in front of her.

Green fields, green such as she had never seen before, emerald green, reached to the cliff edge. Then beyond was a calm blue sea, a paler blue sky with white gulls wheeling and crying above the cliffs. A thin line of white cloud, like a long careless brush-stroke on the horizon, was the only lingering trace of any fog.

She put down her containers and walked slowly, like one enchanted, towards the edge of the cliff. She was cautious too, for the cliffs looked high, running out and falling steeply into the sea to her right, while towards the town to her left the cliffs fell back before running out again beyond the houses, so the farm stood almost midway in the bay.

As she reached the edge she saw that the height of the cliff where she stood was graduated by great falls of earth which lay like a series of broad green steps down to a sandy cove. She was quite sure it was possible to climb down. It was like their own private beach.

She shaded her eyes to see if there was barbed wire or any fortifications against invaders. Over to the right she thought she could see the rounded top of a concrete pillbox and again she wondered if they were near some secret military or, more likely, naval installation – not a very *sensible* place to billet evacuees, but beautiful, so picturesque.

She breathed in deeply. This morning the air was bracing, full of the smell of the sea, good healthy ozone. She wanted to run and fetch Ma but thought she had probably better fill the kettle first. To Ma, a cuppa came before anything in the mornings.

On a practical level, the state of the well was in keeping with the rest of Gerrard's Head. She gasped when she saw the state of the wooden cover, more a danger by its useless rotten presence than the open well, which revealed dark and deep initiated caution. It was impossible to see the bottom or even a distant glimpse of the water. There was no handle or hoist. Paul had obviously just used the same rope he had hauled the bush down the chimney with, for it lay coiled on the wall.

It took several attempts, for the well was deep and though she could hear the bucket hit the water, once there it obviously floated and there was nothing she could do from above to turn it and make it take up water. It was not until she hurled the bucket upside down with all her might that she thought she had succeeded. Pulling again on the rope she found she had captured about a cupful.

She was peering dismally into the bucket when a voice behind her made her start violently.

'Sorry!' said Paul, indicating back along the grassy cliff path towards the village. 'I thought you saw me coming.'

One hand on her thudding heart, she shook her head. 'No, too busy trying to catch some water!' She thought how much more civilised he looked this morning with his cap in his pocket and his hair obviously newly damped down and brushed – or was it that *she* felt so much more uncouth, unwashed and ungroomed?

'It's a knack,' he said, taking the bucket from her. She watched as he retied the rope to it so it looped through the handle but could be lodged on the bottom to hold the bucket upside down as it fell. 'Then as it fills it turns the right way and you can pull it up.'

''Ow do you know when it's full?'

'It's like fishing,' he explained with a grin, 'you can tell when you've got a bite.' He handed her the bucket and rope. 'Drop it down,' he said, 'and I always keep one foot on the other end of the rope.'

She did as she was told. 'Now take up the slack . . .' He leaned over the well wall with her. 'Not too much, just so you can feel the bucket.'

Suddenly the weight on the end of the rope increased and the rope became so taut and heavy she would have lost it if Paul had not grabbed hold. 'Now it's full,' he told her and, grinning, he extended his arm out straight, taking the full weight of the swinging bucket with one hand.

'It certainly is,' she said at last, fearing that if she didn't admire this feat of strength, she might never get the water.

Paul hauled up the bucket hand over hand and, once the brimming container came into sight, he brushed by her, reaching down to grab the handle.

'That all looks 'ard work,' Ma called as she came along the path towards them. 'Morning, Paul. You came just in time. I saw Vi struggling from the window, thought she needed a bit of help.' Her attention then fell on the well cover. 'This needs fixing a bit sharp or we'll be losing Sid!'

'It needs new timber . . .' Paul sounded doubtful as he added, 'I could see Mr Spurrier.'

'Tell 'im it won't look good if he loses an evacuee down his well!' Vi said.

'And 'im a town councillor,' Paul added. 'I'll see what I can do.'

'I suppose the water's all right to drink?' Ma said, peering at the water.

'My ol' man used to say it was the best in Cornwall,' Paul answered.

'It's lovely and clear,' Ma said and certainly it sparkled like crystal in the sunlight. 'Make a good cuppa, d'you reckon? I know after last night we can all do with one.'

Paul's expression was regretful as he asked, 'Did the fire go out? I thought you'd be cosy.'

'We 'ad to put it out when the air raid started,' Vi told him. 'We must 'ave been showing lights all over what with no curtains and sparks shooting up the chimney . . .'

'What raid?' Paul asked, frowning. 'We've never 'ad a raid down 'ere.'

'Well you certainly 'ad one last night,' Ma said. 'Guns and sirens, the lot.'

'Is there a naval base or something near 'ere?' Vi wanted to know.

Paul frowned and stood shaking his head, then he seemed to realise what they were talking about. 'Oh!' he said, his face brightening. 'You mean the maroons on The Long Rocks and – ' he laughed out loud now ' – and the foghorn! That's what you heard. The fog signals! It was thick fog most of the night and the guns would have been going off on the spur of rocks out at sea and the siren you heard would be Pendeen lighthouse.'

'You mean there was no air raid?' Vi asked, while at the same time realising that it had been different but she had not been able to put her finger on why until now. 'I suppose I thought we just couldn't hear the planes or the bombs because of the racket the guns were making.'

'I've never 'eard anything like that lot before,' Ma said.

'We do get a lot of fog,' Paul said, adding in disbelief, 'and you put out the fire.'

'And spent the night huddled together under the stairs,' Vi said. 'That should give all the locals a good laugh.'

'Not if *you* don't tell 'em, it won't,' Paul told her, and taking the kettle he filled this from the bucket. Ma took it without another word and headed back to the house.

'We've been evacuated before,' Vi said, by way of apology, 'nobody liked us much there either.'

'I've never worried much about being liked,' he said, glancing at her quickly before untying the bucket. 'I just get on with what I have to do. I'm ploughing today.' He cast an arm back in the direction he had arrived from and she realised he had come specially to see if they were all right.

'I'm sorry . . . I mean I know you don't have to do all this and we're really grateful. We've got a lot to learn . . .'

'Pity it's not the spring, real nice here then.' There was regret in his voice, a tone of taking a personal responsibility for the shortcomings of his birthplace.

'It's nice today.' She looked out at the calm blue sea. 'Peaceful,' she added ironically, and he laughed, appreciative of her sense of humour.

She watched him go and was sure he could walk many, many miles without tiring. He was strong, muscular – and aware of the fact. For no real reason she found that cautionary, like a vague threat – like the well with the rotten cover. She would mention writing to Roy, she thought, but then if she immediately put herself on the 'spoken for' list that might make Audrey more likely to receive his attentions, his sprigs of heather.

Thoughtfully, she went in to help her mother share the news of their needless panic through the night.

In spite of their broken sleep, as Ma said, they had to 'get stuck in', and by midday their backs ached and they were filthy. A wire brush and black lead had been fetched from the town by Audrey and Sid and the range in the kitchen had been derusted, the flues swept, the grate black-leaded and, with the back boiler filled with water and the fire lit, it was all working. The flames drew under the oven when the damper knob underneath was slid open, and the water was beginning to heat up! It felt like a major victory.

Then Vi, exploring with an old knife declared, 'There's lino on the floor under all this filth!'

'And there it can stay for today,' Ma declared. 'I've 'ad enough hard graft for one day.'

'Right! As soon as the water's hot in that boiler, I'm going to 'ave a stripped wash down and put some clean clothes on. I can't stand being this filthy any longer,' Vi declared.

'It'll have to be in the bucket, then. We've got nothing else.'

'That's OK,' Vi said. 'We can take turns. I'll take a couple of chairs or something upstairs.'

In the end, they wiped down and carried upstairs both an old brass bedstead and an old iron one, plus a couple of chairs. 'That's definitely it for today,' Ma said. 'We'll 'ave our washes, a cuppa and a rest, then I'll get us a meal of some sort.'

Vi had just finished her wash and was brushing her hair when Sid announced, 'There's a lady coming down the lane on a bike!'

Vi peered from the upstairs window and the young woman on the bike saw her, waved, wobbled and had to jump down from her bicycle quickly. Then she waved again and Vi could see she was laughing at her own recklessness. Vi laughed with her and ran down the stairs to meet their visitor.

'Hello,' the young woman called, 'I'm May Minninger. I work for Mrs St John Trewellan. Hello!' she repeated as she propped her bicycle by the wall and held out her hand.

Vi felt an immediate warmth towards this auburn-haired young woman

51

with her warm brown eyes, freckles and open countenance. Here, she felt, was a straightforward person, no worrying undercurrents here.

'I'm her secretary,' she added, as both Ma and Audrey came out to meet their visitor. 'She's gone to London to see her brother, who's home on embarkation leave. She asked me to come and see if there's anything you have need of?' She looked at the trio speculatively and when no one replied, her face fell a little. 'Is there *nothing* I can help you with?' she asked, then, reaching into the basket of her bicycle, she drew out a towel-wrapped bundle. 'Well, I hope you won't take it amiss, but I've brought you a cake.'

'That's kind,' said Ma, 'very kind. I was just going to make a cuppa. You'll come in and 'ave one with us?'

'Thank you very much indeed!' May enthused, beaming on them all, though Vi saw her quick concern for Audrey, whose black-ringed eyes showed the effect of the night's weeping.

In the house she stopped just inside the kitchen where Ma had the kettle on the hob. 'Come through,' Vi said, 'it's a little better in the other room.'

May took in the camp beds, the haphazard jumble of furniture, and walked back into the kitchen and looked around again in there. 'This is where you are living?' She did not wait for an answer, but strode up and down the kitchen. 'You've no pots and pans, no . . . I don't believe this. This is how you were left?' She paused and looked at the Londoners. 'No wonder you couldn't answer – you haven't anything, have you?'

'Not a lot,' Ma said.

'We wanted to stay together . . .' Vi began.

'Yes!' May confirmed. 'But I don't see as that excuses anything!' She looked around with a kind of passionate anxiety and, as Pa would have said, you could fair see the wheels going around!

'Look!' she began again after half a minute's intense cogitation, her eyes going from Ma to Audrey and settling on Vi. 'Could you walk back with me to the Lodge now? It's about two miles. We'll pick up some things and I'll drive you back in the trap. At least cooking utensils and things . . .'

When this was settled, May Minninger sat on one of the camp beds and sipped tea from Sid's cup, relinquished for their visitor, while he in return accepted her slice of the cake. She listened to their story with regular interjections of, 'I really can't believe it!' and finally, 'Auntie Annie will be absolutely furious. She was told the house was furnished.'

Vi saw Ma's gaze fix on their visitor as the aristocratic Mrs Trewellan was referred to as 'Auntie Annie'. Vi caught Ma's attention as it went despairingly from the cups without saucers and the chunks of cake they were devouring. She shook her head, gently reproving her mother for worrying about their current lack of niceties.

Walking back with May pushing her bicycle, Vi learnt more of their new-found friend's background. 'Anne St John Trewellan was my mother's best friend, "Auntie" Annie by adoption – and really I've been tricked!' she announced with a laugh. 'If I'd been a bit younger, my mother would have tried packing me off to Canada or somewhere for the duration, but as she couldn't do that, I was told I could do vital war work down here in Cornwall.'

'Being Mrs Trewellan's secretary?'

'Quite!' May agreed with the query. 'But, you see, the main house, a huge Elizabethan monstrosity, has been given over to the army for training. I understood that there would be some post I could undertake for them. But it's all army run! So I'm sort of secretary-cum-housekeeper-cum-farm manager for Annie. Not that there's not an awful lot to do with Uncle Jimmie being away in the navy.'

'Audrey's father was about to be called up in the Navy . . .' Vi went on to explain Audrey's particular tragedy and how the night before had been a kind of catalyst for the floodgates to open.

'Oh, my dear.' May stood quite still. 'That poor, poor girl.'

They chatted without any reserve and Vi laughed when May unexpectedly called her uncle 'the Commodore'. 'If that's true, don't tell my ma! She has enough trouble coping with your aunt's double-barrelled name!' She explained her ma's awe of the upper classes.

'Upper classes! You're joshing!' May was astonished. 'Heaven preserve us! But you don't feel like that, do you?'

'No, I suppose I'm like my pa. He sees every man as good as another.' She paused, then added her own long-formed opinion, 'And I think a good many of the landed aristocracy did some awful things in olden times to be given their grants of land in the first place.'

'You're right! You're right!' May enthused. 'Fame and fortune depended on being on the side of the right people.'

'Yes,' said Vi doubtfully, then added, 'not sure I don't mean no.'

'Different viewpoints?' May suggested. 'Same conclusion!'

'Same result,' Vi agreed, 'we won't change that.'

'This war might, though,' May suggested.

They had turned left out of the farm drive and continued along the cliff road for about a mile. Now they came to a point where the road swept inland, leaving a raised headland to the solitary occupation of a granite-walled public house. Its aspect was totally grim with black paintwork and a dark grim-looking sign announcing 'Gerrard's Head' above what looked like a severed Spaniard's head complete with bloodied neck.

'Very inviting!' Vi commented. When May looked puzzled, she indicated 'the local hostelry'.

'There's some sort of grim story about the place,' May told her, while indicating that their way was off to the right, 'but our soldiers liven it up in their free time.'

Soon they were walking alongside a high stone wall. When they came to a set of small gates, May said, 'We have to go in this way to the Lodge. The main gates have guards!'

The land here formed a small natural valley and whereas the rest of the land had only scattered wind-sculptured bushes and small trees, here, where there was more protection, were great hedges of rhododendron and many trees like palms such as she had seen in Kew Gardens. It was almost a different atmosphere behind this boundary wall. In some ways, Vi thought, Ma was more correct than Pa. These people with their wealth could make their lives and their homes into different worlds.

'That's the back way to the main house.' May pointed up a narrow drive leading away through the bushes. 'There's actually a barbed-wire gate and a guard further along!' She raised her eyebrows in exasperation. 'But the officers come and go as they like, it seems to me. They are always around at the Lodge with Auntie Annie entertaining groups of them. They never all seem to be at lectures at the same time. Some are quite nice. You may meet some now.'

Vi hoped not. The thought of having an audience of officers while they loaded the trap with household goods was not her idea of a treat. She reproved herself, she'd be thinking like her mother next!

The Lodge nestled its back deeply into a group of pines and rhododendrons. This building was of warm brown stone with deep-set Gothic windows with carved arches above, as great a contrast to the last building they had passed as was possible to find. This had a welcoming feel, the deep porch offered shelter and its two side windows, even in November, had bright yellow flowers lighting up the entrance.

Everywhere seemed quiet. May, propping her cycle near the front door, led the way in. Vi noticed the door was not locked and, as she entered, May called, 'Anyone here?' She turned and grinned. 'Best to make sure before you start talking to yourself or anything!'

It was an elegant house full of old furniture with the wonderful sheen of age and much polishing. There were deep, old-stone inglenook fireplaces in the hallway and in the sitting room which May led the way to, and fires glowed warmly in each one. May was certainly not the only one employed there.

'Hello, old thing.' A tall young man in fine grey cord slacks and blue-grey pullover strolled into the room from the far door.

May went forward immediately, linked arms with him and turned back to Vi. 'This is "my cousin" John Manners. John, meet Violet Tulley.'

Vi wanted to say something about being pleased to meet another of "Auntie Annie's" protégés, but, below the thick shock of black hair, his dark eyes held such a sparkle of roguish good humour she was disconcerted. 'Hello,' she said, inwardly berating herself for such a feeble greeting.

'Hello,' he answered back.

For a second she suspected him of mockery, but then she saw his scrutiny of her held interest, curiosity perhaps, but nothing tongue in cheek.

'We've known each other for ever,' May intervened.

'Since we were young tackers,' he endorsed with a laugh.

Vi looked at him with added interest, remembering the woman in the greengrocery shop using that term, and wondered if he came from this part of the world?

'Story goes he tipped me out of my perambulator when I was six months, and, though he won't admit it, Auntie Annie's obviously pulled all kinds of strings to get him stationed here!'

'It's just not true!' he denied and turned the attack by asking, 'So what are you two up to? I can tell there's something. Furtively sneaking in, wondering if you're alone?'

May explained the situation. John listened carefully without intervention, his glance going from one girl to the other as the story was told.

'I have an hour before my next lecture, I can help you load up,' he offered.

Vi felt it became a little like a cross between a kind of New Year sale in the West End and taking an inventory – with herself as the embarrassed arbitrator, deciding what she thought they really needed and what she felt they really could not take.

'We seem to have two or three of everything when you really look,' May declared. 'I'm amazed, I'm sure we don't use half these things.' She held aloft a small metal gadget with a handle. 'What's this, for Heaven's sake? We've got two of these!'

'Ma uses something like that to cut up parsley,' Vi supplied.

'Oh!' May turned the handle experimentally. 'I don't see how . . .'

'Never mind, if there's two,' John took it from her and added it to the pile of crockery and kitchen utensils they were packing into an enormous clothes basket May had found.

'Don't think we have any parsley . . .' Vi began.

John wagged an enormous wooden spoon at her before tossing it on to 'her' pile. 'Don't you be difficult as well! I've only got about another twenty minutes then I must skedaddle.'

She laughed at him, but admitted, 'I'm beginning to feel very awkward about all these things. I mean, with your aunt not being here . . . I'm not sure we should be doing this.'

'You'll get me into trouble if you don't accept them, seriously,' May urged. 'I mean it.'

Somewhere in the house a telephone bell rang and May rose to go and answer it.

'I'll harness the pony and put the basket aboard, then I must go,' John told her. As she left, he turned to Vi. 'Coming to help?' he asked.

For a second as he held out his hand, she thought to take it in her own, then she recognised the good-mannered arm to shepherd her in the direction they must go. She felt her colour rise and preceded him outside then turned to let him lead the way.

'Do you know anything about horses?' he asked.

'Coming from London, d'you mean?'

'Yes,' he answered in a fairly quizzical way, 'I suppose I do. Most women down here would know how to harness up the family horse, whereas in the city . . .' He stood still and looked down at her. 'Just to get our relationship right from the beginning, tell me, are you touchy about being a woman or about coming from London?'

Relationship! She raised her eyebrows at the word but was cautious and did not wish to make any other stupid assumptions.

'You see,' he went on when she remained silent, 'May would like to be fighting on some battle front or other, so I have to be careful not to slot her into the "home front" too overtly. So *what* about you?'

'I suppose I'm definitely on the home front.' She paused and realised that it had never occurred to her that she had any choice in the matter. 'My pa – who incidentally did used to work with horses – has asked me to look after my ma and brother, and then there's my friend, Audrey.'

'Is your ma not well?'

'She worries a lot.'

'Ah!' He led the way past a small block of stables to a field gate at the far side where he leaned and looked down at her again. 'We have such strong matriarchal figures in our family,' he stated.

Oh! La-de-blooming-da! Vi thought, but somehow, even inside her head, it didn't sound convincing because he stood looking at her so fixedly. She made a stab at being true to the East End. 'You'll know me again,' she said, planning pertness, but achieving a husky whisper.

'So where exactly is this farm they've put you in?' he asked. 'I mean in relation to, say, the Gerrard's Head pub?'

'In relation to, say, the Gerrard's Head pub.' Now she did give in to her gift of mimicry, though her voice didn't quite have the ring she intended. 'The farm is on the cliffs about two miles away.'

'Right,' he said gently, 'so we'd better catch this horse and harness it up.'

Chapter 7

Ma was still in a state of wonder and shock at the things in the clothes basket when they heard a motor vehicle coming up the drive.

'Perhaps it's the beds come!' Sid exclaimed.

'Of course not!' Vi tutted, but followed Sid as he rushed out into the yard. May had not long driven away and she was still reassuring Ma that it was all right for them to have all the kitchen utensils, crockery and cutlery. And not only that, the telephone call May had taken had been from her aunt who, on hearing the state of Gerrard's Head, had sent a message that as soon as she arrived home she would try and persuade the army to release some of her bedroom furniture from the Manor House. 'Apparently there's a lot stored in the attics, the army are using their own beds.'

Sid came back to stand by her side as the van approached at some speed considering the state of the drive, but whoever was at the wheel seemed to know it well and was able to avoid the worst of the potholes. Vi, as her brother moved closer to her, had a sinking feeling she knew who this visitor was.

'Run and tell Ma it's Mr Spurrier – our landlord.' Vi gave Sid a little push on his way as the van drew up in the yard and the furious face of the town butcher turned their way.

'So!' he greeted her. 'Where's the one in charge? Or was it you went tittle-tattling?'

Vi did not answer immediately as she wondered at the speed of events.

'Somebody's seen 'er!' He turned as Audrey and Ma came out of the back door. 'Who's been complaining?' he demanded.

'No one's complained.' Vi stepped forward, suddenly as angry as he was as she saw Ma's hands flutter to her heart and lips. Audrey looked pale but more composed, more herself than at any time since Vi had found her friend in evening dress at the bus stop.

He made a fierce exclamation of disgust and disbelief. 'I've 'ad Mrs St John Trewellan on the telephone telling me of all the things you need – so *someone's* complained.'

I bet that made your ears burn, Vi thought with satisfaction. 'Mrs Trewellan's niece came here this afternoon and took me back to the Lodge to collect some essential household goods they had spare—'

'Oh! So it was you!'

'We asked for nothing!' she retorted as forcefully as his exclamation. 'I told Mrs Trewellan nothing, but she did telephone to her home while I was there. What was said to her was said by her niece.'

'And it would be the truth!' Audrey added in support. 'Anyone with half an eye can see the state of this place.'

'State!' he began, but then all their attentions were drawn to a kind of scuffle and crash by the side of the house. He bounded forward with surprising energy for such a solid stocky man, pouncing like a heavyweight cat after its prey. Moving after him, Vi saw it was Paul who had obviously come along the cliff path again carrying several planks of new wood, which he had now dropped and was pushing urgently into the rough grass at the base of the house wall.

'What the 'ell are you doing 'ere?' Spurrier spluttered and questioned. Vi watched as his workman's eyes became darker and shuttered as the butcher ranted on, accusing him of time wasting and demanding an explanation as to what he was doing with new timber?

'I saw your van along the road when I finished ploughing Monk's Leap, thought I'd save time coming 'ere to ask you about replacing the well cover.'

Vi was impressed by the ease with which the explanations – the obvious lies – came. She was quite sure he'd had no idea his employer was there until he *almost* walked into him in the yard.

'What's wrong with the well cover?'

'It's rotten!' Audrey supplied.

'Didn't think you'd want any more trouble with her ladyship!' Paul volunteered the sarcasm in an obvious attempt to be on his employer's side. Vi watched Mr Spurrier and had to grit her teeth so she did not grin, for the man looked as if he was going to self combust. His face verged on purple and he seemed to be holding his breath.

'If the young lad fell down the well, I mean,' Paul said but his tone and his meaningful nod spoke of another quite different meaning.

The possibility of anyone falling down the well was obviously a secondary consideration! Vi wondered again what serious facts Mrs Trewellan must know to hold such a very big stick over this prosperous butcher?

She watched the two men exchange swift glances. They *both* knew what it was all about. She speculated as to whether they might wheedle the truth out of Paul or if at some stage Mrs Trewellan might tell them?

'I suppose you would be directly responsible for repairs,' she ventured, wondering how far this reluctant landlord could be pushed, 'and that well is dangerous. It does need fixing without delay.'

58

'Responsible?' Cyril Spurrier spat the word towards the Londoners, his glance going over the whole group as if they were beneath contempt. 'What d'you know about responsibility?'

'We can always find out!' Audrey told him. 'You'll find we're better than that,' she tossed a derisory thumb in the direction of the ocean, 'at making waves if we need to.'

Paul glanced with some admiration at this new vocal Audrey, but Spurrier came forward, wagging his short fat finger in her face. 'Don't you threaten me, my girl, it doesn't pay! We work for our living down 'ere, work 'ard – things cost money. We know what we're responsible for.'

He turned back to his van and climbed in. Looking down on his tenants, he added, 'You'll find any repairs will be reflected in rent rises. Think on that! Don't suppose you'll be quite so keen on improvements if you know *you've* got to pay for them!' With that he slammed his van door and revved up. As a final shot, he leaned from the window and pointed at Ma. 'I'll be letting you have a rent book, starting as from yesterday. They'll be no delay on that!' Then he swung his vehicle round in the yard, so they had to draw back to avoid being hit, and drove rapidly away.

'The old bugger!' Audrey said with feeling.

'And so say all of us,' Vi added.

'So we 'ave got to pay rent!' Audrey commented. 'On this dump.'

'We'll be turned out,' Ma worried. 'Split up!'

'No! He won't do that,' Paul said confidently, 'and it only needs cleaning.'

'Oh, yes, that's all!' Audrey retorted, amazed by Paul's judgment. 'It just needs an army to do it, that's all!'

Paul grinned. 'I'll help,' he said.

'Why won't he turn us out?' Vi questioned.

'More than he dare do. He has to keep well in with Mrs Trewellan, very influential people around 'ere the Trewellans.' But he shook his head as they tried to learn more. 'I don't know ye very well yet, do I,' he stated.

He drew their water before he made the well a little more secure by lodging the new wood over the top – and with two buckets, the kettle and several large saucepans filled to the brim, they felt very well provided for. 'I'll bring tools tomorrow and make a start on a proper job.'

'A proper well has –' Sid made a wide circle with his arm, '– like Jack and Jill . . .'

'A winding gear,' Paul supplied, 'but that's—'

'We'll settle for just a lid to keep you out!' Vi interrupted. 'Or you'll be like Ding Dong Bell, Pussy's in the well.'

It was good to say goodnight to Paul with some laughter in the air, and even Ma perked up as she again looked through all the kitchen utensils. Then she set to and made them a delicious vegetable stew, joying in the range working so well and the glow of that fire and the fire in the room around which the camp beds were again gathered. She said nothing about their land-lord and his threats, but Vi knew she would be worrying about it all, mulling it over.

Once the meal was eaten they all lapsed into a state of lethargy. 'It's been a long day, after a long night,' Audrey yawned.

Vi was silent, not because she did not agree, but because her day was packed with so many new experiences, new people, new emotions, new friends. She wondered if that was right? New friends? Or were they just kind people – kind people with excess goods? She, like Ma, needed time to mull everything over. As they prepared for sleep, she thought how she would have loved to have carried her bed upstairs into one of the bedrooms proper and be quite alone.

Sid, kneeling by his bed, fell asleep mid-prayers. Audrey lifted him carefully into his bed and covered him.

Climbing into her own bed, Audrey asked somewhat hesitantly, 'Vi, you're not put out with me because of last night?'

'Me?' Vi was amazed. 'What on earth made you think that?'

'You're so quiet . . .'

'We've worked hard!'

'. . . particularly since you came back with May. But I know I'll sleep now, I won't keep you awake again.'

From her bed Vi told her, 'You can keep me awake any night, love, but it'll be a question of you and whose combined forces tonight. I'm whacked.' Even as she spoke, she knew she had been preoccupied since she came back from the Lodge and Spurrier had left – and she knew, even though she was physic-ally exhausted, she just wanted all the others to go to sleep so she could think in peace.

'So what do you think Mrs Trewellan has over old Spurrier?' Tired as she was, Audrey's mind too was obviously full of questions, though the remark ended in a yawning, 'Paul wasn't going to say was he?'

'He knows though. Perhaps when he does know us better . . .' Vi said, yawning in sympathy. 'He's so certain we won't be turned out. You're good at wheedling secrets out of people, you'll 'ave to see what you can find out.'

'I might just do that,' Audrey promised, 'make 'im my target for tonight!'

'Don't give him the wrong impressions!' Vi warned. 'We have to be careful about giving wrong impressions.'

'He seems harmless enough . . .'

''E's a good lad,' Ma put in, 'needs a bit of mothering by the look of 'im.'

Vi remembered his face when Ma had called him a good boy and thought she was probably right on that score, but as to being harmless – well what man was? They all seemed to bring some kind of trouble or another – heart-break . . . babies . . . making you tongue-tied when you've never been before.

'We'll 'ave to get jobs,' Ma said, 'to pay the rent. We can't expect your pa to send enough money down to keep us all and pay rent. He's got Brierly Street to run.'

No, Vi thought, and they couldn't tell Pa all they had experienced so far – so much it made Number 11 seem so far away and the comfort and care, the closeness of everything and everybody so long ago. It was almost frightening. The whole new evacuation felt like this old stone farmhouse, very uncomfortable, or like Paul's bush, very thorny – this Cockney quartet against the Cornish clan!

Audrey was saying if they had jobs they would really need bikes or something. 'It took nearly half an hour to walk with Sid this morning – and longer back because it was more uphill.'

'Good thing he's asleep or he'd be wanting us to set up with a horse and cart,' Ma said. When there was silence from her daughter, she asked, 'You all right, Vi?'

It took a second to realise she had been spoken to. 'Sleepy,' she answered.

'Sorry, luv,' Ma said, settling down, 'see you in the morning.'

Vi lay, eyes wide open, listening to the quiet crackling of the fire. Tonight, without the fog, it did not seem nearly so cold. Soon she could hear from their quiet breathing that everyone else was asleep.

'A bit audacious I suppose.' May had still been talking about John Manners as they drove home. 'But a great guy,' she had enthused. She had not needed to be told May's opinions about him. They had been obvious to her from the moment she had first seen the way May had linked arms, introducing him as 'her cousin', though the inflexion had implied they were no such thing, any more than May was Mrs Trewellan's niece, apparently.

Talked in inverted commas, these posh folk did. Why couldn't they just be plain straightforward – or did she mean common or garden – folk like they were? She wondered if Audrey would have 'put on an act', tried to be what she wasn't? She remembered her own mimicry and even in the privacy of her bed felt her colour rise.

How stupid. Why should she care? After all, what she recalled so exactly was how May had taken his arm, hanging on it ever so slightly. They had looked like a couple. They were so at ease with each other. But then they should be, of course, if John had tipped May out of her pram at six months! She wondered if that would be about the same time she and Audrey were pretending to be nursemaids, pushing Sid in the Viccy Park and calling him 'Mr Sid'. She turned over quite violently on the protesting camp bed.

So much for her sense of adventure, of wanting to live! As soon as anything different did happen, here she was raking over every shred of conversation she could recall and wishing she'd said and done everything very differently. And she could remember every word, she was sure of that. In fact, she could rerun the whole procedure of fetching Double Life out of his field. Together

61

they had backed the reluctant horse between the trap-shafts, their fingers touching on the nose band as John had sympathised, 'Poor old boy, you thought work was over for today.'

She had passed straps and held reins, having to hide behind the horse's rump to smile when he had complimented her on knowing where things went. She had stood by Pa when he had shown the horse-mad Sid how the coalman's horse was harnessed to its dray. At the time she had protested that normal boys were more interested in cars and motorbikes, now she was surprised how much she remembered. But then she had always soaked up anything her pa had said.

'Do you ride as well?' he asked.

How she had wanted to say, 'Yes. Yes, of course.' Instead, she had told the ridiculous truth. 'Only a donkey at Southend!'

She lay suffused with shame, overwhelmed by the knowledge that she had been guilty of that ridiculous inverted snobbery East Enders were so good at. She made him laugh, yes – but what a fool she'd made of herself. She could imagine him telling his fellow officers. Cockneys, they ride donkeys and eat jellied eels.

He might have ascertained from her exactly where they were living, there had been nothing clever about that – it had been quietly and precisely obtained, a practical piece of information – but there was no way he would ever want to converse with her again.

The more she lay and thought of her behaviour, the more her face burned with shame. She became so hot, she began to wonder if she was ill, physically sick. Maybe she'd caught the flu?

May had said it was a pity people couldn't be exempted from war because of their personality, because John was much too nice a person ever to have to go to war and kill people. 'Though,' May had added, eyes wide, 'I was told he teaches tactics and sabotage!'

John Manners, saboteur! Yes, she thought, and could see his eyes, his high cheekbones, the dark wing of hair falling over his forehead – she could conjure him more easily than she could Roy or Pa. That was a kind of swift sweet sabotage.

But she was tired, exhausted, mind playing stupid tricks and, as she finally felt herself drifting to sleep, she mused that the dangers in Cornwall were strange – not the kind you hid under the stairs from. They came in the shape of very different young men. She dreamt she danced around the edge of a gaping black chasm.

Chapter 8

'I am going ploughing with Paul – with the 'orse! I can, can't I, Ma?'

The three women woke, blinked and tried to pull themselves together as Sid, already dressed, ran into and out of the room.

'I need some croust, Paul says. That's packed-up dinner.'

'In a red and white spotted hanky tied on a stick,' Vi said, turning over with a groan.

'I don't know,' Sid answered. 'Shall I ask him?'

'Where is 'e?' Ma asked. 'And 'ow long 'ave you been up?'

'Outside. Waiting for me!' He danced from foot to foot and agonised, ''E'll go without me!'

Ma struggled out of bed, pulled her outdoor coat over her nightie and pushed her feet into her slippers. The girls could hear them all talking outside, then Sid bounced back in proclaiming, 'We're going to plough The Soldier's Field.'

'Are you?' said Vi with heavy disinterest.

'The Soldier's Field is next to the field called Monk's Leap.'

'Fascinating!'

'Yes! And you've got to bring my croust! Ma sez.'

'Clear off!' she said, adding one of Pa's favourite expressions, 'While you're winning.'

Ma came back some minutes later. 'He's gone off riding the horse like he's king of the country – with a doorstep of bread and marg in his hand.'

'Sounds like Sid's idea of heaven,' Audrey commented.

'I was thinking . . .' Ma brooded, running her fingers along her lips as if she was playing a piano scale. 'Monk's Leap – you reckon that's on the edge of the cliffs?'

'Yeah! Definitely,' Vi agreed, 'shouldn't worry about the well.'

'Vi! You're wicked!' Audrey reprimanded. 'You know your ma worries.'

'Don't fret, Ma, he'll never leave that 'orse's side! Slip back in bed, I'll make us all a cuppa.'

The kettle had been left on the hob all night and was already singing, but Vi was tempted by the sunshine and that view of the sea. She slipped her coat on and, making sure that Paul was well away, she walked round through the yard to the front of the house – and for the first time she wondered why there was no front door? How strange. Gerrard's Head farm seemed to be a house with only *one* way in or out? Something else they must ask Paul about.

It was so still, the sky that pale winter blue, the air so clear with just the slightest suggestion of ice in its rare clarity. The sea was wonderful, dark in the distance and the depths, reflecting the sky nearer the shore, churning white water at the bottom of the cliffs and around the rocks near the shore, shifting planes of deepest to palest aquamarine. She was totally overwhelmed and enchanted by the beauty of it all. Raising her head, she realised she could hear the steady hollow clip-clop of the horse going along the top road in the direction of the Lodge, the way she had walked with May.

She wondered where the fields were Paul was taking Sid to, probably, as Ma said, on the cliffs. Shading her eyes, she looked over towards the headland and could just make out the roof of the public house and, some way before that, she could see a newly turned field which from a distance looked as if it was about to slip off into the sea. Monk's Leap. She decided it would be as well not to mention this, and also that it might be wise to be early taking this 'croust' to make sure Sid was behaving himself and being well supervised. London had its bombs and its traffic hazards but this place was fast adding to its list of unfamiliar traumas and dangers for the unwary. But Vi reassured herself she was not unwary, not this bright clear morning when she was seeing things clearly.

'I reckon we ought to tackle one room at a time,' Ma said as they finished their tea.

'This kitchen floor . . .' Vi began.

'She's got to find out what's underneath. I'd start with the shovel if I were you,' Audrey suggested.

'I'd see what's under this lino first,' Ma said, ''cos if it's anything like a brick or stone floor I'd say let's rip out the lino and clean what's underneath. To be that buried under filth can't be much good!'

'Oh!' Vi was disappointed.

'You have visions of finding an immaculate linoleum square,' Audrey said. 'Think you've come to live in fairyland!'

'That's not true, I've never been like that!' Vi was suddenly very concerned with this exchange. It seemed vitally important to see herself through unbiased eyes. Last night she had realised that in May and John Manners she had found a new touchstone to measure herself against – and she was not comfortable.

'Come on!' Audrey said. 'Aim at a star even if you hit a tree, that's you!'

Vi wondered if Audrey's bereavement was making her bitter? The tears had been shed and now there was a certain tartness in her tone.

'But sometimes it works,' Ma said. 'You've got us to this place.'

'Yeah! And it only needs cleaning,' Audrey repeated Paul's words.

'It needs digging!' Vi decided to let Audrey's remarks go and concentrate on the work.

'Try near the sink first, if it's worn anywhere it'll be there,' Ma suggested.

'The floor's all uneven anyway,' Audrey said, as Vi still worked carefully to reveal the buried linoleum, 'it can't be any good.'

Not convinced, Vi did however do as Ma suggested. Shortly after poking down near the sink, she exclaimed in disappointment. 'Oh! It is worn through and,' she paused to catch hold of a torn corner and lift the old lino, 'underneath looks like stone slabs.'

So, the decision made, they all three began to find and tear up the old floor covering. They tried to keep it in largish strips so two of them could carry it outside complete with the soil it was buried under.

The flagstones underneath had been skilfully laid and, after just a preliminary sweep, were far more homely looking than the compacted earth. The slabs were worn, hollowed where generations of former residents had come in, gone to the fire or to the sink and through to the house.

'Scrubbed they won't look too bad,' Ma declared. 'Come on, I can't wait to get to them.'

'Then the table scrubbed down, we can have our meals in here.' Vi caught her mother's enthusiasm. 'Perhaps we could peg a rug?'

'Dreaming again!' Audrey put in.

'But no old clothes to cut up!'

'Never mind, Ma, first things first,' Vi intervened, 'and what about Sid and his croust? Shall I make him some sandwiches and a bottle of tea?'

'You take 'em, Vi, I'll help your ma scrub.' There was a tiny echo of repentance in Audrey's voice. 'I went shopping while you cleaned the range, so it's only fair.'

Some fifteen minutes later Vi had tidied herself, slipped on her tweed skirt and a green jumper and set off. She would have liked to have tried walking along the cliffs or even the sands part of the way, but the area could hold more dangers than just natural ones. The beaches could be mined, the cliffs watched over by armed sentries. Roy had ended his last letter with the words, 'I'm just off to do a spot of sentry duty. Wish you were here!'

Fool, she thought smiling, wondering if he had yet got her last letter from London telling him they were being evacuated again. She had told him to keep writing to Brierly Street as Pa would forward the letters once they had a proper address. Now she could write to him again giving the farm address.

She contented herself with the road. She might see May again or anyone coming from the Lodge and going into town. She turned to look back towards the farm and the town, then all around over the moors and beaches. For the first time in her life, she was out in the open air with no one else in sight. It was quite weird and she felt a terrible pang of homesickness, longed for the East End, the greetings of neighbours, people on doorsteps, kids making boats and planes from kitchen chairs on pavements, shouts from the street to third-storey tenants. Here it was as if people had hardly touched this land – no traffic, no houses – only the distant Gerrard's Head public house looming on the horizon.

She had been quite ridiculous to wash and change into her good skirt – matching it with a green jumper which brought out the same colour in her hazel eyes – just to walk a bundle of bread and dripping out to her kid brother.

She looked out at the wide expanse of sea. Never had she been able to see so much ocean before. She felt . . . 'I know,' she murmured, feeling tears prick her eyes. 'I feel between the devil of Hitler so I can't be at home, and this deep blue sea – and I don't know what this is about at all. These people? Half don't want us here and the others – are they pretend friends? No sooner are we out of their sight than forgotten?'

'Gawd blimey!' she exclaimed aloud in as broad an accent as she knew, surely she was made of sterner stuff than this! She had better busy herself with all her pa had entrusted to her or she was going to shed tears for a reason she was not prepared to even let herself think about.

There *were* things to be decided on. Ma was right, they would have to find jobs – and a school for Sid, or they'd have the attendance officer after them. Jobs of course would be the other way . . . Into town . . .

For goodness sake! Fiercely she disciplined herself to the task of finding the way to the field where Paul was ploughing. Once on the road it was not always possible to see right to the edge of the cliffs. It might be a matter of some guesswork to find the nearest path down to him and Sid.

She decided she would walk until she came to the next discernible pathway towards the sea, then she would find a way along the cliff top until she came to 'The Soldier's Field'.

The next gateway to the left seemed the most likely, for the gate stood open and centre stage was a large heap of horse dung. 'That way, I think, Dr Watson – and how Pa would like that little lot for his roses. I wonder what he'd make of Cornwall and Gerrard's Head?'

Two fields further on and she could see Sid running alongside Paul as he turned the plough at the far end of the field. Sid had hold of Major's bridle and was helping swing the horse and plough smoothly round and, though she was sure both of them saw her as she waved, neither of them acknowledged her until Major reached the top end of the field nearest to her and Paul reined him to a stop.

'So how are the workers?' she called.

'Hungry!' Sid shouted back. 'Aren't we, Paul?'

66

Paul had brought apples and insisted Vi sit and eat one before she walked back. He also had the end section of a loaf and a large piece of cooked beef. To Vi it looked about half the size of their wartime Sunday dinners. 'I suppose,' she said as he cut a piece off and gave it to Sid, 'that comes of working for a butcher?' She had to prompt him into understanding by a nod at the beef.

'Something like that,' he said with a grin. 'If you ever want some meat I could allus shoot you a rabbit.'

'Ooh! Yes *please*!' Vi and Sid echoed each other's enthusiasm for such a treat.

'My ma can cook a rabbit stew that'd make your mouth water in the next street . . .' She paused, looked round and laughed. 'Well, in Monk's Leap, if that's the name of the next field.'

'Right!' Paul laughed. 'You shall 'ave the next rabbit I shoot.'

'A monk jumped from the cliffs into the sea,' Sid said through a mouthful of meat and bread, 'but . . . but . . . what, Paul?'

'But his long black habit billowed up in the wind and carried him out to them ol'rocks.' Paul nodded out to a group of rocks around which gulls swooped and called.

'And on dark and stormy nights you can still see him flying over them self-same rocks,' Vi added, lightly mimicking his accent.

'She's allus like that!' Sid said, but added in an awed voice as he glanced out to sea, 'We see'd a big black bird over the rocks when Paul told me the first time.'

'And I suppose the soldiers *marched* off the edge into the sea from this field?' Vi said. To end the conversation, she added, 'As long as *you* don't get too near the edge, Sid.'

'No . . .' There was a quiet reflective tone in Paul's voice as he sat on a stone near the wall, bread in one hand and meat in the other. 'No,' he repeated, 'it's a very different story that names this field. Many years ago . . .'

Vi wanted to break in with 'that figures,' but there was a kind of dogged intent to tell his story that reminded her of a man who used to sing at their local in the East End. When he stood up to perform, no one dared do anything but listen, for he was a big strong man with a reputation of violence, so there were no comments, no giggling, and nothing but applause when the dramatic feat was over.

'. . . a local farmer had two sons,' Paul was saying. 'The older one went to South Africa to fight in the Boer War, the other, who the father did not get on with, stayed to farm. The father said that when his other son returned he would have his share and named it for him, "The Soldier's Share". As the years went on, the father got so he could not work at all, so all the work fell on the younger son.'

Paul paused and it seemed to Vi almost as if he was telling his own story, yet that could not be if it was so long ago.

'And the father began to taunt his stay-at-home son and was always being asked to be carried out to this field so he could watch the horizon for the ship bringing his "soldier son" home to claim his land. Then one day the younger son couldn't take it any longer, just upped and left!'

His voice had risen in passion as he told of the younger son's departure. He paused as if suddenly aware of it then, staring out to sea, went on quietly again. 'He left one morning while his father sat in this field looking for the soldier, the elder son who never did come back.'

'Go on!' Sid urged.

'The old man died watching.' He flung an expressive arm out to the middle of the field he was working on.

'And the land?' Vi asked in more practical terms. 'What happened to that? Is this a true story?'

'It's true.' A heavy ring of certainty made them both look at Paul more curiously.

'Did the soldier come back?'

'Not the one the field's named for,' Paul said with a certain finality in his voice, as if declaring this the end of the story – for them anyway.

Then Vi and Paul both were startled as Sid leapt to his feet and pointed dramatically to where a figure rose above the edge of the cliff. At that moment, linked to the story in Sid's mind, Vi could appreciate the ethereal look of the man, who must in reality have been climbing some unseen path but, outlined by the reflected light from the sea, had an unworldly, timeless look as he reached the edge of The Soldier's Field.

'Look! It's the soldier!' Sid said in an awed voice as he watched the man walking towards them. 'He's come for his field.'

Vi shaded her eyes. It was a soldier in uniform and he seemed to be looking their way. Not surprising, Vi thought, considering the way Sid still stood like a permanent finger post.

'It be one of the officers from the Manor House,' Paul said. 'They often walk along here.'

She stood up and gently lowered Sid's arm to his side. 'He's not the right one to be telling these stories to, we'll be having him awake all night talking!'

'I like stories!' Sid voiced his new loyalty to Paul.

Paul looked reproached but did not reply and all three watched as the soldier came waving, hesitantly at first. When he recognised them, he ran more energetically, taking off his cap and throwing it up before himself, catching it at a run. Sid and Vi both laughed at his antic.

Vi's heart began to pound so heavily and so loudly that, though she knew Paul was saying something, she did not hear a word.

'Who is it?' Sid wanted to know.

'You remember the lady who came from the Lodge, who gave us the things for the kitchen? This is that lady's cousin. He's an officer.'

'This is a surprise!' John Manners called. 'Didn't really expect to catch up with you again so soon.'

'I was just explaining who you were, where we'd met,' she said, pitching her voice carefully up to cheerful and unconcerned. She turned to introduce the other two, but Paul was moving away, his food rewrapped in its cloth and his expression only what she could think of as dour.

He turned his back and walked over to slip the nosebag from the horse. Sid followed faithfully but looked back shyly at John.

'That's Sid my brother,' she told John, 'and—'

'Paul Kerrow I've encountered before – a young man with an underdog fixation,' he stated quietly without any note of condemnation, 'but what are you and your brother doing here?'

'My brother's horse mad and Paul's been around at the farmhouse, helping, swept the chimney, chopped wood. I brought Sid's "croust".' She broke off the swirl of information and was so pleased she had changed and had on the green jumper – and she smiled because she was unable to make her face do anything more sophisticated. 'And what about you? What are you doing walking over the cliffs?' Her glance completed the query.

'In full uniform?' he supplied, smiling back at her. 'I've only about twenty minutes before I have to be lecturing a gang of rookies, but I couldn't resist strolling out . . .'

He paused mid-sentence and she lifted her chin enquiringly.

'. . . in your direction as it were.'

She turned quickly to look over towards the headland. *Things*, she told herself, *must not be allowed to get out of hand*. She might allow herself to dream alone in her camp bed at night, but she did not intend to make a fool of herself with an officer who seemed to have quite an understanding with 'his cousin'.

'Is May your cousin?' She was both surprised and then mortified to hear herself ask what had bubbled to the top of her mind.

'Oh, no!' he answered.

When he did not continue, she felt she ought to at least justify the question. 'You both call Mrs Trewellan aunt.'

'Oh! Auntie Annie,' he said laughing. 'She's such an old love, she's Auntie to everybody! But May, well, May *is* special.'

'Yes, I have a special friend,' she interjected while he seemed to be dwelling on May's 'specialness'. 'Known him since we were at school together, Roy, Roy Moore. He's in the army, we write regularly.'

'Lucky Roy,' he said quietly. 'May actually goes back further even than schooldays. Our families have been friends, I think, ever since May's grandmother came over here from America as a young bride in the eighteen nineties and my family rather took her under its wing, taught her the ropes.'

'That is a long time,' she answered cautiously, thinking that was really what

69

she needed someone to teach her the ropes. Talking to him and May was, she thought, like trying to carry a difficult parcel when you were unsure what was inside or how fragile it was.

'Which is the opposite of what I have now,' he answered, glancing at his watch as he asked, 'would you walk *me* part of the way back – if you've time, of course?'

'Ma won't miss me for a bit longer.' She looked over to where Paul and Sid were again busy ploughing, though Sid glanced their way from time to time.

She had the strange feeling that although she would have said they both knew exactly where they were, having declared their special friends, she was at the same time standing at some kind of crossroads. If she stepped over to where John Manners had now taken two paces to lead the way, peace of mind was something she could say goodbye to.

Common sense seemed to be on the side of the Violet Tulley who had refused to be seduced by the charms of officers when they had turned up at the dances in Bethnal Green. The trouble was she felt so removed, so different from that Violet. Some deep inner conviction made her know with every instinct she possessed that if she moved just *one step* to follow, she might well be committing herself to carrying a burden of love which was never to be returned. At least not returned in the way her kind saw as the right way: attraction, walking out, love, marriage, children. She'd read many novels about the 'affairs' of the upper classes, their mistresses on the side.

John held out a hand as he had done in the Lodge when, so foolishly, she had momentarily thought to take it in her own. She just stood with her limbs feeling as if they had turned to solid unjointed wood. 'Not what you feel a young lady should do,' he asked, 'walk a chap back?'

'It's not that,' she began.

He shook his head gently at her. 'There is a war on, you know,' he added.

'Or I wouldn't be here,' she said, taking seriously the phrase that had become a trite colloquial excuse for so many silly things.

'No!' he exclaimed, his voice suddenly full of remorse. 'That was a stupid clumsy remark. Forgive me?' he pleaded, but added quickly, 'Then walk me back!'

She found she had walked forward towards him seemingly without making the decision, and her heart lurched – so much for self-control. She had to follow in file along the edge of the ploughed land but, once out of the 'The Soldier's Field', there was ample room for them to walk side by side along the edge of the cliff.

'So,' he began conversationally, tossing his officer's cap up into the air and catching it as he walked and talked, 'did you have enough pots and pans?'

'Ma was overwhelmed,' she answered, thinking that was just how she felt now, though he apparently found it all so light-hearted as he tossed his hat about. 'She was sure, as I was, that you and May gave us far too much.'

70

'Nonsense.' He stopped to pull a long dry grass. 'I wanted to give you everything.'

She did not answer, remembering how he had thrown everything May had queried into her pile.

'I couldn't get you out of my mind,' he said, swishing his grass over the heads of other grasses.

'You mean that we had so little.'

'I mean . . .' He stopped, threw his hands wide in denial. 'No, none of that occurred to me at all until May was going on about the beds at the Manor. Then I'm not sure it really registered. No. I couldn't get *you* out of my mind.'

'Me! Me?' *Brilliant*, she thought, *what a brilliant conversationalist.*

'You', he answered. 'Of course, you.' Unexpectedly, he swung his cap round over her head and dropped it down on her hair, then straightened the peak. 'May wants to join the forces, did you know?' he added. 'She's sure to bore you to tears about it before long.'

'Then I expect she will go.'

'Yes.' He sounded suddenly reflective. 'The lady usually gets what she wants.'

'So if you were not stationed here . . .' She left the speculation unfinished.

'Hmm! Yes that might be the time she would go I suppose.'

She felt this sudden intrusion of May like a sensation at the bottom of her spine, a qualm of conscience and a confirmation that this was just a moment's flirtation for him. That he should stand so close – she could see how the reflected light from the sea brightened the line of his jaw and cheeks, so close it shortened her breathing – and think of his 'cousin'. She reached up and carefully took off the cap and held it out to him. 'She seems like a lady who knows her mind.'

'Yes,' he acquiesced, but did not relieve her of his cap, 'duty calls. War does not leave much time. We are not in control of our lives, are we?' He looked questioningly into her eyes and the sense of having to grab at any fleeting happiness, of living for the moment not the morrow, was so tangible it seemed to draw them together. At the same moment that he reached for his hat with both hands, she stepped towards him and his hands fell over hers.

They stood for a moment so, then he looked down. 'I'll never ever part with this lucky old hat,' he said, and grinned.

Chapter 9

'Hello! Good morning to you.'

The sound of May's voice calling from the door made Vi pause to compose herself. The spontaneity of their first meeting was tempered now by her walk with John. They had parted as he had taken back his cap. He had walked, then sprinted, to be on time, but had looked back to wave before he passed out of sight. She remembered that the sea breeze had been icy, piercing her clothes and wrapping the tweed skirt around her legs, but she had paid it little mind at the time.

'Good morning, Violet! How are you? My goodness, you've certainly made some progress in here!' May looked around the kitchen, fire bright in the range, stone flags and table scrubbed to a cleanliness only elbow grease and determination could achieve.

'It'll improve now each time,' Ma said, regarding the floor with the air of an expert, 'another few weeks, you'll see.'

The pleasantries exchanged, May had two pieces of news to tell. 'The most immediate is that I met a drover with a couple of huge beasts which he was, until I told him otherwise, bringing here!'

'Beasts?' she queried. 'Cows, you mean.'

'Well . . . steers . . . no, bullocks, I think, is the proper term. Anyway, I told him you wouldn't want them! I left him sending back his lad for correct instructions.' She laughed, then queried, 'I'm right? You're not going in for farming?'

'Not likely!' Ma said. 'Frighten me to death, cows.'

'The other thing is, I heard some of the men talking about some new installations that apparently need camouflaging rather urgently, and that they are looking for women to do the work. I know Vi did say you would be wanting jobs.'

The enthusiasm of their response had May holding up her hands as if to fend them off. 'I'm not sure what it involves, but if you are interested I'll tell the chappie in charge and get back to you. Would you all want to go?'

'Not until we've got Sid settled,' Ma said, 'so say two.'

'And it would depend where it was and whether we could get there,' Vi added.

'My shoe leather's getting real thin,' Audrey said. 'It's all this walking on these rough roads. I can feel every stone.'

'It may be they'll put on transport,' May speculated. 'I'll find out. Righto then! Well, I must be off, old things. Duty calls. Aunt Annie is coming back this afternoon and I have to drive the trap into Penzance to meet her.' Turning to retrieve her bicycle, she added, 'You've another visitor coming now.'

Vi shaded her eyes to see another figure cycling down their drive. 'It's the postlady,' May said. 'Morning Mrs Stevens!'

'Morning, miss,' the stout middle-aged lady in post office regulation jacket, trousers and cap called.

'This is a long way to have to come,' Ma said sympathetically as Mrs Stevens dismounted with a mild skid on the loose stones.

'It is, and it don't seem five minutes since my ol' man was grumbling about having to trail 'ere with the Kerrow's mail. Not that they had much . . .'

'Paul Kerrow?' Ma queried.

'His folks,' Mrs Stevens answered. 'Paul grew up 'ere – well, around 'ere.'

The amendment seemed strange.

'He never said,' Vi commented.

'There'll be a lot that lad won't say,' she said mysteriously, but seemed to close the subject as she delved into the post bag balanced on the front carrier of her bicycle. 'Mrs F Tulley.' She proffered the letter.

Ma took it, looking at the large copperplate handwriting and read, '. . . And All. Mrs F Tulley and All. From your pa!' She put it to her nose and took a deep sniff as if determined to extract every sensation – as if trying to trace some nostalgic whiff of the East End. Then she clasped it to her chest. 'Thank you very much,' she said to Mrs Stevens, as if the woman had personally bought and presented her with a gift.

'You go and read it first, Ma,' Violet told her, 'then you can tell us all the news.'

'I will,' she said eagerly, her voice high like a child's. She turned to go then looked back at Vi, beaming. 'It's thick,' she said squeezing the envelope, 'your pa may have put one in from your Roy.'

Vi's glance went to May who raised her eyebrows and nodded understandingly. 'Letters mean a lot when you're separated from your loved ones.'

Vi felt her heart stand back from May's assumption as their two visitors cycled off together.

'Your pa's not wasted any time, we only telephoned the bus depot with the address that first morning,' Audrey commented then, in a quieter voice, she added, 'and I wonder what's happening in Brierly Street – and everywhere?'

Vi pushed away her own self-centred thoughts and linked arms with her friend as the bleak haunted look came back to her face and it seemed as if she were seeing again the devastation of her home life.

'*I* wonder how old Swanson is getting on without us both?' Vi said to distract her before she began to tremble and shiver – as she had begun to do whenever she relived the trauma of her parents' deaths. 'You know we ought to write to her care of the office. Don't you think so, Aud?'

'They've got some picture postcards in the newsagents,' Audrey said, coming back to the present. 'We could send her one of those – save having to write so much!'

Vi giggled briefly and they linked arms, walking away from the house towards the road, deciding to give Ma time on her own to pore over her letter. 'Now we know the mail actually reaches these out-of-the-way places, we could get Pa to parcel up some of those clothes she brought us. We should have to hand sew, but some of those long full skirts we could use to make ourselves trousers . . .'

'Or divided skirts. Then if we got bicycles . . .'

'Who's dreaming now?' Vi asked, but she gave Audrey's arm a squeeze so she knew there was no retaliation intended.

'I'd like a job to do – take my mind off things.'

'It'd be good for all of us. Ma wants me to go with her to see about school for Sid. We'll soon begin to get ourselves properly organised.' The sight of an army lorry coming toward them made her add, 'Then if we get some beds we can move upstairs and each have proper bedrooms.'

The two soldiers in the lorry slowed down to whistle and wave to the girls. 'Where have you been all our lives?' the driver, a handsome lad with a shock of dark wavy hair above the regulation short back and sides, leaned out to shout as they passed.

'A bit of talent,' Audrey said as they waved back.

'May said a lot of them walk to that Gerrard's Head pub in the evenings.'

Before they could speculate about the possibilities linked to that bit of information, some raucous shouts and animal bellows drew their attention back towards the farm. Two large black beasts came galloping down the hill from the town and, even as they watched, a man running behind bawled at the top of his voice and a fearless black and white collie dog swept in front of the animals, snapping at their muzzles as they attempted to carry on along the road. Consequently, the beasts turned up the farm drive at full speed.

'What?' Vi gasped. 'What does he think he's doing? That must be the man May told us about!'

'Your ma'll be petrified!'

'Come on!'

They ran as fast as they could, but by the time they caught up with the old man in his filthy smock, his boy was in their yard opening a barn door and the animals were inside and the door closed behind them.

74

'What d'you think you're doing?' Vi gasped. 'You've been told you've got it wrong.'

'Don't reckon it's much to do w'you,' he said, turning away. 'I've allus brought 'em 'ere and until I'm told different this'll be where I'll keep bringing 'em!'

'Who's going to look after them – give them food and water?'

'They'll not need a lot where they're going.'

'Where 'ave you come from?' Audrey demanded of the skinny but strangely moon-faced boy, who looked terrified.

'More than 'is job's worth,' the old man declared and, jerking his head at his companion, began to walk back the way he had come.

'What's the big secret?' Vi shouted after him. 'Perhaps we'll ask Mr Spurrier.'

'Aye!' He laughed outrageously without turning to look back. 'You do that!'

'So what d'you think?' Ma asked from the security of the kitchen while the two beasts bellowed from the confines of the barn.

'The man to ask is Paul when he brings Sid back from the fields. Meantime, I think we'll leave 'em alone!' Audrey was decisive on this point.

'Was there a letter from Roy?' Vi asked but Ma shook her head, smiling though as if there were other things. 'So, what's Pa got to say?'

She thrust the pages into Vi's hand. 'Read it,' she said shaking her head, 'read it aloud to all of us.'

Ma's worried frown had them all quickly drawing up chairs to hear what more bad news had come from London. Vi scanned the first page even as she smoothed it, but there was nothing fearful in the opening lines that she could see:

'Dear Flo,
It was a treat to hear that you are settled in a house all together.
Well done, Vi, I am looking forward to hearing all about it when you write.'

'We must get everything today, a notepad, envelopes, pen and ink!' Ma interrupted.

'Well, Ma, you might be surprised to know we've got lodgers! Vi will be even more surprised to know that it's the Moores! Roy's people have lost everything, the shop, home, not a thing left. Fortunately they were under-ground in that new station being made at Bethnal Green. I've let them take on our bedroom. I sleep in Vi's room now. We shall get on all right, I'm sure . . .'

'Mr and Mrs Moore ... lost everything.' Vi paused, a kaleidoscope of memories of the Moore's sitting room through the velour curtain behind the shop, kitchen off, bedrooms upstairs, and Albert and Maggie Moore, Mrs untidy always welcoming, Mr more taciturn, busy. 'I wonder if Roy knows?'

'I wonder what they'll do about the shop and the newspapers? Where will the delivery boys collect the papers from?' Audrey wondered.

They all looked at each other in consternation. There was so much trauma behind the facts Pa had written.

'At least Mr and Mrs Moore are all right – and I'm glad Harold is not on 'is own,' Ma reflected at last, and Vi turned back to the letter.

'You'll never guess who got on my bus the other day – Miss Swanton on her way out to Mr Fieldman's home. Your old office has been bombed and they are working from the boss's home – a right traipse, she said it is.'

'The office gone, too,' Vi repeated and felt her skin grow cold at this added bad news. She remembered the compact suite of rooms, the telephone exchange, the high stools near the ledger benches. 'I wonder if all the files were destroyed? What a job!'

'Perhaps your pa was right to get us out,' Audrey murmured.

'There are lots of notices hanging on ropes outside damaged City offices telling people where they've moved to – must be a nightmare to be a postman! But everyone is helping each other.
Hope Sid is enjoying being in the country, but register him at school as soon as you can. It's important.
Miss you all. Look after them, Vi, there's a gel!
So my old Dutch, all my love, till we meet again . . .
    Your loving husband, Harold.'

There was silence as Vi read the letter through again to herself, then passed it to Audrey, who did the same before passing it back to Ma. She folded it and held it on her lap, then pushed her hand into her apron pocket, drew out and waved a ten-shilling note. 'Pa sent this. We'll get a few bits and pieces in town this afternoon, when I take young Sid up to the school. I hope Mrs Moore's tidier in the 'ouse than she is in the shop.'

Vi did not enlighten her as to the state of the Moore's house, which on the whole she would have judged to be worse than the shop – old stock and out-of-date newspapers seemed to find their way from the shop into the sitting room. But that was all gone. She could sympathise with Ma. It was not a comfortable feeling to think that Roy's parents were now established in her home.

'Do you want me to go and fetch Sid?' Vi asked. 'He'll need cleaning up if you're going to see the headmaster.'

She had hardly finished speaking when the sound of a boot scraping outside had them all turning to see Sid coming into the kitchen. He stopped on the doorstep. 'Wot?' he asked defensively as every gaze fixed on him.

'Wot!' Vi mimicked. 'Wot – nothing. We thought you were gone for the day?'

'A man on a bike came with a message. Paul had to go somewhere. He brought me back to the top of the lane.' He paused disconsolately, then asked, 'What's that noise?'

The noise went on for the remainder of the morning. 'They're hungry and thirsty,' Sid decided. 'Pa said all animals need food and water regular like people. And water's most important – Paul sez.'

'Pity he's not around to give 'em some, then,' Ma said, putting her hands over her ears for a moment.

'I've been thinking,' Vi said, 'do you remember that smell as we tore the lino up out of here?'

'I'll never forget it!' Audrey almost retched. 'It stuck in the back of your throat.'

'Do you also remember Mr Spurrier's shop?'

It was Ma who supplied this answer. 'There was more meat in that window than I've seen since war broke out.'

'And meat comes from . . .'

The animals in the barn sounded as if they were trying to batter their way out.

'It all adds up,' Vi said triumphantly. 'He's slaughtering illegally – and he's been doing it from here. That old man said he's always brought the animals here before – and they wouldn't need anything to eat or drink where they were going. No wonder he didn't want anyone living in this farmhouse!'

'So did Mrs Trewellan know, d'you think?' Audrey wondered.

'Oh, no!' Ma said with complete certainty. 'Not a lady in her position!'

'She certainly has some hold over Mr Spurrier,' Vi was confident.

'She is his landlord,' Ma added. 'I suppose he has to do as he's told.'

Vi privately wondered whether the popular Aunt Annie might not be glad of extra meat to entertain all her 'nephews and nieces'.

The afternoon came and the bullocks continued to bellow their frustration or fear. Ma refused to leave the house in case they managed to batter their way out.

Vi had heard of animals escaping from city abattoirs and running amok. She wondered if these animals caught the smell of others who had been shut up there with the threat of imminent death in their nostrils? Even if that was their fate, surely they should not be kept without food or water all day. To kill to eat was one thing, but to inflict unnecessary suffering quite another. She found herself unable to think about anything else, and the more she thought the more furious she became with their butcher landlord.

Sid suddenly rushed to her crying and, by the look of his swollen eyes, he had been weeping for a long time. 'I've been looking through a crack in the barn door. We have to give them a drink,' he said, opening his mouth to continue the argument, but Vi forestalled him.

'Yes, get the buckets. We'll fill them with water and put them in the yard.'

'Then what?' Audrey asked.

'I don't know. I just know I can't stand them bellowing like that. It's pitiful!'

Ma sniffed loudly. 'If you let them out it's up to you to get them back, that's all I 'ave to say about it – and I'm bolting the door.'

The buckets filled and with Audrey and Ma locked in the house, Vi and Sid carried the water towards the barn – then they stopped. The animals inside seemed first to listen then to bellow louder.

'D'you think they can smell the water?' Vi asked in a whisper. Sid shrugged dramatically.

'Look, perhaps we don't really need to let them out,' Vi compromised. 'You open the door just a bit and keep behind it while I slip the buckets in. Let's 'ave 'em both this side – then it won't take a minute.'

Sid did as he was bid then, pulling back the bolt on the door, waited for the nod from his sister.

'Right!' she breathed, standing with the two buckets ready.

Sid slowly pulled on the door but, as soon as the light streamed in, the animals charged out of their prison, knocking the buckets from Vi's hands and sending Sid flying as the door was thrust wide open.

'Wow!' Sid exclaimed from the ground as the two stampeded out into the yard and up the farm drive towards the road.

'You all right?' Vi asked, rushing to inspect her brother.

'Huh!' he exclaimed as she bent over him. 'You're dripping on me. You're all wet!'

She shoved a hand down and pulled him to his feet. 'Come on, those animals'll be out on the road!'

When they reached the end of the track, the beasts had slowed down and were grazing uneasily on the verge, but keeping a watchful eye on the two of them.

'What you going to do, sis?'

'Let them have a feed, then try to get them back – I suppose.'

They stood for a time letting the bullocks wrap their tongues around and tear out mouthfuls of the long grasses, but when they tried to get to the far side of the beasts to drive them back towards the farm, the animals merely walked further on.

'We're getting nowhere fast!' Vi was beginning to feel really frustrated when Audrey shouted from the now distant driveway.

'What're you doing?'

'It's called "tenting",' Sid shouted back.

'What is?' Vi asked.

'Letting animals eat at the side of the road. Paul said—'

Vi, weary of the whole affair, tutted. 'I can do without a smart-alec kid at the moment.'

'Sid, your ma wants you!' Audrey called.

He gave Vi a triumphant look as if to say 'now you're on your own' and began to walk back. 'I like 'orses best, anyway!'

'His Ma's going to tidy him up and walk him up to the school.'

'He's forgotten about school!'

'And what *are* you going to do with these?' Audrey gestured to the animals.

'I'm beginning to think what I'll do is take them to old Spurrier. It'll be easier than trying to turn them round!'

'Drive them to his shop?' Audrey asked, her voice full of scepticism.

'Why not?' It was bravado at first, but then, as she thought of the way they had just been left shut in a barn with no one intending to care for them, she murmured with more purpose, 'Why not?'

'Vi! You can't!' Audrey exclaimed.

'Can't I? You watch me – and you can help. You only have to walk up to them and they move on.' She showed the truth as she walked towards the nearest beast, but then, becoming over enthusiastic, she waved her arms behind it and it took off at a run, stampeding the other one in front of it.

'Come on!' she shouted.

'I'm not a bleeding cowboy!' Audrey gasped. As the animals careered before them, she added, 'Hope nothing comes the other way.'

Vi wouldn't have admitted it, but she rather hoped something would. They might have some chance of opening a field gate and driving them in with someone or something in front of the animals. But nothing and no one came and, as the hill down into the town came into sight, she began to feel very apprehensive. What if the bullocks charged into town and hurt someone? Would she finish up in court? Pa would be real chuffed if she did something like that!

She ran faster to try to keep up – and the animals looked back at the flying hair and skirts of the two young women, showed the whites of their eyes, and increased their lead into town.

'It's useless!' Audrey shouted. 'And I've got the stitch!'

Vi paused to look back, aware of the pain in her own side.

'Let them go,' Audrey said, collapsing onto the verge, 'someone will catch them. We can go back and make out we know nothing.'

Vi paused in front, panting. She considered the idea, but decided, 'No, I couldn't do that.' She gazed down the hill where the animals were now out of sight. 'We won't catch them up now, but come on,' she said.

When they too reached the bottom of the hill, but before they turned into the village square, they could hear the turmoil.

Exchanging glances, they hurried forward to witness a scene of chaos. The two black bullocks were in the centre, like bulls in a ring, with the spectators either sheltering inside shops or ranked in doorways. Several men stood defending their parked cars, around which the bullocks paced uneasily, snorting and head tossing as they were shooed first one way and then the other. To add to the confusion, on the far road a farm cart was lumbering into the square, and from the Penzance road a pony and trap was coming into view.

It was like a set for an Ealing Comedy, Vi thought, except no one was laughing and no one seemed to know what should happen next. Vi was looking over towards the farm cart, hoping it might just be Paul, or that it might be someone who could handle animals.

'Keep still,' someone advised, 'let them calm down.'

'Drive them into the cricket field!'

'Fetch the constable!'

'What's going on?' From the far side of the square came an even louder bellow and all eyes were turned to Mr Spurrier as he came from his shop. He gesticulated angrily towards the women with their shopping baskets taking refuge, and added, 'Who's holding up my customers? Who's responsible?' He strode towards the middle of the square in his blue striped overall and blood-ied white apron.

'You are!' Vi shouted back, and walking just as rapidly to meet him, she added, 'They're your animals from the farm. Someone came and locked them up in the barn . . .'

For a second he was nonplussed. Vi saw realisation of the truth flicker in his eyes.

'Been a mistake,' he blustered. 'Been a mistake, that's all.'

'Without food and water,' Vi added, not willing to let him off one iota of responsibility. 'He said they wouldn't need—'

'Don't expect Londoners to know much about animals.' Spurrier flung an arm out to include the assembly, his fellow Cornishmen. There were one or two remarks in broad guttural accents which caused much hearty laughter, but which were totally unintelligible to Vi.

'I know when animals are upset and thirsty,' she shouted back at them. 'Even if they're going to be slaughtered, there's no need to make them suffer first.'

'You mind what you're saying.' Spurrier bounced forward, thrusting his face close to hers. 'Remember you're beholden to me. It's me put a roof over your head.'

She was revolted by the closeness of him, could smell the nauseating stench that had risen from the kitchen floor. She forced herself to stand her ground, and stared him straight in the eye. 'I don't think you had much choice about that,' she told him.

He spluttered his rage, his face apoplectic. 'You,' he began, 'you have to learn not to meddle with things that don't concern you!' Then, raising his voice in a sanctimonious manner as if addressing a class of delinquent children, he added for the benefit of the crowd, 'In Cornwall, we teach our young 'uns not to touch things that don't belong to 'em. Perhaps your father never taught you that!' From the pseudo-joviality he directed towards the crowd, his face changed as he suddenly stepped so near that his stomach, his bloodied apron, bumped Vi. 'It's always harder to learn when you're older.' The spittle of rage was on his lips as he added, 'But we'll teach you the ten commandments – don't you fret about that!'

The spectators were definitely on his side now – and there, folding her arms and nodding smugly, was the woman of the sacking apron Vi had encountered in the bakery. It all added fuel to her anger. Her cheeks flamed and her fists clenched. That he should refer to her Pa, disparage her upbringing, was intolerable. She took a step back to give herself room . . .

'I wouldn't call what *they* have done breaking the law, would you, Mr Spurrier?' The new, cultured voice broke Vi's concentration and created an unexpected diversion.

Several men pulled off their caps and women nodded, while Vi was appalled to see that the trap which had approached from the Penzance road was driven by May with Mrs St John Trewellan in the back and John Manners by her side.

It was Mrs Trewellan who had stopped her slapping out at the butcher, but it was John's presence that made her feel as if she had been pushed violently and headlong into a millrace in which she was floundering out of her depth. *Get hold of yourself*, she silently disciplined herself. At least the attention of the crowd had switched to the occupants of the trap. Then her heart tried to leap and plummet at the same time as she realised John was looking fixedly at her, a look of some bewilderment on his face.

He might well frown, she thought, *no good tweed skirt with blending green jumper today. Here I am shouting the odds like a Covent Garden barrow boy, about to throw a punch at the local butcher.*

John was very different too – no smile, no uniform, no cap to throw in the air. His jet-black hair lifted gently in the breeze and he had on fine cord slacks, a Fair-Isle jumper in blues and heather colours, a tweed jacket. His expression might register disapproval or disbelief for her, but she silently acknowledged that he was certainly the only man she knew who looked quite as glamorous out of uniform as in it.

'What are you two girls doing?' he asked as he climbed down from the trap and drew them aside a little as Cyril Spurrier was beckoned over to speak to Mrs Trewellan.

81

'Some man came and put those into one of the barns at the farm. They were bellowing all the time, so we tried to give them a drink and they escaped onto the road – so we drove them here.'

'Well, we ran after them,' Audrey interrupted.

Vi saw the twist of amusement on his lips and his curious glance at Audrey.

'This is my friend Audrey Kingston, more of a sister, really.' She wondered briefly if he might think she was taking a rise out of him and May being 'cousins' and having an 'Auntie Annie'?

'Pleased to meet you, Miss Kingston.' He smiled, then turned and watched as a couple of men took control of the animals. The beleaguered shoppers were beginning to go about their errands again, one or two following the butcher as he returned to his shop. 'With his tail between his legs,' Vi heard herself comment.

'Yes,' John agreed, 'you're certainly making your mark on the local community.'

Before she could react in any way to this remark, Mrs Trewellan's autocratic and authoritarian voice interrupted once more.

'Help those men put the beasts into the village pound until *someone* feels able to lay claim to them.'

More men and a few small boys began to help send the bullocks down a narrow opening by the side of the church to the field behind, where Vi could see what looked like a cricket pavilion.

With these out of the way, May urged the pony a few steps nearer. 'Those must be the same beasts I turned away earlier,' she commented. 'How stupid!'

'Very!' Mrs Trewellan confirmed. She looked tired from her journey, but asked after Ma and Sid and as to whether the beds had arrived from the Manor.

'Leave it to me,' she said, then added, 'get in, John, I'm anxious to be home. Goodbye, m'dears. Don't think another thing about those animals. I think I can safely say you will not be troubled in that way again.'

John gave them both a kind of salute, but as he passed Vi he winked very slowly.

How ridiculous that a wink could make you feel that it was a lifeline, that the flick of an eyelid could make you feel rescued!

'I wonder how London is really looking?' Audrey said wistfully as they watched the little party drive away. 'Funny to think she's just come from there.'

May gave them a little parting flourish of goodbye with the long whip. May was of his world, Vi thought, elegant, at ease, not putting on a show! Her old black skirt suddenly felt wetter and shabbier than ever.

Chapter 10

'Ooh!' Sid groaned, doubling like a stage-ham taking a deep bow.

'It'll go off once you're settled in the class with all your new friends.'

Sid gave Ma a look which could only be described as withering before collapsing back on to his bed and starting on a new tack. 'It's not worth starting before Christmas!'

'There's no way he'll win,' Vi said decisively as the two girls left the house. 'Pa has said he should go, so Ma will see he does! No messing!'

She handed Audrey her packed lunch as they set off. They had both decided to put on their decent coats with more everyday working clothes underneath. May had said the work was definitely camouflaging netting, though she said the site was a secret. They anticipated they would be stitching lengths of green and brown cotton on to nets such as was often seen on the cinema newsreels covering gun emplacements. Best of all was that there *was* transport laid on. They just had to be at the end of their drive at eight o'clock.

'So roll on Christmas,' Audrey said as she shivered inside her thin black city coat.

Vi wondered if her pa might come to Cornwall at Christmas – or at any time? His letter had raised many longings – and fears. They had all contributed to the return letter – hiding their real feelings, making light of the cold and bleakness of Gerrard's Head. Even these kind deceptions made him more remote, for the act acknowledged they no longer shared the detail of their lives with him. Sid, though, had told him about the horse and helping Paul, that would please him. She glanced covertly at Audrey – how did one bear the death of both mother and father? How did one deal with bereavement?

Audrey's face was thinner, she looked older and there was an air of tension inside an overwhelming cocoon of bleakness. 'Sorrowing for my beloved Ma and Pa.' The card Audrey had so very recently written for the wreath. She felt the pain of tears gather again behind her eyes for her friend. All she knew was that she would never be able to bear such a loss herself – and she must do everything she could to help Audrey through this time, forget her own foolish fancies.

'There's a lorry coming from the town, do y'think that's for us?' She pointed to the vehicle that had just come into view.

They watched it draw closer and slow down.

'You lasses for the camouflaging?' The elderly driver, grey hair fringed flat by his cap, peered from his cab – short-sightedly Vi would have said. He jerked a thumb over his shoulder. 'Jump in then.'

The tarpaulin covering over the back of his lorry was a home-made affair thrown over a frame, giving protection to two benches placed along the sides. As Vi and Audrey reached the opening, they could see there were already three other women in there. A small iron step hung below the lorry and a pair of willing hands leaned out to help them in.

'Up you come m'andsome!'

Vi found herself looking into the rosy-cheeked round face of a young woman with a mass of dark hair. Behind her were two older women, one whose pale features were lit by worried almost haunted-looking eyes and beyond her ... was the sour-faced woman of the sacking apron she had crossed swords with in the bakery shop that first day.

'Mornin'!' Vi said very brightly.

'Morning!' the younger woman made just as bright and ringing a reply. 'We can do with a bit of cheer!' Then as if in explanation she added, 'This is Avis, that is Mrs Kerrow and I'm Doris.'

'Hello!' the two of them echoed.

'Mrs *Kerrow*?' Vi queried.

'That's right! Saw you in the bakery.' The woman's tone was uncompromising, her face unsmiling.

'Yes.' Vi too made no concessions in her tone of voice. 'But it was your name, I wondered if Paul Kerrow was any relation.'

Mrs Kerrow grunted deeply in her throat and sniffed but her lips remained firmly closed, neither denying nor confirming the inquiry.

'Hold tight in the back!' the driver called.

He reversed the vehicle down the farm track far enough to allow him to turn, then drove part way back towards the town before branching off on to a road leading down towards the sea. The scenery here was bleak, no craggy rocks to break the skyline, just tiers of sand dunes on the sea side and on the other flat areas of marshy land partly flooded by the tides. Inside the lorry, Vi tried smiling reassuringly at Avis of the haunted eyes, but she, it seemed, was currently under the domination of Mrs Kerrow. *Her* eyes were directed like a searchlight beam, ready to show up any indiscreet bit of conversation which might pass between the two Londoners and her local companions. Vi wondered if Avis was bullied at home or if she had terrible private troubles.

84

She felt that there would be plenty of opportunities of bypassing Mrs Kerrow's steely gaze once they all began to work side by side. There would be time to talk as they sewed, time to befriend Avis.

The lorry lurched off towards the right and came to a sudden halt. "'Ere we are girls!' The driver came down from his cab and helped them down.

'Here we are! Where?' Vi asked as they alighted, it seemed, in the middle of nowhere.

'But where's the factory?' Audrey asked.

'What factory might that be?' their elderly driver asked.

'Where we're going to work!'

'Don't know nothing about that.' The man pushed back his cap and scratched his fringe. 'I was just told to drop you 'ere at these gates. There's no factory – nor anything else as far as anyone supposed to know about, but there's been plenty of coming and going.' He nodded significantly to the well-compacted gateway. 'All I know is I've a contract with the army to bring you 'ere every morning and take you home at dusk each day until the job's done.'

'So where are we supposed to be working?' Doris asked.

'Not outside surely,' Audrey added. 'I'm not dressed for outside.'

'Someone's coming,' Vi said as she saw a man in uniform emerge from behind a line of sand dunes and walk briskly, officiously, towards them.

'Come on! Come on! You're late!' he called.

Just as if he was on a parade ground with a bunch of rookie soldiers, Vi thought.

'There's a war on!'

Doris giggled. 'You sound just like Rob Wilton.'

The sergeant had slightly bulging eyes and his glare seemed fierce as he added, 'No laughing matter! No laughing matter! Serious work to be done, urgent work to be done! Follow me!'

The girls exchanged glances. Half eight until dusk in this bleak place with such a man in charge – Vi reckoned they were going to need each other to keep going. She linked arms with Audrey, then, as Doris stood next to her and smiled, she pushed an arm through her's too, leaving the other 'miserable pair', as she was beginning to think of them, to follow.

The man led them along a sandy road which soon became no more than a track between the dunes. Once they left the shelter of that first row of sand hills, the wind was so strong it took their breath away and they had to lean against it to make progress. The sea rolled and crashed in on to the beach, steel grey waves with foaming white heads driven by an incoming tide and the off-sea wind. The air, fairly forced into their lungs, was heavy with the smell of brine and cold wet sand. Vi thought it must be the coldest most unwelcoming smell in the world, conjuring from her city childhood the marble slabs of fishmongers and glassy-eyed fish among blocks of ice.

She was just beginning to think of protesting to this strutting sergeant in

his army greatcoat who continued to march ahead of them, his only conces-
sion to the weather being that he held onto his forage cap. All right for him!
Glancing back at the two older women she saw they were really struggling
to keep up. Mrs Kerrow looked more as if she might be used to rough
weather and walking than did Avis. This was ridiculous, here they were
following him without any idea of where they were going or how far it was.
She opened her mouth to shout at him, but just as she did so he came to an
abrupt stop.

'Thank goodness,' Doris gasped, 'I was beginning to think I'd joined the
army.'

Vi looked around. 'So where's this building we're going to work in? Or have
you got it so well hidden no one can find it!'

Doris gave a fair impression of giggling and shivering at the same time.

'Building!' he proclaimed. 'Building! This is where you're working.' He
indicated several sand hills.

'What?'

'Where?' There was real trouble in Avis's voice as she fought for breath and
added, 'But I can't see anything!'

'There! There!' The sergeant prodded his finger towards the line of dunes.
'Can't you see! No grass on 'em. Use your eyes.'

Vi suddenly realised that all the rest of the dunes around about were well
grown over with grass, while these stood out because they were bare and
because they were all the same shape and size, unlike the varying wind-blown
irregularities of the sand hills.

'Plant grass?' Mrs Kerrow sounded scandalised – for a moment – then
seemed to accept it as some kind of fate she had come to expect of life.
'Planting grass! Might 'ave known there was a catch.'

'Then we should have been told,' Doris said. 'We'd have come better
prepared.'

'I'm not working in my coat,' Vi declared as her vision of cosy chats as they
stitched away with needle and thread sank reluctantly away. 'It's my one
decent outdoor.'

'Planting grass! planting grass!' The sergeant cut in on their complaints.
'Nobody said anything about planting grass!'

'So what have we got to do?' Audrey asked.

'Watch and listen! Watch and listen!'

'We're all eyes and ears,' Vi told him. He glanced at her sharply but her face
was straight. Then he turned and walked a few steps further to the lea of the
first naked hill and bent down. Doris and Vi simultaneously stuck out their
tongues. Avis almost smiled – but recovered her worried aspect before the
sergeant straightened and came back towards them carrying a box, a pair of
pliers and a roll of wire netting.

'Now I am bemused,' Doris muttered.

'Right!' He held up the pliers as if demonstrating to several hundred. 'I shall show you what to do.' He then proceeded to kick out the roll of wire netting across the sand dune.

'I see what we need the pliers for,' Doris whispered at the same moment as Audrey volunteered for kicking out the wire.

'Right! You can fetch me another roll.' The sergeant, catching Audrey's comment, pointed imperiously in the direction he had carried the first roll from.

'Anything to keep warm.' Audrey shrugged and went, soon coming back with another roll of wire. 'There's hundreds more!' she informed them.

'Right! Unroll it alongside this first one,' the sergeant ordered.

Audrey obliged, kicking it out as if taking personal revenge.

'Now!'

'We're going to learn one of life's mysteries 'ere I can tell,' Vi whispered as the man knelt down and flipped open the lid of what looked like a wooden army ammunition box. He drew out and exhibited a one-inch-wide strip of greenish-brown tin.

'Fascinating!' Vi mouthed to Doris who cringed in the effort not to laugh.

'Your job is to take these bits of wire, put 'em through the edges of each roll of netting to make one whole sheet of netting which, when you have a piece big enough, will be pulled into place over these "dunes" by a caterpillar-tracked vehicle. So make sure each bit's firm, twisted nice and tight but the wire remains flat. Count four meshes of netting and fasten in the next strip.'

The women regarded him in disbelief and he demonstrated again, the same commentary, only slower. 'In! Insert the length of tin under the two side wires of the two strips of netting. Pull! Ensure the tin is pulled halfway, so the wires lie midway across the tin.' His nicotined forefinger prodded the middle wires over the tin strip. 'Putting the two ends of the tin strip together, you takes your pliers and secures the strip close to the ground. Turn the ends in under the wire, don't want any sharp bits on the top.'

'Then it will be pulled into place with a caterpillar-tracked vehicle,' Vi quoted po-faced.

'Corrrrect!' he approved. 'I'll show you once more.'

'Don't bother, we know what to do,' Doris said, 'but what is it for?'

'To reinforce these dunes and the tracks. You'll find more boxes of strips and pliers over there. I'll come back and see how you're doing when I've got my men organised.'

He turned and marched back the way he had come, leaving them with little alternative but to make a start.

'Well, I'm not working in my coat,' Vi said. 'I'll just have to freeze.' She took it off and, folding it carefully right side in, laid it snugly between the grass on one of the other sand hills. Audrey followed as Vi, suddenly curious, pushed her fingers in between the sand and coarse grass. 'There's wire under these,' she whispered. 'What d'you reckon?' Audrey shrugged. 'Radar installations?'

Clambering and slipping around the dunes to pick up their heavy boxes of tin strips and pliers, the five of them surveyed the huge stack of rolls of netting with sinking hearts. Vi reminded herself they wanted the work. The money wasn't bad, was good in fact, twenty shillings a week for each of them – and they were beginning to find out why!

Doris surveyed the sand dunes. 'I wonder what's buried under all those?'

'Probably best not to know,' Avis said and her look made Vi think of everything from ammunitions to bodies!

'We'll ask,' she said. 'He won't tell us – but we'll ask anyway.'

'We might as well get started.' Mrs Kerrow lifted up her coat and from around her waist produced a sacking apron which she proceeded to make into a kneeling pad. 'We'd better pull the wire all out straight first.'

'Suppose so,' Audrey agreed, leading the way and walking up the end of the wire which rerolled itself up again.

At first, while the other four crouched and stooped down, Mrs Kerrow knelt, but before long it was too back-aching for any of them to do anything other than get down on their knees.

'The wind's like a knife,' Audrey said, her hands and body shaking with the cold before they had put in, pulled through and twisted half a dozen strips between them.

'We're going to have to put our coats on,' she decided reluctantly but it was obviously either spoil their coats or risk Audrey or both of them being really ill.

Avis too had stopped work and stood rubbing her knees where the netting was digging into the flesh. 'Here's the sergeant coming back,' she said and dropped immediately back down and commenced work more rapidly than before. Vi was convinced that she must be completely cowed at home. She'd seen more than one woman with a black eye if they dared defy their 'better halves'.

'Look! He's got more soldiers with him.' Audrey pointed. 'Perhaps they're going to help . . .'

The two stood watching as the sergeant again marched along the track, but the soldiers that followed him were carrying spades. 'They're going to make some more,' Audrey said. 'Blimey, how long d'you think this job'll last?'

'Think of the money,' Mrs Kerrow said from where she knelt on her sacking, working on with Avis while the other three stood and watched.

'I'll be better prepared tomorrow, I know that,' Vi decided as she went to retrieve their coats. Then, as the line of soldiers drew nearer and some began calling and whistling over to the women, she waved. Suddenly, a possible solution occurred to her, and she ran over to speak to them.

The sergeant marched on while the men paused in appreciation of the young woman rushing over to meet them.

'This job's going to be better than I thought,' one wit cracked.

'What's up, miss, something wrong?' the first young soldier in the line asked.

'I wondered if you'd help us.' Vi launched straight in before the sergeant could intervene. 'We all came prepared to work inside. Me and my friend have only got our decent going-out coats. But we can't possibly work without coats, we'll catch our deaths.' She paused and the young man who made the first offer she recognised as the one Audrey had called 'a bit of talent' when he had driven past them in the army lorry. 'You can 'ave mine, luv, I'll be warm enough digging.'

'Aye,' his neighbour offered, nodding over to Audrey, 'and yon lass can have mine.'

Another stripped off his coat and indicated Doris, another Avis and another further along added, 'Well we can't leave the old gel out can we,' and piled his on top of the others in Vi's arms. 'Thanks, boys, it won't be forgotten.'

'Dance at our camp next Saturday. How about putting your best coats on and come to that!'

'You and your friends like dancing?'

'We do!' Vi answered immediately enthusiastic then, remembering Audrey's state of mourning, added, 'See what I can do.'

''Ere! What's all this then!' The sergeant came striding back, shouting above the wind, having finally realised he was on his own.

'Women wearing army uniform. Civilians!'

'It's either that or we lose a day's work going home to fetch suitable clothes,' Vi told him. 'I thought this job was urgent.'

Vi gave Audrey the first coat and told her who it belonged to and about the dance. Audrey just shrugged. 'What about you Doris?' Vi asked.

'She's a married woman,' Mrs Kerrow stated, adding the ultimate deterrent, 'with a child.'

'My chap's in the Navy – convoys.'

'So a bit of fun wouldn't hurt would it!' Vi found herself protesting because of the older woman's interference. 'Giving the chaps a few dancing partners – not a crime!'

'It wouldn't feel right,' Doris said, smiling wistfully. 'My Derrick loves dancing.'

'We're not all "good-time girls". Some of us know how to behave.'

'Go on then!' Audrey's explosive challenge startled them all. 'Tell us! Tell us 'ow to behave!' She went to stand over Mrs Kerrow almost threateningly. 'Tell me! 'Ow do I behave when both my parents have been killed? When my 'ome's been flattened – when I've lost everything – 'ow do I behave?'

For a moment Mrs Kerrow looked startled, defensive, then her face hardened. 'Shouting your 'ead off won't help, you stupid bitch! You're not the only one who's lost things!'

'Leave it, Aud, they don't understand.' Vi put her arm around her friend alarmed by the trembling tension she could feel through the army greatcoat.

'What's to understand?' Mrs Kerrow struggled up from her knees, the spittle of rage on her lips. 'You're 'ere and nobody wants you 'ere, bringing your city ways, tempting our lads—'

'You're an unfeeling old cow,' Doris burst in, 'no wonder your son never comes home.'

'You leave my family out of this . . .'

There was a kind of low moan from Avis who still knelt in an attitude of prayer, her pliers clasped between her palms. 'All the wrong people are dying in this war,' she murmured.

'Maybe we should all go dancing,' Doris said quietly as Audrey began to cry softly in Vi's arms, 'take our minds off things.'

Chapter 11

The arguments for them going to the dance built up during the week. First the men were so persuasive, from the loan of coats to small gifts of sweets and chocolate from their NAAFI and the assurances that it was good fun, an early Christmas party not to be missed. There would be a real band not records, plus – and perhaps this was the final perk – there would be three lorries picking up girls from various villages and taking them home when the dance finished prompt at midnight.

Vi was on tenterhooks about the whole affair when May stopped in to see how things were going and to say she and some of the officers from the Manor House always went to these particular camp dances. 'The CO there is a former dance-band leader – we always have great music. There's a fight among the local girls to get tickets.'

Finally it was Ma's quiet comment, 'It'll do no one any harm,' that seemed to make Audrey decide she would go.

'It'll do me a power of good,' Vi commented, holding up the sacking knee-pads they had made. These had become essential wear as the week had gone on – otherwise their knees, like their hands, would have been cut to ribbons. 'I never thought I'd be wearing sackcloth binding up my legs and round my palms – just like old Kerrow that first day in the bread shop. Though I had a terrible bad feeling about that pile of sacks when we first moved in! It'll do us both good to do a little –' she assumed the sergeant's military tone and widened her eyes to a glare – '*In! Pull! Twist! In! Pull! Twist!* on a dance floor to a band.'

Roy loved dancing and was certainly going to *his* camp dances. The sergeant and the job had given Vi plenty to write about in her last letter. She told him all the things she knew would make him laugh. Pa called them 'the double act'. When Roy had been called up she remembered his mother telling her the two of them reminded her of herself and Albert when they were young – 'always clowning around my Albert was.' The seal of approval had been tempered by the taciturn man Albert Moore had become and Roy's

91

mother had added in a confidential whisper, 'that was before his trouble.' Vi later found out that this was a double hernia for which he wore some kind of fierce coiled metal band with pads resembling an ancient instrument of torture. Pa said he could have had an operation, though repeating the suggestion to Mr Moore had brought a sharp 'he hasn't got it!'

Vi reflected he might not have had either if he'd gone for the operation and she improvised a jive to go with the words. 'In! Pull! Twist!' repeating them over and over ever faster.

'Don't she go on,' Sid complained.

'No more than you and your blooming headmaster – we've heard nothing else all week!'

'Well 'ow would you like it if you 'ad to go and dig his garden at break times. *And* he knows about those bullocks! 'E ses we all need keepin' out of mischief – nobody else 'as to dig his blooming garden! It's not fair, Ma!'

'Do you reckon he's being made a scapegoat of?' Vi asked. 'Are you going to see about it, Ma, or shall I?'

'Leave it for now,' her mother urged.

'I think 'e is being singled out,' Audrey said. 'I think we all are. You've only got to listen to Mrs Kerrow.'

'I try not to,' Vi added, 'and what I can't understand is why Paul seems to have totally disappeared this week.'

'I should think he's ashamed of 'er from what you tell me.' Ma put down Sid's socks she was darning. 'Come on let's do something interesting. What y'both going in Saturday.'

'Not that there's a lot of choice,' Vi said without any tone of resentment. 'It'll be best skirt and jumper again for me.' She realised that by the 'again,' she meant that if John Manners was there he would see her in the same clothes once more.

Ma, it seemed, had other ideas and had already been looking through the clothes they had now carefully hung around their living room, the only place they could keep them reasonably aired. The unfurnished upstairs rooms held a permanent smell of the sea fogs that seemed to penetrate even the yard-thick stone walls – and until they had beds and furniture it seemed a useless occupation trying to light fires up there and air them through. Ma said she had a feeling that it would be impossible to keep things aired 'any sense anywhere'. Even the clothes they were so careful with had taken on a damp smell, and when they were held in front of the fire before being put on, all steamed quite dramatically.

Vi set up the long plank of wood they had salvaged from the yard, balancing it between chair-back and table to form an ironing board. She covered this with a blanket borrowed from one of the beds. Audrey had already heated an old flat iron on the fire. This too had been also been retrieved, at first rust-red, from the farmyard where it had obviously spent some years propping open a stable door. Audrey took it off the fire with yet another pad of sacking and used another sack to rub the iron on first to make sure there were no cinders sticking to the bottom. Turning it bottom side up she spat on it but the spittle jumped and fizzed. It was too hot to begin pressing anything, so she held it and retested it after a few minutes.

Ma found out two of her crepe de Chine blouses, one quite lavishly frilled at the neck – and beads, long strings of crystals which shone different colours like prisms as she moved them in the lamplight.

'You'll be like proper flappers.'

'That's a bit dated, Ma,' Vi told her, 'but the beads look nice.'

Audrey finally opted for the frilly blouse and no beads, Vi chose the smaller, prettier string of beads to go over her best green jumper. They had a kind of dress rehearsal before they left the house on the Saturday night.

'Audrey's blouse is the best and Vi's beads sparkle,' Sid summed up.

'Thank you, Hardy Amies!' Vi told him, watching Audrey who still seemed to be in some private turmoil over going out.

'Come on,' she urged pulling her coat on. 'We mustn't keep the lorry waiting or let Doris down.'

'Take the umbrella,' Ma said, 'its bound to be drizzling out there. Got the flashlight? Don't leave it switched on mind.'

'Do you think Doris really will come?' Audrey asked as they linked arms and walked tight together under the umbrella, both grasping the stick while Audrey shone the tiny beam of light down to show the edge of the grass on the drive.

Neither of them were really sure. Ethel Kerrow had made it clear by her remarks such as, 'I don't know what people'll think' and, 'No one's 'eard of such a thing – not in decent quarters,' that Doris had made no secret of her intentions – and the more Mrs Kerrow had shown her prejudices the more determined Doris had seemed to come.

'We'll soon see . . .' Vi began then, peering forward, asked, 'Isn't that a lorry waiting on the road?' They began to run, joggling each other as they both tried to keep their heads under the umbrella. They were breathless and even Audrey was half laughing by the time they reached the road.

'Come on you two!'

'Know that voice,' Vi called, recognising Noel who had volunteered the first greatcoat. 'Good of you to wait.'

'Got half a crown on the two of you turning up,' he told them as they were offered a share of the front seats with Noel and Frank, another of the dune-making party. 'First in get the best,' Frank said as Noel restarted the ten-tonner.

'Frank here reckoned the old biddy'd persuade you not to come,' Noel said, grinning his pleasure that it was not true. It looked hard work as he turned the wide circle of the steering wheel between his hands to bring the lorry from the side to the middle of the road, and Vi suddenly felt tears prick her eyes as it reminded her of Pa and his strong hands gripping and guiding his bus through the streets of London.

'We're wondering if Doris'll turn up,' she shouted to him, then, remembering that John might also come to the dance, her heart rocketed as if this high jolty ride was as exciting as a big dipper at a fairground and the hooded lights of the lorry were picking out the grass and rocks of the roadside as spectacular as a Hollywood extravaganza. She noticed Frank slip his arm around Audrey's waist to steady her on the seat – and Audrey leaned back and enjoyed it. Wonderful!

'I hope she does.' Noel too raised his voice above the engine. 'She's a good sort, makes no secret of the fact that she's married and only out for a nice night dancing. I like that in a woman.'

It seemed a very adult judgment for a soldier who looked so young. 'You married,' Audrey asked.

'No! Give 'im a chance, he's still wet behind the ears,' Frank said and they laughed out of all proportion to the hackneyed old remark.

People are like that, Vi thought, *excitable when they're looking to have a good time.* She snuggled in behind Audrey's shoulder and the door.

'Comfortable?' Audrey asked raising her eyebrows.

'Lovely,' Vi told her, then queried with a grin, 'and you?'

Frank laughed and his arm tightened a little around Audrey's waist. 'Sure she is.'

The old Audrey would have given him back some cheeky remark but now she made no reply – but neither did she move away. Vi felt a sudden unease, she hoped she was not bringing Audrey into any kind of situation she wasn't up to dealing with. But, no, the thought was absurd. Audrey was the experienced one, she wouldn't 'get into trouble'.

The stock phrase for becoming pregnant plus the simple message her Ma had years ago passed on in her quiet worried tone were indelibly printed on her mind: 'Think how disappointed your pa would be if you brought trouble home.' 'Trouble' she very clearly visualised as a bundle wrapped in a shawl. Her ma had used the ultimate deterent to wrong doing – her love for her pa. No way was Violet ever going to do anything to hurt either of them so there was no problem.

When they arrived at the pick-up point in town, some half a dozen girls stood waiting near the shaded light of the telephone box.

'Shall we get out and ride in the back,' Vi wondered, peering through the windscreen and waving. 'I can see Doris.'

'I'd stay where you are, love, we'll be at the camp in about ten minutes.'

They drove on, picking up more young women at two more stops. A fitful moon occasionally lit the sea on their right and it was quite beautiful, though the sound of the women laughing in the back was often raucous. Noel, as if in

94

response, began deliberately hurtling the lorry around some of the corners. The more noise that came from the back the more he did it.

The final swerve took them in at the camp gates. A barbed-wire enclosure holding some twenty-four huts in rows, like a prison camp, she thought. They jerked to a halt before a red and white striped pole and two guards dressed for the special occasion, for as well as uniform and guns their caps were decorated with red and yellow paper streamers.

Everyone's dance ticket was inspected and Noel was instructed to, 'Put 'em down outside the NAAFI and pick 'em up at the same point at midnight.'

'OK, all you Cinderellas, no losing your glass slippers – *or anything else*. See you back here at midnight or yours truly will be in the glasshouse,' Noel called, adding more discreetly to Audrey and Vi, 'see you inside, save's a dance!'

The girls and women all disembarked. In the crowd around the entrance, the two of them looked around for Doris, who they soon saw with another woman in tow. For a second neither of them recognised her – not because she looked so different but because her presence was so unexpected.

'It's Avis!' Vi was astounded.

'Avis?'

Avis, who had carefully set her hair into its marcel waves and certainly had on a little rouge and lipstick, blushed furiously and tossed up her chin defiantly. 'Edwin's away with his work until tomorrow night.'

'And if he hears later?' Vi asked as they were ushered to a small room at one end of the hut that had been transformed for the evening into the ladies' cloakroom with clothes racks and a mirror.

'Live today, let tomorrow take care of itself, you know what you've all been saying all week,' Avis said defensively.

'That's what I say all right!' A woman who Vi judged to be in her late forties pushed through the crowd to the mirror to apply another layer of bright pillarbox-red lipstick.

'They say a lot of these lads could be off to the front anytime.'

'They send them here to climb the cliffs and run on the sands – toughen 'em up.'

'We'll give them a night to remember!' A slim petite blonde demonstrated a few elegant samba steps.

'As long as I don't finish up with anything to remember *them* by I don't care!' The woman putting the finishing touches to her lipstick laughed with uproarous crudity.

'Hark at her,' the blonde commented, 'like a lady until she opens her mouth!'

'That's no lady, that's Gloria! Come on!'

'She'll be wilting over her sewing machine tomorrow!'

A whole crowd who obviously worked together left the cloakroom.

'They're going to have a good time,' Avis said shakily, suddenly reaching for a bentwood chair and sitting down heavily. 'I shouldn't have come. I don't know what made me. I just had this urge.'

'Well you have, so now we'll just enjoy the dancing, then go home and no one will ever know.' Vi reached a hand down to Avis and pulled her to her feet hoping no one would be any the wiser. None of them really knew just what Avis was risking if her chapel lay-reader/inspector for the Ministry of Ag and Fish husband found out. Vi only knew she detested him without ever having met him. It was the honest and naive way Avis repeated his snide and derogatory remarks and took for granted the regime of pandering to his every whim he inflicted on her. Though it did sometimes seem to Vi that Avis repeated what he had said and done to gauge other people's reactions – as if unsure just how hurtful the man was really being.

'Oh, that looks lovely,' Doris said wistfully as the four of them went to stand at one end of the main hut. The floor had been liberally polished with French chalk and some nine or ten couples were already waltzing to 'The Blue Danube'. The ceiling and walls were hung with masses of different coloured crepe paper twisted together into long streamers and great swathes of paper chains which must have taken ages to interlink and glue together. In the centre hung a huge revolving ball made up of tiny mirrors. A spotlight swept around the floor from to time and caught the glass, sending prisms of light like momentary rainbows all around. Best of all was the 'real band'.

Doris sighed as the first waltz finished and the trombonist stood to play in the second dance with a short solo. 'Wish my Derrick was here.'

'This dance please?' A young soldier appeared at Audrey's elbow.

'Never dance with anyone whose name I don't know.'

Audrey's response was automatic, the stock phrase she and Vi had developed when they received an invitation to dance from someone new.

'Cliff,' he replied and offered an arm to escort Audrey to the floor.

'You don't waste any time,' she told him.

'Don't know how much of that we've got do we . . .?'

'Audrey,' she supplied as the two went off into a smooth flowing waltz step.

Vi watched Audrey disappear behind the growing number of couples taking the floor. She supposed that after all the careful effort it had taken to get Audrey there, she was surprised how easily her friend had slipped into not just the dance routine, but the patter. Then from behind them a familiar voice said, 'Good! Thought for sure you would have been snapped up.'

She turned to see Noel grinning all over his face and crooking an arm in her direction. 'May I have the pleasure, Miss Violet Tulley?'

'So,' she queried, 'how come you know my full name and what's yours?'

She supposed he told her but, as he swung her into the first turn, she saw Avis turn abruptly and make for the door. She couldn't be planning to leave, to try to walk home all that way in the dark? But before Vi could do anything the dance step took her round. As she came in sight of the door again, Avis was being escorted back in and towards the floor by a large sergeant major. She gasped, half laughing, half in surprise, as the two of them prepared to enter the dance.

Noel pushed her away a little to look at her face and she realised he had asked her the same question more than once for she caught the repeated pattern of his words.

'Sorry,' she said, 'I was just worried about my friends.'

'They're all dancing,' he reported. 'They'll be no wallflowers at this dance. You girls are in short supply. Is it true your friend has lost her home and her family in the Blitz?'

'Yes, this is the first time we've been to a dance since.' Vi felt sobered by the memory of finding Audrey in her dance dress at the bus stop. She fell silent, but soon the smooth rhythm of the dance and the mesmeric effect of the lights passing over them like coloured hands began to erase the recollection. She began to really enjoy the skill of her partner, glimpsing the band and her friends as they circled – and always glancing at the door when they passed.

'You expecting someone?' He seemed well aware of every move she made.

'Not really.'

'Just hoping then?'

'You're a good dancer,' she told him, lifting her hand from his shoulder to wave at Audrey who actually didn't look too happy.

'Hint taken,' he said without rancour, 'but I tell you what I don't think your friend will want to dance with Frank again.'

'Can't he dance?'

'It's not that. He'll be reminding her who got her ticket for her and got her a lift in the front of the lorry. He likes to establish a little gratitude in his women . . . his wife in particular.'

'Thanks for the tip off,' she was saying when someone approached Noel from behind.

'Excuse me!'

'It's not . . .' Noel began but, glancing at Vi's face as she looked up at John Manners, added a little begrudgingly, 'Oh! Don't know though, reckon she's been waiting for you.'

'Hope that's true,' John said as he took up her hand.

'Don't know why he should say that!' But as his arm went around her waist she directed and placed her hand on his shoulder with some awareness.

'Lordy!' he exclaimed gently. 'You know that made me feel as if I'd been knighted.'

She laughed at the unexpected remark, but what *she* felt as she fitted so perfectly under his shoulder, was that she was coming home to somewhere very special indeed. She brought her wondering thoughts to order. 'Has May come?' she asked.

He inclined his head and they danced on in silence, becoming, it seemed to Vi, ever more aware of each other and oblivious to everything and everyone else. She had the strange feeling that this was the first time she had ever really danced. *Snap out of it*, she silently disciplined herself, *use some common sense, he's got a girl. Think of Roy!*

She knew so little about this man – except that he was different. Perhaps this was his attraction for her. There had to be some reason. She tutted audibly. Looking up she found her own questioning reflected in his face.

'If it's any consolation I don't understand either,' he said very quietly as he drew her closer and she could feel the buttons on his jacket and some of Ma's beads press against her.

'Why you should ask me to dance?' She tried to push away the feeling of momentousness.

'No, I think you know I mean a much bigger question than that.'

She was silent, unable to deny or for a moment find a flippant reply. She wondered just what he did see in her. 'Attraction of opposites!' she supplied.

'Adam and Eve! Of course!'

She felt her face flush, wanted to accuse him of the old one-track mind but that might imply she expected more – whereas really she told herself it was less.

'That wasn't really what I meant.'

'Opposites?' he queried.

She felt he was just playing her along, wished she could see his face clearly but replied, 'Lifestyles . . . backgrounds!'

'Oh those,' he dismissed, 'never think about it.'

'You don't have to if you've got it.'

'And you don't think you have?'

'No,' she replied as the band came to the end of the third waltz and they stood clapping politely as some couples left the floor and the lights came up momentarily.

'You've got something,' he said with the weight of great certainty in his voice and as her lips parted to deny any such thing he overrode it with the invitation, 'Stay together,' as the band struck up 'You Are My Sunshine' for the first of a sequence of quicksteps.

'You're a fighter,' he went on as he took her smoothly into the dance, 'that goes without saying.'

She nearly asked why then remembered the last time he had seen her was on the square as she confronted the butcher.

'You've taken over the care of your family.' He put her away from him a little so he could see her face. 'A big burden for such young shoulders?'

She raised her eyebrows acknowledging the question. 'Twenty, twenty-one next October – not so young.'

He grinned.

'And you?'

'Twenty-six on Christmas Eve,' he told her. 'Not a good date.'

'Did you only get one lot of presents?' she asked lightly.

'No, it had more to do with how sad my mother always became around Christmas and New Year. The special time was always irrevocably linked to the date my father was killed.'

'Oh!' She was instantly sorry for the flippant remark. 'That is sad. What happened?'

'He was a regular soldier, but I hardly remember him. He was killed early in the First World War, January 2nd 1915 to be exact – and my mother died last year without ever in my opinion getting over losing him. So now I really am an orphan.' He looked down at her very seriously then added, 'You know that obligates you to be very specially kind to me.'

She nearly said that he and Audrey should get together but that was not what she wanted at all and then the right moment had passed to say anything.

'I'm not serious you know.' He looked repentent, then added, 'No matter how you treat me I intend to stay around.'

'Anyway,' she told him airily as she tried to reconcile her heart and her head's response, 'I'm kind to everyone.'

'And everything – even bullocks.'

They laughed together then so that several couples turned to look at them.

'And your father . . .?' he asked.

She did not answer because the thought suddenly occurred to her that she had perhaps found someone who really might match up to her pa!

'Violet?'

'He's a bus driver.' She had to make a real effort to make the words come, so involved was she with her thoughts. 'He's a London bus driver.'

'So you worry about him a lot.'

'All the time.'

'Bloody wars,' he said quietly and glancing up she found he was looking way over her head. She in turn studied the way his neck rose so leanly, so strongly from his shirt collar, that there were tiny hairs showing just where his collar came together above his tie. She found herself hoping he wasn't over hairy – then missed a step.

He instantly caught her to him so firmly she lost what little breath she had and then he apologised profusely as if it had been his fault.

'Would you like a drink – give us some time to talk. Pity you haven't got one of those dance cards then I could book every dance.'

She laughed at such a posh notion in wartime and allowed herself to be led from the floor towards the bar at the far end of the room.

'There you are!' May came smiling towards them. 'Spotted you dancing.' She hooked an arm into John's in the same way she had at the Lodge.

'Is Audrey here?' she asked. 'And your other friends?'

99

'Yes.' Vi looked around obligingly but with the definite feeling that she was being hived off, put back with her friends.

'I was just getting us a drink,' John said. 'You like one?'

'We've not had a dance yet.' She pouted prettily at him.

'After a drink then.'

'OK. Fine! There's a table over there look!' She pointed it out to him before releasing his arm.

'So which are your friends?' May asked as they arranged chairs.

Vi was surprised to see Avis still in the arms of a large brawny sergeant. The pair of them looked distinctly uncomfortable as they quickstepped with about as much jerky grace as a clockwork toy around the floor. Yet somehow, Vi decided, they looked right – possibly because they were both so awkward.

'You can't see them,' May prompted.

She waited until Avis and partner disappeared in the growing crowd on the floor. 'No,' she replied, adding conversationally, 'its a great band though. You like dancing?'

'Just watch me when I get on the floor with John!'

'Really!'

May turned her glance from the dancers to Vi and laughed. 'I'm not modest about my dancing, or John's, we're great together.'

The sequence of three quicksteps finished before John had managed to catch the barman's eye. From the platform the band leader announced, 'Welcome all you lads and lasses. We want to keep the party going right from the word go, so *take your partners* for a progressive barn dance. Now, I want no sitters-out – no lingerers at the bar! It's much too early in the night.'

'Come on you old soak!' May cried seizing John as he lowered the three drinks cupped precariously between his hands.

'It's not true,' he protested to Vi as he was dragged away. 'Save me from this white-ribboner!'

Before Vi could do more than separate the three glasses so they stood square, Frank had her by the hand and was leading her into the circle and as it was progressive she allowed him to do so. As the dancers assembled, urged on by the band leader, she could see Noel with Audrey, Doris with a corporal – and Avis still with the same sergeant. Avis, she noticed, continually put her hand before her lips as if in a permanent state of concern. Vi wondered if she was going to think the worry outweighed the 'good time'.

She was watching them when Frank directed her attention over to the left. 'Your partner seems to be enjoying himself.'

It was true. John and May were laughing as they twirled around before changing partners, with John suddenly lifting one hand and arm as if hurling something away, May's head went back once more in amusement.

'Wish you could hear!' It was not so much a question as a sneering comment.

100

'Not at all.' She turned sharply back to her partner as the band began to play the opening bars of another barn dance. 'Nothing to do with me.'

'Not much!' he said. 'Who are you trying to kid.'

She turned her head away from the objectionable man and noticed that Avis and her sergeant had left the floor and were making for one of the small side tables in a corner. The sergeant was offering Avis his handkerchief. She took it quite gracefully and patted her forehead. Avis it seemed had made a conquest. So what! For one measly night what did it matter.

She thankfully proceeded forward, leaving Frank behind. As the men came around, the circle of ladies moved backwards and she found herself facing Noel again. John she glimpsed briefly, a face in the crowd with a variety of partners. The barn dance was followed by the Valetta, then the 'Gay Gordons' and after the whooping and the twirling on the crowded floor most were ready for an interval.

The band leader came to the central microphone again and announced that to give them a breather there would be nice 'smoochy session of foxtrots'. Vi made her way back to where her drink was waiting, but May had caught John as he was leaving the floor and it was obvious she did not intend to be denied.

The syncopated rhythms of the dance throbbed around the hall and John and May were magnificent. The many couples that were already on the floor began to fall away to the sides and soon there were just three couples being cheered on. They could all execute a kind of tap-dance sequence among the more normal steps, though John and May kept it up so long it took Vi's breath away. There were shouts of 'Bravo!' and 'Encore!'

At the end the applause was universal. 'Better than MGM!' someone called. May was victorious and full of chatter, irrepressible. Vi heard herself say, 'That really was dancing the light fantastic,' but the evening was not the same after that. She felt like the one guest at the party who was standing apart, could not give to the good time, as if the memory of those perfectly matched movements were tapped into her memory for ever. May was obviously head over heels in love with John and surely no man could dance like that with a woman he did not care for.

She and John did dance together afterwards and won a spot prize just before midnight, but when time came for the last waltz she saw May coming with her hand already extended to take his arm. She excused herself and went quickly to the cloakroom. When the other girls came in, she told them she was going outside to cool off and wait for their transport.

Then, as they all assembled to climb into the lorry with Noel and Frank, John was suddenly there with a helping hand under her arm. 'Goodnight, Violet, thanks for the dances.'

'Thank you,' she said formally. 'You and May are sensational.'

'You should see her do the Charleston!' he said with a laugh.

Vi just felt glad she had not seen them dancing that sentimental slow last waltz together.

He waited and watched, lifting a hand in salute as the lorry drove away. She positioned her pigskin shoulder bag very straight very squarely on her knees. She was silent all the way back, while Audrey compared partners with Doris and Avis grasped a large khaki handkerchief between both hands.

Chapter 12

Vi was awoken by the sound of Audrey and her ma talking. She lay very still, the only way to ensure any peace in their communal living/bedroom – and she needed a bit longer to come to terms with herself.

In bed by one o'clock, she had still been awake as the December Sunday morning began to edge its grey light in from over the land – and the feeling of despondency and discontent had come with her through the short sleep.

'You were right, it didn't do any 'arm,' Audrey was saying. 'I just danced without thinking about it . . . and it did make me forget for a bit.'

Vi knew she would never forget *that* dance. For hours, as she lay staring at the ceiling, the images of May and John moving together in perfect harmony had flickered in and out of the flames of the dying fire.

Even though the foxtrot that had become a demonstration had been only halfway through the evening, the jollifications afterwards had not been the same. John and May had been feted and continually cornered and questioned about their partnership. It had seemed to Vi they had become public property, all the intimacy of the early evening had disappeared.

In her mind Vi again heard the syncopated beat, saw how John moved with such slick precision, feet, hands, body, elegant line for line, in accord with May's. The excitement as Vi had watched had centred itself disturbingly in her groin, as it did again even on the memory. Last night she had looked away to break the spell and had held herself physically at a distance from him as they performed what seemed very ordinary dance routines afterwards.

But this morning she recognised her fixation for what it was. She was jealous – green-eyed jealous!

But I'm not like that – not like any of those things, she argued with herself, turning violently away from such thoughts – and finding herself the focus of attention.

'Awake at last,' Ma said, moving to the teapot on the hob. 'Both enjoyed yourselves then – met some nice chaps?'

When Vi did not answer immediately, Audrey said she had danced mostly with the driver of the lorry that had picked them up. 'Noel his name is. He's a Dr Barnardo's boy.'

'Not another orphan!' Vi exclaimed without thinking.

'What d'yer mean by that?'

'Oh nothing really. It was just that John Manners was saying *his* parents are both dead.'

'I don't think with his background that counts the same,' Audrey said. 'Anyway Noel isn't an orphan, he has a father and a mother somewhere.'

'Did you 'ave a dance with May's cousin?' Ma asked.

'She did!' Audrey immediately told her, 'Most of the evening in fact.'

'He's a good dancer,' she said defensively, 'and he danced with May too.'

'May's his cousin, that hardly counts,' Audrey said.

'No she's not y'know,' Vi said, crooking her knees and putting her arms around them and holding tight while she waited for Audrey's verdict once she knew the true situation.

'Oh! I see.' She stared into space pursing her lips as she made some reassessment. 'She's more his sort, of course.' Then, glancing at Vi, she added, as if to comfort her friend, 'And you never did like dancing with officers back home, different world you said they came from. You'll have to take up with Frank.'

'Oh thanks very much!' She swung her legs to the floor. 'By the way, he's married did you know? Noel told me to warn you.'

'He needn't worry, he's 'orrible!'

'Any hot water, Ma?' Vi took the kettle and went upstairs to where they had set up a washstand with jug and basin and racks for towels – and the inevitable sacking mat. She stood on the rough hessian her mother had washed to a pale beige and tried to put John Manners out of her mind. *This is your place, me girl – sacking mats, sacking kneepads, sacking bloody aprons.* She plunged her hands into the basin of water. *I wonder if there're any office jobs in Penzance? But how would I get there? How long would it take to save the 'in-pull-twist' money to buy a bike?*

She was hardly dressed when she saw they had a Sunday-morning visitor. She frowned and peered close to the window. 'Doris – with her baby.'

She ran downstairs as quickly as she could, carrying down the pail of dirty water to empty in the outside drain, then stood waiting to greet Doris as she came hurrying up the drive pushing her pram.

'She looks serious,' Audrey said as she and Ma joined her and watched as Doris came unwaving and unsmiling towards them.

'What is it?'

Even as Audrey asked the question, Vi remembered all the other times she had felt uneasy the evening before. 'It's Avis isn't it,' she guessed as Ma stooped into the pram to sweep up a chubby little boy whose big eyes widened even further as he viewed the strangers. 'What's his name?'

'Tommy,' Doris answered abstractedly before going on with the reason for her journey. 'It is Avis . . . how did you guess?' She paused, breathless after her rush up the hill from the town.

'Come and tell us inside.' Ma led the way, carrying Tommy who was intrigued by the flowers and binding on her apron.

'I go to the same chapel as Avis and her husband,' she began when they were all inside. 'He preaches from time to time. He was there this morning. You know Avis said he was away – and, I don't know, there was something about the man, something that made my flesh creep when he looked at me. Anyway, it upset me so much I had to come out part way through the service. I went straight round to Avis's home.' She looked down at the floor, frowning, as if gathering the energy or the words to tell the next part.

'He's done something to her,' she said with certainty. 'She's there but won't come to the door.'

'Did she speak to you?'

'I know I heard a kind of groan and I think I saw her vaguely at the bedroom window – but she wouldn't come to the door.' Doris's eyes were full of trouble. 'I didn't know what else to do. I thought perhaps you might be able to do something.' She looked directly at Vi, adding, 'Her husband's taking the children's service in chapel this afternoon at three.'

There was silence as Vi took in what was being asked of her.

'You shouldn't interfere between man and wife,' Ma commented quietly as Tommy laughed and squirmed on her knee. She nodded at him but spoke directly to her daughter.

'That's the trouble, *nobody's* ever interfered. This isn't the first time. She's covered up with stories of falls downstairs, bumping into cupboard doors . . . and that was when he had no cause!' Doris jumped up and paced around the kitchen. 'I just know for certain by the evil close look on his face he's done something really terrible to Avis.' She paused and tutted. 'She's such a plain, placid soul – wouldn't hurt a fly. Well I think she's stood enough from that pontificating old sod! Stands up there preaching the "good word" and at home he's nothing but a bully and a bastard, throwing his weight about. And why is he exempted from military service anyway? My Derrick's had to go.' She flung up a hand in agitation. 'I tell you why, because he's a low-down, snooping old bugger who goes round spying on farmers and fishermen to make sure they're not giving away half a dozen eggs or the odd herring.' She turned away, gripping the edge of the sink, regaining control, turning back. 'Sorry! Sorry, Mrs Tulley, what must you think of me?'

'She might be real bad,' Audrey speculated.

'You'll know the truth tomorrow when she comes to work,' Ma said.

'If she comes,' Doris said doubtfully. 'I reckon he's given'er a good lacing.'

'You think she'd open up to us if we went this afternoon while he's out again?'

'We could try,' Doris said, sitting down again and sighing relief at Vi. 'I knew you wouldn't let me down – not after seeing you deal with the bullocks and the butcher!'

'You heard about that!'

'Oh, I was there,' she said. 'I thought anyone who could do all that for animals would help. There's things needed sorting out in this community for years – reckon you're the lass to do it.'

'Great,' Vi groaned. 'I'll be real popular . . .' She recollected expressing the same sentiment to her pa when she had seen a thief in her school, a classmate who was letting an innocent friend take the punishment. Pa said it was her duty to go to the teacher. She remembered complaining with those self-same words. She sighed. Pa had also told her that being popular was not as important as feeling right inside herself – feeling she was doing the right thing – no matter what anyone else thought.

It was agreed that Doris should stay and eat with them. They could afford to be generous – there was a rabbit provided by Paul. Not that he had put in an appearance but had sent the highly prized gift of meat with Sid, who even that Sunday morning had gone off (packed up with croust) to help rebuild a stone wall some of Mr Spurrier's animals had knocked down.

They ate well and, putting the pots and pans to steep in the sink, they all walked back towards the town. Ma was to look after Tommy at Doris's cottage while the others, timing their visit to coincide with the beginning of the children's service, went to Avis's house.

The square was quiet, the December afternoon not conducive to casual outings. There were one or two people walking dogs and two children were running up the hill the opposite way out of town towards the chapel and their service.

'It must be the chapel we stayed in our first night,' Vi realised, glancing after the children.

'I heard about that!' Doris exclaimed. 'So *that* was you as well!'

Vi was beginning to think her reputation locally was already past saving. What had she to lose? Not, she told herself, that it had anything to do with it, but somehow the memory of May ever claiming John's arm gave her a feeling of utter, wretched recklessness.

The house was one of many terraced cottages in a backstreet. Avis's differed from the others only because to one side there was a large covered gateway. Doris led the way through one of the large gates, closing it carefully behind them. Beyond was a cobbled path and a neat square of grass, outhouses, a clothesline.

'That's where I think I saw Avis.' Doris pointed up to a tiny paned window above the gateway.

'I think the neighbours will all be at chapel, they have young children,' Doris said as she led the way to the back door and tapped loudly. There was no response. Vi leaned her head to the wood and listened, somewhere in the cottage it sounded like someone moving surreptitiously about or – she frowned – like someone dragging themselves along the floor.

What had the man done? Vi knocked with more urgency, again listening. But this time there was silence. She knocked again and called, 'Avis! It's Vi! Come to the door please, Avis.'

'It's no use,' Doris whispered, 'she's too frightened.'

Vi hammered harder. 'Avis! We're not going away until we've seen you. Are you all right? Avis! We'll still be here when he comes back from chapel if you don't open up.'

All three of them stooped near the door, holding their breath to see if this threat brought the response they wanted. Then all three heard the agonised gasp and half-cry like that of a wounded animal.

'My God!' Audrey breathed as this was followed by a sound that could only be described as whimpering.

'Avis! Open the door!' Doris begged.

'Go away!' The words came in a gasp as if pushed out in one great sob. 'Please.' And this word trailed off into despair.

'Do you think he's locked her in and she can't open the door,' Audrey speculated.

'Avis!' Vi said in a loud firm voice. 'We're not going away until we've seen you're all right. Have you got a key? Avis!'

There was no answer.

'Come to the window,' Vi called. 'We'll talk through the window.'

Another silence. Doris peered into the keyhole. 'There's no key in the lock but its too dark inside to see anything.'

The three of them held their breaths, listening for the slightest sound. Then Vi felt as if her every nerve had been scraped as a chair moved across the floor.

'She's coming,' Audrey whispered and they all moved towards the curtained window. 'I think . . .'

They waited and wondered. 'What is she doing now?' Doris asked as they heard tins being moved and Avis groaning softly with the effort of whatever task she was putting herself through. Doris opened her mouth to call out again but Vi put a hand on her arm. Then they all heard the sound of a key being put into the door.

'Oooh!' The involuntary expression of pain accompanied the hesitant and laborious turning of the key. Vi bit hard into her bottom lip as with each second her anxiety grew.

She saw the door give a little as the lock was released, watched the latch to see it lifted, but when nothing further happened she slowly and carefully put her hand to it. 'We're coming in Avis, all right?'

Inch by inch she opened the door further. The interior of the cottage was dim and for a moment they did not see Avis who stood leaning in the shadow of a tall kitchen dresser.

'My God, what has he done to you!' Doris called out. 'Ooh! My God!'

Avis rocked against the wall. 'I fell . . .' she began, 'down the stairs . . . I—'

'Stop it!' Doris shouted almost hysterically. 'Stop it!'

Vi and Audrey stood shocked by the protest and the sight of the blood matted on Avis's hair and forehead and the bruised eyes. Her right arm was pushed into a cardigan which just hung from one shoulder. Her left arm swung at an awkward angle. She tried to hold the injured arm to herself, to support it in some way, but even as she touched it she moaned in agony.

'Come and sit down,' Vi led her to a chair. Avis uttered a low faltering cry of pain with each breath as she sat down and Vi helped her lift the useless seemingly lead-heavy arm on to her lap.

'Avis,' Vi said gently, forcing herself to hold back the tirade of anger that swept over her as she saw the limb was blue and purple with great wheals of red. She tempered the accusations she wanted to make, controlled her voice. 'Your arm's broken. We'll have to get the doctor.'

'No!' Avis said in great alarm. 'No. I'm all right. It just needs a rest. You mustn't tell anyone. It's just my ring that hurts.'

The three of them were speechless with a new concern as they stared at her hand so swollen the ring was not visible. 'I don't know what to do with it . . .' she said doubling over, rocking in her torment.

'Oh! Her wedding ring,' Doris wailed, 'she must be in agony. It must be cut off.'

'Edwin wouldn't allow that,' Avis gasped.

'Don't think we're very worried about what 'e wants,' Vi said through gritted teeth as she noticed that while the rest of the hand, wrist and arm were all colours, Avis's ring finger was a bloated but deathly white.

'Edwin says I make a fuss.' She paused, then utter panic was in her voice as she added, 'Go before he comes back. I can lock the door again . . . no one need know.'

They all felt overwhelmed by how terrified the woman was of her husband – yet there was no way they could comply with her fearful request. Vi caught Doris's eye and mouthed, 'Go and get the doctor.'

Doris left immediately while Vi stooped over Avis, obscuring her view and occupying her mind with questions. 'When did it happen? Was he at home when you came back after the dance.'

'Do you think she should have tea?' Audrey asked under an incoherent story of surprise and punishment interlaced with remarks like 'said deserved it and more' and 'I'm a wicked woman'.

'Think we should wait now?'

Audrey nodded, the possibility of an operation in both their minds. 'I 'ope he's not long,' she breathed, kneeling by their workmate.

108

'I thought my end had come.'

The sudden lucid sentence brought their attention instantly back to Avis.

'So I told him I'd never enjoyed myself so much in all my life.'

Kneeling by Avis's side, Vi shook her head slowly. 'Not worth this.'

Avis looked at her with a strange calmness and logic. 'Confession – before my end – didn't want to pretend anymore . . .'

'I think you're the one should be preaching at the chapel not your old man! You're the good one,' Audrey decided.

Vi remembered the huge burly sergeant and thought it was a pity he hadn't come home with her. Sometimes goodness needed a bit of strength behind it.

'We'll make sure he never does it again,' Vi muttered with grim determination but Avis gave a short disbelieving laugh. 'It's my lot,' she said, giving way again to the pain from her arm which seemed to come in waves, turning her face from white to grey.

Not if I can help it, Vi thought, wanting to tell her that the worst was over, help was coming, but a glance at the clock also told her that within half an hour her husband too would be on his way back. Just at that moment Audrey whispered conspiratorially, 'I think I can hear someone coming.'

Vi's heart pounded for a moment before she reasoned that if Mr Smith was in charge of the chapel service he couldn't come away early. Hopefully it was Doris with news of the doctor.

Audrey hurried out to the gateway. Vi breathed a silent sigh of relief as she heard Doris and a man's voice as they came into the back yard.

'Now m'dear, what's all this?' The doctor was tall, his manner stern, as well it might be, but Vi felt faith in him as she saw his attention immediately focus on Avis's finger. He moved closer but did not touch the hand, then moved to get another angle on the elbow and forearm, gently lifting the torn sleeve of Avis's blouse to look at the upper arm.

'I'll take you to the hospital myself,' he told her. 'We must get this ring off and the arm X-rayed. Plaster you up, make you good as new.'

'I can't go to hospital, doctor.'

'You really have no choice, my dear. Your new friends here will help and no doubt one of them will stay behind to tell your husband where I've taken you.' He smiled briefly in Vi's direction.

There was just the slightest inflexion in his voice which made Vi scrutinise him carefully. This man knew, or had some inclination, what had happened in this household – in his whole district probably. He knew she and Audrey were new and he hadn't asked any questions about how Avis had sustained the injuries. 'I'll stay,' she volunteered.

Once Avis, arm supported in a sling, was persuaded into the doctor's car with Doris accompanying her, Audrey set off back to Doris's home to let Ma know what was happening – and Vi felt very strange left alone in the cottage.

She lowered herself into the chair where Avis had sat and looked around curiously. It was clean, neat, as she would have expected, but she felt curiously uneasy. Apart from the situation she found herself in, there was something else. She decided it was the tiny feminine touches Avis had tried to put into their home which were totally dominated by the dark masculine furniture. Tiny pink china ornaments were dwarfed by the black oak cupboards and huge dresser.

Along a short arched passageway leading to the front room, she could see the corner of something that shone in the dimness, something that looked so out of place in a home she had to get up and go and see.

She was appalled to find it was exactly what she had imagined. A great brass eagle lectern, upon whose widespread wings stood open a bible of tomelike proportions. There was a chair positioned directly in front for an audience of one. He made Avis listen while he read aloud. Oh yes, she could imagine that! Any man who could do to his wife what he had done last night would want to dictate her every thought. She pushed a foot forward to touch the emblazoned monster. Avis undoubtedly had to clean the thing too!

She felt suffocated by the cottage. She wondered what the monster husband looked like? There was one thing she was going to do before leaving his house. She had seen writing pad and pencil in the kitchen. In large letters she wrote out the only biblical quotation she could remember that seemed suitable. '*Let him who is without sin cast the first stone.*' She put the sheet in the bible like a bookmark and closed the book. She moved one step away then went back, found the paper again and added at the bottom, 'YOU BLOODY OLD HYPOCRITE.'

She closed the back door, aware of the control it took not to bang it with all her might. She shut the big gates with equal control. She did not have long to wait. Soon, family groups in Sunday best began to pass along the main street. One group turned up into the lane. Walking slowly, almost thoughtfully, a couple with two small girls hesitated as they reached the front door of the next cottage.

'I work with Avis, I'm waiting for her husband,' Vi told them as they looked at her curiously.

'It's Mrs Smith, isn't it?' The rotund young woman hurried towards her, her pleasant face serious.

'Yes,' Viv did not hesitate to tell them. These people were neighbours, they must have heard something but had done nothing.

'I told you we should've gone round,' she said to her husband then turned back. 'She never makes any noise that we can hear, but we hear the bangings and thumpings and in the middle of last night it was terrible.'

'Yes.' Vi was not prepared to let them off with anything. 'The doctor has just taken Mrs Smith to hospital.'

'Hospital! Oh dear! I feel terrible now, but one thing,' she said darkly, 'he won't be able to cover this up.'

'Come inside, Polly,' her husband said, ushering the two girls through the front door and holding it open for his wife. 'It's nothing to do with us.'

'And you're waiting to tell him . . .' She turned and raised a dismissive hand to her partner. 'No, I wouldn't miss this for worlds,' she said, then nodding at the closed front door added, 'never wants to make trouble.'

'But you've heard things?' Vi questioned, astonished they could do nothing.

'We've heard the thumping, we've seen the black eyes and the bruises she has, but *always* she says she fell or bumped into something. She's never uttered a word against him!' The woman stopped and nodded to the end of the street. 'Here he comes with his hymn book under his arm. Left to me I'd go to church.'

Vi braced herself, watched the black-suited figure come up the hill towards his home. He was moderately tall with very slightly stooped shoulders, like, she decided, someone being deliberately humble. Even from a distance she hated him.

The two women stood fairly central on the footpath and for a moment Vi thought he was just going to walk straight into them as he had obviously expected *them* to move out of his way. When they did not, he circled rapidly out into the road as if he had just noticed the footpath was fouled.

Vi glimpsed light sandy hair under his black trilby, those light eyelashes that often went with the colouring, fresh-faced, nothing too bestial, until she saw his eyes. These were pale like the lashes, paler even, lacking all colour, all warmth – the cold fish, the dead finger.

His gaze shifted from Vi to his neighbour, 'Do you want to speak to me?'

'I do not!' the woman said emphatically. 'But this young lady has a message for you.'

'I fail to see what message a young stranger can have for me.'

And she felt he had leaned patronisingly over his brass eagle to speak down to her.

'I know your wife,' Vi began.

'Not I presume in the social sense.' He made as if to walk past her.

'I don't go to chapel if that's what you mean,' she said, stepping in front of him again. To open the gate he would have to physically push her out of the way. 'No, I work with your wife.'

'Oh, her work.' He dismissed it, adding condescendingly for the benefit of his neighbour, 'She insists on helping the war effort.' Then, as he fixed Vi with the pale ice of his eyes, he added, 'If there's some message about "work" I'll give it to my wife. She doesn't wish to be disturbed at this time.'

'Why?' She heard her companion draw in her breath and hold it.

'Well . . .' He paused to make a baring of teeth – the shape of a smile. 'She has duties and devotions, such as perhaps you would be unaware.'

'Such as me! Noo, I wouldn't be aware.' Vi felt her anger bubbling over as

111

her words became sarcastic, overemphasised. 'I've no idea how someone who was perfectly well and happy at midnight last night is a few hours later, this good Sunday afternoon, in such a state . . .'

'You've seen my wife?' The question was sharp but cautious.

She had no intention of resolving his doubts so soon. She made no movement of her head, spoke no word denying or confirming, watched him floundering.

'She's very careless you know, has lots of falls. You can ask Mrs Mallan, my neighbour here. I'm quite certain Avis has told her how she has these little accidents.'

Mrs Mallan followed Vi's lead and maintained a stony, motionless silence.

The man assumed indignation, tried to intimidate her with a direct and piercing look. She looked right back.

'Let's get this clear.' A rougher northern accent surfaced as his voice trembled with anger now. 'My wife and my concerns are nothing to do with you, or your sort. You can tell whoever's in charge she'll not be coming to do any more war work,' he paused to regain the pose and the voice, 'of any kind, to mix with people who could have unfortunate, not to say bad, influences on her. Now out of my way. I'll deal with my wife!'

Vi stepped aside and only as he moved briskly into his gateway did she tell him, 'You needn't hurry. Your wife's in hospital.' He missed a stride, faltered as she added, 'But then after what you had *dealt* out to her last night you shouldn't be surprised at that.'

112

Chapter 13

On Monday morning Ethel Kerrow was hardly in the lorry on the way to work before she began to cross-question Vi and Audrey. 'I hear you all went to the dance then!' Vi looked quickly at Doris as she slid along the bench to sit by her. Doris shook her head and had obviously refused to talk to the older woman while they were waiting to be picked up.

'Oh, you needn't tell me anyway. It's all round the place. Told you there'd be nothing but trouble, but would you listen to me?' She paused, obviously eager for every last detail but when nothing was immediately forthcoming, she probed on. 'So how is Avis Smith? In hospital I hear.'

Exactly how Avis was both girls were anxious to know. A message had come from the hospital the previous teatime for them to leave Tommy with Doris's mother-in-law two doors away, so they could walk back to the farm and Sid before dark.

Doris shrugged, raising her eyebrows as if to say Mrs Kerrow was going to hear sooner or later anyway so she might as well tell them all.

'They froze her hand as best they could, with a kind of spray Avis said, and cut her ring off. They let me see her for a minute or two after that.' Doris shook her head, deeply concerned. 'She was still more hassled by the thought of her husband than any pain she was in. Poor maid . . . and she's having an operation today to set her arm. But only her husband'll be allowed to visit tonight.'

'I 'ope someone's around to keep an eye on him,' Vi commented, remembering his cold, cold eyes. She judged him quite capable of hurting Avis as she lay in bed, given the opportunity.

'What even though he put her there!' Audrey exclaimed.

'She put herself there!' Mrs Kerrow stated. 'A married woman going dancing when she *thought* her husband's back was turned.'

At that moment the lorry swung in from the road, pitching down the sandy track, and they were all silent, hanging on to keep their seats and bottling up the storm of rebellious emotions the older woman was brewing.

113

It was no more than she had done all the previous week Vi thought. Stirring them all up into a state of rebellion against the woman herself, the war, against the list of restrictions she gave out as if they were God's law for any married woman – and she in her sacking apron was Moses presenting the tablets of stone. Vi was sure if no fuss had been made neither Doris nor Avis would have gone to the dance – but *every* day the subject had been raised.

They collected their boxes of tin strips and tools in silence and, as they were working either side of the dunelike emplacement, they were out of sight of each other most of the time, but unfortunately not out of hearing.

They were pulling together and re-wiring the netting where it had been damaged as the army pulled it into place. Mrs Kerrow, as if unable to let them work quietly, soon began a steady stream of unsympathetic comments. 'Doris'll be next! Mark my words. When her man fighting on the high seas hears that his wife is out having a good time, there'll be come back.'

'He'll hear as soon as he gets my next letter,' Doris shouted. 'I've told him all about it – and about his mother looking after Tommy for me so I could have a night out with the girls.'

'Can't see it matters who tells him.'

Vi decided the sour-faced old bitch had only to say something about Avis getting what she deserved and she personally would be over the sand heap and down on her so heavy she'd know what it was like to be blitzed.

'It doesn't alter what you did.'

'What I did!' Doris exclaimed. '*What I did!*'

Vi could tell by Doris's voice that she was scrambling to her feet and hurried to follow. The two of them reached the top of the dune together 'I love my Derrick,' Doris shouted down at her tormentor but her voice was suddenly choked with tears, 'and he loves me. 'E wouldn't mind my having a few hours out . . .'

Mrs Kerrow looked up completely undaunted by the two furious young women standing arms akimbo above her. She wagged her pliers up at them. 'Your sort come to a bad end, the pair of you, and no more than you deserve.'

The words acted like a trigger. Almost without thinking, Vi launched herself down towards the woman. What she intended she really had no idea , but in some alarm Mrs Kerrow half rose from her knees – and slipped and rolled over and over, sacking apron over sacking kneepads, to the bottom of the dune.

For a moment there was silence then, as the three of them stood looking, the older woman sat up, waved her pliers threateningly and tried to talk but her mouth was full of sand. She spluttered and coughed. Vi felt a wave of relief that she was not hurt. Then all their frustration with the woman, their pent-up concern, gave way to laughter. The more Ethel Kerrow tried to shout at them, the more they laughed. She stood up and her protective hessian strips hung round her like frayed drapes. They were speechless, hung about each other, their sides ached. Then Doris slipped down to her knees, her shoulders heaving, the laughter giving way to tears – and suddenly all the humour had gone, they were sobered in an instant, it was over.

'What's going on up there?' a man's voice shouted from near the track. 'Is it a private party or can anyone come?'

'It's Noel,' Audrey said, 'he's coming over.'

The three of them brushed themselves down and made themselves as respectable as they could as he climbed up to where they stood. He glanced over to where Mrs Kerrow was now on her feet but still wiping the sand from her mouth and tongue.

''Ere you've not been fighting, have you?' he quipped but when there was no immediate denial he asked more seriously, 'You've not have you?'

'Well not quite,' Vi said.

'Saved by the bell was she? Never mind.' He paused and rubbed his hands together appreciatively. 'We had a good time Saturday night, didn't we.' His smile vanished at the expression that came to their faces. 'Didn't we?' he repeated as if he too now was unsure.

Doris told him all that had happened.

'Blimey,' he muttered, putting his hand into his greatcoat pocket and pulling out a small parcel and a letter. 'I've got a letter for her from Sergeant Wilson. He took it her husband was dead, or out of the frame, because she wouldn't talk about him. What do I do?'

'I'll give it her,' Doris said, holding out her hand, 'but perhaps you should tell the sergeant the situation – but tell him as well that he's ill-treated Avis for years. She's no flighty piece.'

'Right,' he said rather doubtfully, 'if you think that's best. You don't think it'd be better if I just took his letter back and told him?'

Vi too wondered the same and Doris saw her questioning look.

'I remember her saying she had never enjoyed herself so much in all her life,' Doris said with a toss of her head. 'I reckon she's earned a keepsake if nothing more.'

Noel shrugged. 'Old Sergeant Wilson seemed very struck, never known him do anything like this before.' He looked down at the letter which at last changed hands. 'He'd be getting his leg pulled if it wasn't for the fact that he's such an enormous chap *and* he's got five brothers just as huge.'

'Really!' Doris exclaimed ironically. 'Then he's just the sort of man Avis needs.'

Vi had a mental picture of him and his brothers heaving that brass eagle lectern sky-high through Avis's front window. 'Don't let you know who,' she nodded a head towards the dune, 'hear any of this.'

'Or this,' Noel said with a grin, offering Vi the small parcel. 'With Lieutenant Manners' compliments.'

Vi felt her colour flare up as she gazed down at the packet he offered. For a

115

second she felt swept away from them all, as if the wind and the grey sea, the sand beneath her feet were all that existed. She glanced back at Noel who was still smiling.

'Oh, it'll be the spot prize we won. He had it in his pocket,' she said, trying to sound unconcerned as she ended rather lamely, ' I forgot it.'

'So does Sergeant Wilson work with . . .' Doris nodded towards the packet.

'Oh yes, he's the officers' right-hand man up at the Manor where they do this specialist training,' Noel told her, then looking across at Audrey he said, 'There's a dance in the village hall at St Mido next Saturday. Its about three miles in land. We're having another truck, how about it?'

There was never a definite decision made, for their original sergeant instructor came striding along with another batch of soldiers carrying spades. Noel murmured something about being off his route and slipped away as inconspicuously as possible.

Vi had pushed the small brown parcel in her pocket and there it burned until she could bear it no longer. While the others worked on in silence, she slipped away between the natural sand dunes down to the sea and a totally deserted stretch of beach.

She told herself she was a fool because, of course, inside the parcel would be the small paper packet of embroidered handkerchiefs and nothing more. What else was she expecting anyway? Nothing, of course, nothing. Like Audrey said, May was more his sort.

She held the packet in her hands. 'Miss Violet Tulley' it said across the middle, even the address 'Gerrards Head Farm, St Ives Road' and at the top was printed 'PRIVATE'. Even her pessimistic thoughts could not reconcile just a packet of handkerchiefs with the word 'private'. Her hands trembled as she began to slip off the fine white string, pausing once to think to herself that if she never opened it she could not be hurt if it was just 'thanks for the dance, here's the spot prize – and goodbye!'

It's like holding your destiny in your hand, she thought, then exclaimed aloud, 'Oh come on, Tulley, open it and be done . . .' But still she paused long enough to make a kind of apology to Roy, not for what she might find inside but because of what she hoped for.

Inside the brown paper so neatly folded, so carefully cornered, was the cellophane packet of handkerchiefs embroidered with a small corner spray of pink roses and green leaves – and another envelope.

Slowly she put the packet in her pocket and, with fingers that trembled with cold and anticipation, she took out the single sheet of paper.

'Dear Violet, Did I offend you in some way on Saturday evening? If I did I honestly do not know how. *Please* explain. Meet me on Saturday afternoon in Penzance. I have to be at a meeting there in the morning and will stay in town and wait. There is a bus that leaves St Ives and comes past the entrance to

116

your farm at about two fifteen. I will wait for you near the Town Hall where the bus stops. Living in hope, John.'

'You've got it all worked out, Mr Manners,' she breathed. 'Think I'll just jump to your word, you do.' She held the letter gently to her breast and looked out over the grey restless sea. How was she going to get through the week? From Monday to Saturday was a terrible long time, an eternity.

By the time the lorry dropped them off that evening, Vi had already fended off questions from Audrey – had still not yet revealed the Saturday date. While she kept it to herself, it felt curiously unsullied – no one could question the *wisdom* of meeting him, the *reason* for meeting him – or anything else. The secret was hers – for as long as she cared to keep it, for a day or two anyway! But what would she say to him? How would she explain the effect of that extraordinary foxtrot, and May's obvious claim – and Roy?

'Something's happened,' Audrey commented as they neared the house.

'Why? What do you mean?' she asked startled, defensive, thinking Audrey sensed a change in her manner.

'Well look!'

'Oh! There are lights upstairs,' Vi suddenly realised. 'In *both* bedrooms . . . Good job there's no air-raid wardens about. Come on!'

In the kitchen Sid was leaning over the table in an attitude of utter dejection.

'What's up with you?' Vi asked.

'Everything,' he muttered shortly.

'Where's Ma?'

'Upstairs with the beds.'

'The beds!'

The two looked at each other then ran upstairs calling out as they went. 'The beds. The beds have come! Ma where are you?'

They found her in the end bedroom with a pile of bed irons, bed springs and mattresses. 'Is there one each?' Vi wanted to know.

'And an extra,' Ma told them.

'That'll do for Pa when he comes down,' Vi cried. Nothing could depress her now. 'These are not army beds. I reckon they're from the old servant's quarters at the Manor. Poor little tweenies slept on these who never saw their Mas from one year's end to the next. Who's to have which room?'

'We can't sleep upstairs tonight, can we?' Ma said doubtfully.

'I am,' Vi stated, 'that old camp bed has seen the last of me.' She looked round excitedly. 'We can all have a room each.'

'With just *a bed* in each!' Ma pulled a face.

'We could soon buy odd bits and pieces now we're working.' Vi's mood was soaring. John wanted to see her again – and they had a real bed each!

'I don't know about that,' Ma said with such a down note in her voice all activity stopped. 'Sid came home with a thick ear and this . . .' She produced a small book from her pocket.

'Who gave him a thick ear?' Vi wanted to know.

Ma held up the book. 'Mr Spurrier.'

'What right has he to lay hands on my brother?'

'He caught him riding his horse – bareback – just holding on to its mane.'

There was terrible concern in Ma's voice but Vi pulled a face of comic admiration. 'More than I could do. Reckon Pa'd be proud of him.' She laughed but Ma shook her head, worried as always. Audrey wondered how he had managed to mount the great animal.

'Mr Spurrier said he was just on the way to see me, so Sid could save him the trouble. He boxed his ears, which he deserved, and gave him this.' She handed Vi a small printed rent book. 'A pound a week, starting last week – so we're a week behind already.'

'A pound a week!' she gasped in disbelief, 'He has to be joking. This place wasn't fit to put a pig in before we started cleaning it.'

'No,' Audrey reminded them, 'but it was good enough for him to hide his animals in. He was probably making a lot more money from that than having us 'ere. He's not going to do us any favours.'

'Well we're not paying it,' Vi declared, 'not without a fight.'

'He told Sid the rent must be taken to the shop or given to Paul every Friday without fail.' Ma paused, opening the front cover. 'He's written "Private Accommodation" in big red print.'

The little group was solemn as they stared at the thin red book. Vi opened her mouth to say that Pa's capacity for 'fixing things' had landed them in it again, then remembered adding 'The Tulley Family' to the official list of evacuees on the train. What had Cyril Spurrier found out she wondered. Could Pa get into trouble?

'Surely it's not a fair rent.' Vi modified her first indignation. 'The person to ask would be Mrs Trewellan, after all Spurrier's her tenant.'

'Or May,' Audrey suggested. 'She's the lady's secretary.'

'Yes,' she agreed doubtfully then, thinking of the Manor, she asked, 'Who came with the beds?'

'It was only about an hour ago. A sergeant who said he was at the dance, a great big chap he was.'

The girls exchanged glances. 'Sergeant Wilson.'

'Of course, I didn't tell him anything of what happened afterwards,' Ma said and while the other two took in the implications of Avis's sergeant being so near at hand, Ma sat down on the pile of mattresses and bounced. 'These are quality flock you know.'

'He'll know soon enough,' Audrey murmured, then all three turned as Sid came slowly in, sliding round the doorpost, giving a good impression of someone who'd been in trouble.

'Hi, cowboy!' Vi greeted him.

He scowled and rubbed his ear. 'It hurt!'

'No one gave you permission to ride the horse,' Vi told him.

He shrugged. 'I was only going to see if I could find Paul. It's a long way to The Soldier's Field from 'ere – and the horse wasn't doing anything.'

Vi humphed dismissively. 'No excuse.'

'It is if you've been digging the headmaster's garden every break time. 'E keeps me at it, y'know. Watches through the winder while 'e's having his lunch. And *I* was hungry. It makes me 'ungry all the time all this work.'

Vi turned away so he should not see the amusement on her face.

'Paul ses there'll soon be more work because Mrs Trewellan wants to grow more food when the soldiers have gone.'

'What soldiers?' Vi demanded. 'Gone from where?'

'Where the beds came from of course,' Sid said, and joined Ma on the mattresses and began bouncing by her side. Vi was glad of their laughter for she wasn't sure whether she spoke aloud or not. 'Oh no, they can't go.'

'Oy! Leave off!' Ma exclaimed as Sid, whose weight balanced his mother's made her fall sideways on to him as the bouncing became more energetic, more excessive. 'Yes, that's right. The sergeant said it was why the beds were free. They all expect to be leaving soon.'

'Where will they go?' Even as she spoke the words, Vi knew they sounded senseless. There wasn't much doubt where they would all be going.

She was pleased they all decided to sleep upstairs that night. With blankets warmed by the fire and their hotwater bottles put first in Sid's bed and then transferred to the others, they were cosy enough. Ma longed to have her warming pan. 'Work wonders on these cold blankets it would.' She paused then added, 'Wouldn't mind your pa either!'

Vi had not had the heart to say she would have really loved a room to herself. Audrey had assumed they would share and Vi realised her friend really needed not to be alone, while she desperately wished to be.

All through the preparations for bed she felt like a person with an immediate and urgent task to complete, a task that had nothing to do with running in and out of rooms, shading candles and lamps from the windows. There was a decision to be made which needed solitude to make sense of an inner conflict of instinct and loyalty, needed perhaps what there seemed to be so little of, time.

But, when bedtime came, even a shared room was such a joy after the communal cluster around the downstairs fire. They had wondered about lighting fires in the small bedroom fireplaces, just for a kind of celebratory first night, but remembering the mass of stuff Paul had swept from the sitting-room chimney, plus the chore of blacking-out the windows, they decided it was not worth the trouble.

The day's work outside, the harangue with Paul's mother, then the extra

119

energetic work positioning and assembling the beds, and Audrey was soon asleep. Vi too had felt totally exhausted as she fell into bed but the moment her head touched the pillow she was wide awake again.

She lay wondering if she wasn't like Sid, wanting a stolen ride, something she wasn't entitled to, something that belonged to someone else? Or was she more like a rider with a fearsome jump ahead – and courage was needed to make the leap. That thought lingered, niggled.

She rose, amazed how little noise there was after the creaking camp beds. She went to the window and, watching the moon, remembered her walk with Pa in Victoria Park, for it rose like a pale white swan from the mist, swimming up above the grey murk of sea mist to ride high and huge and bright in the December sky. She leaned her forehead on the glass and put a hand to her pounding heart.

What did she feel? Lovelorn – love lost? 'Died and never called me lover.' She murmured her adaptation to the black brooding earth. Then she pressed closer and looked up at the light. Surely she had more courage than that? Even if she got hurt, surely she was honest enough, had courage enough to acknowledge her own feelings.

There came a moment of realisation. To love at all was to care too much, to always risk being hurt – to be ever afraid for the loved one. But surely, surely, not for oneself – or that wasn't true love.

She rolled her forehead on the cold glass. Courage to risk all, to give all. Courage to heed her heart not her head – was that what she was deciding?

Chapter 14

'You haven't met him, Ma.'

'No, but I've met Roy plenty of times!' It was as near to sarcasm as she had ever heard her mother go.

'I know,' Vi acknowledged miserably, 'but . . .'

'And Mr and Mrs Moore living with your Pa! What a time to choose.'

'If May's not his cousin then she's certainly sweet on him too,' Audrey contributed with a shake of her head.

'You shouldn't think of coming between such high-up people. No good'll come of letting Roy down either when he's off fighting for his country and heaven knows what might happen to him.'

'Oh, Ma!' she protested. 'No one knows what will happen to any of us.'

'They're different class, Vi! You've nothing in common.'

'That's what I mean to find out when I meet him on Saturday.'

'So you've got a proper date!' Audrey exclaimed.

'I've known all week there was something different about you,' Ma declared. 'Dreaming about.'

'I think it is different,' Vi said, 'that's why I'm going Saturday afternoon to find out for sure.'

'I don't know what your pa would say.'

She had not answered that old bit of blackmail but all her ma had said weighed heavily on her conscience.

She knew she had lost weight from worrying, several pounds probably. As she sat down on the bus, her skirt felt as if the band hardly touched her waist. Audrey had seen her off with the legendary, 'Don't do anything I wouldn't do!'

'Was there ever anything?' she had quipped back and for a moment they were back on the old jokey wavelength of the East End. But it passed as quickly as it came and Vi had lifted her hand solemnly as the bus drew away. She glanced over at the farmhouse on the cliff-edge and knew Ma would be watching either from outside or from one of the bedrooms, perhaps hoping for a last minute change of mind.

Passing through the village and the turning for Avis's cottage, she was delighted to think that their friend had escaped, at least for the time being. At the instigation of the doctor, who Vi had come to respect more and more, Avis had been discharged on the Wednesday into the care of an old school friend who now lived at Plymouth. On Thursday, Sergeant Wilson had again come to the farm, this time specifically for news of Avis. Ma had directed him to Doris's address. Thursday evening he had arrived at Doris's and she in turn had unhesitatingly given him Avis's address at Plymouth. Speculation among the three of them as to whether he would do anything more had occupied much of the time they spent *out* of the hearing of Ethel.

It had, Vi reflected, helped the week along. She wriggled uncomfortably in the bus seat, aware it was her own bones that hurt against the hard leather seat. *I'm all angles*, she decided as the bus turned from the lane into the main road downhill into Penzance. Memories of May's assets revealed so beautifully as she had tap-stepped and twisted her shoulders did not help.

Her heart quickened as she realised the other passengers were all gathering up their bags and packages preparing to get off. They must be nearly at the terminus. Would he be there? Not the time to be thinking of May and all her advantages!

Even before she rose to join the steady stream of people leaving the bus, she glimpsed him standing close by the stone wall of the Market Hall – tall, dark, dignified, more daunting in uniform. By the time she reached the bottom of the bus steps, she felt she needed to concentrate to walk in an upright dignified manner, to hold her head at the right angle, to breathe even.

'Hello!' he said.

'Hello.'

'You came. Thanks. I've been standing here wondering what I would do if you didn't come.'

'I would have let you know – somehow – if I hadn't intended to come.'

He smiled down at her. 'Yes, I guess you would too. Thanks.'

She glanced at him, wondering if he was pulling her leg by thanking her?

'Would you like to walk down to the sea and along the quay. I thought we could talk better there.' Two naval ratings walked past and he returned their salutes. 'Less interruptions.'

They made their way from the main street down a cobbled sideway at the bottom of which Vi could see the sea and the great stone harbour wall out to her right. They walked a calculated yard apart, and it was as if both kept the neutrality of that distance, neither straying nearer, nor drifting further away.

Once they had crossed the main road and were near the deserted harbour walls, John asked, 'What was it then? What did I do? We started off so well on Saturday night – then you changed, turned into the ice maiden.'

'I ...' She remembered her resolve to be honest, fearless – but for a

122

moment her voice failed, developed a stammer. She'd never stammered before in all her life. 'I . . . I . . . I . . .' She closed her mouth firmly then reminded herself whose daughter she was, what she was about. 'It was watching you dance with May. It made me feel no one could dance with a girl like that – and not love her.' The last three words broke free and came out with a terrible rush.

He stopped walking as if astounded by her answer, then a brief startled laugh escaped his lips. 'I do love May,' he agreed, 'of course I do. Love her like a sister.'

'But she's not.'

'She's as near to as I'll ever get. We practically grew up in each other's perambulators! It would be incestuous for me to think of May and any other kind of love.'

'And May?' They both hesitated as they came to a flight of steps up to the top of the broad quay wall. Vi turned towards him to ask, 'Do you know how May feels?' The instinctive act brought her very close to him, brought too a terrible yearning sadness in the wake of her questioning – and his silence. Heart's desire admitted in the silence of the night before, now so close and unattained.

He seemed to study her face for his answer, or was it, she wondered, a recollection of May's he was searching. 'I had always assumed she felt the same.' He frowned. 'She does, surely?'

'I didn't think so – the dance showed what I'd always thought from the moment I saw you both together for the first time.'

'And that is?'

Vi remembered that first time, the way May had moved across the kitchen to link arms with John, to her mind proclaiming them a couple. 'That is,' her voice was low, weighted with what she saw as the unfortunate truth, 'you belong to each other, are as good as engaged.'

'M' dear girl.' John caught her hand. 'Nothing could be further from the truth. May and I – why – we're too much alike, too much akin.'

She regarded him solemnly, so aware of her hand in the warmth of his, but she knew her face must still reveal the chill of her doubts. She recalled how much she had herself liked May when they first met. A straightforward person, she had thought, with no hidden undercurrents. No they were definitely not hidden – May's feelings were, to Vi's mind, all too obvious.

'She can't be thinking on those lines,' he protested, 'not old May?'

'It's what I feel.'

'But it's not anything like I feel,' he said with such sudden intensity that she felt her heart surge. She swallowed quickly but, before she could speak again, he held her hand and ran swiftly up the steps pulling her after him. 'Come on.' He drew her further along, walking her into the wind along to the very end of the stone bastion, to where, on one side, lay the calm waters of the

123

inner harbour and, beyond, the choppy white-crested surging tides led out to the widest part of the English Channel and then to the Atlantic Ocean. He turned to face her.

'Violet, my life changed the moment you walked into the Lodge, then I remember watching your face as we tossed those stupid things into that basket!'

'That's one of the . . .' She almost tutted with momentary exasperation. 'They weren't stupid things to me. They were things that cost money, things we couldn't 'ave bought.'

He silenced her as, impulsively, he took her fingers to his lips and kissed them extravagantly with an energy that demanded she listen.

'They could as easily have been the Crown Jewels or brass fathings, I wouldn't have noticed,' he told her. 'Don't you understand, it was as if I'd been searching all my life for someone – and suddenly there you were! Like, like the final piece in a jigsaw that made my life complete.' He looked down at her, then cupped her face in both his hands. 'You have the most wonderful expression on your face and what I want to say to you is – why do you think I've brought you to the end of this pier? There's no escape, girl. You have to jump in at the deep end, admit you at least *like* me, that there's some attraction for you.'

She had more than already admitted that to herself. She wanted to believe him, wanted it all to be true.

'Believe me,' he assured her, 'you've assumed and seen things that are not there!'

'You *think* are not there,' she amended.

'They are not as far as I am concerned, isn't that all that matters at this point. Vi, I shouldn't tell you this but we may not be here much longer. I don't want to be sent away and regret for the rest of my life that I never told you how I feel about you. Can't we just take it along, see how things go, how we get on – just spend whatever time we can together. That's not asking too much is it?'

She looked up at him and smiled. 'No, I don't think it is.'

'You don't!' He swept off his cap. 'I wished I dare hurl this far out to sea to celebrate.' He grasped both her hands. 'So there's . . .'

'A dance at St Mido on Saturday,' Vi supplied.

'And my birthday party, so that's two definite dates for your diary.'

'I've never had a diary in my life,' she said as he questioned her wry expression.

'We must put that right then,' he said, 'because there'll be a lot of things I'll want you to remember.'

'I've a good memory.'

'I hope so,' he said and, pulling her towards him, he kissed her gently on the mouth with a tender quake of restraint.

124

The touch was light but she felt as if some faint charge of electricity arced between them. And out of nowhere came the thought that if Roy was there he too would have to salute as the naval ratings had done.

'Aren't you worried about being seen – in uniform I mean.'

He nodded behind her towards the land and she gasped, hardly believing that landwards all was obscured and before them the sea was clear. At that moment the warning guns and sirens which had so disturbed their first night in Cornwall began to boom out. 'This is a great place for bleeding fog!'

He laughed out loud. 'Violet doesn't suit you really, you're neither sweet nor retiring. And . . .'

Before she became upset by her slip into the East End vernacular or his judgment on her name he added, 'And I think I love you in a quite unsisterly fashion.' Though it almost seemed in contradiction to his remark, he kissed her on the cheek. 'I think we'd better walk back while we can still see.'

The walk back was eerie.

'What are you thinking,' he asked as she walked by his side, hand pulled through his arm and held tightly by his.

'I'm remembering a walk in my local park in Bethnal Green with my pa. It was misty that day too,' she remembered. 'It was the day I rebelled about being evacuated.'

'Glad your pa won!'

Then Vi's heart somersaulted as, with his officer's cane, he tipped his cap on to the back of his head. She saw in the action more than an echo of the way Pa had flicked his soft cap to the back of his head and spun an imaginary cane as they had strutted together in Viccy Park.

'That must have been a special walk,' he said when she was still silent as they came to the steps. He went first and held out his hand to help her.

'A very special walk,' she confirmed, extending her hand to his with a smile, 'we both made big decisions.'

'I want to ask,' he said as they reached the bottom of the steps already slippery with a sheen of mist and he gently pulled her to face him.

'I don't mind.' She smiled up at him and put one hand on each of his lapels. 'I remember Pa talking about duty, the way his duty to King and Country was keeping the buses running and his duty to his family was to send them out of the danger of bombing.'

'I hope I'll meet him one day. He sounds a splendid fella!'

'He is.'

'And your decision?'

'That if ever there was going to be a "fella" in my life he was going to have to be pretty special to compare with my pa!' She laughed gently at the look of dismay on his face before she added, 'And I think he is.'

Chapter 15

'And then he kissed her, folks,' Vi told the seagulls swooping round the well the next morning, '*and* I've written it in my diary.'

She put down the bucket and the kettle and folded her arms around herself, aware there was one more gorgeous thing she had not written down and did not intend to tell even the birds. She lifted her head to the blue December sky, the white gulls drifting and calling. 'But you can come with me if you like,' she told them, stretching her arms upwards in invitation, letting her mind dwell on how happy she was, how blue the sky was, how the brilliant clear winter sun streaked burnished patterns on the restless sea, how very beautiful that world was.

She relived those moments from the time he had taken her into his arms at the bottom of the quay steps. The second kiss had grown from the same tremulous tenderness of the first to a mutual confident desire. 'Foxtrot!' she shouted up at the gulls who, startled, screamed back at her. 'Phewy!'

Dances did not have a kiss that was so tenderly fiery, so precious their lips had clung long, long, to the sweet sensation. Then only slowly, so slowly, had he drawn away, as if he too felt a sudden parting would be too painful, the separation unsupportable.

'I think we'd better go shopping for that diary,' he had said.

Almost as precious was the recollection of buying the diary together. The way he consulted her, called her 'old thing' as if they had belonged to each other for a far greater span of life than minutes. Vi was very aware that the demeanour of the shop assistant changed as Lieutenant John Manners exuded charm and good manners. Vi, in the aura of his presence, was treated with equal deference – nothing was too much trouble. A diary for 1941 was obtained – and the assistant searched the drawers under the counter and came up with one for the current year. 'Please accept this, then if you need to jot things down for the coming festive season . . .' She had handed it to Vi but simpered at John.

What do I care! Vi thought.

'You're 'appy this morning.'

She span round, heart thumping. Paul stood leaning on the wall of the house, just watching.

'How long 'ave you been there?'

He shrugged, heaving himself upright. 'Not long.'

'So what are you doing here this morning?' she asked sharply.

'Come for the rent,' he replied, grinning.

'Sid took it to the shop on his way to school,' she told him.

'I know,' he said, 'only kidding. You going to the dance at St Milo Saturday?'

'I may be.' She turned away, indignant he should joke about the rent. She busied herself, prepared to draw the morning's water. She was very aware of him as he approached behind her and, as she hooked the bucket on to the windlass he had fitted, she also knew that they were in his debt, much in his debt. She realised she was laying herself open to an unwanted invitation and quickly amended her statement. 'We . . . yes, I am. I think we both will. You going?'

'I heard you went to the camp dance.'

'I suppose your mother told you,' she said and awaited his response.

He scowled and his gaze wavered and fell. He scuffled his boots uneasily in the dust. 'No,' he said truculently, 'why should she?'

'You do know we work with her?'

His startled and amazed look told her he had no idea, made her state without thinking, 'So you don't live at home?'

'I lives where I want to,' he stated, 'and it's no business of nobody.'

'So if you didn't know, where have you been all this time?' She regretted the forthrightness as she cobbled together an explanation. 'I mean we thought it was because of something your mother had told you that was making you stay away.' She had a vivid recollection of Ethel tumbling head over sacking.

'You missed me then?' His look under his dark brows was watchful, probed for any significance in her answer.

'Well, Ma has!' She made her tone as light as possible. 'Where 'ave you been?' She turned to look him in the eye and again his gaze dropped.

'I 'ad some urgent work to do for the boss – away.'

A sudden intuition told her that what he had been doing was preparing some other out of the way place for the slaughtering of animals to fill his boss's shop with meat. To know she had caused Cyril Spurrier some considerable trouble helped balance her anger about the rent, and she could feel some pity for this young man with his boots and overcoat cobbled together with string, trapped between an unpleasant boss and Ethel! 'So your mother's not told you she knows us?' It seemed the safest question.

'I don't often see my parents.'

'Your father's alive?' Her reaction was automatic, she was so astonished.

127

She had never heard anyone talk of a Mr Kerrow, least of all his wife.

'He was last time I saw him.'

It was such a strange and unfeeling answer she did not reply, merely stood back and tacitly accepted his offer to draw the water, then followed him as he carried it back to the house.

'Why has this house only one door at the back?' Somehow the questions she could not pursue demanded she make a different challenge. 'Was it because of the weather, the winds from the sea?'

'No, it was so that my grandfather could keep a check on his sons' comings and goings. He filled the front door in.' He gestured to where, between the two main front windows, the blocks of stone looked slightly more haphazard than the rest of the building. 'There was a porch too,' he added scuffing his boot to reveal a paved rectangle under the gritty dust.

A weird man from a weirder family, Vi thought, and hoped he would never turn up at any function she and John attended. He hardly seemed the sort to socialise, living rough when he had a – well, perhaps home might be too grand a word – but he certainly had a mother and a father who presumably lived together somewhere in the area. It would be interesting to know where that was *and* where Spurrier's new hideout was. That could really be a useful ace to have up the Tulley sleeve.

She found herself very curious about this untalked of father and in her mind linked it with the story he had told of The Soldier's Field. She wondered if there was any relation between the tale and the truth? But she kept these questions strictly to herself, no way did she want Paul hanging around for long and she certainly wanted him well out of the way before the afternoon.

But once inside he lingered, cleaning and priming their oil lamps and, to her consternation, Ma told him if he wasn't working he was welcome to stay for Sunday lunch. Seeing her daughter's face as Paul went eagerly off to renew their wood pile, she took the opportunity to quietly remind her that the meat from two rabbits he had already shot for them had made several meals.

'Well, I don't want him messing around following me!' she hissed back.

Ma sighed heavily. 'So where are you going?'

'Just a walk,' she whispered urgently under the noise of Paul dropping the wood beside the fireplace.

After their meal she made Ma sit down while she cleared away. Audrey and Sid had become intrigued by a piece of purple crystal Paul produced from his pocket and were eager to go and explore an area of old tin workings nearby for more of the amethyst-like quartz. She refused their pressing invitation to go with them, grateful for once that Sid made such a fuss about setting off without wasting a minute. Paul, to give him credit, was obviously anxious neither of them should go alone. 'There's old shafts to the tin mines, doesn't do to go wondering about.'

Never were dishes stacked so quickly. The draining board full, she reached for the tea towel. Ma's hand reached it at the same moment. 'So you found out what you wanted to know?' she asked.

Vi nodded.

'And?'

She frowned down at the mutually held tea towel. 'It's not something I can help – and he may have to go away quite soon.'

'Vi!' There was such anxiety, such caring, such questioning in the way her mother spoke her name.

'I know, Ma. I know all the pitfalls. I won't let you down and I'll be honest with Roy. You never know he might 'ave met someone else!' For a moment she tried to make light of the situation by suggesting such a convenient hurt-free solution, but it fell short of the whole truth and she added quietly, 'I love this man, Ma, I know I do.'

'He's not just stringing you along, here today, gone tomorrow? Making a fool of you?'

'No, I'm sure, really sure.'

'I can't stop you, can't keep you under lock and key. Go on off you go.'

'I . . .' she began.

'While there's no one to follow you.'

'Ma! It'll be all right!'

Ma shook her head but flapped the tea towel, shooing her on her way before turning away to start drying the dishes.

Vi had previously made out a little-used path which split from the cliff-top path and seemed to run along the middle of the two tier-like structure of the cliffs to the right of the farmhouse. She used this now, out of sight of everything except the sea below her and an overhang of green-edged cliff above. She hurried, feet nimbler with practise, but it felt as if her heart was way out in front of her, leading the way.

She caught sight of John almost in the same way as Sid had first done – in outline – but approaching from below she saw him silhouetted against the sky. He was shading his eyes looking along the top path.

'The soldier, the soldier's come,' Sid had cried and her heart felt as if it bounded forward and upward with the same sentiment. He was indeed come.

Almost as if he sensed rather than saw her, he looked down. She laughed as she saw his mouth open in surprise and pleasure. Then the next moment he was bounding recklessly down towards her.

'I didn't think you'd see me,' she gasped as he reached her and she steadied him on the narrow way. 'I thought I'd surprise you.'

'You always surprise me. But I still sense when you're near.' He kissed her gently on the lips, then his tone deepened to a theatrical note. 'Every fibre of my being knows, shouts with the message.'

She laughed. 'What message?' she asked, safe in his arms, able to play coy.

'The message that says "this is the woman" and you know, old thing, the

129

Gods grumble at the trouble its taken them to bring us together.' He sounded as if he was fooling but she had already come to realise that whenever he called her 'old thing' it was like a promise, an oath of dedication to her. It was both a very strange but very special privilege.

'Everything would have been against us ever meeting if it wasn't for the war . . .'

'Yes, old Mars has done a good job.' He looked skywards. 'Thanks, old boy!'

'You are a fool,' she said, leaning closer to him. 'But if you could just arrange for your god to finish the war now we have met, that would be just the ticket.'

'Not *my* god. We share everything now, gods, kisses . . .' He stooped carefully because of their precarious position to peck her lips quickly again. 'Everything.'

'But you don't think the war will be over for a long time?'

'Need a miracle. Things are getting worse on all fronts.' He took her hand and held it gently between both of his. It was meant to comfort her but to Vi it was reminiscent of one passing on bad news. 'You look so defiant, so full of pluck,' he added.

It did not help the stir of unease she felt, everything seemed so precarious, a sudden wind squall making them hold each other more firmly. Then the war brought separation – Ma and Pa – and more permanent partings, like Audrey and . . .

'Now I've made you look stricken,' he said then added, 'don't let's waste this time we do have.'

'Time,' she repeated, leaving the word hanging without conclusion, remembering Sergeant Wilson's remark about there being plenty of beds to spare at the Manor soon. 'I wish,' she went on passionately, 'that we could pin time down, stop it at certain good points.'

'How I wish,' he agreed. 'And how long shall we make this afternoon?'

She glanced up above his head. 'Until the gulls stop flying,' she whispered.

'Agreed,' he said softly, then with a low laugh tangled in a sigh added, 'one of the most awful teachers at prep school only ever said one thing to me that stuck, that it was "impossible to waste time without damaging eternity." Don't let's waste it on the impossible, old thing, let's just take what there is – and store the memories.'

Memories, she thought, were about the past and about parting. She searched his face and realised he was dealing in the true world and she with dreams. He sensed he might need every memory, every good time to balance bad. She remembered a quotation gleaned from her Friday afternoons at school, when each child had to learn and recite a piece of poetry before being allowed to go home.

'We look before and after
And pine for what is not
Our sincerest laughter
With some pain is fraught;
Our sweetest songs are those that tell
of saddest thought.'

'Shelley,' she added.

'That's cheery,' he said, grasping her hand with a new resolution. 'Now we'll both go and throw ourselves into the ocean. Or – alternatively – we'll paddle.'

'In December!' she protested as, holding her hand, he began rapidly picking their way down between rocks and the prickly bushes towards the beach, giving no time now for any more sad introspection.

'I've swum here on my birthday and the day after, Christmas Day.'

'Are the beaches safe?' she gasped, though no one would have heard. She had hardly time to breathe as they laughed, half falling, half slipping down towards the beach as the waves came rapidly closer.

'All right?' he asked as they landed at the bottom of the cliff, but hardly pausing, he began to pull off his shoes and socks. 'The last one in the sea's a cissy!'

She shook her head at his antics, at the fact that he really did mean to go into the water. He ran halfway down to the sea, stopped to roll up his trousers above his knees, then went on shouting and hallooing. 'Like someone let out,' as her ma would have said. Let out from where Vi had never wondered until now, but watching John's antics as the cold water reached his feet, it was obviously from a madhouse.

She was grateful that she could undo her stockings and push them into her pocket without him seeing for there was no thought but that she would follow him. Then, once the feel of the cold wet sand hit her bare feet, she too raced like a mad thing to join him, screaming as she ran into the water at the same moment as a wave raced up the beach – and immediately the bottom of her best skirt was wet.

She held it up, demanding, 'Who's idea was this?'

He cocked his head sideways, studying her from top to toe. 'I claim all credit.' He laughed as she stepped back as another wave swirled up her calves.

'Come on,' he said holding out his hand. 'Let's walk along the edge of the sea.' He gestured towards the far curve of boulders and where above on the cliff she could make out the black tarred roof of the forbidding Gerrard's Head public house.

She reached out her hand, smiling, remembering the first time he had held out his hand in the Lodge kitchen. She had nearly taken it then.

131

'You really must learn not to smile at me like that,' he told her. 'You can't imagine what it does to me.'

'I'll choose my moments more carefully,' she told him glibly but she knew that choosing had nothing to do with it. This was not a matter of a reasoned choice, a thing for the best, an option. Whether she liked it or not, her heart or her nature or something bigger than herself had already chosen for her.

'Promise.'

His look was so intense, so meaningful she could not answer. She nodded a little breathlessly and, pulling on his hand, began to walk in the shallows, kicking at the sheen of water bright on the flattened sand before the next wave brought replenishment.

They walked on holding hands at the bright sea's edge, the afternoon full of the water's blather – far out boisterous, pushy, at their feet gentle submissive, content – as they were.

'We'll have time to walk to the rocks and back before it begins to get dark,' he said.

'I wondered if the beaches were safe. I mean is it all right for us to walk on them? I know Sid would love it.'

'There's barbed wire on some, but nothing to worry about. Nothing you can't see, nothing hidden, not here anyway.'

'You heard about the work Audrey and I are doing? *We* seem to be hiding things.'

'Sounds jolly hard work,' he said noncommittally and she felt him gently smooth over the rough scratches on her hands. Stooping, he picked up a small black stone streaked with bright gold. He dropped it into her palm and she stopped to study it.

'It's money,' she said and caught herself before she added that it helped pay the rent.

'What did you do in London? Did you work there?'

She bent to wash sand from the pebble. 'Yes,' she said, looking sharply up at him. 'Us East Enders do tend to have to work.'

'Right,' he said unabashed, 'so what did you do?'

'Do you think this is what they call fool's gold?' She ran a finger along the bright vein. 'I worked in an accountant's office. I was thinking of doing my exams, becoming qualified. I'd just been given the opportunity to do that.'

'So what the war gives with one hand, it takes away with the other.'

She dropped the pebble from one palm to the other. 'I don't think the two things quite compare.'

He looked quizzical, smiling.

'I mean its not every day one has the chance to . . .' she pushed the stone into her skirt pocket and began to run, calling back over her shoulder, '. . . become an accountant.'

He caught her halfway to the end of the cove, laughing, breathless, both quickly sobered by the other's closeness. Vi, with a sudden feeling that she was both aware of and at one with the whole universe, turned to him and raised her arms above her head, wanting to embrace the world.

'Oh, Violet,' he whispered, 'you're like a precocious tantalising fairy.' He paused to kiss below her ear. 'Flying off across the beach, teasing.' He paused to bite gently at her earlobe. 'Tormenting . . .'

She laughed shakily. There was nothing fairy-like about the effect he was having on her, for while the wind and the sea were cold, where their bodies touched seemed to her like fire. She understood why he had put her away from him under the town harbour wall and taken her shopping! She could so easily have lost all inhibitions – his closeness, the smell of him like fresh heather wind blown from the sweetest of moors mingled with the aroma of newly pressed linen. Almost as if to enhance the impression, he reached into his pocket and took out a blazing white handkerchief.

'You've sand on your cheek,' he said, gently brushing it away. She remembered the khaki handkerchief Avis had clutched on the way home from the dance. That hadn't brought much joy, but she would stake her life that Avis still had it. She wondered if John had khaki handkerchiefs when he was in uniform?

He kissed her sweetly on the lips, leaving her longing shamelessly for a more passionate embrace then, slipping his arm around her waist, they walked slowly on, very close, their mood much more sober now. She watched their mutual shadow moving before them. Everything had significance for her. The faint warmth of the winter sun, the chill of the sea around their feet, a sheet of light like enchantment over the flat wet sheet of sand they trod. The feeling of inviolability was not lost until they neared the end of the beach.

'The tide's turned,' John said and they stood judging the waves beginning to hurtle up the crags, spilling white foam back into the sea to form the far end of the cove. 'And this beach runs very level to the cliffs. We mustn't be too long turning back. I know from experience.'

She slipped an arm around his waist, as if to make an extra bond no element could break, and stood a moment longer inhaling deeply, catching the smell of the salt spray in the wind.

'Violet . . .' he began.

When he did not continue, she said, 'I'll feel more like myself if you call me Vi.'

'Vi.' He paused again and she looked up to find him staring way out to the horizon, such a look of yearning about his expression that, without thinking, she tugged at his jacket to distract him. What she saw in his eyes was the fear of uncertainty.

She caught his hand. 'John,' she said, quietly her voice little louder than the sound of the waves soughing up around their feet, 'take today, this afternoon.'

'You promised until the gulls stopped flying,' he whispered huskily.

'Until there are no more gulls either of us can ever see.'

The words 'until death do us part' hung between them unsaid.

'Would you have your photograph taken for me? There are some quite decent studios in Penzance.'

There were so many implications in this simple request and she acknowledged that the very least of which was the fact that she could not afford a studio portrait.

'And,' he added 'you will write to me?'

She felt an anger then, the kind of rage she had seen in Audrey, futile anger against the unchangeable, the inevitable.

'Do you know something, I mean about being posted?'

'Everywhere you go there are rumours. It's really no use trying to second guess the army, but I just need to know things between *us* are arranged for certain.'

'Of course.' She remembered how practical her pa had been, sending them away, his loved ones, 'making certain' they were safe. But before she could be any more introspective, John drew her attention away from the sea and up towards the cliff top near Gerrard's Head pub. 'Someone's waving. It's your friend . . .'

'And Sid.'

'Isn't that Kerrow with them?'

'They've been looking for amethyst crystals,' she said, waving enthusiastically back at Sid who was obviously shouting something. She made wide erasing movements of her hands and arms to show him they could not hear.

Audrey waved understanding and spoke to Sid, who lifted a more dismissive hand. Paul stood quite still behind the other two, staring down in such a concentrated way it seemed he was reading some important personal message in what he saw. Then, quite deliberately, he moved behind Audrey and looped an arm around her waist. They saw Audrey turn in surprise and the arm was removed.

By her side John tutted. 'He's a strange cove. I once saw him lose his temper with that horse he works. Thought he was going to back the beast and his cart over the cliff top, but before I got to him he was kicking four kinds of hell out of the cart wheel.'

They looked up at the figures on the cliff top a moment longer. Audrey and Sid gave a final wave, while Paul was on Audrey's heels never more than a pace behind. 'He's a weird man.' Now it was Vi's turn to tut her disapproval. 'But having met his mother we're not surprised!'

'Come on,' John said, taking and swinging her hand. 'Time and tide . . . and so on. But I'm free Saturday and if I write to you before that, Mrs Thingy the postwoman will have to deliver – and if you happened to have a letter ready . . .'

Chapter 16

She began compiling the first letter as they parted at the top of the farm drive. Then there had been so many things to say chasing around in her head, so many amusing versions full of humour and sincerity, but when the opportunity came to put the words on to paper it felt as if she was charged with carving words in stone. It was all so much more significant when set down. How did one make sure the messages carried the intended tone and meaning? A joke might be taken the wrong way, or – worse – a word of affection might be seen as a hook to exact some return the other party was not yet ready to give. She would hate to be thought guilty of that!

What a problem, she thought then grinned as she thought of Mr Rubenstein the tailor and, mimicking the old jew whispered, 'Such problems, such happy troubles you 'ave!'

It would be easier if she had a letter to answer, but this was to be an exchange. She wasted two pages from the lined notepad before she shook her head and decided this would not do. She had to be completely honest, had to feel right inside. That thought gave her pause. She laid down her pen and thought about feeling right inside. Then after staring out of the window for some time she began.

'Dear John,
As I write to you I can see the glow of the moon on the sea. I have brought a little table and a candle into one of the bedrooms overlooking the cove so I can write in peace.
I am not finding this an easy letter because I still find it difficult to believe we are . . .

She hesitated a long time before she penned the next words.

. . . so attracted to each other, when everything is against such a wonderful thing happening. Like you say – if it wasn't for the war we certainly would

135

never have met. When we are apart I wonder what we have in common? I suppose the only thing I can say is that "it feels right" inside me, "it feels right" when I think of you, when we are together nothing and no one else really matters.'

She paused there to feel really guilty about May and Roy. She put her pen down to think seriously about Roy. Of all the boys at school, she had liked him the best – tall, sandy-haired, freckled, smiling. She would always have a soft spot for Roy. But of all the men in the world? It could only ever be John. Vi picked up her pen and unconsciously poked blue-black holes in the pad's sheet of blotting paper. If May really loved John in the same way? She thought of all the hurt this falling in love could cause.

It took some long time to continue and then it was only after doing a kind of mental girding up in the manner of her ma with her wrap around apron when there was much to do and the going hard.

'Everytime I see a gull swooping over the sea I think of you and my heart flies like the bird. I see my ma looking curiously at me from time to time. I think I must be starry-eyed!'

Unsure when this letter would be collected by the unsuspecting postlady, she left it unsealed and added a little more on Monday evening to say that it looked as if the others would *not* be going to the dance at St Milo after all as nobody seemed keen. She stamped the letter and left it with Ma for Mrs Stevens 'in case she comes with any post.'

Ma had glanced at the address, raised her eyebrows, but made absolutely no comment, which Vi was thankful for. She could torture herself quite enough.

That same morning Doris was obviously agog with something to tell them but it was equally obvious both to them and to Mrs Kerrow that she was waiting until the older woman was out of the way.

They had to wait until she disappeared in the direction of the portable lavatory set up behind the dunes. All three watched impatiently until she was out of sight then downed tools. 'Tell us before we all die of curiosity,' Vi demanded.

'Well,' Doris began with an expansive gesture reminiscent of a conjurer about to let a very large rabbit out of a bag, 'I've had a message from Avis. She wants to see us all at the dance at St Milo Saturday!'

Disbelief was mixed with the feeling that they had not heard correctly.

'What!'

'You have to be joking!'

Doris shook her head vigorously. 'No, honest, this friend she is staying with came special on the train all the way from Plymouth to deliver the message.'

'So what's going on?' Audrey asked in awed tones of no one in particular. 'She must still have her arm in a sling, and after what happened . . .'

'She won't be thinking of letting her husband know that's for sure,' Doris said.

'Did this friend tell you anything else?'

'No that's all. She'd come special to deliver the message because she said,' Doris paused to give full effect to the words, ' "we don't want anything written down"!'

'Crimey! Do you think she's going to divorce him?' Vi speculated. 'She could plead mental and physical cruelty.'

'You don't know anybody who's divorced. That's only for people with plenty of money.' Audrey dismissed the idea out of hand.

Vi shrugged her admission that she was unable to think of anyone off hand. They fell to speculating whether Avis wanted them to help her make peace with her husband. Doris was adamant. 'She wouldn't go to another dance for that!' Perhaps she wanted them to go to the cottage and get her clothes? Or tell her husband she was never coming back.

'I'll volunteer for that!' Vi said.

'I suppose it settles one thing!' Doris said. 'We'll all be going to the St Milo dance!'

The discussion ended as they saw Ethel Kerrow had emerged from the nearby dunes. Vi wondered if she had been standing just out of sight listening? It would be like her.

Thursday's post brought a letter in answer to her's. John was *pleased* no one wanted to go to the dance. 'I'd much rather have you all to myself. I'll meet you off that same bus in Penzance on Saturday. I have tickets for a musical and plans!'

Now she was in a quandary – not about what to do, but how to tell Audrey and Doris that she would not after all be going to St Milo. She wondered whether to tell them both at work Friday morning or to let Audrey know right away at home. Her first loyalty – well, after Pa and John – was to her friend. In the end it was Sid who sparked the revelation.

He sat at the kitchen table, grading the small pieces of blue and mauve crystal he and Paul had found – not on the Sunday expedition but when Sid had joined him after school, scattering seaweed on The Soldier's Field. 'They're like teeth, look!' He held up the sharp fragments.

'Just like fangs,' Vi answered.

'It was funny when we saw you,' he went on in that reflective tone of voice she knew usually meant some embarrassing revelation. 'We were in The Soldier's Field and you were with the soldier on the beach.'

'Yes,' she replied cautiously, 'I suppose so, if you think about it.'

'I think Paul wanted to be like the soldier, cos we all saw you kissing – dead sloppy it was!' He looked at her and grinned. 'You've gone all red!'

'You'd make a good spy you!' she told him.

'And 'e put his arm around Audrey!' Sid added his final bit of information for Ma's benefit.

'Not for long!' Audrey put in.

'Is he your boyfriend now?'

'Thanks – but no thanks!' Audrey stated. 'I don't intend to take up with anyone who's stuck in this dead and alive 'ole!'

It hardly seemed the appropriate moment, but if she didn't tell all soon it was going to be too late. 'I had a letter from John Manners this morning . . .'

'We all know that,' Audrey said drily. 'You've spent hours this week upstairs either writing or reading letters!'

'The thing is he wants me to meet him in Penzance again Saturday – and he's bought tickets for a show . . .'

For a moment there was silence, then Audrey exclaimed, 'You mean you're *not* going to the dance?' Audrey looked her old self, indignant, vocal if things did not go her way. She asked, 'What about Avis? She's expecting *all* of us.'

'You and Doris can tell me what she wants us to do. I'll help whatever. It's too late now to let John know we've changed our minds again about the dance. I told him at the beginning of the week that we wouldn't be going.'

'You could stand him up,' Audrey said bluntly.

'I don't want to stand him up,' she said slowly and deliberately.

Audrey tutted her annoyance and drummed her fists lightly on the table. 'He's exactly the sort of chap you always reckoned you didn't like! He's an officer! You never went out with officers – it's *me* who ought to be going out with him!'

There was a moment's silence. If there had been any light-hearted intention in the outburst it was lost in the petulance of the voice.

'Do you want Vi's soldier?' Sid asked, attempting at the same time to keep two pieces of stone in his mouth like fangs.

'No thanks!' Audrey snapped. 'For second-or third-hand things. I'm going to bed.'

When she had gone, Ma jerked her head at Sid. 'Time you went up.'

Vi listened as her mother went upstairs and settled her brother. She knew from the silence that she would be listening to his prayers. All in all, not a very congenial evening. She wondered if Ma would be happy to stay in Cornwall if Pa was with them. Pa as farmer. She could see that. He would be good – good with animals that's for sure. She felt Ma had stopped fussing quite so much about her son, daughter and Audrey and now reserved most of her worrying for Pa in London, in the Blitz. She sighed deeply. Would she soon be one of the women on the home front with their men in the front line of the action?

She listened to Ma coming down the stairs and thought how heavy her footsteps sounded for so light a woman, but as her mother came back into the kitchen she knew it was weariness not weight that laboured her pace.

'Ma? You think I'm wrong, that I'm letting the others down?'

'Whatever you do now it'll be letting someone down.' She sank carefully down into her chair again.

'You all right, Ma?'

'Tired.'

'You've scrubbed our bedroom floor again,' Vi said and, when her mother's face brightened because she had noticed, she added, 'everything is beginning to look really clean.'

'I wondered,' she said, 'I just wondered if your pa might manage to come down for Christmas. No . . .' She paused and shook her head. 'Just a wild dream.'

'It's his turn to be off this year, I remember that. You never know!' Vi paused. 'Ma, *you* don't mind me meeting this chap – you can trust me.'

Ma shook her head at her girl. 'Not only that, I rely on you.'

Vi went quickly to kneel at Ma's feet and put her hands on her knees. 'I won't ever let you down,' she said earnestly.

'Your pa told me that before we set off,' she said with a smile.

'You think about him a lot.'

Ma sighed. 'My heart,' she paused and pressed her hand over her chest as if to still a great pounding, 'when a letter comes but then I think by the time I read it something could have happened to him.'

'That's my ma, worrying away!' Vi said affectionately and, settling more comfortably, asked, 'Tell me about you and Pa before you were married.'

'Well, we were both working class,' she began, but when her daughter would have protested she added quickly, 'no listen. We both came from poor families but after that everything was against us. Your Pa's family were strict Catholics from Ireland years back—'

'I never knew that.'

'Oh, generations back, but I was from a Methodist Chapel background. You'd 'ave thought I come from Timbucktoo! Not only that, but we lived *miles* apart. A right route march it was for us to get together! And that was the easy bit, getting days off at the same time was a pain in the neck.' She was smiling as she warmed to her subject. 'But then the biggest trouble we 'ad was *my* pa! He was a *real* worrier, always telling me some Jack the Ripper would get me as I wandered about the streets. He was always turning up at places to ferry me 'ome!' She laughed out loud at the recollections. 'Me and your pa, we used to be furious, but we daren't let my ol' man see!'

'I reckon I'm the luckiest girl in the world to 'ave parents like you and Pa. John's lost both his.'

'You'll 'ave to bring him to see me for a chat and a cuppa.' No sooner was the invitation out of her mouth than she covered her lips with her hands. 'What am I saying! He'll recognise all the cups and saucers and things!'

'Oh, Ma! What does that matter – but what about Audrey?'

'Bit surprised at her outburst,' Ma said reflectively. 'Know she's your best friend but she always been a jealous madam, you know. People don't change. Jealous when young, jealous when old; jealous when glad, jealous when sad.'

'Losing her ma and pa . . .'

'Yes, she didn't 'ave time to grieve, poor gel. There'll be outbursts, the sooner the better for her, maybe.'

The look they exchanged held the mutual understanding that they might both be in for a difficult time with Audrey Kingston.

The following morning at work she certainly felt Audrey voiced her grievance to an unnecessary degree – and in front of Paul's mother. She either lost control of her tongue or forgot they had kept as much as they could from Ethel Kerrow – or she simply did not care. Vi could see the older woman lapping up and mulling over everything that was said.

Once Doris realised the man she was going to meet was the officer who had stood looking so woefully after Vi and the lorry as they left the camp dance, she gave a loud 'Ah!' of realisation and seemed perfectly happy. 'As long as Audrey comes and I don't have to go on my own, no hassle.'

Vi thought she had put all the 'hassle' behind her as she finally boarded the bus for Penzance. She slipped into the vacant front seat. She would see John quicker and be off the bus first, but someone called her name from further back. She turned to see May waving to her.

May gestured her to come join her and moved up to the window on her double seat. With the utmost reluctance and with a sinking heart she rose, pinned a smile on her face and went to sit by May.

'Hello!' May enthused. 'And where are you off to?'

'I might ask you the same,' she countered, 'don't often see you on the bus.'

'That's because you've not been on it much.' May laughed. 'I come into town quite regularly on Saturdays.'

'This is only my second time,' she admitted.

'There you are then.' May was bright, chatty, full of questions about the work, not realising it was out-of-doors. 'I feel quite guilty too that I've not been to see your mother again.'

Vi felt guilty for quite another reason but May's conversation flowed so fast she could not find time to frame the right words to tell May that John was meeting her off the bus.

As they drew into the town May looked out of the window and waved. 'Oh good, John's here! Usually if we're coming in we travel together. *And* he's not in uniform. Great!' She half rose waiting for Vi to get to her feet, which she did and as May bustled out of the seat she automatically stood back to let her go first.

140

'Hi!' She heard May's greeting. 'Didn't know you were coming in today.'

'Nor me you,' he answered. 'I'm waiting for Vi actually.' He nodded and smiled at Vi as she slowly followed down the steps.

'Hello, old thing,' he greeted Vi.

She thought it was like watching a light being blown out, as May's cheery top-of-the-world brightness turned to a pallor which was almost grey. She felt it was like observing someone become bereaved, an intrusion. 'Oh, I see. Sorry!' She waved an airy hand and turned quickly away. 'My mistake.'

The two watched her go, stumbling a little in her haste as she took a side way sloping steeply down to the harbour. 'I wonder why she's going that way?' John mused. 'Doesn't usually.'

Vi was appalled. It just bore out all she had guessed – no, known. 'I don't suppose she knows where she is going. Don't you see, she thought you were meeting *her* off the bus.'

'I've never done that.'

'You've travelled in with her though.'

'Because we were both coming . . .'

'May is in love with you,' she stated with quiet certainty. 'I knew from the first moment I saw the two of you together.'

'No, no,' he said, still dismissive of the idea. 'I'm sure you're wrong. She'd be surprised, of course.'

'We can agree about that.' Vi was surprised he could not see what she found so obvious. One moment May was bright, sunny, full of life, the next she had stumbled blindly off down a side street looking like one bereft. 'Perhaps you just don't want to see it,' she added.

He did not answer as they turned and began to walk down past the many and varied shops either side the steep town street.

'Do I take that as a yes. Yes, you don't want to admit it.'

'I don't want to see May hurt,' he answered.

'Nor me!' she answered emphatically.

'But if what you say is true what can we do?'

'Be honest, acknowledge her feelings. Not . . .' She paused, unable to put into words how she felt but trying to show him as she went on, 'I don't think I'll ever forget the way she went off by herself just then.'

'I'll talk to her,' he promised, 'but don't let it spoil our day. You know, old thing, I can't help my feelings either.'

'No,' she admitted taking the elbow he crooked at her, 'or me.'

She felt her hand and arm pressed more closely to his side beneath his and understood the real meaning for poor May's exclamation when she saw he was not in uniform. Then, as he gave her hand an extra squeeze, she could feel guilty about May no longer. She thought if anyone asked what she was walking on she would probably say 'clouds' and she found if difficult to stop smiling. She was aware of people glancing their way and one or two smiled back indulgently, knowingly. So even strangers could tell, she thought.

She was so lost in the experience of just walking in a state of bliss, it made her start when he suddenly stopped and declared, 'This is the place.'

She found they were before a grey-painted shop front which proclaimed Theodore Timson, Photographic Studio. He was heading her for the door when she pulled back. 'How much will it cost?' she asked.

'It's for me, I shall pay,' he said and, opening the door in front of her, they were both so startled by the loud and clamorous shop bell above their heads that they scuttled in and closed the door quickly. The bell continued to jangle furiously above the door, dancing about on its spring like some minature whirling dervish. John pulled a face and reached up to hold it still. At that moment a middle-aged woman with faded red hair, dressed in emerald green velvet, came from the back of the shop. The smile on her face froze as she saw what he was doing.

'Sorry,' he said releasing the bell as if it was hot. Vi bit her lip to control a giggle which threatened to become out of control.

The lady of the shop became increasingly on her guard as, shown upstairs into the studio, they both collapsed into laughter at the sight of the photographic backdrop behind the central piano stool. This, she told them stiffly, was very popular but she also had velvet drapes which were considered elegant, that was if they 'preferred something less out of doors and realistic'. They assured her that the seascape with outsize seagulls was fine, 'just the ticket'. She pursed her lips and refrained from asking why then it had sent them into near hysterics. Instead she informed them stonily, 'Mr Timson is away serving his country, photographing the war for posterity.'

Why this should also send them into waves of giggles, Vi guessed all three would find difficult to explain. Mrs Timson was obviously relieved when this particular commission was over – one of each of them seated alone, then the piano stool was banished as they opted to stand, Vi slightly in front of John.

'My husband trained me fully before he had to go,' she told them defensively as she escorted them to the door.

'Oh dear, that was awful,' Vi declared once they were outside and the door closed very firmly after them. 'I ache with trying not to laugh. Poor woman!'

'I didn't even notice you trying!' he joked. 'Can you imagine her husband "photographing the war". I bet he has to make it all stand still and smile before he can begin. He probably has a green velvet suit.'

'Stop it!' Vi implored holding her sides.'But those seagulls!'

'Realistic seagulls!' He arched his arms like wings and lumbered a few paces as if trying to get airborne.

They were in the mood to be intoxicated by anything. All through the rest of the day, one or other of them bubbled over into laughter that had nothing to do with the stolid Chelsea buns at the teashop or the progress of the

Gilbert & Sullivan Players in the *Mikado*. It was not really until they caught the last bus from town and sat close together on the back seat that their mood changed.

Perhaps it was the darkness and the near empty bus, or the way John overlapped her shoulder with his and held her hand as the bus, even older than the one she had first come to Penzance on, took the hairpin bends of the coast road. They were silent too as if their own irrepressible high spirits and the nonsense they had talked had worn them out.

It was enough to sit close, to be together quietly, and a great feeling of contentment swept over her as she thought that she might one day really be the 'old thing' by his side. She gazed with a secret added intensity out of the window, but, with a feeling of some disappointment, recognised the shape of the one crooked bush bending over away from the sea winds which grew near the farm drive.

'Nearly there,' she said reluctantly, just as the old chap who lurched arthritically up and down the bus with his ticket machine and money bag called, 'Next stop Gerrards Farm.' He had obviously remembered her and where she got off. She supposed all evacuees must stick out like sore thumbs to the locals.

'I'm getting off here too,' John told her.

'Oh, but . . .' Her voice protested but her face beamed as she added, 'You'll have to walk if you do.'

He stooped to her ear as he let her lead the way down the aisle. 'It'll be worth every step.'

She wished she could stop this silly habit of blushing. She smiled at the conductor who grinned back as he saw them down the steps, his hand poised to ring the bell. 'Goodnight, m'maid, watch your step! Goodnight, sir.'

The headlights and the noise of the engine faded quickly into the distance and they were quite alone. They stood by the side of the road, letting their eyes become accustomed to the night. She became aware of the sound of the sea, the noise that varied with wind and tide but which was a constant in her life now, just as the noise of the passing traffic and the delivery drays had been in Bethnal Green. She felt the wind, keen, cold, on her face, smelt the sea and the damp bracken, and all the more keenly because of the warmth of his hand around hers.

'Come off the road a little, there might be another vehicle along.' He drew her into the gateway opposite the farm drive.

He enfolded her close to him, very close. She felt as if every inch of her body was a sensor, aware, responsive. She looked up over his shoulder and was amazed how large and bright the stars were and there was a thin sliver of moon. 'Oh!' she exclaimed softly. 'It's a new moon.'

'New moon, new beginning.' He glanced up at the sky then his voice deepened as he went on, 'This is a beginning such as I've never ever thought to

143

find. I didn't know there was such a feeling. I do know I've never really been in love before.'

She garnered the words in silent wonder.

'I love you, Vi,' he repeated. 'From that first moment my heart became,' he looked up to the heavens, 'as wide as the sky and as studded with all those stars, all bright treasures that belong to a girl named Violet Tulley.'

Half of her stubborn nature wanted to argue against such a description, such romantic images, but, lifting her head and staring upwards she could believe herself there with the stars.

'I feel you may fly away if I don't hold you tight,' he said, then added her name questioningly, 'Vi?'

'I love you.' Prompted, she answered with eager honesty. 'I love you,' she repeated. 'I do love you.' It was as if all dammed-up emotions had found sudden release. 'I want to shout it out aloud.'

'You'd better not,' he advised and bent to kiss her on the lips. This was a very different kiss to the tentative testing of reactions. This had an assurance, went to the core of her being, evoked all those responses single girls should not have and left them both tremorous and breathless.

'I can see a light across in your farmyard,' he told her and she automatically knew he had seen it some moments before. 'It looks like someone with a torch.'

'Oh!' She tutted her annoyance. 'Ma would know the time the bus was due. I suppose she's wondering . . .'

'Of course, she's bound to worry about you.'

'Worry and my ma are bosom friends.'

He laughed, kissed her lingeringly once more, melting her every thought in her desire to be of him and with him for ever and ever . . .

'I'll walk you part way down your drive then be away.' His tone became more businesslike as he added, 'On a day-to-day basis I'm not too sure of my duties—but I can't wait until next Saturday to see you again. So can we write, it worked last week.'

'Poor postwoman.' She bit back the questions, the worries, the urge to confront him with Sergeant Wilson's statement that there would be plenty of spare beds at the Manor soon. Not too soon, she prayed.

'You have a torch?' he asked very gently, as if aware of her inner conflict.

'Never travel without,' she said breezily, taking the small pocket light from her shoulder bag.

'Goodnight, my love. I'll be waving even though you can't see.'

Their lips and arms and hands became wayward, lingering, until, from the farm, she too saw the searching beam of a flashlight and heard someone call. John kissed her hand and was gone. She stood and waved into the darkness.

As she approached the farmyard a voice called out. 'That you, Vi?'

'Audrey?' She hurried forward then, by her own torchlight, saw there was a jeep in the yard. 'Is there something wrong?'

Audrey was obviously agitated but as she led the way to the back door it became clear that it was Vi she was annoyed with.

'Where 'ave you been. The bus came ages ago.'

'What's the matter?' She repeated her question more firmly. 'Didn't you go to the dance?'

'Oh yes, we *went*!' Audrey sounded peevish and unhappy as she opened the door and led the way in. 'But we're all back waiting for *you*.'

The kitchen appeared full of people who, unlike Audrey, were obviously in good spirits as a minor cheer went up as she entered.

''Ere she is at last!' Doris declared, beaming at her. 'Come on you're missing all the excitement.'

'Excitement? What's going on? What's happened?' she demanded, though the presence of George Wilson standing possessively over the kitchen chair occupied by Avis made it was obvious *who* the exhilaration was all about.

Vi felt she too could have cheered as she saw the difference in the woman. Though her arm was still encased in plaster and supported on a slender sling, gone was the cowed, battered woman she had helped into the doctor's car. Her pleasant face had taken on a kind of calm beauty, even her hair seemed blonder, brighter. Avis rose to meet her and folded her free arm around her neck. 'This is my saviour.' For a second the description flashed a picture of that great brass lectern before she went on, 'I had to come see you and say a proper thank you.'

'And I want to shake your hand, m'dear,' Sergeant Wilson said, burying her hand in his huge fist. A warm, caring handshake and a direct honest look made her rejoice for Avis—but at the same time she *was* still married to that bible-thumping hypocrite.

'So what happened?' Vi wanted to know. 'You all went to the dance, but you must have left early.'

'We left early because of our friend Mrs Kerrow,' Doris said with weighty meaning. 'There was a commotion at the door just after we arrived. It was the "right reverend" trying to get in without a ticket.'

'So she *did* listen,' Vi interrupted.

'And made it her business to go tittle-tattling.'

'The old cow!'

'Vi!' Ma reprimanded, nodding at their guests.

'She is, Mrs Tulley, there's no other word for 'er.' Doris endorsed. 'But we smuggled Avis out the kitchen door and we were away—quick.' She wiped a pretended film of sweat from her brow.

'George is taking me straight back to Plymouth tonight.' Avis smiled up at her friends. 'And I don't intend to come back again—ever.'

George Wilson cleared his throat quietly and took up the story. 'I have forty-eight hours embarkation leave and tomorrow I'm taking Avis to meet my brothers and my mother. I want her to stay with them for the duration of the war. We have a business, a garage, and Avis could help if she wanted to. There'll be a flat empty above the shop. Our mechanic's just been called up and his wife's going back north to her mother.'

Vi only half heard the details—forty-eight hours embarkation leave! Forty-eight hours. Did that mean Saturday and Sunday, leave Monday? John had said his duties were uncertain, but uncertain in hours! No surely, surely not. No it couldn't include John. No, of course not otherwise he would have been on that special leave loved one's must dread to hear named.

'Sounds like you've got it made,' Audrey said. Vi hoped it was only she who caught the edge of bitterness in her friend's voice.

Avis smiled apologetically, as if she too had caught some edge of grouchiness. 'I was sorry about the dance. But I'm going to ask one of you to do something else for me. You see I am going to break my wedding vows and I may be heading for eternal damnation . . .'

'God's unjust if he ever dammed you for not staying with that devil,' Ma unexpectedly contributed.

'Thank you, Mrs Tulley, but my guilt is with me, and there's this one thing I'm finding difficult.' She paused to reach down for her handbag and George Wilson was obviously as much in the dark about this as they were. 'I want to be rid of this and I can't bring myself to just throw it away.'

She drew out a small handkerchief, while deeper in the bag Vi glimpsed a larger khaki one. She laid the small lace square on the table and opened it to reveal her split wedding ring.

The room was silent as they all looked down at the ring, severed and prised wide apart. She remembered the finger swollen so much the ring had been invisible.

'It says it all really, doesn't it?' Vi said.

'Throw it in the sea,' Doris said, 'hurl it off the cliffs.'

Vi thought of all the seashore had come to mean to her and did not speak.

'Give it him back,' Audrey suggested.

'Yes,' she heard herself agree.

'In an envelope through his letterbox,' Doris added. 'I'll take it!'

Chapter 17

Vi see-sawed between joy and dread, one emotion bumping out the other with all the force of the playground ride: her time with John, the photographic studio; the homecoming, the crowd of visitors, Avis so changed! Men on embarkation leave, separations; the memory of May's face as she turned away.

By Monday morning she was almost looking forward to confronting Ethel Kerrow – someone she could justifiably vent her anger on! There could have been such dire consequences of the woman's interference. As it was, Audrey still seemed uptight about her lost night out. Then, as they waited for their lift, she finally revealed that just as Avis's husband arrived, Noel had been boasting that he bet he could give her the best night of her life. Vi huffed in surprise.

'*You* don't know!' Audrey retorted, retaliating when there was no attack. Then, as they saw the lorry coming towards them, she added 'What's up with him?' as, instead of drawing up so they could climb in the back, the driver stopped and leaned forward to speak to them, holding out two envelopes.

'You've been paid off,' he told them.

'Why what have we done?' they asked, crowding to his door.

'No, no,' he said, pushing back his cap. 'Everybody's been finished for the time being. They've not said but I reckon its because the equipment's coming in. The army's there in force this morning with great transport lorries. Don't want us civvies to see what they're up to. It's air defences of some kind,' he added, 'and a gun or two.'

The girls took their envelopes and tore them open, each revealing to the other a ten shilling note.

Vi searched inside her envelope. 'That's it!'

'They might have made it a quid, miserable gits.' 'Well I'm going to find something else,' Audrey declared. 'Do you know of anything?'

'They'll be plenty o' planting and picking coming along after Christmas,' he told them, putting his lorry into gear. 'Meantime, if I hear of anything . . .'

'I like 'aving a bit of my own money,' Audrey muttered.

Vi shared her sentiments, adding the old cry, 'if we could only get bikes!'

'Noel's got a bike. He cycled to the dance on it.'

With this repeated mentioned of the man, Vi began to understand. 'You seeing 'im again?'

'We didn't 'ave much time to arrange anything—but yes, six o'clock tonight outside the Gerrard's Head pub along the way.'

'Oh! That place!'

'Where else would you suggest in this Godforsaken 'ole, where else is there?'

They trudged back towards the house. 'I like Noel,' Vi said. 'He seems an honest chap, no secrets.'

'Not like some—or wives like others!' Audrey linked arms, companionably mollified by Vi's approval. 'It makes me feel I've come back to life a bit, having a chap again.'

'So I don't 'ave to go to school either!' Sid tried on as they arrived back at the house and placed their pay-off money on the table.

Ma didn't bother to answer him. Her daughter knew she would already be worrying about the rent.

'Shall I walk 'im up, save you?' she offered as Ma began to pull on her coat. 'And pick that money up. I've still got a couple of bob.' She prompted Audrey with a look.

'And me,' her friend obliged.

'I've one or two things to get and I see a few people at the shops who pass the time of day . . .'

'We could ask if there are any jobs going in the shops,' Audrey suggested. 'We're going to miss this money now *and* just when I've taken my shoes to the menders!'

Ma reached forward and took the two ten-shilling notes. 'I'll pick your shoes up.'

Vi thought of the post which might arrive quite soon. She had a letter she could finish and another to write which needed a lot of thought. 'You go. I'll stay and do some of the chores.'

Audrey shrugged. 'Please yourself, but I'm going.'

She watched them go, Ma bustling them along so Sid should not be late, then she rushed to her writing table to add a postscript to her letter, telling John that their work had been finished so she was free every day. She had barely finished adding three exclamation marks after this piece of information when some noise outside alerted her. She prayed it wasn't Paul. She gave an involuntary shiver as she wondered how he would take Audrey having a fella as well? Then came the unmistakeable sound of someone alighting from a bicycle. Sticking the envelope down as she ran downstairs, she flung herself out of the kitchen door, her face glowing with

148

anticipation, her hand half outstretched to pass over her letter.

'Oh!' Both girls exclaimed in surprise.

'I came to see your mother,' May said, 'an overdue call. I thought you would be at work.'

Vi laughed shakily. 'I thought you were the postlady.'

'She is on her way, I passed her.' May spoke and smiled formally, strictly controlled.

As controlled Vi thought, in this sad role as she had been in the happy syncopated steps of the dance. It would be easier if she didn't like this normally frank, open-hearted young woman. She found her pallor shocking and could not escape the fact that May's look of desolation made her appear older, ten years older. They were silent and still, one holding her bicycle, one a letter and neither meeting the other's eye.

'You must think me an awful fool,' May said at last, 'taking for granted . . . Well, what I had assumed all my life I suppose.'

Vi wanted to explain that *she had* understood, that it had all been very plain to everyone except to John. 'May, I . . . for a long time I thought you were really his cousin. I mean you both called Mrs Trewellan "auntie".'

'I know, that was the trouble.' She looked up and there was a new hardness in her eyes. 'I too had assumed a relationship, but unfortunately for me it wasn't the same one John assumed.' She bent over her bicycle and fidgeted her front wheel with a gentle agitation of the handlebars. 'I've not given this all up without a fight you know.' There was a silence and a stillness in which only the wind blew a little stronger from the sea as if to urge them into action again.

'I realised afterwards that you probably knew how I felt. I remembered you had seemed a little put out when I was on the bus, a bit abstracted when we were talking. When you know the whole truth these incidents all fit into place don't they?'

'I told John he was—'

'Wrong to think of me as a sister?' May laughed bitterly. 'He was so very wrong and I think I did finally make him realise that late last night.' She looked frankly at Vi. 'I threw myself at him as they say. I went to his room, invaded the security of the Manor. That actually didn't take much doing.' She paused and gave a short sobbing laugh which shocked Vi because it held so much hurt, so much rejection. 'He turned me out when I had made clear why I was there and how I felt . . .'

'You went . . .'

'Shock you does it? I'd do it again, every night, if I thought . . . But if I'm honest . . .' She took time, as if gathering courage for this final admission. 'If I'm honest, there was a time before all this when I sensed something had happened, something was different. It was when I realised he had stopped calling me "old thing". I know that sounds stupid . . .' She stopped as she

149

caught the stricken expression on Vi's face. 'He calls you that doesn't he?'

'He does,' she admitted, wondering if there had after all been a transfer of affections? Would John have married May if she had not come on the scene?

'I hope every time he says it you think of me,' May said, for once real bitterness in her voice.

She found herself wanting to take a defensive step back startled by the unexpected harshness and remembered John's judgment that May usually got what she wanted. This time she had not. Vi stood her ground, forced to realise once more this man was not for sharing – neither of them wanted that.

'So all or nothing,' May suddenly declared as if her thoughts were running along the same emotional path. 'I'm going to do the other thing I wanted to do. I'm joining the WRENS. I go up to London tomorrow. I shall stay with friends and go and have a word with Uncle Jimmie – he's at the Admiralty – and take it from there. So this is probably goodbye. I can't bring myself to think of the possibilities after the war, who will be where? We shall see . . .' She paused to look at Vi who read the clear message that she thought the evacuee might long have returned to where she really belonged.

'Or how the country's values have changed.' Vi wanted to remind her of the new equality they had talked about, but there was too much to say, no time, and perhaps no point.

'I don't think we'll shake hands,' May said finally, 'we'll keep our integrity.'

'Good luck, May,' she said, keeping her own.

'Give my best to your mother, tell her I'm sorry to have missed her.'

The two looked straight into each other's eyes. There was neither absolute winner nor absolute loser. Vi realised that even in success there was the burden of making another lose.

Alone, Vi found it difficult to concentrate. She began the chores – throwing back eiderdowns, blankets, sheets, shaking and pommelling up the mattresses – but she still found herself concerned with May's parting look. It had also held a particular quality which she remembered being directed at her before. It was a kind of interrogation, an assessment – then she remembered. It was when she had been interviewed by old Mr Fieldman for the job with the accountants. So what position had May been unable to think of her in – John's wife presumably? 'We shall see,' she repeated May's questioning words, then again adding her own determination, 'We shall see!'

She sat on the edge of Ma's bed, imagining the mortification of being put out of a man's room when you'd gone to . . . She tried to imagine surrendering her own virginity. She tried to imagine wanting any man to make love to you – and him refusing. Her experience was that it was more a matter of keeping them in their place – and it wasn't something she felt Audrey had always done.

No wonder May was bitter and had decided to go away immediately, leaving the coast clear. Vi needed to talk to someone. Audrey would be more sympathetic now she had a chap of her own. She itched for them to come back.

She prowled around the house, went outside, scoured the lane, the cliffs, the moors for some sight of life. Even Paul Kerrow would have been almost welcome. No wonder Ma wanted to walk up to the village with Sid, see a few people. After the Green this place was like a desert – OK a picturesque desert, but definitely a desert.

It already seemed like an eternity when she heard someone else in the drive. She rushed out, thinking it must be Ma and Audrey back, only to see the stout figure of Mrs Stevens propping up her husband's red post-office bike. Her hand flew to her pocket. She had forgotten all about her letter.

'One to go is there,' she said before taking the letter and the two-pence halfpenny for the stamp, aware, it seemed to Vi, exactly where and who it was to without looking. 'And there's one for your ma.'

The letter had a London postmark, though it was not Pa's writing, but any letter was an event. Now she was more anxious than ever that the other two should return. She did try to write to Roy and made penance for her failure by black-leading the range, her least favourite chore.

When Ma and Audrey returned home the letter that had arrived was immediately opened and threw further gloom over the household. It was a thank-you letter, but from Roy's parents. Maggie Moore wrote saying how grateful she and Albert were 'for giving us free run of your home'. She gave not very reassuring details to the houseproud of how the newspaper business was for the time being run from the front of the house in Brierly Street 'until some sort of shoring up can make the front bit of the old shop safe. The newsboys think it's great having a fire to warm themselves at.'

That depressed Ma, the thought of all those muddy boots in her front parlour. The next part sobered Vi. 'Tell Vi to write to our Roy, he says he's not heard for a bit. Letters are important when you're away. You must have plenty you can tell him, Vi, about your experiences in the country!'

'I've been trying to find the right words to do just that,' Vi said quietly as Ma continued reading.

'Your Harold says to tell you we still manage to get down the Old Vic from time to time. There's still a bit of a sing-song there of a Saturday in spite of old Hitler.'

'Could do with a milk stout to drown my sorrows,' Ma said, refolding the letter and offering it to Vi who shook her head.

'Why don't you and Vi walk along to the Gerrard's Head with me tonight for a quick one,' Audrey suggested. 'I'm meeting a chap . . .'

Ma of course wanted to know who he was and what Vi thought, but the suggestion that she might go for a drink was not received with much enthusiasm. 'It's Monday, that wouldn't 'ardly seen right even back 'ome – and 'ere? I just don't think the men take their womenfolk out down 'ere.' She shook her

151

head. 'Don't think so – and there's Sid. It'll be dark almost before you set off. Will this chap bring you back? Bring him in lets 'ave a gander at 'im!'

'OK.' Audrey shrugged. 'Do you good though and why should we care what the locals think!'

Audrey was better tempered all day and volunteered to go and meet Sid again in the afternoon, leaving Vi resolved to write her letter.

'Take a cup of tea up with you, that might help,' Ma suggested when they were alone.

'What's best, Ma? How on earth shall I tell him? I do have to tell him.'

'Yes.' Ma bit her lip and shook her head. 'I think . . . I mean he's away fighting. I think you should tell him gradually.'

'Let him down gradually.' Vi fully realised the meaning of the phrase for the first time. 'Perhaps,' she said, 'it'll be the only way I'll ever be able to tell him. I mean I really do like old Roy.'

'And if this other man hadn't come along . . .'

'But he has.' Vi drank her tea before going to discard all her earlier attempts to write to Roy, pages strewn with phrases like 'there does not seem any easy way', 'it seems like fate' and 'not something I planned or could help' and wrote her first breaking it to him gently letter.

'Dear Roy,

Hope you are keeping well and not quite so bored out of your mind as you were when you last wrote! We had a letter from your ma today, saying how they were faring running the business from our house! Can imagine how your dad likes that!

Are you still enjoying the dances you manage to have. We've been to one or two here and met various fellas, real nice some of them. Audrey has a date tonight with a chap called Noel. I went more for the officer type!'

She wondered why she always had to make it a joke with Roy, no matter what.

'His name is John!'

Always the exclamation mark. Roy wasn't stupid, surely he might guess something. She hoped so as she went on then about Sid and school, how he said he was a 'marked man,' always picked out if there was any trouble, always getting the blame. She finished and folded the letter, knowing it was not right easier for her, *perhaps* kinder to Roy. She would wait until she felt this first letter had reached him, then write again, more fully—the full truth.

Sid came running in well ahead of Audrey. 'Paul's going up the road with a load of hay. If I run I can catch up with him!'

'Thought you were always hungry?' Vi challenged.

'Can I take it with me?'

'Take your school trousers off, put your old boots on.' Ma raised her voice above his groans. 'And I've made you a dripping sandwich to last till dinner-time. Now don't you be too long, we shan't wait.'

'He'll be way up toward Gerrard's Head by now,' Audrey warned.

'I don't care,' he shouted, racing off as fast as his legs would carry him.

'Hello and goodbye, Sid,' Vi said.

An hour and a half later, Ma had already poured extra boiling water into the casserole twice and Sid had not returned. In the end she served their meal, putting his share back into the covered dish. Audrey was changed ready for her date and it nearly was dark.

'We'll walk up towards the pub with you,' Ma decided. 'That was the way Paul was going with the cart?'

Vi was not sorry Ma had bought new batteries for the flashlight, though she had grumbled about the cost. She took out the old batteries and put them on the side of the kitchen range to warm up – 'give 'em a bit more life for just round the farm.'

Ma gave the light an experimental swish around as they reached the top of the drive.

'Stand and listen for a minute,' Vi suggested. 'We'd hear the horse and cart a long way off.'

The constancy of the waves seemed to emphasise the overall silence, the feeling of solitude.

'I think we should shout,' Audrey suggested.

'Sid! Sid! Where are you?'

They walked along shouting from time to time and, though she didn't voice her growing concern, Vi could not help thinking of the mining shafts that abounded on the cliffs. Some had a vestige of barbed wire to warn walkers, others nothing more than a pile of rocks overgrown with brambles.

'Surely Paul wouldn't have just left him somewhere out in the wilds,' Audrey said. 'He's always brought him at least to the top of the drive.'

'I don't like it,' Ma said. 'Something's happened.'

More dramatic things began to occur to Vi as she remembered what John had said about thinking Paul might back his horse and cart over the cliff in his temper.

'We're nearly at the Gerrard's Head,' Audrey said after another session of shouting.

'Listen!' Vi ordered. 'I thought I heard someone calling.'

They stood and they could hear someone, but it was a man's voice. Then a bicycle lamp came wavering along the road towards them.

'I think it's Noel,' Audrey said.

Meeting by the light of one bicycle lamp and one flashlight made the introductions brief and the emergency soon told.

'Split in two's will be the best bet,' Noel said. 'There's a path round the back of the pub and along the cliffs. I know that. You two ladies could go further along the road – and keep shouting.'

'What d'you think?' Ma asked fearfully.

'Its not a nice place to be lost at night. Come on, Audrey, you come with me.'

Vi linked arms with Ma and they walked up to the top of the Gerrard's Head road, calling, listening. It was colder and much more windy on the fully exposed headland. They could sense rather than see the great expanse of sea – and in between a vast expanse of moors and an odd farm building or two, which shone up as Vi took the light from Ma and swung it all around in a wide arc over the cliffs and paths, hoping there were no enemy planes, shipping *or* air-raid wardens about. 'Sid! Sid!' She cupped her hands over her mouth and shouted as loudly as she could towards the cliffs and then inland to the higher moors on the other side of the road.

Ma began to walk on and Vi wondered just how far it might be wise to go or whether it wouldn't be better to try to find Paul? But where? She didn't even know where the horse was stabled. Then she stopped, lifting her head, listening intently. 'Wait, Ma, can you hear something!'

'It's Audrey and her chap shouting,' Ma said after a minute.

'No . . . the other way . . . listen!' They listened again and Vi shouted once more. 'Sid! Can you hear me? It's Vi! Where are you?'

Against the wind from the sea came a distant shout. They couldn't make out the words, but Ma immediately decided it was Sid.

'Sid!' Vi hurried down from the headland and directed her voice towards the high moors. 'Keep shouting so we can find you.'

'Vi! Vi! Vi!'

'That's m'boy!' she said, allowing herself a smile now as the shouts went on and on. 'Come on.' She took her mother firmly by the arm and walked back along the road towards the pub until they found a path running inland. She paused to gauge Sid's continuing shouts and led the way. 'He's up here.'

The path climbed steeply, gorse and bambles got higher and the path narrower the further they went, but Sid's cries definitely sounded louder. At last they came to a huge outcrop of rock around which the land was quite bare, the soil so shallow it allowed only the sparsest of grasses to grow. Other paths seemed to lead away from it. Vi could see that they might all three soon be lost if they were not careful. 'Ma,' she ordered, 'just stay here and don't move. Then we'll know which path we came up and I'll be able to find you easily.'

'All right,' Ma said. 'If you're sure.'

'Just don't move an inch!' Vi emphasised. 'Or we may all be lost.'

'I won't.'

Vi heard the tremor and the apprehension in her voice. 'He's near somewhere, keep still and listen. I'll call to you when I find him *but stay still.*'

She went forward alone and it was wierd approaching these great rocks with only the thin beam of the pocket torch to guide her.

'Sid! Where are you? Are you near rocks? Can you see my flashlight?'

'I'm at the top.' His voice was thin, high, full of panic.

The voice sounded above her and instinctively she shouted back. 'Stand still, Sid! Stand quite still until I shine the light.'

She shone the beam in front to the rock, then up – and up. 'My God!' she breathed as she saw a black figure outlined by the torch. A figure on the edge of a drop of some twenty feet of sheer rock.

'Sid keep quite still until I reach you. I'll have to find a way round the other side.'

He said something else and behind her she heard Ma's voice distantly querulous with questioning, but she replied to neither in the urgency to find a way round and up. In the dark, and hurrying over what appeared to be the flat grassy parts, she stumbled and fell to her knees several times but her aim was to circle and climb and climb. Then as the grassy parts disappeared and the rocks became steeper, she paused to still her breath and calm her voice.

'Sid, without moving an inch call to me again and keep calling until I reach you.'

The last few yards did not take long once she realised he was quite near behind a shoulder of rock. He had mistaken his way and wandered along a ledge which ended at another rock face. Without a light it would have been impossible but she soon had him by the wrist and pulled him carefully back to the safer side of the massif.

He gave a sort of sobbing cry once there and she held him tight for a moment before anxiously shining the light over him. His face was deathly white, his hands frozen and his knees were both bleeding. 'I couldn't find my way back.'

'What were you doing up there? Thank God you had the sense to keep still!' But when he attempted to explain she silenced him brusquely. 'Come on, Ma's waiting down below and Audrey and her chap are searching the cliffs. We'll save the explanations until we're home.' She felt furious with him now he was safe and once they were back where Ma waited shivering in the cold, Vi went ahead, the pace too brisk and the path too narrow to allow for more than walking and breathing.

Once they were back on the roadway, Sid began to cry in earnest but Vi hurried them still so she could let Audrey and Noel know her brother was safe. As they approached the public house she noted how effective the black-out was. The deep stone windows were well curtained within and outside a kind of wooden-roofed shelter had been erected with an extra outer door so no light escaped as customers came and went. She hoped no one had seen their torch beam flashing around the peninsular! Think they were signalling to enemy ships!

155

As they reached the door they heard footsteps and Noel's voice.

'We've found him,' she called.

By the light of the torch, they took in the state of the shivering boy with cut hands and knees and Vi too, her stockings laddered and her knees bleeding.

'Come on!' Noel said and pushed inside the first of the two doors. Immediately they could hear laughter, good-natured banter and, by the pauses and then the cheers, it was clear some kind of darts match was being played in the bar.

'I'll have a word with the landlady,' Noel said, pushing through the front door proper and holding it open. As this led directly into the bar, their appearance caused at first a fall in the conversation, then total silence as all eyes turned their way.

'We've had a boy lost on the moors, just found him. D'you think he could come in a minute or two to recover.'

The landlady, who had turned laughing from the soldiers and locals playing darts, became a stony-faced proprietor viewing with displeasure the three women and the boy who stood dishevelled in her doorway, letting in the cold among other undesirable things.

'What's anybody doing letting a child out on the moors this time o'night!'

It was not a question, it was a judgment. Vi's reply was immediate. 'We were stupid enough to let him out with a local.'

She would have turned away but there was half uproar, half cheer, from the men in the bar. 'Come on, Maude, you can't turn them out. Look at the state of the boy!'

Maude bridled and came grumbling to lift her counter flap. 'Come through to the kitchen, boy.' Noel edged Ma and Audrey through into the parlour. 'I'll get you a drink before you set off home,' he told Vi as it became clear only those who were obviously bleeding were to be let through into the private quarters.

'So who's "the local" who got you lost?'

'He told me to go home,' Sid explained to Vi.

'Ah! And you didn't do as you were told!' The landlady seized on the admission. 'Thought there'd be something.' She handed Vi a clean piece of rag for a flannel and poured hot water into a basin, then looked up sharply as Noel appeared at the door with a bottle of pop and a bag of crisps.

'He can have these in 'ere can't he, missus, while we all have a drink in the back parlour?'

The acquiescence was not exactly gracious and, though Ma had a milk stout and Vi drank a port and lemon, they soon left Audrey and Noel to their evening.

'We'll tell you the full story another time,' Vi said as they collected Sid from the kitchen.

'So what did happen?' Ma demanded later as Sid got undressed before the kitchen fire.

'You ran after Paul with his cart load of hay,' Vi prompted.

'Yes!' There was suddenly a trace of aggression in Sid's voice. He had cried on his mother's shoulder but now, warm and fed, he became what he obviously mainly felt – and that was aggrieved. 'Paul *always* let's me go with 'im. I 'ad to run halfway to that pub and 'e wouldn't let me get on the cart. 'E told me go 'ome!' The hurt and the surprise were still in his voice, in the way he clasped his hands between his knees and crouched nearer the fire. 'So I followed 'im. He saw me once. He was just slowing down to turn inland past Gerrard's Head. He stopped and shouted, told me to clear off and . . .' He paused shaking his head as if not quite believing what had happened next. Then, eyes wide, he faced his mother and sister before going on. 'And he threw stones at me! But I was too far away. Told me to go 'ome and stop there!'

'So what did you do then?' Vi asked.

'I made sure he didn't see me again.'

Vi bit her lip but Ma shook her head in concern as she asked, 'So you still followed him?'

'He went to some barns ever such a long way away. I hid round the back. There were animals there, Vi, bellowing like they did here, but Paul took the hay into them and he gave them water. It was dark when he'd finished and when I tried to follow him down the path I got lost.'

'That's very interesting,' Vi mused, 'but I wouldn't tell Paul you followed him all the way to the barns.'

'I'm not!' Sid said decisively. 'He'd go crackers.'

157

Chapter 18

'You look as grey as the morning,' Ma told Sid as he looked up from his porridge. 'Washed your face?'

'We'll take him to school,' Audrey announced, one of the decisions made as the two got dressed.

'We're going to have a proper search for jobs and find out about buses into Penzance.'

'We'll not come back until we've found something.' Audrey had come back invigorated from her date with Noel.

'This morning I wouldn't be sorry.' Ma peered through the window at the swirling banks of mist accompanied by sheeting rain. 'But you'll get wet through.'

'This is the wettest place in the world.' Sid leaned over to join up threads of condensation running down the window. 'I could stay with you, Ma,' he volunteered, then added more fiercely, 'I can go to school by myself! I know the way.'

'Don't draw on the windows unless you're going to clean them – when you get home from school.'

'Ma!' he appealed. 'Everyone else goes by themselves! They call me names . . .'

'You'd probably get lost!' Vi commented as she pulled on her coat.

'That's not fair!' he wailed. 'I only got lost because—'

'You didn't do as you were told,' Ma said, handing him his raincoat.

''E didn't 'ave to throw stones.'

'No and two bits of bad behaviour didn't make a good one.' Ma pulled him into his coat. 'Do your buttons up!'

'If you see anything I can do,' Ma said to the two girls. 'Might be some Christmas jobs.' She stood at the door and handed out umbrellas, calling after Sid, 'Soldiers don't put their hands in their pockets either!'

The driving onslaught of the rain had lessened a little and out at sea they glimpsed a convoy of battle-grey ships arrowing out away across the slate-

158

grey ocean, quickly gone like ghosts into the mist. Sid was soon marching along in front of the other two, shouting orders to himself until in the murky distance he caught sight of a horse and cart approaching. Immediately he fell back in line with the two girls. 'It's Paul with Major.'

'Be interesting to see what he has to say for himself,' Vi said.

As the two parties neared each other, Major pulled the cart away from the side of the road and headed for Sid.

'He knows who spoils him,' Paul said, reining in. 'Mornin' girls!'

Neither answered, the tacit feeling being to give him enough rope and see what the consequences were.

'Not saying much this morning?' His gaze went to Sid who was now fondling the horse's nose and giving him a crust he had in his pocket.

'Not much of a morning,' Vi replied enigmatically.

'Coming along Monk's Leap after school then.' He addressed this next remark to Sid. 'You can help me spread some seaweed on the field, can do with a good man in charge of the horse.'

'You'll want him today then?' Audrey questioned.

'Too late last night for him to be out if that's what you're getting at.'

'So you threw stones at him?' Vi said unsmilingly.

Paul laughed. 'I weren't aiming to hit 'im. No chance, m'andsome, just scare 'e off.'

'You *might* have hit me,' Sid complained.

'No chance,' he said shaking his head at Sid who stood looking hurt and resentful.

'Come on,' Paul urged, 'my grandma threw stones at me all the time.'

They were all three so astonished by this remark no one replied.

'Well you'll know where I'll be if you want to come.' Paul slapped the reins on Major's back and drove on.

The watched him go, whispering to each other.

'His *grandmother* did he say?'

'Did he mean it, sis?'

'Sounds as if he comes of a long line of . . .' Vi sniffed rather than labelled the family in front of Sid. 'His grandfather, or great-grandfather, bricked up that front door.'

'Bet they all interbred,' Audrey said darkly.

'What's interbred?'

'It makes people throw stones,' Vi answered quickly. 'Come on or you'll be late for school.'

'So he can't help it?' Sid was still questioning as they delivered him to the school gates. He turned back to say, 'Perhaps I should go to look after Major.'

The two gave a gasp of exasperated laughter as two women, bulky with dark clothes and shopping baskets, glanced curiously at the two London girls and nodded meaningfully at each other. The sniffs were audible above the clump of their stout shoes.

'I don't know about looking after,' Vi said loudly, 'I think some round here want permanently locking up.'

'Mind, I don't suppose it's as bad being 'ere as it was at Dunkirk,' Audrey added for good measure.

'Do we feel better for that?' Vi queried.

'Yeah!' Audrey linked arms with her.

They did a tour of the shops, the public houses, the chip shop and the teashop but found no hope of work, not even temporary, and were shown out of the teashop so quickly Audrey asked, 'You've not stood in anything 'ave you?'

'I'd like to stamp *on* a few things,' Vi answered as the door of the tearoom was closed so quickly behind her it half pushed her out into the road.

'Take your bleeding 'urry,' Audrey shouted through the glass at the po-faced uniformed waitress.

'Don't want to wear a stupid hat like that anyway,' Vi said as they began to trudge back along the road. 'At least I found out when the buses run. We could catch the early bus every morning . . .'

Not a great enthusiast for exercise, Audrey groaned. 'At least we can get properly tarted up to go into town, we must look a right pair of scarecrows this morning.'

The thought had them standing staring at each other, wet through, hair dangling from under their knitted berets, coat collars misshapen by the rain. 'No wonder they shut us out of the teashop . . .'

'Look a right pair of old bath buns!'

They began to laugh and to run in the rain, shouting, then kicking at the puddles – two London street urchins rebelling in a deserted Cornish lane. Vi thought momentarily of the punishment they were giving their shoes, but dismissed the prudence. They needed this break-out, this moment of foolishness. They paused only when they were out of breath and they saw an army lorry coming towards them.

'Anyone we know d'you think,' Audrey wondered.

'Hope not, not looking like this.' But as the lorry approached Audrey was soon waving. 'It's Noel!' she said. 'Hope nothing's gone wrong for tonight.'

'Tonight?'

'Yes I'm meeting him at Gerrard's Head again,' Audrey said over her shoulder as she hurried to the slowing lorry.

'Your ma said you were walking, thought I could give you a lift.'

'You been to the house?'

'Yeah! Jump in!' He began the difficult manoeuvre of turning the lorry on the narrow road, working hard at the great steering wheel as he told them of work he had heard about – their reaction immediate and violent nearly had him off the road.

'Camouflaging!'

'You have to be joking!'

'Not out in all weathers again!'

'Nah! This is inside. The Women's Voluntary Service have been doing it but can't keep pace. They want to set on two women – so I immediately thought of you two. It's in an old army building stitching strips of material on roping netting. I'm often by that way, can usually bet on a cuppa there.'

'Sounds OK,' Audrey said. 'Inside, its what we expected before. What's the pay and is transport laid on?'

'Put your shirt on it being the same as before,' he guessed, then, glancing at Vi, added, 'You not so keen?'

'She's—'

'I fancied a job in town, in Penzance,' Vi interrupted, 'something more permanent if I could get it.'

'You both worked for an accountant . . .'

'I wouldn't mind getting up at the crack of dawn if I could get a decent office job,' Vi added.

'I mustn't be too late back at camp.' He stopped at the top of the drive. 'You 'ave to know how to hedge your bets!'

Vi liked this young man with his gambling sayings and left him and Audrey to have a quick private word.

'Is there something wrong?' Ma asked, meeting her on the doorstep.

'What do you mean?'

'Audrey's chap comes looking for you both, even goes after you and brings you home . . .'

'He's come to tell us about a couple of jobs – camouflaging again but inside, and we could start right away.'

'So why so down?'

She was suddenly aware how much she did wish to try for work in an office, using her skills again. She explained about their plans to go into Penzance the next day. To her surprise, Ma blessed it immediately with the final seal of approval, 'Your pa would like that.' She broke into a wide smile. 'And come and see what's turned up!' She led the way to the kitchen where a tea chest stood in the middle of the floor spilling out clothes.

'Oooh!' Vi exclaimed. 'Pa's sent the clothes from Miss Swanton.'

'And . . .' From the far side of the box, Ma revealed tinned peaches, Spam and four large bars of chocolate.

'Ma! How did 'e get it all?' she exclaimed then tutted. 'But he would wouldn't he, he's a right fixer.'

The two of then had a little hug and a dance, then Ma drew back exclaiming, 'You'd better get that coat off and on a hanger if its going to look any sense for job hunting tomorrow.' She paused to nod towards the table and the fanned pages of his letter. 'He says he's sorry you're wasting your brains down 'ere.'

161

She went over to touch the letter, the tender gesture touching Vi so keenly. 'And look!' From a chair she lifted her sewing basket which had always had pride of place on a small stool near the kitchen fire in Brierly Street. Opening it, she displayed an array of new cards and skeins of wool, bobbins of cotton, packets of needles and a long paper strip of lines of pins. 'He's restocked it all.'

Vi shook her head and laughed. Just how did he manage to do these things – the chocolate, the tinned goods – with everything so scarce and him having to work double shifts because of the manpower shortage.

'The things were all carefully packed in the clothes, but . . .'

'But?' It was Vi's turn to query her mother's sudden downcast look.

Ma went to the mantlepiece and lifted down two small objects. They were her bead hatpin cushion and her white pottery ring tree from her dressing table. 'He sent these too . . . and I wish he hadn't.'

'I suppose he never thought about us having nothing but beds.'

'It's not that.' Ma struggled to find words as she held the two objects in her hands. 'These belong at 'ome in Brierley Street, like I do. It's somehow making it worse sending more things that don't belong!'

'He'd be trying to think of something, anything and everything, he could pack in that chest to please you.' She put her arm over her ma's shoulders as she sighed heavily and her hands moved slightly as she appeared to weigh and value the two objects sent from her dressing table. Then she turned an agonised look at her daughter before turning to reach up and put the two little things between the vases. 'And 'e's working Christmas.'

'Perhaps it'll be better for him to come in the spring,' Vi suggested. 'Everyone says how beautiful it is here then.' But the suggestion only made her feel bleak, only reminded her of everyone going away, of the convoy steaming out to the great ocean, of Sergeant Wilson, of May . . . all going . . . going to a war Winston Churchill said they must fight to the end. He had promised blood, sweat toil and tears when he first spoke in the House of Commons as prime minister and after Dunkirk he had pledged the whole country to fight to the end, there would be no surrender. Only a few weeks before he had acknowledged death and sorrow as the lot of the people he rallied. A splendour of words, a rallying cry from the wireless that was turning all their lives topsy turvy. Next spring would be an empty promise for so many.

'I'm never easy without him by my side.'

She heard Ma speak as she stood with her back to her daughter, her hands gripping the edge of the high mantle so she seemed to hang crucified there. Vi knew it was true, Ma never really relaxed unless Pa was in his chair by her side, settled for the evening. He used to pull her leg – 'Stop worryin', gel, the door's shut, we're all safely gathered in.'

'You've got me,' Vi said.

'Your pa said that in his letter too.' She let her hands fall to her sides, turned and, as they heard Audrey coming back, said quickly, 'And thank the good Lord for that, thank God.'

Audrey came hurrying in, shedding her wet clothes, full of the news that Noel was going to try to come back at the same time tomorrow morning and take them over to see the WVS lady.

'What about Penzance?' Vi asked.

'Well, if we can get it I'd sooner do this job Noel's finding out about.'

'We've been having a bit of a talk about that,' Ma explained. 'I wouldn't mind taking on a job, give Vi time to have a look round.'

'Suits me,' Audrey said. 'Vi can keep house until she lands the job she wants. Noel's coming on his bike to pick me up again tonight by the way.'

'Perhaps we'll soon all have bikes!' Vi said. 'And you haven't seen what's come yet!'

They were soon all involved in the excitement of the tea chest and its contents.

'Harold's sent something for everyone really. There's even a parcel for Sid.'

'I'd save it for Christmas for him,' Vi suggested. 'He'll be pleased enough with a bar of chocolate now.'

The rest of the day passed in plans for the remaking of the clothes. The newspapers Pa had packed around some of things was pressed flat to be used for paper patterns.

'And,' Ma said triumphantly as the last of the clothes were refolded and the tea chest finally emptied, 'this on its side, with a curtain across the front is our new clothes cupboard.'

'Wish we had three,' Audrey said.

'One's better than none,' Ma said with the utmost satisfaction, adding, 'and it's such a blessing your office manager was always a decent size. These skirts unpicked, pressed and recut'll make two for the likes of us!'

The two girls giggled, remembering the awe, the grudging respect their old office warrior had demanded and received from them.

'She turned out to be quite human didn't she?' Audrey said.

'Yeah,' Vi agreed, holding up an angora jumper, 'larger than life but twice as generous!'

Vi went to sleep that night with the anticipation that there really should be a letter from John in the morning. She looked across to the sleeping form of her friend. Having a fella again had certainly cheered Audrey up. Then there was the real prospect of work for two of them and her shoes were drying downstairs stuffed with the remnants of the newspaper that could not be salvaged, her coat had been pulled into shape and carefully placed on a hanger. Her skirt and blouse were clean, pressed, ready to 'knock'em dead' in Penzance. Events were moving.

She planned – if she managed to secure a position and knew what her wage would be – to spend all the rest of her money, except the bus fare back, to buy John a birthday present. She hoped any interviews would leave her plenty of time to look around the shops. She wondered about something with a seagull on it?

Chapter 19

Noel had been early to pick up Ma and Audrey and had left saying it was possible that they might even start work that day. Sid, hearing half a word about being allowed to walk to school on his own, set off at a run, determined that should there be any change of heart he would be too far away to hear about it.

Vi decided she would wait for the post then aim to catch the midday bus into Penzance. She busied herself pulling out the threads of cotton from the unpicked garments then carefully washing and hanging out the odd-shaped rectangles on the line they had rigged facing the sea. Today was a complete contrast to the grey day before. The wind held the pieces horizontally for many long seconds before slapping them sharply in a sea breeze so full of the ozone Pa seemed to envy them so much.

She suddenly glimpsed the unmistakeable figure of the postwoman cycling along the top road and ran, meeting her halfway down the drive.

'Reckon this'll be what your waiting for.' She beamed, her round cheeks aglow with the wind and the effort. When her nod to the letter brought no information, she set off readily enough with another question. 'You'm ready for Christmas then? Be difficult cooking with everything short, though I eard as 'ow you had a big parcel from Lunnon yesterday.'

'Clothes, Mrs Stevens,' Vi said resisting the postwoman's curiosity as she handed over her letter to go to John and pushed his letter into her skirt pocket. 'A bit of make do and mend. I've washed some pieces, you'd see them on the line as you came along.'

'Thought you'd got some odd bits and pieces!' Mrs Stevens laughed loudly, good-naturedly. 'My son's reared some geese. Could put your name on one for Christmas – he'd not overcharge.'

With a promise to see what her ma said, she saw Mrs Stevens off, warming to this loud, laughing postlady. Curiosity was a kind of interest after all and the offer of a Christmas goose was obviously kindly meant. If she got a job and Ma and Audrey were working, poultry at Christmas might be a possibility. She could imagine Sid's face and the smell – roast goose!

The idea of Christmas treats went with her to the quiet of the kitchen. She drew out John's letter with all the anticipation of a child – but the first words had her quickly on her feet in astonishment, so out of the blue were the contents. The more she read, the more astounded she grew. She read it once, twice, only the third time beginning to appreciate all it did contain.

'Darling Vi,
You will have been as surprised and upset as I was to hear of May's decision. Nothing anyone could say would dissuade her and I realise that your judgment was the right one all along. I will tell you more of this when I see you – suffice it to say now that I just could not let her go off to London on her own.'

Vi paused again at this same point. It was difficult to accept this. Did it change anything between herself and John?

'I have managed to secure a week's leave and plan to be back Thursday. I shall be in touch immediately I'm home.'

A week's leave! That was convenient – a week's leave when he had been so unsure of his hours, his duties.

'Meantime I hope you have not found a new post? Read on, old thing, there's a reason for that remark! Now May has gone, Aunt Annie, or to give her full title, Mrs Caroline St John Trewellan will definitely need someone else. Accounting is, and will be more so as time goes on, a big part of the estate work. If you could manage it, go up to the Lodge any afternoon after you receive this letter (this very day if you can manage it, my love). Aunt Annie says she will be at home every afternoon this week and would like to interview you.
Heaven knows I don't want to rush you into anything – but if you'd consider this post I'd feel that at least it would encourage you to stay around near my home and not rush back to your beloved Pa. You see how well I am coming to know you.
One day I want to walk with you in your Viccy Park but if I have to go away to this wretched war I could imagine you so much better if you were looking after Auntie Annie and had seagulls flying around your dear head.
All my love,
    Yours, John.'

She questioned the swift departure to London, the convenient week's leave. She sat some time rereading bits but decided the most important paragraph was the last. 'Right!' she decided, refolding the letter. 'In with both feet, Violet Tulley. Off to see "Auntie Annie" this afternoon.'

She walked to the Lodge with the sea over to her left, sparkling and beautiful, white horses whipped up on waters reflecting the deep winter-blue sky, while near the cliffs the waves churned and swirled up and up in green and white spume. In the cliff-top fields Paul was ploughing. She thought he was lucky to work with such beauty around him. How could anyone help but feel good.

She was sure he was looking her way and she waved. Not until that second did she remember the stone-throwing. At the cliff edge, Paul reined in the horse and lifted his arm slowly as if unsure of his current rank in the Tulley's popularity stakes. She walked quickly on. She must remind Sid not to tell Paul he knew where the barns and animals were. She was sure this was Cyril Spurrier's new hiding place for his illegal slaughtering. She was also sure that it might be very useful to have this knowledge like an ace up their sleeves.

She turned into the Lodge gates, noticing on this second visit that it had a painted name plate on the open gate – 'Llewellyn Manor Lodge'. So its official title was somewhat posher that just 'the Lodge'. It also reminded her she should have been rehearsing what she was going to say to Mrs Trewellan, what book-keeping system she had practised at Chase & Fieldman's. She should also have given a thought to how much might be a fair wage down here. The landed gentry did not have a great reputation for high wages as far as she'd ever heard, but she ought to get at least a pound a week, twenty-five shillings if she was really lucky.

She felt a little like Alice re-entering Wonderland. The sheltering effect of the rhododendrons and the pines so short a distance from the windblown cliff road was like magic, or privilege. She wondered how much Mrs T knew of her friendship with John? She calculated she might be allowed to trip prettily for a time on the edge of being – what? – 'taken up' by John and employed by the estate, but there was a yawning gulf between good works for evacuees and any kind of real devotion for and from one of their kind. She might not share Ma's inferiority complex, love might well colour her world, but it did not make her a fool. Neither did she intend to be looked down on or patronised by anyone.

Reaching the house, she again wondered what John could mean about 'staying around near his home'? Was this area his real home? Perhaps she was about to find out more. There was, she supposed, always the possibility that Mrs Trewellan of the tweeds and weighty tipping of the buggy was his real aunt. Heaven forbid!

There were bright brown autumn leaves and berried holly in the deep window recesses of Llewellyn Lodge porch, she wondered vaguely if flower arranging had been one of May's talents? She pulled the handle of the bell and heard it jangle deep inside. She remembered the deep stone fireplaces in the hall and sitting room and the welcoming fires that had glowed there, then there was the wonderful old furniture, the deep polish – there must be other help.

She heard a brisk step approaching the door and Mrs Trewellan herself greeted her.

'Ah! Come in.' She turned immediately and led the way to the sitting room, adding over her shoulder. 'You're prompt.'

'I need a job,' she answered. If Mrs Trewellan was able to dispense with preliminaries so was she. 'I intended to go into Penzance this afternoon to look for one there – then John's letter arrived.'

'How are things at Gerrard's Farm?'

Vi felt there was more than one layer to this budding conversation.

'Your mother and your friend, and your brother, of course.' Mrs Trewellan went on leading the way but ignored the businesslike desk and waved to an easy chair, and taking one opposite herself, she sank down into it. Vi thought she did so with some degree of weary resignation – or was it irritation?

'Fine,' she said, thinking that she might have preferred the more upright chairs for this encounter, 'thank you, Mrs Trewellan, though I'd like sometime to talk to you about the rent Mr Spurrier is asking.'

'Rent! Doesn't he have the rent paid through the evacuating authority?' She frowned severely as if this new topic was certainly an irritation.

'It isn't quite that simple,' she said cautiously, then once launched heard herself babbling. 'I suppose because we insisted on staying together – Ma doesn't want any trouble – we're quite willing to pay a reasonable rent. But we did clean the place up, we have made it habitable – from whatever it was used for before . . .'

'Yes.' The affirmative was weighty. Mrs Trewellan regarded her solemnly then asked, 'What do you want me to do?'

'Adjudicate as to what is a fair rent.'

'I'll talk to Spurrier, see what he thinks he's up to.'

Vi cleared her throat, straight talking demanded a more detailed reply. 'There's something you should know first.' She told briefly of her father fixing it for the family to replace another who were unable to travel.

'I see, or I think I do.' She looked fixedly at her until Vi began to wonder just what kind of fool she was, telling this to one of the organisers of the local evacuee reception committee.

'John told me you are as devoted to your pa as *I* know you are to the rest of your family,' Mrs Trewellan said at last, shaking her head slightly as she added, 'devotion often demands an impossible price of people.'

'I'm sure it was unofficial,' she said, pushing to the back of her mind the memory of being in the train toilet and adding their name to the list. 'We'd rather pay any rent than get Pa into trouble – but I hate to see us being taken for fools by . . .'

'Such as Cyril Spurrier,' Mrs Trewellan finished for her. 'Don't worry I can be tactful – firm but tactful! I've certainly learned that skill over this last twenty-five years.'

She was puzzled as to what 'twenty-five years' referred to. She wasn't referring to how long the family had owned the Manor House. She'd understood from Paul that the Trewellan name and village went back into the mists of time, like some of the legends he related.

'John tells me you worked for an accountant in London,' she said, pausing. Then she looked sharply at Vi as if with a new intention. 'You know, I don't think I'm going to be very tactful after all. I'm not a fool and I don't take you for one. I know May wanted to get into the war, but I also know why she's taken the decision into her own hands now. I'll also tell you that I believed, as May did, that she and John would eventually marry. Everyone assumes the same, they've been—'

Vi was on her feet. 'I can understand how you feel. Perhaps I don't understand why you sent for me on the pretence of interviewing me – unless it's to warn me off.'

'Sit down.' Mrs Trewellan waved away the idea. 'You have a lot of lessons to learn. Never assume things against yourself, there'll be enough without imagining them.'

It was as much her matter-of-fact tone of voice as the words that made her sit down again. It was as if the older woman not only completely understood but had trodden some similar path, though why such an idea should enter Vi's mind she had no idea. Mrs St John Trewellan looked every inch an aristocrat.

'I think before we go any further there are some things you must know. My husband is John's father's younger brother.'

'Then you are his real aunt,' she gasped, feeling utterly stupid that she had, even for a second, imagined this woman to be anything other than a lady born and bred. It must have been as big a shock to Mrs Trewellan as it had been to May to realise that a cosy marriage within their own circle was not after all such a certainty.

'I am indeed,' Mrs Trewellan confirmed, 'and you are here because John asked me to see you, but that's not to say I would have had any prejudice against interviewing you anyway – if I'd known your skills.'

Vi bit back the retort 'that's big of you' as it teetered on her lips and saw Mrs Trewellan assess the effort it cost her to stay seated.

'And there's much more you should know. I may be Mrs Trewellan with Trewellan Manor up the drive and Trewellan village along the road but I no more belong to this part of the world than you do. I'm a Londoner like you and my place really should be near my husband while he's at the Admiralty. Would you like some tea?'

Vi floundered now, at once slapped down, then invited to tea! She acknowledged both that and the invitation with a dumb nod as Mrs Trewellan took up and rang a small silver bell from the arm of her chair.

'What I'm doing down here is what I've been doing more or less since John was a toddler, and that is guarding his interest.' She spoke meditatively, as if she reviewed the facts for her own benefit as much as for her visitor. 'John is our only nephew, my sister-in-law's only child – we've not been a productive lot. We have no children and perhaps John told you he was as good as orphaned when his father died.'

'John told me his father was killed in the First World War,' she confirmed.

They paused as a buxom, middle-aged woman Vi thought she might have seen about the village came in to take Mrs Trewellan's order for tea. 'For two of course, Alice,' she added, pausing until the woman had closed the door behind herself.

'He would have been too loyal to tell you that his mother was totally useless after Greville's death. She never coped again. My husband and I were already godparents but we became John's official guardians shortly after we lost Greville – though we never gave up our London home.' She gave an ironic little laugh before adding, 'Keeping John's interests together down here became like a sacred trust.'

'John's interests?'

'He was just ready to take over everything – let us "retire" – when the war came along.'

And me, Violet thought, the Cockney spanner in the Cornish works.

'The Trewellan estate, John's inheritance from the family,' Mrs Trewellan went on to answer her question. 'My husband was the younger brother and frankly not interested in any of this. He's a navy man, went to naval college, enlisted as a boy. The only thing he enjoys down here is messing about in boats. It gets into men's souls. If you're around long enough you'll find that out about John too – there's a lot of the frustrated pirate in him!'

'I'm only "around" now because you asked me here, Mrs Trewellan.'

'I know, m'dear. I meant because of all the things that could happen to anyone, or even all of us before this wretched war is over.' She paused again as Alice came with the tea tray. Vi smiled at the woman but as their eyes met she recognised her as one of the women who had passed Audrey and herself outside the school. The animosity of the returned stare assured Vi she had an enemy here before she started, if she ever started!

'I had a telephone call just before you arrived,' Mrs Trewellan went on after the door had closed, 'from May. Our London home has been badly damaged by the Luftwaffe, fire more than blast I understand. Fortunately my husband was at the Admiralty all night and John and May were with friends. No one has been hurt – only my pride and my precious possessions, all we've collected over the years. I feel sort of violated. Stupid to be attached to *things*.'

170

She paused. 'We packed some and put them in bank vaults but . . .' She appeared to recollect herself. 'I hope your London home is still in tact.'

Vi thought of 11 Brierly Street and of the possessions they all had there – but none so precious as Pa. 'I'm so sorry,' she said, 'you must want to go and see.'

'If there is anything fortunate in the affair it is that John and May are there to help my husband sort things out. He'd be useless on his own – ships in convoys fine, but chairs and cabinets . . . Will you pour out for us?'

The fine china service rattled a little but she managed. Mrs Trewellan thanked her and after sipping several times, brought herself back to the subject of the interview. 'You were going to take your accountancy examinations if you had stayed in London?'

'Yes, if it hadn't been for the war,' she stated, 'but I do have my employer's home address if you would like to contact him for a reference. Our old office has been bombed out.'

Mrs Trewellan tutted in sympathy but accepted the offer of the address. 'Let me show you the office we've set up next to the sitting room here and you can tell me what you think of our systems.'

The ledgers and records revealed that the 'estate' consisted not just of farms with tenants but tin mining and fish marketing interests. It was quite a sizeable business empire. Vi was at once numb with the shock of John's wealth as well as full of professional admiration for Mrs Trewellan's grasp of it all. But she could immediately see where the book-keeping fell a long way short of efficient. She made one or two immediate suggestions which were greeted with the comments that they 'all seemed common sense!'

John's aunt led the way back to the easy chairs and Vi was silent as she was obviously reaching some decision. 'It's rather an unusual situation,' she began, 'you would obviously suit me down to the ground . . . But . . .'

Vi lifted her chin as if in preparation for the final blow, the final judgment that would say that while the war was undoubtedly sweeping away barriers and standards, the fact that it had washed up Violet Tulley was hardly good enough.

'I believe in taking up references, which I shall do, and . . .' Mrs Trewellan paused slowly, entwining and clasping her fingers. 'The other thing I know for a certainty is that if I put obstacles in the way of what John wishes he will only want it all the more.'

Vi knew what was coming. She'd heard of this ploy before in her own neighbourhood – Bethnal Green had its own particular standards. You put the undesirable acquaintance against the other's home background, so it came to be realised what a misfit the intended was. *Now* she understood May's comment about 'the possibilities after the war, who will be where?'

It felt like a challenge. One thing she wondered, had John deliberately not told her of his real position in case it had frightened her away? She knew that, having come this far, she could not retreat. That wasn't something she knew how to do. *As good as anyone*, she told herself, then aloud asked, 'So I have a chance of the job?'

'Subject to a satisfactory reference, I'd like you to start as soon as possible. I desperately need someone here to answer the telephone and deal with callers. The sooner I replace May, the sooner I can go to London and sort out what's left of my poor home.'

Vi was silent.

'Is something wrong?'

'I'm sure you'll find my reference all right, but we haven't said anything about pay,' she answered quietly. 'I don't intend to come as a kind of free apprentice girlfriend.'

'Fifteen shillings a week,' Mrs Trewellan answered as slick as any true Cockney dealer.

'I did get quite a bit more in London,' she said coolly. 'Twenty-five shillings.'

'London wages hardly apply here.' Her lips were tight, controlled, as she made her final offer. 'A pound, you cycle home and are here at nine o'clock tomorrow.'

'I haven't—'

'The bicycle goes with the job.'

Chapter 20

Thursday came and there was no news of John's return. Friday morning Vi cycled to the Lodge in a state of apprehensive excitement – eager to see him, eager to have answers, eager to confront him with all he had not told her. If he had arrived on Thursday's late train she might see him immediately, or at least his aunt would have news of him.

She arrived to find Alice at the door – in charge.

'My Charlie's driven Mrs Trewellan to catch the early train to London. I'm to keep an eye on *everything*.' She nodded briskly to emphasise the fact that the instruction would definitely include Vi. She reached behind Vi's back to polish the door handle as if she wished she could eliminate this London intruder as easily as her fingermarks on the brass.

'Has something happened?'

'Nothing I suppose that need concern you,' Alice said, 'there was a phone call.'

'Thank you, Alice,' she answered, mimicking the exact tones Mrs Trewellan used, 'you may carry on then.'

'It's the carrying on others do that concerns me,' she snapped and for a moment looked as if she were about to engage in a full-scale onslaught. Instead she turned abruptly and went back to her kitchen.

Vi hurried through to her desk looking for a note, some message, instruction, or explanation from Mrs Trewellan – but there was nothing. Something more must have happened – and John it seemed was not back.

She fidgeted with the papers and account books, with the work she was already involved in, bringing together several farm records into a master ledger. Try to work, work and wait. She wouldn't give Alice any satisfaction by making any further enquiry of her. Mrs Trewellan was a polite old pussycat compared with the thorny Alice. She tried to concentrate on the figures before her. Heaven knows there was enough to do and she hadn't begun to learn to deal with the enquiries that came in daily about repairs, disputes, complaints. They would pile up while Mrs T was away.

And John? How was it he could just stay away when it suited him? Or wasn't he able to come back? Images of people trapped in bombed buildings had her pacing the room. She wished she had someone to share her worries with but even if she went back to the farm for the day she'd be on her own. Anyway, she wouldn't give Alice the chance of being able to report that she had left her post.

Ma and Audrey were the happiest they had been since their evacuation, both really enjoying the sociable atmosphere as they worked together. 'It's how we imagined it would be on the first job,' Audrey said, 'and guess what! They need someone else, so I'm going to let Doris know!' And Sid, he was happy running off all over on his own.

She suddenly envied them, felt beleaguered at this desk, in this house, or was she just out of her league – without John here certainly no one else wanted her around. The unease became a more positive thing and she suddenly sensed she was being watched. Glancing up, she saw Alice in the garden, arms akimbo, watching her through the window.

She jumped up again, a straight open fight she understood. She mirror-imaged the pose of the woman outside – and they stood so, ridiculous, ungiving until they both heard the sound of Charlie coming back with the trap. Vi knew she could win now, Alice would go and see her husband, check the old man had done the job right. He worked as gardener-handyman and Vi had already twice seen him skulking in the rhododendrons out of his wife's sight.

She was right. Alice gave up with an irritable toss of her head and departed. Vi still stood at the window in the same stance, vaguely listening for Charlie's inquisition to begin, then gave an exasperated sigh at the futility of the vendetta.

'That sounded heartfelt,' a man's voice said from the doorway.

She span round. 'John?' She queried the possibility of the tall rather weary-looking figure. 'John! I didn't hear you, where have you sprung from?'

'First things first,' he said, came forward and took her into his arms, holding her tight and long, as if just savouring her nearness, then pushing his face down into her neck, he murmured, 'you don't know how good it is to see you, to hold you again. It's like a cure, we should bottle it.'

She surrendered herself to him with a gurgle of swift laughter then was silent for long, unthinking, uncritical moments, aware only of the feel of him, the smooth strong cloth of his uniform against her cheek and a vague smell that suggested utter weariness, like she remembered on wardens and workers in the Blitz. She clung tighter, as if to aid her understanding. Brickdust and perspiration, she thought. There was so much to be explained, but most important he was home. 'What's happened? Have you just come back?'

'This very minute,' he said, 'in the trap with Charlie. Auntie Annie went off, we just had time for a short chat . . .'

'Oh!' she said, but there were more pressing questions. 'Something's hap-

174

pened, hasn't it? You stayed longer than you said and your aunt wasn't planning to go today.'

'Yes.' He turned away, walked two paces to look out of the window as he told her. 'Some people were found in the cellar of their home under the burnt-out section.' She could see his jaw muscles flexing as he clenched his teeth. 'It was a good deep arched cellar, strong as a bridge. We all used it if there was a raid while we were in town. My uncle allowed one of our old maids to take her daughter and her grandchildren down there regularly because she hated sleeping in the crowded tube stations so much. The smoke I think had got them first, or I hope to God it had.'

'You saw . . .'

'I helped get them out – and identify them. I knew them all – such a bloody waste of young lives.'

'Perhaps a good thing so many children have been evacuated,' she mused aloud.

'The bombing's terrible. I never realised. London seems totally devastated. It's more in the front line than . . .' He turned as he spoke and saw the alarm on her face. 'No, Brierly Street's all right, old thing. Not touched. I went to see on your behalf. I couldn't remember the number, but I found it . . .'

'You . . .'

'I saw this man coming along in a bus driver's uniform . . .' He spread his hands wide. 'I couldn't just let him walk by. I asked him if he was Mr Tulley.' He smiled at her. 'He said "yes", pushed back his cap and looked exactly like you are doing now.'

'You met my pa,' she said, wanting to laugh and cry at the same time, 'just like that, in the street, I can't believe it.'

'Walking home to eleven Brierly Street, large as life and twice as handsome!'

'John don't joke about this. Is he really all right? Does he look . . .'

'He looks fine. He took me home and fussed over me. I think I came in for all the attention he really wanted to lavish on you, your mother and brother. He couldn't stop asking questions. He asked me if I was a friend of yours?'

'And what did you say?'

'I said of course, why else would I look up on her pa, and he agreed with me. "That's right," he said. We both felt sort of overjoyed I think. We kept patting each other on the back to a quite extraordinary extent.'

It seemed bizarre in the calm quiet of the Lodge, listening to him describing Albert and Maggie Moore, Roy's parents, sorting newspapers in the front room. She wondered if Pa had explained precisely who they were? But John was racing on about her pa lighting the fire, making tea, producing a parcel of sausages from his workbag and frying them up.'

'Don't make fun of my pa or my home – ever!'

He stopped mid-detail of the excellence of the sausages plus bread fried in their fat. 'Vi,' he shook his head at her severely, 'don't ever think such a thing. Don't suggest it.' He took both her hands. 'There's so much disaster and heartache, when something good happens, it just makes you feel light-headed. You want people to share your enjoyment. Then coming home and finding you here, knowing you came so quickly. I love you, love you, love you.' He squeezed and shook her hands with each repeated phrase.

Before he could embrace her again she stepped back out of range. 'There are other things.'

'What is it?' he asked. 'What have I done?'

'Or not done would be more to the point. You didn't tell me Mrs St John Trewellan is your real aunt and that you own half of Cornwall.'

'A slight exaggeration and it never seemed to come into the conversation,' he said, shrugging lightly, unconcerned. 'Did it matter?'

'Matter?' It was her turn to purse her lips, taking a comic suck at the air. 'Nooo, it doesn't matter. Your aunt obviously thinks I'm a gold-digger, Alice thinks I should be either shot or hung and what the rest of your friends and acquaintances think – well, I can guess.'

'I love you.'

'Daring to throw my cap at the lord of the manor – and you are, aren't you? That's what you are.' She had said the words unwittingly but now the truth of them made her angry with him all over again, standing there looking as if all this was quite by the way, of no importance.

'I love you.'

'So now I know what you are, and you know exactly where I spring from. The East End, Bethnal Green.'

'I love you.'

'Well, I don't love you.' She rounded on him fairly now. 'I don't even know who you are! It makes me want to kick your bleeding shins!'

'Really! Well I feel a bit light-headed with lack of sleep and no breakfast – could do with some more of your pa's sausages really – so go ahead if it'll help.' He collapsed back into a chair thrust out his long legs and held up his arms as in surrender.

'It might, it just might!' For a moment she contemplated throwing herself at him, pummelling him with her fists. But, seeing him relax in the chair – head back, the light emphasising the long weary lines etching his cheeks – seeing how pale he was, she decided not to. Instead, she knelt by him, put her arms around his waist and her head on his chest. He let his arms fall slowly around her again, like a shawl, she thought, warm and gentle. She must really try to be different, to be more tender.

'So why me? Why me and not May?' She moved her cheek on the roughness of his jacket, inhaled the faintly soapy smell of wool overlaid by that of travel, dust and cigarette smoke.

'Ah!' he exclaimed, teasing. 'There's a question.'

176

'No, I need to know.'

'Humm!'

Now she pummelled gently at his side.

'May's a beautiful schemer, the sort of sister every man should have to help him through his schooldays. I learned a lot from May about how a woman's mind works, the tactics of getting your own way.'

She was silent, wondering if he fell for the scheming type? She fell to reasoning with herself that it *was* usually for the benefit of others that she could be devious. She looked up to find him grinning down at her.

'You're what my uncle would call "heart-led and conscience-stricken".'

'I don't—'

'Well, you quite rightly fall in love with me. Then you worry about it. Now, if you suddenly discovered my family were totally impoverished that would put your mind at rest!'

'Oh yes, that's another thing. How come your name is John Manners – if your family name is Trewellan?'

'John Greville Manners Trewellan,' he said.

Vi was silent, transfixed for a moment by this latest piece of information, then breathed, 'Wot a moniker!'

He guffawed, gently jolting her on his chest but not opening his mouth. It was the laugh of one whose body is totally exhausted and, having relaxed, finds it difficult to make much further effort.

'Tulley, Trewellan, the initial's the same,' he said and, leaning sideways in the chair, he pushed a hand into his trouser pocket and brought out a small box. 'This was my mother's. I want you to have it.'

'But . . .' She hesitated to take the black velvet-covered box. Even the box, she thought, was old, square, quality.

He placed it in her palm. 'Open it.'

She pressed the tiny gold rod which protruded from the side and opened the box slowly, like one saying 'Open Sesame' for the first time. She gasped as she looked inside. Glittering between black velvet and gold-lettered satin was a diamond brooch in the shape of an elaborate 'T'.

'Lucky that wasn't it, same initial. Put it on, old thing.'

She was totally overwhelmed. 'It must be so valuable.'

'It wants wearing, not locking up in a vault.'

Very gingerly, she unpinned the brooch from the velvet and gasped as the sunlight caught the stones and made a galaxy of prisms. 'It's so beautiful. I really . . .' She glanced up, shaking her head at the total unacceptability of such a gift. But his eyes were closed and, though she took his hand and gently said his name, he did not stir. His face had relaxed and he seemed to smile as he slept.

She knelt holding his gift, amazed at the quality but more amazed at the thought that not only he had been involved in digging people from buildings and seeing May off to the war, he had also fetched this piece of jewellery from a vault *and* been to her home and seen her pa!

The last thought made her go to stand before the mirror above the fireplace and very carefully pin the brooch on her jumper. Just at that moment there was a tap on the door and Alice entered.

'There's a messenger come down from the Manor for Mr John,' she began, then her eyes were riveted first on the brooch, then on the exhausted sleeping figure.

Her instinct was to tell the woman that, no she hadn't knocked him out and robbed him but, as Alice came further into the room as if she would disturb John, Vi stepped forward, urgently waving her away.

'No,' she whispered, 'whoever it is will have to come back, or leave his message,' Vi told her. 'John's exhausted. I'm going to let him sleep where he is for a while.'

Alice had left her with difficulty, tearing her gaze from Vi's bosom and herself from the room – but it seemed to Vi she had crossed some kind of Rubicon. She had given a direct order and Alice had obeyed, ungraciously, not in the same fawning manner she obeyed Mrs T – which Vi despised – but she had obeyed.

Vi went quietly to her desk, sometimes working, sometimes just watching him as he slept on silently, unstirring. She worried about him being cramped when he woke and once had to make sure he was still breathing because he was so motionless. Even peering closely, it was difficult to see his chest moving. She ignored her allotted lunch break so as not to disturb him, but not long afterwards she heard the front door bell and Alice tramp to answer it. Again the door was tapped, and this time Alice looked more certain of her errand. 'Mr John's commanding officer, Major Fitson, is here and must speak to him.'

'I'll call him in a few minutes,' she said. 'I'll rouse him and then come and fetch the Major.' She stood motionless until Alice turned and left to deliver her message.

She knelt again before the chair, 'Come on,' she breathed, 'you have me ordering Majors about now as well as Alice.' She touched his hands, and his cheeks, whispered, then said his name more loudly. Without her being conscious that he had woken, he suddenly seized her arms, gripping her so tightly it made her wince. 'John, its me, Vi. Vi!' she insisted.

'Oh God. I'm sorry,' he exclaimed as full consciousness and recognition came. He slackened his grip but did not release her. 'I must have fallen asleep, I'm sorry. Do you like it?' he asked, seeing the brooch on her jumper.

'Now I'm used to the idea.' When he looked puzzled, she added, 'You've been asleep five hours. I'm only waking you now because your Major's waiting to see you.'

'Waiting?' He frowned, looked at his wristwatch in disbelief. 'You robbed me of all that time in your company,' he accused.

178

'No,' she told him, 'I was here, watching over you, guarding you from Alice. Now she does think I've robbed you.' She put her hand over the brooch.

John stretched. 'Alice has always been more of a social snob than anyone in the family – but duty calls then.'

'I'll get something to eat . . .'

'Best let me see what's on with the bossman first.' He kissed her briefly on the nose then, rubbing his hand over his stubble, added, 'I must be revolting.'

'I've seen you looking better.'

'Vote of confidence accepted – see you later, you flatterer you.'

They grinned at each other, kissed, leaning over to touch lips, and he went out to meet his officer.

It was beginning to get dark when the telephone rang. It was John, though he sounded distant, official, as if there were other people who could hear what he said.

'Go along home at your usual time, old thing.'

'John?'

'Don't worry,' he said and put down the telephone.

She was home first, even before Sid, it seemed, for the usual tumble of school clothes where he changed before rushing out to find Paul were not there. She hoped he arrived home before Ma. There was a casserole of vegetables in the oven and, as instructed, Vi found and added two small leftover back portions from a rabbit Paul had shot for them earlier in the week. She topped up the gravy too with a little more water from the kettle. She changed, laid the table, made up the fire, thought of the poem Ma used to say at Brierly Street, and all the time she could hear John's voice say, 'Go along home, old thing. Don't worry.' She wondered if there could be two words more designed to make you do just the opposite.

She told herself she might have wondered before, but *now* she worried. Men were embarking for war – women too, May included . . . She wondered about Noel. Would Audrey have heard anything from him? She found herself upstairs again, checking on the diamond brooch as if unsure it had really happened. 'You never expected to find yourself in a place like this,' she told the small velvet box as it stood mid-centre of the tea chest that Ma was in the middle of converting into a clothes store.

It was really only when she heard the lorry bring the others home that she remembered about Pa – she had all that to tell. Though the whereabouts of Sid would be the first concern. The thought had hardly come to her mind when there was a clump of shoes up the stairs, followed by Sid's voice with that familiar note of trouble in it. 'Sis?' Then his head appeared around the bedroom door.

'What've you done?' she asked, adding to prompt a speedy reply, 'Ma's on her way down the drive.'

179

He came in and stuck out his bum in her direction. His school trousers had a large V-shaped tear and were filthy.

'Get 'em off quick. They're got to be mended washed and pressed before tomorrow morning.' She hurried to help him into his old trousers. 'We'll eat first, everyone'll feel better then.'

'Do you 'ave to tell?' he asked without too much enthusiasm for the coming evening.

'Wot d'you think?' she asked with a nod to the state of the trousers. 'And hurry up I've things to tell you all – about Pa.'

The meal eaten and all the stories told, Vi rather hesitantly produced the brooch.

Ma held it reverently. 'And he told Pa he was your chap?'

She nodded excitedly.

'You and an officer – a landowner!' Audrey exclaimed. 'Is this the Violet Tulley who helped me push Mr Sidney around in the pram! You used to hate that game, just *pretending* we were nursemaids to the gentry.'

'I know, I know, all you're saying.'

'So Mrs Trewellan is his aunt and Trewellan village and all that is to do with his family,' Audrey repeated, gingerly taking the brooch Ma offered for her to hold.

'Did you really used to call me Mr Sidney?' Sid asked. 'I could tell my mates that at school.'

'I wouldn't if you want to keep them mates,' Vi warned. 'Don't take kindly to us having airs and graces the locals.'

'I reckon,' Audrey went on, weighing the brooch as if making a valuation, 'if he's handing out the family jewels you've as good as got him in the bag.'

Ma looked at her with eyes full of questions and worries. 'I 'ope you're not going to get hurt.'

'I love him,' she said simply with a shrug of accepting the inevitable. 'I'm sure I love him as much as you love Pa.'

'That's all right then,' Ma said and folded her hands across her apron in satisfaction. 'This evacuation ain't such a bad lark – if only we didn't 'ave to 'ave the war as well.' Ma didn't often philosophise, didn't often have such an air of contentment about her. 'Isn't it nice to think your John saw my Harold and they 'ad something to eat together?'

'Sausages!' Sid exclaimed. 'I wish I'd been there.'

'And me,' Ma echoed quietly.

'It makes me wonder where I'll end up,' Audrey added wistfully, returning the brooch into Vi's hands.

Chapter 21

Cycling to the Lodge the next morning, Vi was early and anxious but there was something more – an unease, some disturbance of the morning, another sound drifting in the air on the edge of hearing? She tried to listen, identify – the waves, the wind, the movement of her tyres over the road, the occasional ricochet of a pebble. She stopped pedalling as she reached a slight decline but the ticking of the freewheel still did not allow her to hear properly.

Even though she was so keen to arrive, to see if there was a message, or, better still, if John himself was waiting for her, she stopped her bicycle.

She decided it might be some kind of farm machinery for it sounded as if it was crushing something between stones with a regular beat. It was slowly coming closer so it did seem that she and whatever it was were going to meet. She pedalled on, wondering if it was a steam engine of some kind?

Then, as she neared the drive, she recognised the sound for what it was – many boots in unison, men marching in columns. She stood watching the curve of the cliff-top road, holding her bicycle, a reception party of one, remembering all the ranks of soldiers and evacuees she had seen marching to the stations in London. Men en route for war, others, like herself, banished to wait in unfamiliar places. Was this what Major Fitson had wanted John for, was this the meaning behind the firm but subdued 'go home, old thing.'

Round the corner came the first column, in full marching order, rifles, khaki webbing with munition pouches on their chests, bayonets, water bottles, large packs on their backs. Soldiers marching in ranks had been part of her City life since she left school, waved at by girls, crawled behind by City traffic, always given a kind of send-off by whoever was around. There was nothing here to mark their progress and she gasped as column after column came on towards her. The noise seemed to deafen her, to crush her with disabling force – all these men, these young men.

'Wish us luck then?' one called to her as they passed.

She swallowed hard. 'I do,' she said but it was no more than a whisper, her throat tight. Then, as if one at least saw and understood, a tender clear voice

181

began to sing words learned from an earlier generation who had fought the previous war to end all wars.

'Keep the Home Fires Burning' the young sweet tenor urged and before many lines the yearning words were taken up. The melody spread and swelled to the group, from unit to unit, seeming to Vi at one moment tuneful with hope, then deep and gruff with sorrow as, trapped within the metrical beat of their own tramping feet, they were carried relentlessly on and away.

She had to dash the tears from her eyes so she could see clearly, but no one above the rank of sergeant appeared to be marching with the men. Then, as the song ended, someone began to whistle 'Colonel Bogey' and they seemed to march away quicker, swagger with the whistle and the lusty, 'And the same to you.' She stood on and on, listening long after they were again out of sight. She began to wonder if she was going to see John any more? Had the officers gone first? How did the army work?

When finally she pushed her cycle up the drive to the Lodge, Alice came bustling out the front door, hat and coat on, full of importance.

'*You'll* not be wanted! At least not for long, I've had a message. I've sent my husband away – need the place for extra work connected with that lot leaving. I've not to come again until I hear from Mrs Trewellan.' She cocked her head first towards the Manor House and then after the distant troops. 'Reckon you've wasted a lot of your time coming 'ere at all.'

'I'll probably 'ave more of that than you do so don't fret yourself.' She pushed the cycle quickly past the woman not wishing her to see she was upset.

'At least I know *where* I belong,' Alice shouted after her.

'I'll remind you should you ever forget,' Vi shouted back.

Angry was not the best frame of mind to park your bike and enter some-one else's empty house, to find the flower vases had been removed from the porch, that though the door was open and the key in the lock, there were no fires lit. Alice's extreme efficiency added to her sense of bleakness. But it was very odd, she thought, to take over another house when so many men were obviously moving out. That it might be for something very secret, and prob-ably not for long, was all she could think. From what she had heard, Mrs Trewellan certainly made frequent trips to London but never stayed more than a couple of days. They surely couldn't take both her homes . . .

She decided that if her desk was cleared, the farm accounts put out of the way, then she presumed she should go home, but all the ledgers were as she had left them – and Alice could certainly have been trusted to have locked her out unless specifically told not to do so.

Wait and see – and work – and she soon decided to light the fires. They were laid and whoever was coming would surely prefer to be warm. If no one turned up by early afternoon, she'd just let them go out.

She revived the wood-burning stove in the kitchen and was making herself tea when she heard a vehicle screech to a halt on the gravel drive. She ran through to the hall and met John in full uniform rushing in at the front door. Behind him, she could see a jeep with the driver waiting, grinning, engine running before John flung closed the door.

'John . . . ?'

He grabbed her hands. 'Don't talk, old thing, just listen. I'm off to Penzance station to see some of the men away. They're on the move, and me soon . . . but not quite yet. I'm coming back here. You'll wait?'

She nodded dumbly, thinking, *Keep the home fires burning*. Thinking, *He already looks lost to me with his uniform and his swagger stick. He belongs to the army, to his country, to the war*. 'Is anyone else coming here. Alice said—'

'I'll explain later.' He grinned, that fleeting boyish roguery out of place on the lean-faced officer – gleaming Sam Browne belt, holster, lanyard, revolver, turning her heart with the agony, the coming trauma. 'You'll be all right here on your own?' He queried the look on her face. 'Until I get back.'

'Of course,' she told him briskly. 'Go on. The quicker you go, the quicker you'll be back.'

'That's the spirit!' He gave her a swift hug, kissed her briefly on the lips, turned and was out the door. The jeep drove away in a flurry of gravel, with John's arm lifted briefly from the sidelight.

'That's keeping a stiff upper lip,' she told herself, 'sending 'em off with a smile.' She turned and, seeing her beret had fallen from the hall chair, kicked it hard – twice, three times – then picked it up, dusted it down and laid it carefully on top of her coat. 'I was in and out of his arms so quick I feel almost spat out,' she explained. 'And my arms . . . so empty now. What you've never had you never miss, but . . .' She folded her own arms around herself, dreading a worse parting to come but when? Did 'and me soon' mean on the next train? Tomorrow? Next week?

She tried to work just to fill the emptiness, the empty house. She wondered if waiting for someone and not knowing when or if they would return from the war was as bad or worse than knowing the final truth. She thought of Audrey and the bleak look of real bereavement that came unwittingly to her face so often. 'No,' she decided, 'while there's life – or not news of death – there's hope.' Even people who had telegrams "missing presumed dead" hoped.

Then she gasped as a huge blot from the nib of her fountain pen dropped down on to the new ledger. This concentrated her mind. She picked up her blotting paper and, with the corner, very carefully inserted it into the middle of the blob of ink, and allowed it to be drawn up into the paper, limiting the extent of the damage. In the drawer was a very hard, dirty ink eraser which she dropped back. She could have wished for the bottles of the ink-eradicating fluids from the old London office. This carelessness made her really cross with herself, spoiling the look of the immaculate ledger. 'Harriet would not be pleased,' she decided, 'and neither am I.'

She strode about, then went to the kitchen. It was cosy now and, with her head full of all the old warnings from her grandmother about chilblains, she slipped off her shoes and lodged her feet on the hot oven door. She might eat her sandwiches early. She thought of the small greaseproof-wrapped parcel in her coat pocket. She wondered about putting her coat and hat on and going outside, looking up and down the road for a while – but she reminded herself she was being paid to work. She tutted again at the thought of the blot and went back to her ledger.

'A blot right on the name of Trewellan.' She shook her head. She had not realised until that moment. 'Payment to the Trewellan Greater Farm', she had headed the page and the blot was centre name. She could take it as an omen. Alice certainly would.

Then, hand on ledger, she stood stock-still, listening. A vehicle drew up in the drive, a door slammed and she heard John's voice call to his driver. 'Give me as long as you can.'

The words seemed to encapsulate everything and she was overwhelmed by the thought of all she – all the world – was embarked upon – and by the thought that she had not as yet begun the difficult part. She answered when he called but waited where she was taking the extra seconds to try to order her feelings.

He came throwing his cap and stick on to a chair. 'What is it?' he asked. 'Has someone telephoned already?'

'No, nothing's happened.' She shook her head then laughed shakily. 'Well, I've blotted your name. Look!'

He came and put his arms around her waist, looking down over her shoulder and she leaned back against him. 'Good gracious,' he said gently, 'but do you know what, it won't be near so noticeable by the time you've written in the whole page.'

'John.' She turned in his arms, trying to push away thoughts that this moment might be all they ever had. 'I do love you. No matter what ever anyone ever says or thinks, I love just you.'

'And you must always remember, old thing,' he began holding her with a close cherishing, 'that "just me" is what my past has made me, just as "just you" is all that your ma and pa and Bethnal Green made you. I love all that because it made you. I'd like you to love Trewellan – even the spiky Alice in time – because it's part of what I am.'

'Yes, I'll try always to remember,' she told him, adding with mock seriousness, 'Alice may be the biggest stumbling block. When will the other people be here?'

'What other—'

'Alice said . . .'

'Ah! I just had to get her out of the way somehow. I could hardly . . .'

'Admit you wanted your girlfriend on her own in your aunt's home!' *This is being in love*, she thought, *white lies, the oldest game in the world.* 'But she said a day or two.'

'I had this awful feeling she wouldn't have let me get away with it, and you have to exaggerate with Alice. If I say a day or two she will at least stay away until teatime. It's true,' he added as she shook her head at him. 'She's still got a cricket bat she confiscated when I was fifteen.'

'You are a fool!' She punched at him, then wished she hadn't. Pa said it was a stupid habit to get into – led to trouble – but that was married people.

'If we're going to box I'll take this harness off, for a while anyway.' He began to unbuckle his belt.

'Let me do it,' she said taking over. 'I saw a film once about knights of old and their ladies having to help them off with their armour.'

'They also used to have to help them bathe, but I'll let you off that one this time.'

'Is that true though?'

'Yes, I'm sure. May was the expert on ancient history. She'd tell you in a flash.' He turned to throw his jacket, belt and holster on to the chair.

'Yes, I'm sure of that.' She must stop feeling she had fallen into an unseen rut everytime he mentioned May. She would, Vi supposed, be part of this past she had to grow to cherish, along with Alice.

'I need a drink.' He went to the sideboard cellaret, questioned her with a look but she shook her head. 'Seeing men off you've trained for months and wondering if and when you'll ever see most of them again is not the best way to spend a morning.'

In the hall the telephone suddenly jangled, making Vi start and John swear. 'It'll be for me,' he told her, taking his brandy with him.

He came back after no more than two yeses and a no. She waited, holding her breath. 'I have to go to London tomorrow on the early train,' he told her and she sat down quickly on the arm of the chair, her knees unsteady. 'This is why I wanted to see you today. I have to fly out in two days, but I've permission to go to London first. I must see my aunt and one or two other people, there are things to settle before I go. I want to ask you to come with me.'

'To London?'

'We could see your pa of course – then when I've gone . . .'

'John . . .' For all her stoicism, all her resolve, tears sprang to her eyes and ran unheeded down her cheeks. 'I can't bear this, I can't bear to think this may be all.' She wanted to say that all she would have would be a diary, a brooch and a broken heart for the rest of her life.

He took her back into his arms, took a khaki handkerchief of fine soft cotton and blotted her tears. 'I am rather hoping I'll come back,' he told her.

'I'm rather hoping that too,' she told him, trying to smile.

'Tears make your eyes very bright.'

'And red!'

185

'Quick, kiss me before the rot sets in.'

Once their lips met, there was no more pretence, no more fooling. Their feelings flamed and, when finally their lips parted, it was with the mutual knowledge that this was not enough. 'I have a bedroom here,' he said.

Her only answer was to take his hand as if she would lead the way, though she did not know it. When he lifted and laid her on the bed she told him as much. 'Trust me,' he said, 'just let it happen.' He put his hand forward on to her breast with a kind of exploratory gentleness. 'You're not afraid? Tell me if you want me to stop.' Then, as drew nearer to her, he slipped his hand inside her jumper, adding gruffly, 'But tell me soon.'

'I wouldn't do that,' she told him, 'and I'm not afraid.' Inside her head she defied all the warnings she'd ever had and pledged that this was her bed and she'd take whatever consequences.

'I'll never do anything to harm you,' he breathed, bending to put his lips in the cup of her shoulder. 'Never.'

He was so gentle she wanted to cry, her arousal so complete it all felt so right so natural and she so complete in his love.

'Sweet Violet,' he whispered when he lay still. 'I do love you.'

So that, she thought triumphantly, was married love. *I'm a real blot on his family now*, she thought. *And, Alice, I'll take some rubbing out.* 'And I love you too,' she said aloud, joying in the words, making the admission as if it were to the world.

'Until?' he prompted.

'The seagulls stop flying,' she said, then they both fell to giggling about the lady photographer.

'And I have the prints you know,' he was saying when the sound of his jeep sweeping back into the drive scattering the gravel instantly sobered them. He leaned over to kiss her once more. 'I'll bring them later if I may – to show your mother?'

She nodded her head as they dressed and he went to the door. She heard him tell his driver he would be two minutes. He came back with his jacket half on, carrying his Sam Browne and holster. She helped him button his jacket, buckle his belt, and this time the new intimacy made a stronger bond, the action more poignant. It felt more like fable, knights and ladies.

'Bye, old thing, see you later at the farm. Not sure about time, but this evening because of the train tomorrow?'

'I understand,' she said, 'I'll talk to Ma as soon as she's home.'

Chapter 22

There were, she learned, other officers from the Manor travelling together in another first-class compartment and, after a couple of hours as the train left Cornwall behind, John explained he needed to ask his fellow officers a favour before he could make plans for their time in London.

Left alone, she wondered about a small hotel with the two of them together, signing in as Mr and Mrs John Smith, buying a curtain ring at Woolworths. Audrey had once told her in excited whispers of 'an affair' arranged like that. She closed her eyes as the speed of the express began to blur the images outside the window, but immediately her mind was full of its own images, echoing with the voices of Ma, Sid and Audrey when they had arrived home the evening before and she had told them of John's coming visit – and the proposed trip to London. She felt they had looked at her with disbelief and that Ma might at any moment reach up and feel her brow for signs of a fever.

When John had arrived carrying a box of toys and books he had unearthed from the Manor House attics, this event seemed to make the other more acceptable – and Sid had been like one possessed. A football, books such as *The Boys' Favourite Story Book, Boys' Book of Adventures, Boys' Campfire Yarns*, a cricket ball and stumps – she and John had exchanged private smiles at the lack of a bat – a couple of jigsaws and, to Sid's great joy, a box of soldiers, – guardsmen in red, right legs stretched out, marching off their stands, rifles on shoulders.

It had certainly served to moderate any awkwardness Ma had felt in the presence of John Manners Trewellan. Sid's enthusiasm was too overwhelming, his pleasure infected them all – except Audrey. She had provided the one sour note with the comment, 'That knocks on the head anything we could do for Christmas.' She also exclaimed, 'Who's paying?' when John broached the subject of Vi going with him to London.

She remembered that he had shown his innate authority as he allowed his voice to raise the merest fraction, otherwise ignoring the comment and going on, 'My regiment is on embarkation leave but some of us have to go out ahead . . .' Vi's heart had plummeted as he had added 'quite soon'.

There had been little sleep after John had gone. Ma had suddenly become so excited at the thought of Vi actually going to see her pa. She had sat on and on, her four steel knitting needles flashing in the lamplight to finish the pair of socks that had been for Christmas originally, but which now Vi was to take with her – and all the time she remembered things for Vi to look for, to check up on. 'See what crockery he's letting Mr & Mrs Moore use. See its the second best out of the front room china cabinet.' 'Check he's letting the coalman drop a bag in every week.' 'Have a look round the Green see what's what.' 'Go see our neighbours of course *and* wouldn't it be nice if you came across Miss Swanton, you tell her about the job you've got and that we're remaking her clothes.'

Sid should have been long asleep when he wandered sleepily down, clutching the box of soldiers in one hand and, in the other, 'My best amethyst pieces for Pa. Tell him they're my fangs, show him how to put them in his mouth,' he ordered. 'And tell him all about Major and that I go to school by myself at last!'

'Give her time to catch breath when she's back home.' Audrey had ushered him back to bed and, significantly it seemed to the other two, she stayed upstairs herself.

When finally Vi had gone to bed, her candle flickering across the still form of her friend, she had cautiously whispered Audrey's name, adding the promise, 'I'll go to the cemetery.'

Audrey immediately propped herself up in bed. 'Thanks,' she said and, reaching over, released into Vi's hand a hot half-crown she must have been clutching for a long time. 'Will you buy a Christmas wreath and lay it for me?' she asked. When they had both settled for sleep, she added very quietly, 'You've found your fella'.

Vi found her thoughts, the words, arranging themselves into a pattern and fitting to the tiddle-de-dum, tiddle-de-dee rhythm of the wheels over the rails: John's kit up above; the one that I love. Bombs blast and fire; back to see Pa. She remembered the crowded journey down, washing nappies in the toilet. She wondered what had happened to the girl called Mary, with her sister's baby, Wendy?

She awoke as the carriage door was slid open and looked up to see John smiling down at her. 'So that's all fine! My friends'll take my kit to the barracks so I can go with you to your home first and can show my face later.'

'I could just find my way home from Paddington Station. I don't want to be in your way.'

'No chance, old thing. We're going to be late in and it'll be dark quite soon. I'm not letting you out of my sight for a moment longer than really necessary.' He took her hand, moving it gently, threading his fingers through hers as if memorising both the look and the feel. 'I want to ask Auntie Annie to show you all over the Manor while its empty briefly, tell you how it was, and, once the army have finished with the place, I want you to help us put it back into order.'

He paused to look at her and she felt her throat tighten, thicken with emotion, and she had to grit her teeth not to cry. 'After the war . . .' He shook his head, as if abandoning what he had planned to say and going urgently on with what he needed to say, 'I want you to wait for me, Violet. I promised myself I wouldn't ask this because it's not fair.'

'You don't have to ask, I would wait for you anyway. I love *you* I don't want anyone else.' She thought she sounded almost foot-stamping petulant and added more gently, 'Tell me just what you want me to do.'

'Learn as much as you can, business, house. Aunt Annie will be your friend I know. Promise you will stay at Trewellan until I come back from overseas.'

'I promise.'

'And I want you to meet Uncle Jimmie too – he's a great guy!' He relaxed back into his seat. 'We have a lot to do.'

And little time to do it, she thought. *Memories, that's what we have to make, memories to store for barren days – but will there be enough to last?* 'We have to make every second count don't we?' It was more pledge than question.

Paddington Station was awash with uniforms, men and women from every branch of the services, most of them laden with their kit. Vi briefly met John's companions who took over John's holdall and went on their way with a cheery, 'See you later, old boy! Don't do anything we wouldn't!'

As they made their way to the exit it was the smell that Vi remembered, the wet smell of woollen uniforms, the smoke and soot not getting less as they left the trains but greater as they reached the fog-laden darkness outside.

'Stay here, I'll try to find a taxi,' John told her.

The fog was much worse than she had imagined. Cars crawled by, their headlights behind their narrow slotted shields almost useless. People moved like dark anxious ghosts and she could hear the eerie clip-clop of a carthorse echoing like a film gimmick in a Victorian chiller. She knew they would not reach Bethnal Green and Brierly Street that night.

John was back quickly. 'The fog's quite bad and there was a raid earlier, I've been advised to find a room and stay overnight where we can. The policeman at the taxi rank says everything's stopped we've no chance unless we walk.'

'Take us all night in this,' she said. 'Where are your friends?'

'Disappeared!'

'Good!' They both laughed but she momentarily remembered Ma's look of trust as she had nodded her consent to the journey. The next moment she had her arm tucked in John's and they were off to find accommodation. She thought of the Woolworth's ring and decided it would be as well to keep her gloves on – then she giggled, breakfast might be difficult.

189

'What's funny?' he demanded.

'Tell you later!' she said hanging on his arm as fog brought anonymity and they avoided lamps and puddles and other people.

'I know a small hotel somewhere here,' he said, hesitating at a corner. 'This way I think.'

He led her into a doorway through heavy plush curtains to a swing door and into a quiet carpeted lobby. A stoop-backed, white-haired man in blue red-piped uniform sat behind a desk.

'Good evening,' John said, 'the fog's benighted my wife and I. Could you find us a room?'

'No problem there, sir, these nights people go out of London to sleep. Dinner's over but I could warm you some soup.' He seemed pleased to have someone to talk to and kept up a non-stop flow as he led the way to a lift that operated with a brass lever larger than most tram's. 'Thought we were in for another bad raid like last Wednesday, sir. Were you in town? The fires got the better of the Fire Service in parts. But I reckon now the weather's changed, the fog and cold'll keep them away a bit. I hear the ice is worse the other side the channel.'

He led them to a first-floor room with a double bed, pink drapes and an eiderdown that was pink, fat and resplendent on the bed. John helped pick up the matches the man dropped lighting the gasfire and tipped him generously as he left. He told them their soup would be ready in the dining room in ten minutes.

'Someone should tell him about careless talk costing lives,' Vi said as soon as he'd gone, then, slipping off her gloves, hat, coat, shoes, she threw herself on and into the great fat eiderdown. 'Oh the bliss of lying flat after that train. My head still feels as if its hurtling along! Ten and a half hours!'

'We mustn't forget the soup,' he said, lying down beside her with a sigh of relief, stretching his back, hands under his head. He contemplated the suitcase on the stand at the end of the bed. 'What a good thing we had your case, otherwise he might have thought . . .'

'We were up to no good.' She turned on her side to look at him. 'Is he receptionist, porter and chef or,' she assumed an American accent, 'just the oldest bellhop in town?'

John laughed. 'You'll really get on with Aunt Annie when she gets to know you properly.'

'Does she like a joke?' she asked, then made her own judgment that she was certainly not a snob.

'Nobody more.'

'Will Alice allow such carrying-on?'

'There'll be some encounters worth recording! Write to me everyday? Tell me everything, keep me up to date with Trewellan.'

'Of course and I shall keep my diary.'

He caught her hand and lifted her arm full stretch. 'Violet Tulley, compromised beyond redemption, loved until the seagulls stop flying, repeat after me: I promise . . .'

'I promise . . .'

'To love John Manners Trewellan . . .'

'To love John Manners Trewellan . . .'

'Until . . .'

'Not until.' She pulled her arm back down to the bed. 'Just forever. There are no conditions with my love.'

He propped himself up on his elbow and looked down at her. 'You make me feel very humble.' He bent and kissed her with the utmost teasing lightness.

'This is an affair, isn't it?' she whispered contentedly. 'I feel like I'm in a film. I think it's the eiderdown.'

The following morning, John insisted he saw her home before he rushed over to report to his billets and see if his instructions had arrived. They managed to pick up a taxi outside the hotel. John handed in their case and told the address, the driver answered, 'Don't know how far I'll get, governor, but do my best.'

'Why?' Vi leaned forward to ask.

'You weren't in the East End last Wednesday night then!' he stated. 'More fires than ever, the west end of the Green was a sea of flames and Bethnal Green Road, well, that was bleeding on fire wasn't it. The wood blocks which surface it were on fire, burnt right through to the concrete underneath.'

John glanced at Vi who had pushed herself back defensively into a corner of the cab.

'We 'ad hundreds, possibly thousands of incendiaries. The Fire Service and Civil Defence had no chance of keeping up with 'em.'

'Just do your best then, old boy,' John told him, closing the glass screen to cut off his flow of news.

'If anything had happened to your Pa you would have heard before now. It was a week ago this raid they're all talking about.'

'Yes, I'm all right,' she told him but at the back of her mind she remembered Ma saying that by the time a letter reached her something *could* have happened – but they sent telegrams with bad news didn't they? The war was bringing many heart-rending stories of letters from the front arriving after the dreaded buff envelope with the news of a death. A stream of bad options paraded themselves through her mind.

The driver joined the Mile End Road and took them into the Green as if surreptitiously, weaving this way and that, talking to himself as if remembering the hazards through the maze of streets. Vi stared miserably out of the window, so many gaps in the houses, homes blown back to piles of bricks, sections of masonry, splintered debris. It was difficult at times to recognise the district she had grown up in but then suddenly she exclaimed, 'Oh! Globe Road!' as the taxi drew to a halt and the driver reached over his shoulder to open the glass division. 'This is about as far as I can get!'

'Wait for me will you,' John asked.

'Fine by me, governor,' the driver nodded. 'I'll just turn round and be over the road.'

'It's not far from here,' she said, wanting to ask if Brierly Street was all right but at the same time impatient to be away to look for herself.

She wanted to run on, leave John with the case, but he held on to her hand and hurried with her. There seemed to be barricades of bomb-blasted ruins, the rubble so high and extensive it spilled over pavement and road. Here London was like a front line and there was this no-man's-land she had to cross to get home – and cross it she was determined to do, whatever it took, which-ever way she had to twist and turn or climb and slide. There were workmen still clearing pavements and she saw in their weary patient labour the differ-ence between them and herself. She had no sense of relief that she had sur-vived this latest onslaught, her feelings were of anger, of impotent fury, com-ing back to see what had been inflicted on the streets where she had played.

The streets approaching Vi's home looked as if they had been in a fire-storm, nothing seemed whole or clean. It was possible to trace the direction of the wind-driven flames by the charred and soot-stained walls, the empty windows the destroyed entrances.

She half realised that she was running, John too. Brierly Street at last. She sobbed with relief and amazement. It was all still standing, there had been fires, but still standing. 'Thank God! Thank God!' she heard herself repeating automatically, 'I couldn't have faced Ma if it had gone.'

'Come on, old thing, steady up now. Don't want to arrive in a lather.' He tucked her arm under his.

'This is about where I first met your pa. He was coming from the other direction,' he said as Vi now slowed to snail's pace taking in every detail of their neighbours' houses. Number 11 appeared quite untouched and there was a pile of canvas newspaper bags outside. 'Of course,' she said, 'Mr and Mrs Moore.'

She ran across and tapped on the front-room window, then the door, but no one was in. 'Ma gave me her key.'

Inside Vi found the house so changed, so lacking her mother's hand. The cosy old range in the back kitchen badly needed a black lead, cold grey ashes in the grate. The gas stove was spotted and greasy, a very dirty frying-pan on the top. The whole house smelt unaired and neglected. Then she realised John was spinning his cap and she remembered he had to go.

'I'll be back as soon as I can,' he told her. Her look begged answer to the question she did not voice. 'No way will I leave without seeing you again, even if I have to desert.'

'No.' She shook her head at him. 'I know you better than that, you'll never do anything less than your duty.'

'I'd risk hell and high water to be by your side,' he said with conviction.

'And if I can find anything to eat in the pantry I'll have supper waiting for you and we'll find somewhere for you to sleep – it might only be under the same roof mind.'

When he had gone, a more detailed inspection revealed that Pa was not having much home life. The Moores might be living there, but Mrs Moore certainly had not taken over the housekeeping, though their clothes hung in his bedroom and Pa was sleeping in Vi's. She was putting her case unopened on to Sid's bed when she heard a noise downstairs. 'Hello!' she called, 'Who's there.'

Mrs. Moore and she confronted each other on the stairs, each with the same expression of right and possession on their faces. Mrs Moore, still carrying some of the newspaper bags the boys had thrown down, was astonished when she saw who it was. 'Heh! Violet! I couldn't think who it might be upstairs! 'Ave you come 'ome?'

'Only for a bit Mrs Moore. You and Mr Moore all right? How's Pa?' she asked.

'He won't let me do for 'im y'know – not that I've much time.'

Or much inclination, Vi thought as the newsagent's wife told how they were struggling to keep the newspaper rounds going. 'It's important now the shop's gone, important for our Roy when he comes 'ome – important for you too.'

She hadn't looked for this moment coming so soon, hadn't really let herself think about it, there had not seemed time. 'Mrs Moore I'm here with another fella – I've sort of written to Roy.'

They had walked down the stairs and were in the hall now. She saw Mrs Moore's back stiffen and she stood still and rigid for long seconds before turning back on her. 'My Albert said there was something when that toffee-nosed officer came! But no, *I* said, no she wouldn't do that to our Roy while he's away fighting for his country!'

'It wasn't something I planned. It just happened.'

'You just *let* it 'appen.' Mrs Moore turned away from her rejection and hurt in the judgment that what she had to do was more important than Violet Tulley. 'I've papers to deliver.'

Vi had known it was not going to be easy and dreaded the return of the waspish Mr Moore. She threw herself into restoring the house to its former state, black-leading, tutting over the near empty state of the coal shed in the back yard and feeling a real sense of achievement when she managed to hail their old coalman and buy two bags. By the time Pa was due home there was a leek and bacon pie in the oven, the kitchen was cosy and spanking clean, just as Ma would have wished.

193

She heard him coming and impulsively opened the back door and hid behind it, peeping through the crack to watch his first reactions.

His step slowed, then he came into her view. He paused on the threshold, sniffed the air, took in the transformation before he sensed someone nearby. He turned cautiously to see his daughter, taking long seconds to believe what he saw. 'Your Ma?' he queried immediately.

'Just me, Pa. I've come up with John, you met him . . .'

'Ah!' He shrugged and half pulled a face as he held out his arms – nothing was to be allowed to spoil this moment of reunion. She ran to bear hug him. He held her tight, rocking her about, at the same time exclaiming over the smell of the meal, the fire, everything aglow. 'You've been busy! But Ma and Sid, and Audrey, everyone all right?'

She led him into the kitchen, took his coat, bag and cap and hung them up for him behind the kitchen door.

'This is a bit more like it!' he exclaimed. 'This is a bit like home!'

They stood for a moment doing nothing more than beaming at each other across the table set for three. 'You've grown up,' he said quietly and laughed a little when she blushed. 'He's a nice chap, but what about Roy?'

'I've tried to explain to his mother . . .'

'You've seen Maggie?'

'And I've sort of half broken the news to Roy. I wrote and said I had met John.' She paused, her heart full of her other news. 'He's asked me to wait for him.'

Pa looked at her, shaking his head just once, just a fraction. 'You'll need to be grown up then,' he said quietly.

'Yes.' She turned to pick up the kettle before she asked, 'Do you like him Pa?'

Pa answered without having to consider. 'Not from the same stable as us lot, but a winner! Could cause a lot of trouble – and not just on his side. What about Ma? Don't suppose she's too easy about things!'

'I think she knows how I feel. She told me about your courting days.'

'Did she by heaven!' He paused, surprised, half laughing. 'Well, like they say, love conquers all!'

'Pa, he's going straight overseas from London. That's why I came so we could have a bit more time together.'

Pa tutted then gave vent to a gasp of utter exasperation. 'This bleedin' awful war!' He slightly raised one arm, it was a familiar invitation from her childhood and she slipped under his shoulder, arm around his waist. She looked up into his face. 'You look tired, Pa,' she said, 'and in need of a good wash. Then a good meal and a good old catch-up gossip in front of the fire.'

'Sounds good to me.' He kissed her lightly on her cheek. 'So are you looking after them all for me?' They never stopped talking all the time he took advantage of the copper full of hot water she had heated for him and

194

had a bath in the back kitchen. They were silenced only once by the slamming of first their front door and then their front parlour door. The Moores were back but obviously not in the mood for confrontation.

John returned just before she was beginning to think her pie would spoil. She helped him out of his greatcoat in the hall where they lingered to exchange an embrace and a kiss. 'I can stay over,' he whispered.

Just at that moment Mr and Mrs Moore emerged from the front room, carrying blankets on the way to begin queuing for admission to the underground for the night.

'My taximan said there'll be no raid tonight,' John said with quizzical light-heartedness. 'He said he's heard the weather's so bad on the continent the planes can't get off the ground.'

'Tittle tattle lost the battle!' Mrs Moore said fiercely. ''Ow can 'e know!' She huffed and heaved her bedding through the front door leaving her husband to follow.

'I apologise,' John said to Mr Moore as he followed his wife. 'It was repeated as a joke. I thought it was funny.'

'There's a lot you bleeding hoity-toity lot think's funny.' Mr Moore was suddenly back on the doorstep, shouting, seemingly beside himself with fury. 'You'll laugh on the other side of your faces when this lot's over. You can afford to laugh at 'ome, playing fast and loose with such as our lad's girl while he's fighting. Bloody shirker! That's what you lot are.'

'What's all this?' Pa came through from the kitchen. 'Hello, John.' The two automatically shook hands.

Mr Moore snorted his disapproval. 'I see 'ow the land lies! Come on Maggie we're not wanted 'ere. We'll move out as soon as may be.'

Vi had many things she wanted to protest about but Pa answered quickly. 'Perhaps that'll be best.'

As the door closed behind them John began to apologise. 'I obviously should never have come here.'

'The man's his own worst enemy,' Pa said, 'though life's not doing him and Maggie any favours just now.'

'He shouldn't have called you a shirker,' Vi said gravely. 'I won't forgive him for that.'

'He looks ill,' John ventured. 'Don't like to think of them having to move out because of something I've caused.'

Pa waved a dismissive hand. 'Don't worry, me and Maggie'll sort things out between us. She carries him and the business if the truth's known,' he confided as they returned to the brightness of the kitchen fire. 'Poor old Maggie. She's all in at the end of each day but he insists they rush down to queue at the underground early every night.'

'I can't see any point if there's not been an air-raid warning,' Vi said.

'Become a way of life for a good many. Though they do say you only get

195

killed if its got your number on it. You wouldn't believe in such daftness?' Pa directed at John.

'It seems to me fate decrees some things, people meeting . . .'

'Aah!' Pa exclaimed, looking over at Vi, and they all laughed, as if now they had the house to themselves they could relax properly, be themselves. From then on the evening was cosy before the fire. The meal eaten, Vi's deep rich pastry on the pie (made with all Pa's unused fat ration) praised beyond all, John talked to Pa about his wish for her to stay at Trewellan. 'And believe me, sir, your whole family's safer down there.'

'Harold,' he corrected before going on. 'I ache to see Ma and my lad but I wouldn't wish any of them back to this, *and* as soon as you're away I want Vi back out of harm's way.'

'Still the same old bossy object, aren't you ,' Vi put in, feeling uneasy, this man-to-man decision rang with too many echoes of her earlier sending away.

'I'd like to take your daughter to meet my uncle and to stay at a friend's place for a night if you've no objection.'

'So I understand your aunt and uncle to be . . .'

'My nearest surviving family.'

'Are you telling me your intentions are serious to my gel?'

'Pa!'

'If I return safely, very serious,' John said, 'but I don't want to compromise Violet in any way.'

'You just make sure you don't,' Pa said with emphasis.

'Oh Pa!'

'He knows what I mean.'

So do I, she thought, *and you're too late, Pa m'lad*. Suddenly she realised that he was assuming they had arrived just that day. She hoped they never got down to discussing just when they had reached the city.

'Your daughter will come to no harm at my hands, sir.'

She remained silent but, as both men looked at her, she felt curiously balanced between them, loving them both so much. Then she smiled as the thought came that the girl in her was something no one could spoil or touch because that part was over – complete – would always belong to Pa. The rest of her life, the woman, which hopefully would have proper time to bloom and blossom, belonged to John. She looked from one to the other still smiling and saw how her smile affected them both.

'She's a bit of a charmer, isn't she?' Pa stated.

John cleared his throat. 'She's wonderful!'

'Right!' she proclaimed, grinning as she saw John actually blush. 'Now you two have decided about me – let's sort the beds out! You can sleep on your own bed with the Moores gone. I'll have my own and John can have Sid's.'

'You're the bossy object!' Pa retaliated. 'Don't know who you take after!

196

And I hope you know what you're taking on.' He wagged a finger at John. 'Your life'll never be the same again!'

'I'm counting on that,' he answered quietly.

They spent that night at Brierly Street, kissing goodnight on the landing, pledging love and scuttling to their respective beds as her father cleared his throat noisily. The next day they were up early enough to see Pa off to work an early shift, John even walking part of the way along the road with him. She went to the front door and watched them striding out together, her heart warming to their affability. Then Pa suddenly stopped and half turned towards John who caught his elbow and, after a few seconds, persuaded him on his way. But the two walked slower then, heads down as if in more serious talk. She instinctively stepped back out of sight into the hall, leaned on the wall and wondered what could have been said to so stagger Pa in his tracks?

When he walked back alone and when they left the house a short time later, John carrying her case, he was silent, sombre, brooding. The mood would have been easy to take up as she saw how different 'the everyday' was in the Green. She supposed it was because so many people had moved out, been evacuated, called-up – and the debris, even a torn and abandoned firehose still in a gutter. And what, she wondered *had* he told Pa? 'John?' she began.

'Vi!' he countered and tried a smile.

'I think you might as well tell me now.'

'Meaning?'

'Meaning, I've never seen a better picture of a man with something on his mind – or his conscience. If you've changed your mind about what you want us to do . . .'

'Not changed my mind, just not strictly told the truth – well not until just now to your pa – and then it wasn't everything.'

'For goodness sake.' She stopped in the middle of the pavement. 'I'm going no further 'til I know.'

He came to stand very close to her. 'I leave tomorrow,' he said in a very low voice.

She felt she had come to a division between light and utter blackness. She wanted to argue her corner as if there was some hope of making him change his mind, as if it was his decision to go or stay.

'We have until midday tomorrow,' he was saying, 'and I want to take you to see my aunt and uncle now . . . then I have the use of a friend's flat while he's away . . .' She felt his hand under her elbow.

'You told Pa this morning.'

'That I had just another twenty-four hours, yes.'

It felt, she thought, like a death sentence – and perhaps that was what it was. She realised they were walking again but felt numb, cold. For John it could be a death sentence. She might never see him again after tomorrow.

'You're shivering.'

197

She thought she might never feel warm again. 'I thought we might have Christmas together – and your birthday. Counting my chickens!' She tried desperately to smile up at him but as their eyes met, the look they exchanged was branded into her memory – it was at once bond and pall, it was at once pledge and duplicity. They knew their own powerlessness as they were sucked relentlessly to the very lip of the war machine.

'I feel guilty telling a white lie to your pa, not telling him the friend's place was an empty apartment.'

'All's fair in love and war – and we have both.'

'Yes we have both, so perhaps he'd forgive me.'

They had everything but time and that was something no one could fix.

'Look,' he interrupted her thoughts as he saw a bus coming, 'we're at a stop.'

She wished they could catch a plane, fly away to the end of the world, just the two of them. They went upstairs and stared silently out of the window, gripping hands in the space between them. *We always do this on buses*, she thought, and the tear pains built up to a terrible pressure behind her nose because it was twice they had done so. But there wasn't even time to cry for he was already standing waiting for her to precede him. 'We'll walk from here.' And they were getting off the bus, cutting through a narrow street to a crescent of Georgian houses.

The large-end-terraced house was badly bomb damaged and had a removal van standing outside. It was to this part of the row John took her. The front portico was scarred and chipped as was the whole facia of the building, but at least it was still standing. Once inside the front door the damage was evident. To their right it was possible to see through to the garden and a deep hole surrounded by rubble showed where the cellar must have been. There had been shoring up inside, and there were voices and work still going on. She recognised Mrs Trewellan's voice and held back. 'Does you aunt know I'm in London?' she asked.

He nodded reassuringly at her, then took her hand and pulled her onwards.

In what had obviously been a dining-room they found Mrs Trewellan in slacks, directing the removal of the largest grandfather clock she had ever seen.

Catching sight of them, she called, 'Hello, you two, come and look at this! I think the house must have been built around the clock.'

A tall ambling kind of man came through from another room carrying a blanket. He waved to John. 'Hello, my boy!'

'Uncle James, I'd like you to meet Violet.'

'Ah, you're the lass we've had warning shots over the bows from Alice about!' His hand was large, warm, and his eyes very like John's as he smiled down at her. 'This war's a bugger, isn't it? Look at the state of this place – and Annie going on and on!' He raised his eyebrows as his wife came and swept the blanket from his arm.

'These men have a lot to do.'

'I've got to get back to the Admiralty!'

His wife waved away his reason for any haste and they all stood and watched as the four men lowered the great heavy carcase down on to its face on the blanket, then the four men struggled away with it to the waiting van. 'Another war casualty,' James Trewellan stated, then turned to his nephew. 'So, this is it then, m'boy!' He held out his hands to John, grasped and shook him with a kind of hearty compassion, then took the young man into his arms. 'No time for high jinks! Heh, boy! Not till after the war, then watch out Alice and Trewellan!'

Vi caught the glimpse of moisture in his eye as the two men parted, one, it occurred to her, already old in the game of life and warfare and manoeuvres while the other was going in as fresh front-line material, cannon-fodder they had called the young soldiers in the First World War. She turned away so she did not immediately realise John's uncle now reached for her hand.

'While you are here you must get my Annie to show you photographs of herself when she was your age,' he said with a knowing nod. 'Chin up, m'dear.'

He was away just like that. She felt he ought to have changed into gold-braided uniform or summoned a limousine, after all he was a Commodore. Perhaps he had his uniform at the office, then she thought what a stupid thing to be troubling herself about.

His wife watched him go then turned to John and Violet. 'So.'

'I'm going to say goodbye now, Aunt Anne, no point in double doses.'

His aunt held out her arms and they embraced for a long moment. 'God speed! Come back safe to us.'

Vi saw his aunt's hand caress and pat his shoulders as if he was only her small charge again and the hand trembled as it reached his cheek.

'Let us know where to write as soon as you can,' she said as she released him and turned to Vi. 'Goodbye, my dear, we'll pick up the threads when we both get back to Cornwall – other things more important now.'

She gave Vi's hand a quick shake then, in the moment of parting, nephew and aunt were in each other's arms again.

'Goodbye, dear, dear Aunt Annie,' he said, then broke away and, catching Vi's hand, walked resolutely out of the room, out of the devastated house into the quiet elegant street. Vi was very aware that his aunt was left all alone there standing in the ruins of her home . . .

Chapter 23

The apartment was in a street of smaller Georgian houses with a kind of faded elegance – high ceilings, moulded and carved covings and ceiling roses from which she felt elegant chandeliers must have hung pre-war. 'It was my friend's parents' home. He inherited and split it up. Keeps just this one top floor for himself when he's in town. He's in Canada at the moment, helping to train their air force.'

Vi wandered around, through a large sitting room with a grand piano, to a dining room, beyond a kitchen, two bedrooms and an enormous bathroom, with a bath in proportion. She wandered back to the kitchen and saw John was unpacking things from a small hamper. She went forward, curious, and read the name on the basketwork: 'Fortnum & Mason'.

'I got them to put together a kind of Christmas hamper for me. Not quite like the old days but good enough – and, you see, I know you can cook.'

There was wine and two baby woodcock ready dressed for the oven with stuffings and sauces in bottles and jars, whole white English peaches in Madeira wine, a tiny Christmas pudding, crystalised fruits, biscuits, cheese.

'I didn't know you could still buy such things,' she said but then, sparked to enthusiasm by the sight of a rather superior gas stove, she added, 'I could make us Christmas dinner, everything's here. Oh, but no vegetables, no potatoes . . .'

'I could fetch some quite quickly.'

'Right, I'll find what needs to go on first. What time does sir wish to eat?'

'Early! I think we should combine lunch, tea and dinner in one binge, get it over with.'

'Agreed!'

He kissed her neck as she exclaimed over the seemingly never-ending goodies. 'Port *and* brandy. Just for two of us!' While she was unpacking, busy, it was possible to keep the pain away, prop it up with an effort of will like a tarpaulin against the weather, but once he had left to shop, she closed her eyes and felt the misery fall over her shoulders like a weighted pall.

She went from room to room, trying to find some ease, some best way of dealing with this time – this little time. So if she cried what would that achieve? Red eyes, a miserable evening, a miserable 'last supper' – she wished she didn't think things like that.

'Come on, Violet Tulley,' she admonished herself through gritted teeth, 'you're made of sterner stuff.' She looked out on her city from this unfamiliar high viewpoint, for a moment unable to pinpoint where she was, not remembering which sand-bagged and boarded-up shop and office fronts they had passed on the way here, which spire belonged to which church. Then, in the distance, she located the dome of St Paul's and her heart gave a silly leap, like she'd found a friend. 'God keep you safe too,' she whispered and felt an unlooked-for moment of sheer national pride in the glories of London and the dogged endurance of Londoners.

She thought of her gran – and her ma – and went through the physical movements she saw her do so often – tightening that wraparound apron, girding up her emotional loins.

'Right!' She marched back to the kitchen and took up a woodcock in each hand. 'You'd better be good, this has to be the best meal he's ever eaten. I bet it's cost enough!'

The tiny birds were in the oven when he returned, loaded with a Christmas tree, tinsel, holly. 'Come on,' he called, carrying the lot into the sitting room, 'help me decorate the tree.' He produced a box of fairy lights.

'Yes, lovely!' she eyed him from the doorway. 'And the potatoes?'

'Ah! I did start off all right, I bought,' he paused to dive into a paper carrier bag, 'parsnips, will they do?'

'Just parsnips?'

'I saw the Christmas trees.'

'Give 'em here. We'll have to be like Marie Antoinette – "let them eat cake".'

'Can I help?' he asked.

'No, you're better at the fancy stuff. You decorate, I'll peel.'

She decided to roast half and boil half, that way there would be variety, she thought. She wandered back to the sitting room, surprised to find him looking out of the window into the early December dusk, leaning on the sill, his shoulders slightly hunched. 'What is it?' she asked quietly.

'I hadn't realised just how dark a city could be, how effective a good blackout is. If you didn't look very carefully it could be deserted. All the shop lights gone, the car lights no more than peepholes at ground level.'

'Open the window,' she said, 'it's all still there.' He pushed up the sash and they leaned out. 'Close your eyes,' she ordered.

The square below was not busy, they could hear people walking just below, a newspaper seller at the street corner, but in the background was the muffled roar of the metropolis traffic. 'It's all still going on.'

'Keep the wheels turning while I'm away won't you,' he said, pulling her into his arms. 'Perhaps we won't bother with eating,' he said.

'Oh yes we will,' she whispered back, 'we're not wasting all that lot.'

It was almost, she thought, like preparing for a ceremony, not the real festival of Christmas, but their private time together, their one festive meal, their one night in this place. She was finishing the final preparations for the meal when she suddenly heard the piano.

She went through to the sitting room. The blackout curtains were closed now and the tree was lit by the small bulbs which had silvered cardboard stars behind each red, blue, yellow and green light. He was playing a piece which seemed to her totally beautiful and most wonderfully romantic. She walked to him and the passion of the piece seem to increase. She stood in the curve of the grand piano and looked upon him so she would never forget. He seemed at once absorbed in the music, part of it, yet she knew he looked at and played for her.

When he lifted his hands from the keys, they were both still as the spell of the music lingered even after the sound had fallen into the shadowy corners of the room, into their memories.

'What was that? It was beautiful.'

'The overture to "Romeo and Juliet" by Tchaikovsky.'

'I didn't know you could play the piano,' she murmured, suddenly daunted by how much she did not know about him. 'You play so well.' *And dance so well*, she thought.

'My mother taught me. She was rippingly good at the piano.'

Ripping. She wanted to throw the word back at him, suddenly she felt awkward with him. He sensed it immediatley 'Vi?'

'I no good at anything really,' she mused. 'No social graces. I can't even sing in tune, do you know that.'

He laughed. 'I won't ask you to entertain the guests then.' He paused and sniffed. 'But I had thought I might get you to cook for me sometimes.'

'Oh no!' The unmistakeable smell of burning parsnips invaded her nostrils. She rushed back to the kitchen, half threw the hot saucepan to the sink and doused the charred contents. 'So! We'll just be having crispy roast parsnips.'

He kept making uproarious jokes at her expense and she realised with a sense of shock that she was in danger of becoming quite upset. She had wanted to do so well for him, cared too much what he said. Driven half between tears and laughter, she turned to confront him and saw the desperate bleakness behind the comedy, the sad clown in motley, saw his fooling for what it was, his need not to let there be too big a gap to think too deeply, not yet, it was too soon. They had at once so many hours to pass and so few. She tried to chase him out of the kitchen but he refused and insisted on eating on the small table there. 'Come on it'll save time.'

The mention of the word aloud rather sobered them and he sat down while

202

she served the game and vegetable with a red wine and giblet gravy that had come ready bottled in the hamper.

'Hmm!' he said. 'This is delicious, we must always have parsnip chips at Christmas.'

'Well, we always shall if you do the shopping.'

'Shall we take the bits and pieces into the sitting room and have an orgy in front of the fire. I'll take these,' he picked up the port and brandy, 'and go and make it comfortable.'

When she carried through the tray of sweet goodies, the only lights were those on the tree and the warm glow from the gas fire which he had turned full on. All the cushions from all the chairs were heaped on the floor.

'Our Bacchanalian feast!' He came to take the tray, then poured two glasses of port and waited until she had rearranged the cushions to her satisfaction.

Seated close in this new informality, she felt there was a homely intimacy: the total privacy; warm lights; the deep red wine; the huge soft cushions and the hush. All she could hear was the very faint hissing roar of the gas fire.

'Comfy?' he asked slipping his arm around her shoulders.

She didn't answer, too busy studying him in the soft flattering light. He was so handsome, so aristocratic. It wasn't in her nature to feel humble but if she ever did . . .

He looked down at her quizzically and grinned. 'You know you look like someone trying to think their way into the role of the little Victorian matchseller.'

She laughed and would have protested but he went on. 'Don't ever pretend with anyone, Violet, part of your charm is your honesty. Demure you are not!'

'I'm not sure what to say to that.' She let her head fall to his chest, thinking there were one or two dishonest things she could quote – but knowing in a way that wasn't quite what he meant.

'Just be yourself always, promise?'

She lifted her face to him and he kissed her lightly then gently ordered, 'Drink your port or put your glass down.'

She drained the glass and he took it, reaching across her to put it on the tray. 'I love you, love you,' he breathed as he looked down on her.

'I love you, John Manners . . .'

'Trewellan,' he added.

'Hmm, yes, there are one or two things . . .'

'My honesty is not up for questioning, I hope!'

'If the old cap fits,' she said and, seeing his officer's cap behind her on a chair, she hooked it up on one finger and twirled it.

Immediately, it was as if they both remembered the cliffs, The Soldier's Field and the way he had thrown his cap into the air. He reached over to take it from her and kissed her more seriously.

203

Much later in bed, they were both awoken by the sound of the air-raid siren.

'What do you want to do?' he asked. 'The nearest shelter is an underground but there's a cellar here.'

'Stay where we are unless it gets bad,' she said.

He rose and went to the window, opened the curtains. 'The searchlights are not up . . .' he began, then stopped. 'They are now, sweeping away to the right.'

She joined him and they watched as the beams of light swept behind St Paul's, describing the dome as they moved across the sky like pencils finding the pictures in a magic drawing book, hatching out the background of sky and barrage-balloons behind the great cathedral.

In the far distance there seemed to be something happening, but nothing near the City as yet. 'Perhaps an odd Jerry going home getting rid of his bombs, just dropping them at random.'

'Poor old Random,' she said, shivering. It was becoming a stale wartime joke, but he laughed, picked her up and put her back into bed. 'Do you want a brandy, warm you up?'

'I'd rather have another port if you're having something.'

He came back with balloon glasses of port and dishes of peaches. They sat up wrapped in blankets finishing the fruit and sipping their drinks. She found the sweet peaches delicious and the drink soothing. It made her sleepy and yet she wanted to be in his arms again, melting into them.

She fell into a strange half-dreamy state, unreal, like a picture she had once seen of lovers entwined underwater. This was how she felt as they lay together, languid at first, then surfacing to a wild excitement as he caressed her, feeling him like another swimmer, naked, painted in contours under her hands as he moved. Then they fell from the maelstrom into a deep and wonderful invulnerable world of love and sleep, drowning time.

She woke to hear John exclaim, 'My God, it's half past eleven.'

'Oh!' She rose and for a moment her head throbbed but she told it firmly she had no time for such nonsense as a bad head. 'What time . . .?'

'There's something I want you to do for me this morning, something—'

He stopped short, looking at her sitting up, her shoulders naked above the covers. 'I want you . . .' He hesitated, then began again. 'I want you to take me for a walk in your Victoria Park.'

'Oh John! That's back near Brierly Street.'

'Yep! So up you get lazy little matchgirl.'

'Are you trying to give me an inferiority complex?'

'Not so long as you remember who your lord and master is.'

She threw a pillow at him and knew this was all again a game, words to fill spaces, trips to fill time.

'We must clear up here first,' she said, looking round at the debris. 'We have made a mess. We didn't even wash up last night.'

He looked at his watch. 'That could be a problem. Could we get someone to do it? I don't have to hand a key in or anything. I was going to ask you to take it and give it to Aunt Annie for safe-keeping.'

'I could come back later then . . .'

'Would you, old thing, I really don't want to waste time now. I really do want to walk you over to that red pavillion you've talked about.'

'John, I . . .' She was not sure this was a good idea. Victoria Park was already a place of some emotional memories.

'Please!'

He seemed really anxious now about the time and somehow she felt it detached him one small notch from her. She decided they would leave her case behind – no need to carry that around the Park – but he said she ought take it, he would carry it.

I have to come back. But she didn't voice the argument because she didn't know where she had to come back *from* at the end – a railway station most likely. *Oh God!* she prayed fervently, *give me strength.*

He caught her hand before they locked up, pulled her close. 'This may be our last private kiss,' he said.

'Oh, John, come back to me.'

'Trust me, old thing, the thought of you waiting will bring me through anything. You will wait?'

'For as long as it takes.'

'For as long as those stupid seagulls keep flying.'

'Much longer than that.'

Again they took the bus part way then walked into the park by the same entrance she and Pa had used the day she had been reconciled to the thought of being evacuated – if they hadn't she would never have met John.

'I always used to envy girls who walked with their chaps in this park, sitting on those little benches beneath the trees, smooching away.'

'I can't believe I've never been here before.' He turned the case to point at the lake. 'You've made it all so familiar to me.'

She was telling him of the fright they had had when the park keeper shouted at them and they had fled over this self-same bridge, tipping Sid out of his pram. She looked up to see if he was laughing and saw he was looking straight ahead. She turned to follow his gaze. Standing in front of the red pagoda she saw Pa a second before he saw them, and he was looking at his watch.

Her steps slowed as Pa saw them and straightened up, lifting his chin. But he waited where he was. She turned to look at John, searching his face as he stood holding her case. 'You're leaving me here, aren't you?'

She saw his jaw muscles flex as he nodded. 'Yes, this is goodbye, old thing.

My sweet Violet, I want you to take your case and go to your father and don't look after me as I go. I couldn't bear it.'

The weight of the case fell from his hand to her's and he gave her a gentle turn to face her fully to her father. 'No looking back,' he said.

Chapter 24

'Get your case packed, Vi.'

Pa had gone from Bethnal Green underground station, where they had spent the night, to walk towards the City to see the extent of the damage. He returned grim-faced. This first raid after the respite all over the Christmas holidays had caught London napping.

December 29th, the last Sunday of 1940, had meant offices, warehouses and churches were still locked up and fire watchers were still at home relaxing in the peace and the seeming goodwill of the enemy – or perhaps it was only the result of that spell of terrible weather keeping planes grounded. Somehow they had been lulled into the sense that they would also see in the New Year without another air attack.

'So is it bad?' she asked, not rising from her ma's chair by the fire.

'You're not the only girl left behind y'know,' he told her. 'One of thousands, hundreds of thousands, you are – wives and mothers getting on with their lives – coping.'

She did not move. It felt just like old times, her and Pa on opposite sides of a decision.

'Vi!' he exclaimed. She knew he was both worrying about Ma and reaching exasperation with her moping around. He had at first accepted her argument that the army was unpredictable and John *might* come back for a time. She in turn had busied herself clearing the apartment, bringing back everything, even the Christmas tree, to Brierly Street, setting it up, making a decent Christmas for Pa. The Moores had kept to their own rooms. Last night's raid though had been a kind of turning point.

'It doesn't make me feel any better.'.

'No and it doesn't make you unique either. Come on, snap out of it. We've all jobs to do.' He reached down his work haversack and threw it on the table. 'If you can't think of your ma, think of John. Get back there, start learning more about his life. Make yourself the sort of girl he'll want to have for his wife. Learn his business, learn his life. You'll never have a better opportunity with all the men away and his aunt in charge.'

'I know it'll be easier with Roy's mum and dad if I'm not here.'

'That's not the point!' He spread the *News Chronicle* he had bought out on the table. 'We nearly all went up in smoke last night.' He smoothed the newspaper flat. 'The river was so low the fireboats couldn't get in to reach the City fires and a lot of the shore-based pumps couldn't reach the water.' He lifted his eyes from the paper to add, 'While I was out I met a chap who was fire-watching on the roof of the Bank of England. He said he'll never forget the roaring of the flames. It shook him, I can tell you. He said he thought the whole of London was going up. He hadn't expected to see the morning. They reckon it was a miracle St Paul's was saved.'

'St Paul's?' Vi could visualise the dome as she and John had seen it on their last night, in black outline with the searchlights beyond.

'Yes, dozens of incendaries hit it. One lodged halfway through the dome and began to melt the lead. They couldn't get anywhere near it with stirrup – pumps. Then somehow it fell *outwards* onto the parapet and fizzled out.' Pa shrugged. 'You tell me how! Some things are meant to be – others we can help along.'

They were both silent, both deliberating. At last, Vi got up and took the kettle from the hob. 'Cuppa?' She should get on with her life, Pa was right. St Paul's had been saved, now she had to deserve her other prayers to be answered. She should stir herself, go back to her responsibilities.

'Sorry I've been such a wet blanket,' she said as Pa handed over her case before she joined the crush for the Penzance train at Paddington. The second day of the New Year was seeing a lot of people returning to their duties after the holidays – troops to southern postings, land girls to West country farms. Vi stood aside from the crush for the doors to exchange a last few words.

'You had me worried for a time! But I'm sorry for going on at you. Everyone's getting so tired – and I miss your ma.' He gripped her forearm as he spoke.

'If I tell her *that* she'll be back!'

He pulled a face and they both laughed wryly. 'Tell her I'll definitely be down in the spring – have a week or two with you all.'

'OK, Pa.' They kissed and hugged and she climbed aboard at the end of the queue, settling her case in the corridor where she could lodge her bottom on it, not bothering to try to find a seat in the crowded train. 'I'll get one later,' she assured him as he looked concerned for her and was about to try to fix something with the passing guard. 'They'll thin out.'

The end of her journey was as solitary as the beginning had been crowded. By the time the train reached Penzance, the passengers were few. There were three people on the late bus out of the town, then she was on her own and the walk uphill to the farm in the dark, with only her pencil flashlight for company and her case to carry, took her last bit of energy.

'Who's there!' Ma's startled voice reached her as her case banged into the door before she could control it.

'Hello, Ma, I'm back!' The warmth of the kitchen greeted her and the lingering smell of a meal made her realise how hungry she was.

'Vi? Vi! Thank God! You all right? You look all in. Get your coat off, get sat down. I'll make a cuppa. How's Pa?'

They hugged each other, asked and answered a great number of shortfire questions for quick reassurance. Details could come later. 'You all right really? And John?'

'Gone!' She pressed her lips together, tiredness would have made it easy to cry and Ma in turn looked so stricken, reminding her of that last look of concern Pa had worn seeing her off. 'But we have to go on don't we. So how have you all been?'

'Sid must be hard on or he would have been down. He's missed you, we all 'ave. Though Audrey . . .' She paused and shrugged. 'I'm glad you're back, might be able to put a bit of sense back into her head.'

'Is she out?'

'On the bike! Not been in much since you went, parties over Christmas, then New Year, tonight to the pub with that Noel.'

'So how often has she been off *on the bike?*' This was the Trewellan bike and her responsibility.

'First time tonight. Don't think she'll make a habit of it – she's not that brave in the dark – but she's talked that silly at work. Felt quite ashamed of 'er, going into details about what she and these men friends do, kissing and carrying on all the time to hear her. Don't know what her ma and pa would've said.'

Not a lot, Vi thought. *They were used to it.* Then she remembered the message for her ma. 'Pa said to tell you he is definitely coming down for a holiday in the spring.'

Ma's face lit up like it was Christmas all over again and obviously nothing else interested her quite so much after this. 'Spring would be March do you think?'

'Well really, Ma, it could be March April or May . . .'

'Not May,' Ma insisted. 'I don't think May's spring, more early summer. Don't you think?'

Vi felt a wave of love for her mother's air of intense calculation over the matter. 'Yes,' she agreed, 'March and April are more spring.'

Ma's beam returned. *She'll be working out the weeks and days*, Vi thought and tried to ignore the plummet of her heart as she wondered how long her own wait would be.

'I was so pleased you were with your pa at Christmas. We 'ad the goose from the postlady.' She drooled at the memory. 'But we missed you. Sid missed you.'

It was Sid who woke her the next morning, dressed ready to go off to school. She struggled out of sleep to sit up as he hovered in the doorway. Audrey's bed, she noticed, was empty. She had neither heard her come home or get up.

'Sis?' he queried.

'Hello, Sid. All right?' That he patently was not. She patted the side of her bed. 'What is it? Come and tell me.'

'I might be going to prison.' He leaned back on her as she put her arm around his shoulders. 'I've not told Ma – or anyone – except Paul knows. I've broke Mr Spurrier's cart. It was an accident, but it broke the shafts and Major fell over!' His face was grief-stricken.

'Is Major all right?'

He nodded. 'But I think the cart's 'ad it.'

Downstairs, Ma called to remind him of the time.

'You don't go to prison for accidents,' she reassured him, reaching for her handbag. 'Talk to me again when you come home this afternoon. And Pa sent you this to spend.' She dropped a shilling into his hand.

'A whole shilling!'

'Yes, a whole shilling!'

It brought a glimmer of a smile but he was very solemn, very grown up as he added, 'I'll see you later then, sis. I come 'ome round the back lanes so I don't 'ave to pass his shop.'

'Do you indeed,' she murmured as he clattered downstairs.

Audrey put her head in next. 'Welcome back! At last! We've got to go to catch the lift. 'Ave a proper natter tonight. Did you . . .?'

'Christmas Eve.' Vi confirmed her visit to the city cemetery. 'I got a real nice wreath, holly and laurel with lots of berries.'

'Thanks, kid.' Audrey came to give her a swift kiss.

She was struck by some change in her friend, a ragged-edged feel to her manner. 'I borrowed your bike last night. I knew you wouldn't mind. Can I do the same tonight?'

Vi hesitated just a second and Audrey pursed her lips and jumped up from the bed. 'Oh, it doesn't matter anyway. There's always someone who'll walk me home.'

'Give me a chance to say yes or no,' Vi said, laughing, not wanting there to be any disagreement – not this quickly. 'As long as you take care of it I suppose its all right.'

Ma too came upstairs as Audrey clattered down, leaving Vi protesting that she hadn't said no and that Audrey could have the bike.

'What's up?' Ma asked.

Vi mouthed back, 'The bike.'

Ma shrugged and asked. 'Are you working today?'

'I'll go up this afternoon to see what's what.'

210

'Can you warm some plates for when we come back. We'll have a treat tonight, fish and chips – there's a shop where the girls get the lorry to stop on the way home.'

'Great!' She felt she should be pleased to be so involved back in their lives so quickly, but there was a kind of pilgrimage she had to make before she would feel in tune with Cornwall again.

She took the bike, which she examined for damage, and cycled towards Trewellan, but rode looking at things with new eyes, with the eyes of one who must report to an owner, spin words for a lover. She swept the cycle round off the road down the bumpy track towards The Soldier's Field. This was the mecca she was drawn to, this place of their first meeting, this place where seagulls slowly scythed the salt-laden air, crying and mewing their melancholy calls. She stood alone on the cliff top and her gaze went out to the wide empty sea, but she saw the soldier who had appeared as Sid had cried out, 'He's come, he's come.' He had indeed come. She remembered their walk when he had thrown his cap up into the air, had put it on her head – and she thought separation must be like drowning, for all their past times together came before her mind's eye.

She would write tonight, tell John about coming to this place. And there would be more to tell when she had been to the Lodge – even if it was only that Alice had tried to turn her out!

She parked the cycle and went to the front door as usual. She rang but there was no answer, though there were flowers in the porch again. She was just about to go round to the back when she heard footsteps on the gravel coming from the rear. It was Alice.

'We're not working!' she announced, accompanying the message with a flap of the tea towel she was carrying.

Vi worked hard not to narrow her eyes and go straight into the attack. 'Mrs Trewellan?' she queried.

'The master's 'ere on leave and won't want employees around!'

'On the contrary, young Alice,' the commodore said, breaking his way through some of his wife's rhododendrons on the other side of the doorway. 'This young lady we definitely want around.' He turned to Vi. 'Hello, old thing, jolly nice to see you again. You didn't expect to see me though, I'll be bound.'

He took her arm and led her down the drive. 'We'll walk up to the Manor House. Annie's there.' He turned to shoo Alice off with much the same gesture she had demonstrated with the tea towel, confiding once they were out of earshot, 'They're all bloody scared of Alice y'know.'

She had warmed to James Trewellan in London but his unexpected appearance from the shrubbery left her startled and a little speechless.

'You all right, old thing?' he asked. 'Didn't have too rough a time in London? The bombing, I mean – know it was bad saying goodbye to the boy. Bloody war!'

211

'Things are getting bad aren't they?' What she really wanted to say was that John called her 'old thing'.

'Dark days, old thing, dark days.'

They walked on in silence until they reached the Manor and as they approached a knocking at a first-floor window attracted them.

'Wanted first-floor front,' James said obediently, setting off in that direction, ushering Vi before himself in through the front door.

The hallway was light and handsome with a high gallery directly opposite the door and a great window above with stained glass – St Francis of Assisi in the centre with birds and animals coming to him.

'You like it?' he asked. 'Too many deer and fawns, I always think.'

'But what a wonderful first impression,' she said, half lifting her hands in response to the light and the colour it gave to the entrance.

'I'll let you into a secret now,' he said, 'those are exactly the words John used to describe how he felt when he first met you.'

She glanced at him quickly, thinking he was joking. But he confirmed his seriousness with a nod. 'John is as certain about you as I was about Annie when we first met. 'Love at first sight.' He cast a hand towards the window. 'Now, if someone could portray that!'

From upstairs his wife called down and, when they did not appear upstairs, she came out on to the first-floor gallery.

'Hello! Hello, my dear, safely back! Good, we've a lot to do tomorrow. I want to go over this place and make a list of what's been damaged before the next army detachment takes over. We need to know who to claim what from when the time comes.'

She leaned over the balustrade. 'What are you up to?' she asked her husband as he stood quite still and drew from his inner jacket pocket a large but rather battered looking wallet.

'Showing our young friend what I fell for when you were her age!'

'Jimmie! You've not brought those! You wouldn't!' She came protesting down the stairs.

'I've brought them specially to show this young lady. John's orders.'

'John would not be that devious! It's you, you old scoundrel.'

He laughed, pulled out a photograph and gave it to Vi. It was of a young woman in her late teens in a knee-length ballet skirt posed on one toe point in a perfect arabesque. Knowing it was Mrs Trewellan, she could see the facial resemblance immediately.

'That is beautiful,' she said dutifully.

'And this.' He handed over a portrait showing his wife on stage in a dramatic pose, hand on heart. Then came more stage shots and portraits and cuttings of shows in London at the beginning of the century 'starring Anne Caroline Barry'.

'Oh!' Now she looked at Mrs Trewellan in true amazement. 'You really were on the stage! How wonderful!'

The former Anne Caroline Barry was looking through the exhibits now with every sign of nostalgia.

'I was,' she said hanging on her husband's arm, 'until this beast came and dragged me away.'

'My little Annie had an awful lot to put up with when we married. Times have changed now, but, I tell you what, she plays the part of aristocrat so well I thought she might frighten you to death – so . . .'

'You do,' Violet confirmed. 'I mean – well, born and bred I thought.'

'As long as you don't give me away to Alice!'

'No fear!' she replied with relish. 'I'll just enjoy the situation more that's all.'

'That's what we wanted!' James said, looking at his wife as if requiring her to make acknowledgement of the mutual wish. She smiled briefly but nodded in agreement. 'So back they go.' He carefully gathered all the papers and portraits together and put them into the wallet. 'I'll take them back to London with me. Can't risk young Alice snooping around, finding out Annie here is only playing the role of country lady!' He roared with laughter.

'I'll soon wipe the smile off your face,' his wife said, 'come and see the damage to the cornice in the main bedroom.'

It was the damage to Spurrier's cart that concerned Vi as she waited for Sid to come home from school. She had replenished the fire and laid the table for the evening meal when Sid finally put in an appearance, but the last thing he now seemed to want to do was talk about it.

'Pa always says problems are best out in the open,' she prompted him.

'Nope, it's OK, sis, it's sorted.'

'Sorted! So has the cart healed up by magic during the day?'

'No! Paul's mending it. He's not going to tell. I just have to do him favours?'

'What kind of favours?' she asked with discreet lack of emphasis.

'I've just got to keep telling him when Audrey is going out, when she goes dancing, to the pub and that . . .'

'I think if Audrey wants him to know where she's going she'll tell him herself.'

'Sis! I'll be in terrible trouble if anyone finds out about the cart. I 'ave to tell.'

'No, I don't think so! That's worse than telling tales at school, much worse.'

'' E won't mend it if I don't spill the beans. It was my fault!'

'How did the cart get broken? How could *you* possibly do it?'

A glazed stubborn look came over Sid's face.

'Look, you tell me everything. How was it your fault?'

'I was late from school and Paul was in a bad temper because the cart had got stuck twice at the bottom of the field. That was my fault . . .' He inter-cepted the question, going on with emphasis, '*Because* it's my job to shout at Major and keep him going as he turns the corners because its boggy down at the cliff edge and the cart gets stuck.'

'Can't he stop before he gets to the boggy bit?'

Sid looked at her as if only a girl could ask such a question. 'The seaweed has to go *all over* the field.'

Vi refrained from asking why they couldn't carry it from the cart to the edge of the field.

'I worked twice as hard because I was late and because Paul always stops to have a bite of tea soon after I get there – and I'm always starving hungry after the digging at dinner time, then running home, then going to the field, then running up and down. Starving!'

Sid's voice became low and grim as he went on. 'Paul said to get his croust bag from under the hedge. When I got it, he said throw it up to him because he wasn't going to give me anything today, I hadn't earned it. I was so mad and so hungry I threw it at him – but it went the wrong way, hit Major on the head and it frightened him.' Sid's eyes were full of trouble now and his voice rose with the relived drama. 'He slipped and slid down sideways and broke the shaft. Paul said sometimes a horse gets impaled when the shafts break, that means—'

'I know what it means,' she cut in. 'When did this happen?'

'Last week.'

Vi calculated that if Paul had told his employer they would have heard from Mr Spurrier long before. Paul was keeping this to hold over Sid's head for his own ends. 'Two can play at that game,' she murmured.

'What you going to do, sis?'

'Put matters right. It was an accident, you didn't mean to break the cart or frighten Major.'

'No, but—'

'There's no buts, I'll see Paul.' He looked at her in some alarm. 'Don't worry anymore about it – and there'll be no need to tell any more tales about Audrey. If she wants to tell Paul where she's going fine – but *you* certainly shouldn't!'

Audrey came home full of talk about the rumour that women were going to be called up. 'I'd go like a shot,' she said, 'see a bit of life.'

'I think what we're doing would be counted as war work,' Ma said, looking over at her daughter.

'Worry about it when it happens,' Vi told her. 'These are the best fish and chips I've ever tasted. The fish!'

'Fresh caught that's why. Paul ses the shop buys it every day from the quayside.'

Paul, she thought, seems to be having quite a lot to say one way and another. When Ma went upstairs to supervise Sid's bedtime, she told Audrey what Sid had said.

'I'm flattered then,' Audrey said with a shrug.

'Flattered! You have to be kidding! And he's holding Sid to ransom!'

Audrey blew dismissively through her lips. 'So what. I don't mind him knowing where I'm going! When I'm out it makes me forget things for a bit – and if Noel gets sent away I'll want a stand in, till he comes back!'

'You could be a bit particular though.'

'Meaning?'

'I should imagine there's only one thing Paul Kerrow would be after.'

'Aren't they all! You can't tell me you and John haven't? In London by yourselves, stands to reason.'

Upstairs they heard Ma moving about. Vi was silent and Audrey took her advantage one step further. 'I've just started enjoying myself – and why shouldn't I?'

It was the look of recklessness in her eye that made Vi retort, 'Well in future tell Paul yourself, don't rely on a boy telling tales.'

'Don't worry. I suppose you'll be staying in, just waiting. I think you'll be the fool. After the war they'll all close ranks again, probably never accept you even if he comes back. You'll never be one of them.'

Vi felt rigid with the hurt of the words so carelessly spoken. She refused to contemplate her world should he never come back. In that moment she decided she would never tell Audrey, or even Ma, about Mrs Trewellan's stage career before she married. It was her first act of loyalty to John's family.

Chapter 25

John's first letters were a masterpiece of the censor's art, the zealous removal of any words that might give information to the enemy should the Army Post Office mail be intercepted. While the actual sentences that had been decimated might make some kind of sense without revealing anything, those written on the back of the same page were often totally scrambled by the gaps.

'They've got special scissors haven't they?' Sid said. 'Square, you know, like those the grocery shops cut your coupons out with.'

'I reckon you could be right,' she agreed holding up one page where a whole sentence had been cut out in a perfect neat rectangle so only the plain margin of the paper kept it hanging together.

She spent hours going over them, writing back, advising that if he wrote so the lines did not correspond front and back of the paper she'd be able to understand much more.

They had one major victory in his fourth letter, though it was actually the seventh to arrive. He had put in the mystic words, 'The dances here seem to be next door but one to the flamenco.'

She and her brother had become cooperators and compilers of a series of wall maps in Sid's bedroom. They cut line drawings of battle areas from newspaper reports and Sid had painstakingly traced maps from his school atlas then made flags with pieces of paper and pins from Ma's sewing box. They shared any news they could glean about the progress of the war, the movements of troops, victories, defeats.

'I'm sure that's a Spanish gipsy dance.' She put her finger in the middle of the country's outline.

'I'll find out for sure from school,' he said eagerly.

'So next door *but one* has to be Greece.' Vi slid her finger across the map. 'I think John's in Greece.'

'Yes,' Sid nodded in solemn confirmation. 'I think so. It's a secret message to us.'

Then, looking at his maps, at the position of Greece with the long island of Crete at its foot, she felt what was no secret was that Greece was fast becoming hemmed in by enemy flags – Roumania and Bulgaria, which Sid had recently flagged as on the side of the enemy, hung above, while Italy lay to the west – bleaguered was the word the newspapers used. She shivered, suddenly terribly apprehensive, terribly afraid.

Sid unexpectedly reached for and gripped her hand. 'Sis, if Pa had been in the army he would've fixed it better.'

'Course!' she agreed, startled and moved by his unexpected gesture, reminded involuntarily of when she had taken his hand before they plunged down a Southend helter-skelter. Now the need for reassurance was hers. She squeezed his hand back. 'He'll be interested in all this work you've done.'

'He'll like Major.' Sid's eyes shone at the prospect of Pa coming. 'When?'

'Can't be too long if its going to be in the spring. We're in the middle of April now. Any day I think!'

'Any day . . .' Sid repeated excitedly, then they both looked to the door as a movement attracted their attention.

Audrey stood leaning in the doorway, but as their attention was drawn to her, she rolled on her shoulder around the door jamb, away out of the room, out of their sight.

'Audrey?' Vi queried. 'What's the matter?' There was no reply.

'Doesn't she want Pa to come?' Sid queried.

'It won't be that,' she reassured him, but when she called again they heard Audrey going downstairs. She felt guilty of neglect, her work on the Trewellan Estate had left them for the first time in their lives without the mutual subject of the same job. Ma listened agog to any news she brought from the Manor, the new troops arriving, some of the problems of running an estate.

'It's not all sunshine and flowers . . .' she had said.

'My heart bleeds for 'em!' Audrey had interrupted.

She was careful after that, didn't talk about Mrs Trewellan when Audrey was around, which anyway had become less and less often as she dated Noel until he too was drafted overseas. Then, as the weather had improved, she 'switched to the local talent'. It was Paul who took her for a drink to the Gerrard's Head where the visiting forces again outnumbered the more conservative locals, though if any chance came she joined up with others to go on to local and camp dances. Paul had either to go along or she left him in the pub. According to reports she never lacked for a dance partner. Often dumped but dogged, Paul seemed to Vi like a scavenger, ever at the farm, ever shyly watchful for scraps, opportunities to be part of their lives.

'She's gone quite wild since she knew you and John were serious,' Ma said quietly. 'Is there some special reason?'

She was going to just deny there could be, but then she remembered their games in the park, how Audrey had always liked to think she was connected with the upper classes, the London dances where the attention of an officer had Audrey on cloud nine. She became aware Ma was watching her closely. 'Life's strange isn't it,' she said. 'Audrey was always the one who liked the officers.'

'She's not going to get one the way she's behaving.'

'Perhaps I'll try to go out with her more. I wouldn't mind walking up to Gerrard's Head for a drink.'

'Now the nights are lighter I wouldn't mind going, then when your pa comes we could all go. I'll suggest it at work Monday. Perhaps if it's a nice night Doris would have a walk over. She's trying to do a deal on a bicycle for Audrey. Some old boy living in their street does old bikes up and he's got a good one for five shillings if Audrey wants it.'

Doris arrived on the bike just before six on the following Wednesday evening. 'Ruining my reputation you Londoners, taking me to public houses for drinks!' she said cheerfully. ''Ow's things then, Vi? Lovely to see you again, m'andsome.'

They were soon established with halves of shandy in one corner of the snug, where, to Ma's disgust, drinks were a halfpenny each more than in the bar. 'Never mind we can talk better in here, not worry about being overheard. I want to hear about Avis, is there any news?'

Doris cleared her throat. 'She's at his home.' She nodded significantly and they nodded back not wanting her to breathe Sergeant Wilson's name aloud. 'And getting on famously, come into her own in her overalls selling petrol and running the office for them.'

'The war's brought some good then,' Audrey was saying as a soldier came hesitantly through from the bar. He stood in the doorway and cleared his throat.

'It's not private,' Vi told him, 'you can come in.'

'I'm looking for Audrey,' he said, 'only I have some news for her. I don't know her other name. She used to meet my mate Noel Parker here.' Then Vi saw he recognised Audrey and she saw him draw in a deep breath like one about to plunge into deep waters. She found herself holding Audrey's unresponsive hand as they waited for the news the sober-faced young man had to give.

'I'm sorry to tell you, Noel Parker was killed in action a week ago,' he said. 'Only I thought you would like to know.'

'But he's only been gone a little while!' Audrey almost snapped back, sounding petulant, resentful. The young man said he was sorry, nodded deeply and backed himself out of the bar parlour.

Doris got to her feet. 'I'll go thank him for coming.'

'I don't think it's right,' Audrey said. 'It can't be right!'

Vi could understand this protest ... this useless anger. 'Were you really fond of him?' she asked, going on as she remembered the quicksilver, open-

218

hearted young man, 'I liked him, his gambling sayings, odds on this, bet yer that! He was always . . .'

Audrey said something which stopped her mid-sentence, yet she hadn't really heard, or she'd been unable to take in what she had heard. 'I'm expecting his baby,' Audrey repeated.

'Oh, my God!' Ma exclaimed and flopped back on the long wall bench, eyes closed as if in a faint.

'Someone else!' Audrey exclaimed in a kind of wild bewilderment. 'I can't have lost someone else!'

Vi felt torn between trying to see if Ma was all right and reaching out to Audrey, wanting to hold her, pat her back. At the same time she was aware that the landlady had hovered in the doorway of the parlour, as if trying to monitor what the commotion was in her best room.

Doris came back and looked bemused by the new drama she found. She rushed to Ma and helped support her. 'What's happened to your mother?' Doris asked. 'Why . . .?'

Audrey startled them by jumping to her feet, knocking over her untouched drink as she pushed blindly by the table and out.

The tight-lipped landlady was there immediately cloth in hand, her thick corseted bulk leaning over, mopping up.

'My mother needs some air,' Vi protested, 'can we just get by.'

The landlady arranged the towel she carried in a circle around the spilled drink then without a word went to hold open the door for them.

'Thank you so much,' Vi said, waiting to see if she made any comment, ready for her now that Ma seemed recovered and was walking normally on Doris's arm.

The soldier who had given them the news came to open the front door and, behind them, she heard him telling the landlady that the girl who had rushed out first, her boyfriend had been killed in action.

Audrey was some way ahead of them and nearly running. It was clearly no use all of them trying to catch her up.

'Hope she don't do nothing stupid,' Doris said.

'Wish my Harold would hurry up and get here,' Ma said. 'He'll help us sort things out.'

'Not much he can do, Ma. The only good thing is we've got plenty of room at the farmhouse.'

'And I've got all my Tommy's things she can borrow.'

Vi was suddenly struck by the thought that her father would not consider this 'looking after them all'. 'We must try and get some things sorted before Pa arrives,' she said with urgent determination. 'Don't want his holiday spoilt.'

'We'll manage,' Ma said. 'I suppose we'll manage, somehow. At least you've got a good job, Vi, and she'll 'ave to stay home while we work, that's all. As time goes on . . .'

219

It conjured a picture of Audrey heavily pregnant. Vi wondered how the neighbourhood and the Trewellan family would eventually take the news, when there was no more hiding the fact? 'Cockneys abuse local hospitality!' a newspaper headline had only recently announced.

'Perhaps she won't want the bike,' Doris said.

'Oh, we'll still have it,' Ma said. 'Do for me. There'll be more going up and down to the shops, the chemists and the doctor's.'

'Didn't know you *could* ride a bike,' Vi said.

'Well . . . I'd soon learn. I must have 'ad a go as a girl?'

They shared a brief laugh but it lightened their step a little, sent them on a bit quicker, made it possible to think of the problems ahead. Spare bedrooms were uppermost in Vi's mind, they had those. She could bring her writing table into her bedroom and Audrey and her baby could have the other. She felt a slight pang of guilt as she thought of taking advantage of the situation to gain a bedroom to herself, so she could set out her letter table and have their photograph set up on it and see it when she was in bed.

But a baby! Noel's baby. How would she have felt if – if she was having John's baby. Alarm and a kind of pleasurable triumph seemed to fight for predominance. She was glad she wasn't but if anything happened to John would that make her feel differently? If . . . Ah no, she stopped the thought short, would not go down that what-if way. She had begun to learn to turn her thoughts to someone else, someone else's needs and troubles, when dread threatened to swamp her yearning for John, when as now the seagulls swirled and called over the cliffs making the ache for him unbearable.

She looked ahead to where, instead of going down the farm drive, Audrey was carrying straight on. It looked as if she was going to have many other things to take her mind off her own worries.

'Where's she going?' Doris questioned as if to herself.

'Look,' Vi decided, 'I'll run on and catch up with her, bring her home.'

'Go on,' Ma urged as Audrey began to descend the long curving hill down to the town, began to be out of sight.

She ran, remembering how they had both chased the bullocks, the new trouble made that seem a careless lifetime ago. She ran until she reached the end of the farm drive, then she paused for breath because she could see Audrey not far ahead, talking to Paul who was coming up the hill driving Major with Sid on board. As she watched, he reined in then bent to give her a hand and haul her up beside them on the cart. There was something in the way she wriggled in between Sid and Paul, some coquettish wriggle of her backside that told more of calculation than grief.

'Don't be a fool,' Vi heard herself say. 'Don't be a fool.'

By the time Pa was due to arrive, she and Doris had repeated the words to

Audrey many times. She in turn had told them to mind their own business, to keep quiet about *everything*. Paul began to be ever more around, usually leaning in the doorway of the kitchen drinking tea Ma always put in his hand. 'Does he know,' she asked Vi.

'I shouldn't think so. Perhaps I should tell him – scare him off – he scares me.' She was surprised at the words that tailed her own sentence.

Finally, as she returned from her walk to The Soldier's Field, soaking in the sights and sounds of sea and land so she could describe them to John, she came unexpectedly upon the two of them in each other's arms near the well. She swept past, determined to tackle Audrey as soon as possible.

'Does he know? What the hell do you think you're doing. Don't you know he's . . .'

'What?' Audrey demanded fiercely. 'Go on! What?'

A great many words and phrases suggested themselves, all extreme, about oddness and menace, about throwing stones and using kids to spy and being unpredictable. She paused to wonder if she was prejudiced, then said most of them anyway, finishing with, 'I know you'd be better off on your own than with him, that's all!'

'That's all? *Surely* you can think of more than that!'

'Yes! All his odd relations!' She gestured in the direction of the bricked-up door. 'His mother!' She tossed her arms upwards. 'I'd love her for a mother-in-law! And his father, we've never even seen his father . . .'

'I have.'

'You have! Where?'

'At his home. He's in a wheelchair.'

'What were you doing at his home. Where *is* his home?' She was beginning to feel totally exasperated with this girl everyone was doing their best to help.

'The far side of town. Paul took me to meet him.'

'Am I missing something here? Is there something between the lines something that's being censored out?'

'Yes,' Audrey suddenly shouted back at her. 'I'm tired of hearing you all making arrangements, rearranging rooms, borrowing stuff from Doris. Everytime Sid's out of hearing, the topic of conversation is me! Well, not me, what you are all arranging for me! I'm tired of being the one everyone's sorry for! Well you can forget it. I've decided to take what there is, what I can't lose. Paul's exempt, he's not going away. He's asked me to marry him and I've said yes.'

'And the baby?' she asked quietly.

'It could be his and he'll never know any different.'

There was such brash recklessness in her voice, in her intentions, that Vi shook her head and begged, 'Please don't do it, Audrey.' But even as she asked, she saw in the toss of the red hair, in the aversion of her face, the

221

schoolgirl who had before any of them dressed up and made-up and dared to walk in Viccy Park with a man.

'We've been thinking if we get a special licence your father might give me away while he's here. That'd be nice, wouldn't it.'

She did not answer.

The next day Pa's letter came to say he would be there in two weeks. He had been waiting until some new women drivers had completed their courses so he could take two whole weeks' holiday together. He would travel down on May 3rd.

They declared a kind of truce. Ma, in any case, was so overwhelmed at the thought of seeing Harold again it was difficult to talk to her about anything other than the work they were doing on yet another bedroom, so that Sid would have his own room, leaving Ma and Pa on their own.

Sid and Vi suddenly decided to weed all around the front of the house and set flowers near the well, wishing they had thought of it before. John's aunt gave her clumps of pinks, forget-me-nots and aubretia and Vi willed the wild foxgloves to be in full pink, white and mauve bloom along the stone hedges. Ma saved rations, tried to stock up a little, asked Paul to be sure to bring a couple of rabbits while he was there.

'Do better than that for you, m'handsome,' he said and tapped the side of his nose.

Two days before Pa arrived, he brought a brace of mallards. Vi found Sid stroking their emerald and blue gloss where they hung in the outhouse. 'I don't like things to die,' he said but she whispered him a secret which had his eyes shining again and him bursting to tell everyone. 'Won't Pa be 'mazed!' he exclaimed. 'He will,' she agreed with confidence.

Chapter 26

They were at the station much too early, Ma, Sid and Vi. Sid had plagued them with nonstop questions but suddenly, as the train was signalled and they could actually hear it coming, he fell silent. His unwavering gaze and attention focused on the train, slowly growing larger as it came almost head on towards them along the last straight stretch and in under the canopy into Penzance station, bellowing out a last excess of steam within an inch of the end of line buffers.

Vi did not believe any of them drew breath as they watched the passengers disembarking. 'There's Pa. There he is,' she exclaimed, her voice gruff with the waiting tension.

'Pa! Pa!' Sid flew along the platform to him, at him. Cases were dropped as Pa caught him in his arms, swung him round to the danger of a passing porter. Then he came carrying him, hurrying to them. He stood Sid down and caught Vi and Ma in his arms, then released Vi and held Ma tight for long seconds, then swung her off her feet and around, so they were all laughing and shouting with excitement.

Then he stood back and looked at them all. 'My, you've all got some roses in your cheeks, you look ten years younger Flo.'

'Oh, go on with you.' But she bridled and blushed like a young maid.

Sid was struggling to lift one of the cases. Vi went to help him. 'What've you brought, Pa? This case weighs a ton!'

'Among other things, my tools. Thought there'd be a few jobs I could do while I'm 'ere.'

'We've got a special surprise for you,' Sid told him, hauling on his hand. 'Come on! Vi's been practising.'

'Oh, what's this then?' he asked Ma, but she shook her head at him.

'It's their surprise.'

Sid danced away in front as Pa refused to be drawn away from Ma. The young boy kept looking back as if to make sure his pa really was with them. 'His name's Double Life,' he shouted, 'and he belongs to our soldier's auntie.'

'John's aunt,' Vi explained as they reached the pony and trap.

'My guy, this is something,' Pa exclaimed. 'This is class.' He walked all round the little trap, saw them all aboard, lifting Ma in, cases on the floor in the middle, then went to the horse's head. 'Hello, old fella, you ready for home then?' The pony snickered a soft reply and, as Pa ran his hand up under the mane, it visibly leaned towards him.

He watched as Vi unhitched the reins and took up the long whip, clicking her tongue she drove off at a steady trot from the seafront station along the coast road. They all talked, Sid was irrepressible giving Pa no time to answer his questions as he gave out his own flood of news. Vi felt it was a good thing he did not know about Audrey.

'You look tired, Harold,' Ma said.

'It's going to be nice to sleep in a bed and know I haven't got to get up for work or for Jerry.' Then, as if he could bear to be a passenger no longer, he leaned over and took the reins from his daughter. The leathers seemed to fall into his palms as if they had always been there. Even the pony held its head higher and heeded the rein with greater attention, as if it too knew it was in the hands of an expert. 'You couldn't have given me a better present if you'd thought all year. It's worth coming three hundred odd miles for this.'

'Paul's got a horse,' Sid began again.

'Do give Pa a rest,' Vi said quickly, too quickly, but cutting off the ultimate dampener that he also had a cart. Instead she added, 'I mean let Pa just enjoy driving in peace.'

She had also instructed Audrey not to burden Pa with 'all the gory details' as soon as he arrived and she noticed Ma's frown as they heard Audrey coming home from work. Vi had felt many reservations about Audrey in the last few weeks, but her greeting of Pa left no room for either complaint or reserve.

'Oh, Mr Tulley!' she shouted and ran to give him a great hug and a kiss. 'What would we do without you! It's so good to see you again, isn't it?' She turned to the rest of them as if for confirmation.

'It's bloomin' good to be 'ere I'll tell you, and I'm going to make the most of it.'

For a moment they all held their breath as if waiting for Audrey to say more than they wanted on this first evening. 'Well, we've all got plans for you,' she said. 'Haven't we folks?'

'I'm not going to school for one thing.'

'Good try, old son,' Pa said, laughing. 'You've just had Easter holidays and Whitsun's only around the corner. Tell you what, I'll meet you out and you can show me round the place.'

'I could take you to meet Paul and Major! Before school . . .'

'After,' Pa ruled. 'I'll be too tired to be up that early – but I *could* find the strength to open those cases.'

224

'Yeah!' Sid exclaimed, diving on his father. 'What've you brought?'

'All sorts,' he said, snapping open the huge battered leather case, heavy when empty but ponderously so now. 'But first. . .' He drew out a neatly wrapped brown paper parcel, quite large, important looking, and handed it to Ma.

'What's this?' she asked as the parcel was placed on her knee. Pa did not speak but nodded to her to open it. She did so wonderingly and ever more so, as mouth open, she pulled from inside a tailored navy skirt and jacket. She stood up and held the skirt against herself, slipped on the jacket. It fit perfectly. They were all speechless at this triumph of Pa's fixing abilities. 'But you can't just buy . . .'

'No coupons required!' Pa laughed, enjoying his wife's delighted bewilderment. 'Don't you recognise my navy suit?'

'Your suit, but . . .'

'My suit turned and remade by Mr Rubenstein! He knew your measurements and he wouldn't take a brass farthing for doing it.' Pa put on the tones of Mr Rubenstein. 'For your lady I do for nothing. What do I want with more money at my age? Heh?' They all laughed at the accuracy of the impersonation and Vi had that comfortable feeling of confidence that her pa would repay the old tailor in some way. He could be relied on for that.

Now were pulled out tinned foods, oranges and dried egg, then nylons for Vi and Audrey. 'Pa?' Vi queried.

'Don't ask!' he told her. 'A friend of a friend, of a friend, who delivers biscuits from a factory!'

Then he stood erect and looked at his son hands behind his back. 'Well, old lad, all those things Vi's soldier brought you . . .' He let his voice trail off and shrugged his shoulders.

Sid frowned but stood up straight. 'That's right, Pa, I've 'ad a lot.'

'So I bought you something for your horse. They're old mind, from an old baker who used to come round the Green.' Looped on the forefinger of each hand, he held out two beautiful horse brasses, one a star in a circle, the other an encircled sheaf of wheat, both polished until they gleamed.

'Wow!' Other words seem to fail him, but Vi saw her pa's pleasure in his son, in his joy in the present or his willingness to have received nothing.

'I'll show you how they fix on Major's harness.'

'Wow! Thanks, Pa!' He held the brasses either side his head.

'You only want your fangs in,' Vi told him.

The banter and the exchange of news as they picked up the threads of each other's daily lives made it very late when finally bedtime was declared. Though as they went upstairs, Sid insisted Pa saw his wall maps and told of John's 'secret message'. Both brother and sister waited to see if he agreed with their interpretation. His finger went towards the long broken outline of Greece and held there as he too assessed the enemy flags all around. 'Letters getting through are they?' he asked.

'More and more out of order and very late,' she told him.

Even when they were all in bed and the long spring evening had given way to darkness, Vi felt the whole house had a different, more contented, more complete feeling because her pa was there. She curled herself up tight, think-ing of Ma and Pa together and she wondered if they would make love – not as she and John had of course, or she supposed not. How long, she wondered, did such passionate love go on for? How many years would there still be when he returned?

She thought they would all sleep late, but when she went to the well the next morning Pa was already there, soaking up the early morning sun, draw-ing the sea air deep into his lungs. He turned as she approached and lifted his arm, she went to stand with her arm around his waist, his around her shoul-der. 'My,' he said, 'this is some place, some view.'

'It's all right now, Pa, but its been rough, rough for Ma. Bad weather, no furniture and the place was filthy when we first moved in.'

'You'd never know now. Ma's worked her magic on that. I'll have to see if I can make you some rails and shelves for your clothes upstairs, put some hooks up in the kitchen for the saucepans and lids.' He looked down. 'And you've been planting flowers. I know Ma didn't do that.'

'No, me and Sid. He's beginning to settle, to make friends and he loves that old horse – if only you were here to stay.'

'If only. My guy, I'd go for that!'

She pointed out the cliff-top path and the one halfway down from which she had recently found an easy winding way right down to the beach. 'You can walk either of those and this stretch of beach is safe, no mines or anything.'

'Like there's not a war on down here,' he said wonderingly. 'Though there is something you've not told me yet. Something you all know, except Sid, or by now he'd have blurted it out.'

'Let's just walk a little way before we go in to make everyone a cuppa.'

'Well?' he prompted as he followed her towards the beach.

'Audrey's expecting.'

She heard his footsteps stop behind her. She turned back as he stood stunned by the news, then he swore softly under his breath before demanding, 'So who is he?'

She told him about Noel – then about Paul. She told him of her own feelings and fears about Paul.

'But she says this baby could be his?' He thought for some time after she had confirmed this was what Audrey *said*. 'Sid seems to spend a lot of time with him and your ma says how good he's been to you all.'

She did not answer, weighing the value of telling Pa of the stone-throwing, of how she had confronted Paul about the cart and his threats to tell Mr Spurrier about it. 'You tell and I tell what I know,' she had threatened. 'Only

I'll go to the police. Why should your boss make money out of the war and rationing! And you're worse! Trying to blackmail people into doing what they don't want to do!'

He had not spoken directly to her since, but the cart had reappeared mended and Sid obviously felt on good terms with the Cornishman again – something she doubted she ever would be. Like Ethel Kerrow, he did not like to be got the better of. She guessed he would always be looking for revenge.

'So is Paul likely to be around today?' Pa asked. 'Has he been invited tonight to share in these ducks he's supplied?'

'Yes, Ma invited him – as usual – but he'll be around anyway.'

'I think I'll try to see him on his own. If you spot him around let me know, no time to be wasted. Christmas she told you it could have happened?'

Mid-morning Vi saw Paul working in the fields towards the town, lifting stones back into place on the hedges, working his way around the boundaries. She told Pa, and he and Ma, who had already spent some time discussing Audrey, walked together along the cliffs towards the young man. They held hands like young lovers, she thought, and already, in spite of this new trouble, Pa looked more rested, his eyes less dark-ringed.

She watched them reach Paul, saw him stop work and walk away with them, out of sight. She went thoughtfully back upstairs to unlock the leather stationery folder John's aunt had given her as a Christmas gift. She had formed the habit of writing in the folder several times in a day, even taking it to the Lodge stowed in the bicycle basket. Often she wrote to John of events yet to come and her expectations, then adding what was often a funny reversal of how events turned out. She wrote now of the coming dinner party ending with the words 'great discussion expected!'

But by dinnertime, when the house was aromatic with roasting duck and sage and onion stuffing, the matter had not so much been discussed as the Tulleys told what Audrey and Paul had arranged. As Pa said, 'You've not been idle!' when Paul repeated the news over the meal that he had a special licence for the two of them to be married at Penzance Registry Office two weeks on Saturday and he had the offer of a cottage the far side of Gerrard's Head from his employer, Mr Spurrier.

Vi glanced at him. He looked victorious, sounded quite triumphant while Audrey, even though she had insisted this was what she wanted, now looked neither as Paul became more talkative than she had ever heard him before.

He was at the house more after that evening, bringing wood for Pa to make shelves, even stout dowelling for clothes rails. By the time the middle weekend of Pa's holiday came, in no time at all it seemed, Vi was curious to know his verdict about Paul.

'I'd like to meet his parents.' Pa answered her doubts with his statement. 'I've asked, being as I'm sort of standing in for her own father but . . .'

227

'But?' she queried.

'I'm being fobbed off. All the talk is of meeting them at the wedding. Not . . .' He paused to rub his hand around his chin. She could hear the roughness, it was a gesture he had made every day at Brierly Street just before he shaved. 'Not that I feel I can do much about it, considering how keen Audrey is to be married to him. I've told her we'd look after her and her baby – but she definitely doesn't want that. She wants her own home and life, which I can understand.'

'So you don't like him, Pa?'

'Ma's told me how good he's been to you, the jobs he's done, but there's –' He cut himself off short as if annoyed with his own chatter. 'No, is the answer I'm trying to circle around – but no I don't. He's deep.'

'Yes,' she agreed, 'and his depths are . . . not nice.'

'All we can do is be there for her if things go wrong.' He looped an arm around her shoulders. 'Come on,' he said, 'I've promised to play cricket with Sid on the beach.' He picked up a bat he had shaped from a piece of leftover shelving. 'He's gone to get the rest of the gear.'

'We'll all play,' Vi decided. 'I'll go and get Ma and Audrey.'

There was much protesting from the women but, with Sid's help, they were persuaded they would enjoy fielding if nothing else. When they arrived on the hard wet sand the tide had just left, Audrey declared if she was being made to field she was having a bat as well.

'OK, then we'll play properly with sides – me and Sid against you three,' Pa said.

With much blustering that two men could outplay three women any day, Pa won the toss and Sid insisted his father should go in first bat. Vi was to bowl with Audrey behind the wicket and Ma would be responsible sea-side fielding. 'But if you hit it in the water you're fetching it out!'

The first ball Vi threw down, Pa hit with all his force. The ball sailed up high towards Ma but she was watching her husband as the force of the hard cricket ball on the unsprung piece of wood had him pretending to vibrate violently all over, even as his team mate screamed for him to run, which he eventually did, still twitching and jerking. Ma dropped the ball she saw only belatedly. Then Vi, having berated Ma for her butter-fingers, dropped it. As it was finally thrown in, she was laughing so much as Pa lined himself up for the next bowl like a crooked old man.

The game never recovered as each in turn found the hard ball on the bat made them react with flinching comic reactions as their fingers tingled or arms jerked if they hit the solid ball. Sid, having protested for some time that it was a serious match, in the end was clowning as much as the rest of them.

'We'll get a soft ball for the next game,' Pa declared wiping the sweat from his forehead and the tears of laughter from his eyes. Then he shaded his eyes and frowned, looking up towards the house. 'Someone's standing by the well looking this way, a woman.'

Vi too shaded her eyes. 'It's John's aunt! She did say she would like to meet you, Pa.'

She waved to let Mrs Trewellan know they had seen her.

'Don't go,' Sid wailed. 'It's my bat!'

'I'll give you three balls,' Audrey offered.

'We'll follow you.' Ma nodded Pa and Vi on the way. Vi was tempted to tell him about Mrs Trewellan's stage career as they walked up the winding path, but, glancing up, she felt John's aunt was watching them with such intensity there was even a danger she would guess what she was saying. Perhaps she was just making a distant summing up of her pa. She had talked about his coming enough.

'I must remember to thank her for letting you borrow the pony and trap,' Pa said as they approached. Then he too seemed arrested by the stillness of the woman as she stood one hand on the well wall as if for support and the solemn, stricken expression on her face.

'Oh no!' Vi heard herself exclaim even before she saw the buff coloured envelope in Mrs Trewellan's hand.

'It came about an hour ago.'

Feeling suddenly as if she and the whole world had turned to solid ice, Vi watched her own hand go out to take the telegram form. She was not sure she read it.

'Missing in action.'

'What does that mean?'

'I rang Jimmie right away. He says it means he is unaccounted for. Not among the dead or wounded, not reported as having been captured. He'll try to find out more from people he knows in the War Office. He's going to ring me back at midday.'

'Unaccounted for?'

'M'dear . . .'

She watched Mrs Trewellan's lips moving, frowned and tried to concentrate. What did it mean? It couldn't be true. She vaguely realised that Pa and John's aunt had briefly introduced themselves, were asking her things, making decisions about going back to the Lodge. Then she heard Mrs Trewellan's voice break. 'He was like a son to me, the boy I never had. What are we going to do?'

'Not give up hope,' Pa told her, offering her his arm to lean on as she stepped away from the well.

Never give up until the ball stops rolling. Vi remembered hearing Noel say that, but it had stopped rolling for him.

'I wondered if you would like to come back with me to the Lodge and wait for my husband's call so we both know as much as possible.'

229

'Yes please.' It was the only thing she felt certain about. She did want to know as much as possible.

Ma, Sid and Audrey stood in a sad line, only the breeze moved the women's skirts as Sid nervously tossed the cricket ball, John's cricket ball, from hand to hand his eyes riveted to his sister's face. Ma's hand was on his forearm as if restraining him from either unappropriate movement or speech. Pa took charge of the pony and drove them up away to the Lodge. No one waved or spoke. Vi felt she saw everything with startling clarity, every minute detail etched into her memory – for weren't these the first moments of her life without the certainty of John's existence. He was unaccounted for. Everything else had hard solid outlines while she herself was like a formless nonentity.

She watched Alice bringing in tea for them all; she saw the woman's compassion when she looked at John's aunt, she saw her eyes did not lift to meet Pa's face or her own. *Poor woman*, she thought and was not sure why.

Then the sound they all waited for startled her but Mrs Trewellan, seated next to the telephone, answered it immediately. Vi watched as she stood solemnly nodding her head. 'Yes, I understand. Yes, Violet's here now.' She broke off and held out the receiver. 'Jimmie wants to speak to you.'

Her hand trembled so much she had to steady the receiver to her ear with both hands.

'Bear up old thing, for Annie's sake.' His words, his deep warm voice broke through the icy coldness and some realisation of what it might all mean began to seep through. 'She'll be brave for a time, then go to pieces. Will you stay with her tonight?'

'Of course,' she answered without thought. 'Do you know any more?' she asked, surprised how ordinary her voice sounded, just like it always did. 'What does it mean, missing?'

'That they know nothing for sure except that he is not with his unit. M'dear, there's a big retreat but many men are escaping south, over the water, the navy's there.' She was alerted by the rapidity of this piece of information and the tone – it was a clue like the flamenco. She knew she must remember those brief few words as he went on in more general terms about how many men would be missing. 'This is mountainous terrain, many more will be unaccounted for because they will be hiding from the enemy, possibly with guerilla bands.' She listened on to his fervent words about carrying on, helping Annie, keeping things together.

The two women looked at each other in silence as the receiver was replaced.

'He must be safe,' Mrs Trewellan said at last in no more than a whisper. 'I will have wasted an awful lot of my life down here if he doesn't come back.'

'And the rest of my life will not be worth living,' Vi stated.

'Much too soon for either of you to start talking like that, to start thinking about him not coming back,' Pa urged.

But the two women looked at each other with more understanding of what each felt. 'Life's funny isn't it?' Vi said, turning away to the window as the irony of it all made tears threaten. 'I wish with all my heart I was like Audrey, expecting her chap's baby. Then I'd have *something*.'

'Then we'd both have something,' Mrs Trewellan said quietly.

Vi felt a hand on her shoulder. She turned and the two held each other, patting each other's back in the universal instinctive gesture of giving comfort when words had no more to offer.

Chapter 27

Vi began to feel she might well lose her sanity as she continually churned over possibilities, looked at Sid's maps, at the mountains of Greece. The Pindus Mountains, she read, thinking of a man fighting there, lying wounded. Was there snow? Was it hot, arid like a desert? Then there was the coastline so broken. The escape route? The Ionian Islands with the long island of Crete lying to the south – what dangers there? Were there sharks? Snipers? Mines on the beaches?

She tried desperately to think herself into a foreign land, knowing nothing but this corner of England and London. At the same time there were the realities of Audrey's wedding on Saturday, Pa's departure on Sunday *and* being businesslike for the sake of John's aunt. Quite suddenly, and just as the Commodore had predicted, she had gone to pieces – but in her own peculiar way. How did one get through these times?

Vi had stayed at the Lodge that first night, neither of them retiring until the early hours of the morning. When, by mid-morning, John's aunt had not come down, Alice had prepared a tray and taken it to her room. She had found her mistress lying rigid as if in some kind of fit, unspeaking and eyes closed, alarming them both with her unresponsiveness. Like someone professionally laid-out was the unwitting thought that came to Vi as she sent Alice to telephone for the family doctor.

She took up the inert hand and cradled it tightly between her own. 'Mrs Trewellan, come on, luv, time to be up and about,' she urged and wondered if the Commodore would have expected this reaction? Then another thought occurred to her.

'This, Anne Caroline Barry,' she said in as firm a voice as she could muster, 'is very theatrical!' She felt some change in the hand she held, as if some small electric charge had stirred it to life, and the eyes snapped open, fixing her with an aggressive stare. 'Don't call me "luv",' she snapped, but the barriers between them were falling fast and as they both heard Alice coming back upstairs a look of panic crossed the patient's face. When Alice came bustling into the room, she found the mistress she was devoted to just beginning to come round.

But if John's aunt could get through the days by playing a part, Vi knew she could only survive if she was herself – and this state of indecision, of replaying all the options was tearing her mind to bits.

On Thursday Mrs Trewellan decided that what she needed to do was to go to London to her husband. 'Just to collapse and really be myself for a day or two. I won't stay long, m'dear, and while your pa's here seems a good time. We'll speak on the telephone each day – if you don't mind.'

On Friday morning Sam took John's aunt to the station, Vi immediately began tidying her desk, piling the letters ready to be posted neatly on one corner, then called through to Alice. 'I'm going out, Alice, not sure how long I shall be.' *Or where I'm going*, she added silently.

Then, without giving Alice time to make any coherent comment, she was away on her bicycle, aware from the exclamation behind her that Alice was outside, probably hands on hips. She turned right, away from the farm, laboured uphill past the pub, beyond the turning to Spurrier's latest hide-out, on to the wildest part of the coast. All the time she pedalled, she kept thinking if only she knew for sure then it would be easy, no problem.

In the distance she saw people working in a line across a field strewn with baskets, potato picking. Inland the moors were high with rocky crags like the ones she and Sid had negotiated. She turned away on to a side track towards the sea. For a time it was like a cart track, then the ferns and gorse and thorny ropes of briar forced her to dismount. To go further she had to abandon her bicycle. She leaned it against a great thorny gorse bush and walked carefully on to the very edge of the cliffs. They were high here, very high, great steep vertical spines of rock down to the beach. Near where she emerged was a precarious ledge, a cup of grass, some four feet below the top of the cliff, just a jump down.

That she decided was where she wanted to be. She stepped off the cliff out into the air – and landed – and staggered – and screamed, her panic mingling with the gull's as it rose from under her feet. She felt its wings slap her legs, chest, face, as if it climbed more than flew over her to escape, beating her back. And she found herself pressed against the cliff face sliding down into the green scoop of grass as her knees gave way, her heart pounding.

She gripped her knees and pressed her forehead on to her arms, tight and tense. What a stupid thing to do. But she was not sure what she had intended, though she knew the gull had saved her from going over. 'Oh God!' she exclaimed, tension giving way to tears. She sobbed, free of all restraint, free of the danger of being overheard or interrupted, sobbed the ragged loud cries of one whose heart is breaking.

'But,' she gasped mopping the flood of tears with fingers and palms, 'I don't know! I don't *know!*'

233

Saved by a seagull? Was it a sign? She gave a brief gasp of laughter, she wasn't one who looked for such explanations. 'And I'm probably sitting on its nest.' She felt quickly, only grass. Her weeping was quieter now, for tears cannot go on for ever. She lifted her head and, looking out towards the sea, wiped the final blur from her eyes on a sopping handkerchief and felt that in a clumsy dangerous way she had found some of the relief she had sought.

Calmer now, she began to feel the peace of this place, as physically cut off from the world as she felt mentally detached from it. Completely and utterly alone except for the gulls. She watched them now, clamouring and calling as they flew in to perch on the cliff face. Big, soft grey and white birds, strong, graceful, gliding to and from nests, she supposed, busy raising families.

She hugged her knees tighter. *I can't believe I shall never see his face again, never sit on a bus with our hands clasped between us, never see again the naked curve of his back in the firelight, never hear the sweet music his fingers could command. I don't believe all that is gone. It can't be.* It can't be.

'No,' she ordered herself, this was just a different helter-skelter rushing her nowhere. She had to reason her life out, do what was best. She gave a brief tremorous laugh as she acknowledged just how like Pa she must be, reasoning things out, making little grunting noises to himself as he settled a point to his satisfaction. She recalled his solitary and painful decision to send them here and the price he was daily paying in the joyless house that was now number 11 Brierly Street.

It was time to do her own reasoning.

One gull in particular caught her eye as it came near, almost above her, floating with effortless grace on the breeze, approaching, turning away, lifting white and beautiful against the dark cliff. She wondered if it was her gull.

So many questions, so many doubts – but there were things she did know for certain. She knew it was possible to love only with hope – and beyond – beyond hope, beyond the grave, beyond death, she knew that was possible. If she never saw John again, the love they had shared was still theirs for ever.

Hundreds of women, thousands even, hundreds of thousands Pa had said, must be yearning for news of their menfolk – mothers for sons, wives for husbands, sisters for brothers. She made pause to thank God Sid was so young. And hadn't she decided long ago that real love was to care too much, to ever risk being hurt, to be afraid for the loved one, but not for one's self. What had seemed to need courage then, braving his family, being honest with Roy and May, those mountains had been cut down to something more the size of large foothills.

'Keep up, old thing.' She repeated Commodore Trewellan's words aloud. 'Keep up.' Keeping up, keeping up appearances, putting on a show – doing things in a bit of a style. Yes, this would be her way. To survive she would not only keep going, she would do things with a bit of style.

She would still write to John every day, still post letters even if they did come back. But she would also keep a diary, a much bigger thing than the one he had bought her, a notebook, a page for each day's events: family matters, hers and his; business affairs, the complaints of the tenants, the work they needed doing, what was done and what left; profit and loss – she knew about those. And Alice's doings, that should also fill a line or two.

Pa kept saying, 'He's missing, not reported killed. Hang on to that.' He tried to raise a smile. 'Don't get off until the bus reaches the terminus.' 'Make him proud of all he hears of you when he comes back.' So many things Pa kept saying, never giving up on her. 'Work's the best time-killer, useful work well done.'

He had dug and planted a plot of land in front of the farmhouse, begun a vegetable garden, and obviously intended to leave it in the charge of Sid and herself. Gardening, her job at the Lodge, Audrey's baby, there was going to be plenty she could busy herself with. This felt right for her, to be up and doing. She stood up and felt a little dizzy on this airy ledge with a swirl of gulls overhead, heads lowered as if watching her. Very cautiously, heart thumping, she climbed back to the cliff top.

She felt she had learned several salutary lessons and before she retrieved her bicycle there was something else she could do. This wilder more remote section of coast was, she understood, where Audrey was going to live. She scrambled up a rough pile of rocks and debris, but climbed with caution for she realised it could be a derelict mine shaft. Turning when she was some ten feet up, she found there was not much doubt where or which cottage it might be, for there was only one, set down square it seemed in the middle of the natural wilderness of low bushes, wild flowers and granite outcrops.

The day before, Paul had arrived with a cart piled with furniture he had bought at a local auction. Pa and Ma had come with him to this cottage that Cyril Spurrier had agreed he and his bride could have. Now she would go and find out why Pa had been so noncommittal, while Ma had just looked more and more worried, constantly repeating in ever more anxious tones, 'To have a baby there . . .'

Audrey had reasserted that it was only walking distance away.

That might be so, she thought, if you had a whole day to spare, and unless time was taken to clear briars and rocks from the paths, Audrey was never going to be able to push a pram from the cottage to the road.

The cottage was no more than a granite square with a low tile and concrete-wash roof, looking like an ancient bunker from some ancient war. Someone could be beleaguered here all right! It was a place for a recluse, not for the Audrey Kingston Vi had known all her life.

She fought her way along disused tracks to the door, feeling very much an intruder, though it was obvious no one was around. She thumbed down the latch and the door yielded. She stepped in on to a hard-packed earth floor. 'Oh dear!' she exclaimed as she also saw the stone sink on brick piers –

though there was a small hand pump over it – a range which someone had attempted to clean. There was a deal table, two chairs and a small dresser. All needed a lot of work to make them wholesome. 'We've done all this once.'

She wandered on through the house. The other downstairs room was empty. Upstairs, one room was furnished with the double bed, wardrobe and dressing table. These were the items Paul had bought at the sale. The other room she expected to be empty but, surprisingly, there was an ancient oak single bed on which was a mattress, black ticking pillows, a couple of grey blankets and several coats.

She moved further into the room. There was no doubt at all that someone had been sleeping here fairly regularly. On the bare floor at the far side of the bed there was a candlestick, matches. It could surely only be Paul. This cottage was the answer to the question of where he went when the weather was bad. She had long ago come to the conclusion he slept out when the season was right. It suited him to be out, waiting for dawn to shoot game and rabbits which he gave to them in return for meals – and other favours – or which he sold in the town.

She was leaving the cottage, planning how best to help bring some kind of homeliness to the place, when she paused, listening to the distant sound of a man's voice, raised, bellowing. She had no doubt but that it was Paul bringing another load of goods to the cottage. With a shudder she thought that no one would hear however much anyone shouted in this cottage. This was isolation. If you were in trouble this was desolation . . .

She walked as quickly as she could back towards her cycle, scratching her legs and snagging her skirt. She began to realise that she was being reckless in response to the irate cries of the man coming towards her along the overgrown track from the road. Her stockings were torn and her calves bleeding and she was out of breath. She paused to pull herself together, to take some rational account of the situation.

Paul was driving Major with the cart loaded again with furniture – a rocking chair and a small gate-legged table she could see over his shoulder as he stood on the cart urging the animal on against the wheel-clogging mass of briars and gorse.

She watched for a moment, appalled, and John's description of him came vividly back to her. 'He seems kind enough in the normal way but I once saw him lose his temper . . . I believe he's a man to walk around very warily.'

But as Vi came up to the frenzied man who was prodding his animal's rump with a stout length of wood, wariness was not the emotion that surfaced.

'You bleeding madman! What do you think you're doing? Stop it! Do you hear me! Stop it!' She was bellowing now but at first she knew he was not even aware that she was there.

The double shouting alarmed the horse though and he gave a half leap as if to try to clear some of the obstacles that impeded his load. The only effect it had was to make Paul lose his balance a little and as he stooped to grab the side of the cart he saw her.

'He can't pull the cart through this lot! Use your brains if you have any?'

'Get out of my way!'

She stood firm as he spaced the words with threat.

'How did you get the last lot of furniture there?' she demanded. 'Not on the cart!'

'No,' he roared, ' I carried the bloody stuff and I ain't carrying no more!' Gerrup!' He raised the length of wood he carried.

'If you strike that horse I'll . . .' She knew the threat had to carry weight, knew physical strength was on his side. 'I'll tell your butcher boss how careless you've been, that we all know where his secret slaughterhouse is. That should finish his business.' She warmed to her story now. 'Then I'll get your deferment cancelled, that shouldn't be difficult.'

'Got a bit of influence now, have you? Think your chap's got a chance of coming back then!'

She could not believe even he would stoop this low. She went forward to speak more directly at him. 'I'd sooner gamble on John coming back, than on Audrey's chances of being happy with you.'

'Once we're married that'll be nothing to do with such as you.'

There was a tone in his voice that brought back a vivid picture of Avis's kitchen, of that huge dark dresser with its tiny china ornaments, of a woman's vulnerability to a strong and violent man.

'Until then,' she said, fury shaking her voice, 'you'll carry the furniture from here and I'm waiting to see you do.'

He tried to bluster and bluff, to threaten and frighten her away, but she stood arms folded and waited for him to carry the furniture from that point. He attempted to push her aside as finally he unloaded the pieces. 'You're not married to Audrey yet and unless you're going to drag her out from under my father's nose you'd better watch yourself.'

She thought it was the first time she had ever heard a man really snarl.

When finally he was carrying the last piece to the cottage, Vi, more at ease now with horses, managed to back Major until she could turn him ready for the return journey. Even so she felt uneasy to see even an animal go off in the man's care.

She cycled home determined they must stop the wedding, determined to enlist Pa's help, but it was Audrey who was at home and she immediately launched into a eulogy for the furniture Paul had managed to get that day from his parents. Vi cut her short. 'I know I've seen it all.'

'When?'

'Look!' Audrey's voice was low and furious after she had listened to all Vi had seen and said. 'I don't care what you *think* you know or how much *you*

237

dislike Paul. I'm marrying him on Saturday and setting up my own place. I can handle him and I want my own house, my own life!'

Vi rehearsed ways of warning Paul he had better treat her friend well or else! But he did not come to Gerrard's Head again before the wedding and all was last-minute preparation and rush. Pa's departure on the Sunday also acted as a restraint to raising more problems that would certainly cause more desperate worry but probably have no answers. Her only comfort was that she decided, welcome or not, Paul was going to see a lot more of her at his cottage. She could cycle there from the Lodge each day before going home.

The wedding day dawned bright and warm and Pa and Sam were responsible for the first of the day's surprises. Sam had, with the telephoned blessings of Lady Trewellan, agreed to act as footman. Not only that, he and Pa had unearthed black and gold coach paint from the Manor stables and had refurbished the trap. So, while Ma, Vi and Sid were to travel into Penzance on the bus, Pa and Audrey would arrive in some style.

There were gasps of pleasure when the spanking outfit arrived at the farm. The new paint gleamed in the sunlight and there were ribbons and bunches of pink and white moss roses tied to the front and sides of the trap, while Sam was resplendent in white shirt, black trousers and black waistcoat with shiny brass buttons.

'What a sight to behold!' Ma exclaimed and before the day had fairly begun there were tears.

Vi went upstairs before she left the house and found Audrey dressed in the pale green shot-silk suit given by Doris and altered by Ma, who had also made a round pillbox hat of matching ribbons on a petersham base. Her face was very pale except for the splash of bright lipstick but her hair burned glossy auburn under the hat and its trailing ribbons.

'Wish me luck then,' Audrey said as the two stood looking at each other.

'Goes without saying, my luv.' She went to her and kissed her cheeks. 'Mustn't rumple you. You look beautiful.'

'Green's my colour isn't it,' she said with a brave attempt at pertness, but she stood very still, her bouquet of white roses was on the bed lying slightly upended on to the blooms.

'Yes.' Vi remembered the green dance dress the morning after her parents had been killed. That had been left at Brierly Street. 'Don't forget the Tulleys are always on your side, always here.'

'Once you get an idea into your head, you never let go do you, Vi?'

'No! Never give up!'

They laughed then. 'No hard feelings?' Audrey asked as Ma called that they ought to be leaving to walk up to the bus stop.

'Oh no! Never! Never! Friends for ever!'

They did Audrey proud, that was for sure – the trap, the Tulleys, all smart as any new paint. Doris and the new friends they had made at work had been invited, even Mrs Kerrow seemed under instruction be pleasant. They were introduced to a big old man in a wheelchair, Paul's father, crippled with arthritis. Vi stood next to him as the ceremony finished, the Registrar declaring Paul and Audrey man and wife. 'Poor girl,' he murmured, 'she doesn't know what she's taken on.'

She was astonished *he* should breathe such a remark but it was too late for more soul-searching. Then Pa invited them all to make their way to The Turk's Head where he had arranged a small celebration drink and buffet for everyone. 'Told you these Cockneys know how to enjoy themselves,' she heard Doris boast to another one of Audrey's new workmates.

When all the glasses were charged, all the plates full of fish paste or egg and cress sandwiches Pa raised his voice to officially toast the bride and groom.

'In my role as best man and father by adoption to this beautiful young lady, I'm wishing her all the luck in the world and, as I go back to London tomorrow, I'm asking all you Cornish friends to take care of her and all mine. And I reckon we should all eat together, have a few more drinks together and before anyone leaves we should sing "Auld Lang Syne" together.'

Ma cried when it came to that time, cried as she watched Sam drive the couple away to go to their new home, but she cried with her gaze fixed more on her husband than anyone else.

That night when all the festivities, all the talking – and all Pa's packing – were done, Vi lay listening to the sound of Pa and Ma talking softly in bed, of Ma still crying softly. She turned her head to the wall and silently let her own tears fall for many things and many people and she wondered how they would all sleep, but it seemed not many minutes later that her alarm clock was going off and before she was dressed she heard Sam again arriving with the trap.

'Always prompt!' the Commodore had said about Sam, then added to her in a whisper, 'Always ready to be out of young Alice's way for as long as possible.'

Pa had said he would go to the station alone, say his goodbyes at the house, but she had seen Ma's face look so stricken she had implored, 'Come on, Pa, that's not our way is it! And you'll never be able to put Sam off, you've made a real friend there.'

So they found themselves assembled on the station platform in the morning light that even in May was only just dawn, waiting for the minutes to tick away on the station clock.

Vi looked at her mother and could read her thoughts. *Don't leave me! Don't go!*

Pa stood and held Ma's hand really tight as he talked to Sid and Vi and they listened, watching the activity on the platform, the preparations for the departure of the train from this end of line station.

'I'm proud of you getting on with life again. It's all you can do, Vi, all you

239

can do, but remember you are setting an example to those around you. You never know what young Sid here may face one day. You have to show him the way to do it – and you are. I'm proud of you all.'

'All aboard, m'andsome!' The same bow-legged old porter who had been on duty the day they arrived now came to see Pa aboard, sympathetic but always one eye on the driver leaning out of his cab and hand on handle waiting to close the door.

Pa kissed his son and daughter, then held his wife for long intense seconds before releasing her so quickly she staggered a little, then he was on board and the door slammed to. The whistle blew, the green flag waved and the train gave those first great sobs of steam that always seemed so final to Vi, no turning back now. She and Sid ran a little way with the train, while Ma stood quite still waving a small white handkerchief at the last.

Vi thought how strange it was that they had come to this place the day after the funeral of Audrey's parents and now Pa was going back to London the day after Audrey's wedding. How strange. A sudden shiver overtook her in the deep shade of the covered station. Outside the sun was up and bright but its warmth did not reach them. How long would these separations, this awful war, go on?

Chapter 28

'Jimmie was devastated – especially knowing John was involved . . . somewhere.' Mrs Trewellan was looking out of the sitting-room window at the Dower House, where pink rambler roses hung full blown in the June sunshine. 'He said they evacuated over sixteen thousand men – but twelve thousand were left behind. Four nights the navy went into Crete. Lost three cruisers, six destroyers and many other ships were badly damaged, including the fleet's only aircraft carrier.'

'He couldn't have any direct news?' Vi felt obliged to ask.

John's aunt turned back, shaking her head, inhaling fiercely from the cigarette in the long amber holder she had brought back from London. Vi wondered if it was a symbol to her of happier times, something to cling on to. It certainly did not fit the 'county lady' role – Alice's covert glances were uneasy and disapproving.

'Jimmie says he believes John may yet be free and fighting with Greek or Cretan guerillas in the mountains.'

Vi wrote in her notebook that she thought his aunt might have had a breakdown while away in London. 'It's her eyes – and I'm sure she did not intend to stay away so long. She was very apologetic when she came back about leaving me in charge so long. But I did all right! Never lost a farm, or a tenant, or came to blows with Alice – not quite! The other thing that is going "all right" seems to be Audrey and Paul! They are like a pair of love-doves with a new nest. He's taking bits and pieces back to improve the cottage all the time – and Audrey is blossoming nicely!' She paused after writing that, but these notebooks were fast becoming the *whole* truth 'as Violet Tulley sees it' and she added, 'But I feel it's all so brittle and could break at any time if things don't go *just* his way – that temper we've both seen lurks not too far below the Kerrow surface.'

She had just begun the fifth notebook when, on Saturday September 13th 1941, Paul came to the farm his face beaming. 'It's a girl,' he told them, 'in the night. I've to go to the chemist but the midwife's still there. She'll wait while one of you gets there.'

Paul had never acknowledged the fact that Audrey had asked Vi to go and stay with her for the first few weeks after her confinement and didn't do so now. Vi prepared to leave straight away while Ma cross-questioned him about mother and baby, weight and names.

'Oh, I don't know these things,' he answered.

'But Audrey's all right?' Vi pressed him.

'Why shouldn't she be!' he replied.

'I bet the baby's about as heavy as Major's nosebag when its full,' Sid offered before the silence became awkward, going through the gestures of holding up and weighing the feed-bag.

'Sounds about right,' Paul grinned.

Vi collected what clothes she needed, her writing folder and current notebook, and cycled off immediately towards the point. Ma insisted she also take the matinee coat and bootees she had crocheted along with her love and promises to walk over to see how they were coping the following day.

'Meet Noelle Margaret,' Audrey said as Violet leaned over the bed to hold back the enveloping shawl and view the tiny red face with flat fringe of dark hair.

'She's beautiful and are you all right?' Receiving a reassuring nod, she queried, 'Noel?'

'I told the midwife it was to be Noel if was a boy and she said it was a girl's name too and you could add another "le" to make it look more feminine written down. So that's what I've decided – it seems only fair after all. After the father – and my mother.'

'What about Paul?' she questioned, alarmed by what seemed total fool-hardiness. 'He doesn't know?'

'No, and never will. Don't worry, I'm not quite such a fool.'

'But he knew about Noel.'

'I just said I always liked the name. He's got nothing to complain about. He's never had it so good, never been so comfortable or looked after.'

She looked so confident, not so pale now after the summer sun. Her hair, always her most sensational feature, was long now. It lay over her shoulder in a red cloud. With a pang Vi thought she ought to have found herself someone so much better – the aristocrat she had always fancied. 'No, but don't risk making him suspicious or jealous,' she warned.

'You know what I've told you, I can handle him. I've got him eating out of my hand, and now this little mite . . .' She looked down at the bundle in her arms with such tenderness, Vi's heart leapt in both joy and overwhelming concern for them both. 'I've no regrets, you know, the war took her dad but this is next best.'

That night Vi wrote in the notebook: 'I must be very selfish because all I could think is I hope I never have to make do with second best.' Then she began a new paragraph. 'I have in the end had quite a "forgiving" letter from Roy. He says that after all no one can be *forced* to be in love with someone and he hoped we would still be friends and he told me he had written to his parents to tell them how he feels.'

The notebooks became the archives for all her personal thoughts, events large and small, her immediate world, his home, and world events.

'December 7th 1941, Pearl Harbour – wherever that is. Sid has found a story in one of your *Yarns for Boys* books called "The Pearl Fishermen." He thinks it must be where Pearl Harbour is. I don't know, perhaps he's right. It's brought the Yanks into the war. His maps with Japan overrunning the Far East really do make it look like a World War.'

'I can't believe so long has gone by without any news of you. You really are missing – and me – I'm missing my life, my love. "No news is good news" – even Alice has said that to me – *to me*. These old sayings must have a lot of truth in them or we wouldn't keep repeating them generations after generations – would we!'

'September 13th 1942. Noelle's first birthday and what a happy nature the child has. At least Audrey is living. I'm sure Paul is more morose though and do I imagine it or does even little Noelle regard him more solemnly than she does other people? I think he's jealous of the baby.'

'What strange places we hear about and learn to say. Sid is fascinated by names. I hear him muttering "Guadalcanal". It is a name that has been in the news since thousands of Yanks were sent there. Now, here we are in January 1943 and I think the Japs are getting the worst of it at "Guadalcanal". It seems a long time since I wasn't sure whether "Penzance" was a real place or not.'

'February 1st. Heard from Pa today that Mr Moore has died, apparently he was taken into hospital a few days ago and it was something to do with his long-standing rupture. Mrs Moore is determined to move back into the shop – it is under reconstruction – and keep the business going for Roy.'

'Another bit of news – the Yanks are not only at Sid's Guadalcanal they are at the Manor House too! I am appointed in an official capacity to liaise with the Yankee Army – sort of like May used to do. Incidentally, both Ma and your aunt saw May in London over last Christmas. She said she is "having a great war". Ma is very unsettled now after her trip to London. She was distressed by the state of her home and is convinced the bombing of London is largely over. I can see her deciding to go home anytime – if it was not for me and Sid she'd already be away I'm sure!'

'Another thing about the Yanks at the Hall (sounds like a film title) – some are nice guys and I do try to keep my distance a bit, but – and this is going to make me sound like what my Gran would have called "a brazen hussy" – but I wish I had a ring – your ring – sort of give myself official status. There is this feeling that Yanks think of any girl as "fair game" – not true of all, just most!'

'Never thought that just buying the notebooks would be a problem. Have enlisted Mrs Stevens the postlady – she's great at getting us things, willing too! Have begun to write on the front and back covers, so this gives thirty-two days' news in one book. I am on my twenty-eighth exercise-book! Piled on my table it reminds me of school with all the class books ready for marking! It makes my heart go into a great yearning to count them – so I must go on writing quickly.'

'Our great family news is that Pa is coming down for Easter again. He can't wait and neither can we. Ma is most put out because she has just discovered that Easter Sunday is not until the 25th of April this year – as late as it can be! Poor Ma! Poor me – how long will I have to wait for you? Heard of someone in Penzance being notified their husband was a POW three years after he went missing. You have been missing for one year, nine months and five days.'

'February 13th 1943 – not a Friday but unlucky for some. Baby Noelle has a bruised arm and while Audrey says she fell and I know that is bound to happen with a toddler, this bruise goes right around the arm, more as if someone has grasped it hard. What convinces me it is Paul who's responsible is the way the child looks at him when he comes in. She reverts to going along on her bottom and shuffles away behind things. Things will come to a head. Audrey will be pushed to *something*. She no longer defends Paul, she no longer talks about him! I am definitely telling Pa *everything* when he comes down. I have to.'

'March 7th 1943. London. Brierly Street. Where do I start? How can I bear to write it? My pa is dead! My pa – I cannot believe it. I can't believe I'll never see him again.'

Tears dropped to the page and Vi put down the pen, the awful sobbing pain that began like a great fist clenched in her stomach came again. She could not believe this emptiness that was real loss, real death – not missing, not not-knowing – but knowing, knowing for sure that the awful pain was to be without relief, without reprieve.

The kaleidoscope of misery caught her up once again, replayed all the shock, the hurt and the sorrowing which had begun with the policeman coming to the farm. 'But he's coming for Easter.' 'Another year Easter could have been this early – he could have been here!' The disbelief, the journey to London, trying to buy a newspaper on the way to see if there was any news. Arriving late at night to hear the story from a thinner, more dishevelled Mrs Moore as they sat around the kitchen range – with Pa's workbag hanging in its usual place behind the door.

'It was the rumours that did it.' Mrs Moore sat shaking her head, looking, Vi thought, as incredibly weary and as emotionally spent as they were. 'I 'ave to tell you this, it's what made it 'appen,' she said as if asking tolerance for what might seem like needless introduction.

'The numbers going down the Bethnal tube station had dropped no end. Well, we'd 'ad no real bombing to speak of since well before my Bert died – but he made me promise I would always go down until the war was over. But that night was just after that big raid on Berlin and Jerry threatened reprisals. The warning went at about quarter past eight and immediately hundreds of people began to flock down. I was there in my place as usual. In ten minutes people were flooding in like they did when the Blitz was at its worst. Then what happened was some rockets were fired from a new gun emplacement in Victoria Park. They made such a racket that everyone thought it was bombs falling. It made everyone twice as eager to get down the stairs.'

She paused and sighed deeply. 'Someone fell on the stairs – we heard the shouts and commotions – but there was nothing anyone could do. As the uproar got worse it seemed to make those outside more anxious to get in – pushing and screaming to get out of danger – as they thought.'

'Soon there was a solid mass of bodies at the bottom of the stairs – and still people were pushing in.'

They sat in stunned silence until Maggie recovered enough to go on. 'I didn't know Harold had been trapped until the next day – when the police brought the message. They found his workbag with his name in, then came to enquire.' All their eyes went to the bag on the door. 'I looked in to make sure it was his. It 'ad his name in like they said – and he hadn't come 'ome and 'e wasn't at work. They wanted me to identify – but I said best wait for you.'

Without thought beyond finding out all there could possibly be to know, Vi went to the door and took down the bag, she looked at Ma then unbuckled the strap. It wasn't easy – the thick tough black leather was distorted, all out of shape – but it was Pa's all right: his flask, crushed, pieces of silvered glass falling from the shattered sides as she lifted it. Underneath there was a brown wrapped parcel.

'I did look,' Mrs Moore said as Vi unfolded the paper. 'I knew he'd gone after work to fetch something he wanted to take to Cornwall with him.'

Broken to fragments but the parts recognisable was a small pull-along child's toy, a wooden horse painted black and white, the four small red wheels, though broken from the splintered stand, were the only things still whole. No fixing this . . . Then, as Ma began to sob, all three of them were in each other's arms, trying to comfort each other from the depths of their own particular misery.

'Monday March 8th 1943. Today Ma and I went to the hospital mortuary. I suppose I did have some hope until then. I thought he might have been knocked down and wandered away having lost his memory. But it was Pa, I suppose. No, I know it was Pa's body, but it was not the Pa I knew. This man had fought for his life – it showed – and his poor face was like his bag out of true.'

'Wednesday March 10th. Pa's funeral. I never knew he had so many friends, the church was full, the path to the church lined with men from the bus depot, even a woman who just used to travel on his bus came. She bought a bunch of violets. All passed in a kind of cold misery. I don't know how we all got through it, except we were all looking out for each other. Sid broke out into such great sobs at the graveside it startled us all – and when we came back here I saw without Ma having to say anything that she will not go back to Cornwall now.'

'March 11th. Ma and I decided we must attend the official enquiry into the disaster set up by Herbert Morrison, the Home Secretary.'

'March 17th – this was the last day. Eighty witnesses with Mr Dunne, one of the Magistrates of the Metropolitan Police Courts, in charge. Some witnesses said it was a woman with a child in her arms who fell first. Others said she was carrying a parcel, others that she had both. Mr Lawrence Rivers Dunne's conclusion was that, "This disaster was caused by a number of people losing their self-control at a particularly unfortunate place and time." I felt as if there was hysterical laughter going on in my brain to hear such words. He made it sound as if had there been "self-control and practical common sense" my pa would not have died. I felt he was blaming Pa! I thought I was taking care of Ma until that moment, but she took my hand and led me out.'

'A hundred and seventy-three people died, not from enemy action but from being crushed and suffocated by each other in our own Bethnal Green tube station.'

She sat staring at the words, again her mind rebelled, her stomach knotted and hot tears flooded over her cheeks. *I can't believe my pa has gone for ever.*

'Can't you fix it, Pa!' She tried to visualise him as he had always been and could not see his face. The only thing about him she could see clearly was his hands – good well-shaped hands, calloused by the steering wheel of the bus constantly running through them – working hands – never to touch her again. She could not imagine how Ma must feel – and Sid, poor boy. They had both hero-worshipped their father. She wiped her face, so many tears, too many soaked handkerchiefs.

She must go downstairs again, help make tea for all these people who kept coming to offer their condolences. She could not leave it all to Maggie, who, God knows, had trouble enough of her own. The door was knocked again as she went down the stairs.

She opened it wearily and for a moment did not recognise the tall figure that stood there. She stepped back automatically, inviting whoever it was in, only realising it was John's uncle as he stood in the hall.

'Hello, old thing,' he said gently, 'nice to see you.' He held his hands out and she automatically put hers into them. They enveloped her with the kind of caring she had known in John's touch. Didn't someone say the handshake revealed the man? He stooped and kissed her cheek. 'I am so sorry to hear about your father. Would your mother accept my condolences?'

She led the Commodore through to her Ma and brother. He stooped over Ma's hand and solemnly shook hands with Sid. 'Man of the family now, old boy,' he said to him and Sid raised his chin though his lip quivered.

'That's right, sir.'

'I don't want to intrude at this close family time but my news, I think, must not wait.' He looked at Vi. 'Sit down, m'dear. John is a prisoner of war. We've had confirmation today.'

Chapter 29

'My darling Vi,

I write this letter with a bit more hope that it *will* reach Blighty now that the Red Cross are getting letters *and parcels* through to us – some of the parcels have been a long time on the way! But some of the goodies are OK and some we're eating anyway.

Darling! Darling! Darling! A WHOLE BUNDLE of your letters has *just* been handed over to me. I know I should never have doubted that you would be writing – but it's a long time without news isn't it. This sudden arrival has knocked me for six and to catch the next collection I am now going to have to finish this letter quickly. I will begin my new letter immediately, in time for the next post, whenever that might be! Imagine me now about to indulge myself in your words! So many letters! Joy! Joy! Joy! There are gulls here, flying of course. All my love to you – with hopes this letter will reach you. Perhaps you haven't received any of my letters??? If not *you* may receive a bundle!

Until later, old thing, now I can't wait to get into your letters. Special regards to your pa, ma and Sid. In case post to Auntie Annie hasn't got through either let her know you've heard won't you!'

Yours for ever and ever with all the love in this crazy world.

John.'

It had been readdressed by Mrs Trewellan. Vi recognised the handwriting, so she guessed it would be Mrs Stevens, their invaluable postlady, who had had the good sense not to push it through into an empty farmhouse.

She pressed it to her lips, to her heart, then to her forehead and held it there, as if to let there be immediate answer to all that he had written – so he might know all the turmoil as she wondered if life had a predestined pattern, a cruel pattern, giving you this, taking away that – swings and roundabouts – malicious and merciful in turn. So much he did not know.

Even the letters delivered to Brierly Street that morning seemed designed to make her feel she was all wrong, in the wrong place, made her want to rush back to Cornwall when her mother's need for her – and her need for her mother – were still paramount.

The two other letters had come in one envelope from Audrey – one for Ma and one for herself. The letter to Ma had been full of sympathy, of her distress at the loss for all of them, and for herself – 'one more on my list.' The letter to Vi was full of regrets that at first she had not really taken in the news when Vi had cycled over, leaving again in a matter of minutes to prepare for the journey to London. Most of all she seemed to regret not being able to come to the funeral. 'I hadn't the fare or no one would have stopped me. I would have got away somehow. I'd still like to come.'

There was no mention of her husband contributing any money to the fare and 'I would have got away somehow'? She imagined Audrey writing the letters secretly, baby Noelle standing at her knee, big-eyed, gripping her skirt. They had certainly left Audrey isolated – at the mercy of an unpredictable man, to say the best of Paul Kerrow.

That evening Vi walked to the local telephone box and rang Mrs Trewellan. Her heart warmed to John's aunt as she exclaimed in delight, 'I recognised the handwriting, of course. Wasn't it wonderful just to see that!'

She told of the bundle of letters John had just received and they speculated whether they would receive stacks of back mail. 'Not that I care about that as long as we know he's alive and well.'

'He does sound himself, in spirits, though they've obviously not had enough to eat.'

'When are you travelling back?', Mrs Trewellan asked and, when Vi did not reply immediately, she added, 'Is there some problem?'

'My mother is determined to stay in London now.'

'I can understand that.' Her own yearning to return permanently to London showed. 'Jimmie says the bombing's eased – so what will you do?'

'John thinks I'm still in Cornwall and doesn't know about my father. While Audrey is . . .'

'Audrey is in need of help,' Mrs Trewellan said bluntly. 'She needs a friend badly I would say. I saw her shopping today – and there's beginning to be talk, according to Alice.'

'He's not striking her!' Vi interrupted.

There was a pause at the other end of the line. 'There are many other ways of being unkind. Mrs Stevens tutts and shakes her head whenever Kerrow's mentioned – but I just don't know. To be honest my dear, *I'm* certainly missing you and not just because the work is piling up. Early days to say this, but when you feel you can leave your mother I'd be delighted for you to live-in. I could make you very comfortable with your own bedroom and sitting room. You know we have plenty of room.'

'I couldn't leave yet, but if the work's too much I'm sure Audrey would be able to help. You know we worked in the same accountants' office. She'd know the systems I've set up. She'd be glad to earn a little.'

Mrs Trewellan hesitated. 'I could ask, and Alice could look after the little one for an hour or two.'

'It would get Audrey out of the house for a bit and that can help, can't it?' She wondered how Alice would like minding a toddler, half Cockney.

When she returned to the house, she found Ma with Audrey's letters still open on the table. Beside it was her handbag. 'You know the bus depot had a collection for Pa, I could send Audrey's train fare.'

They both sat looking at the letters, knowing that Harold Tulley would have approved of some of his memorial money being used that way. Then, as they sat on, Vi told her that she had suggested Mrs Trewellan might employ Audrey for a few hours each week. And then perhaps it was because their thoughts ever turned back to her father she went on to tell of her encounter with Paul, the horse and the furniture.

'Harold wouldn't 'ave liked that!' Ma said emphatically. 'Anyone who ill-treated a horse was lower than the low in his eyes.'

'I'd like to think Audrey had some money in her purse – she always liked to have her own money, just . . .' She did not expand on the thought, didn't need to.

'We mustn't interfere between man and wife though.' Ma shook her head, convinced this would be wrong, yet she was fingering a large, white five-pound note she had extracted from an envelope in her handbag.

'I think that's a bit old-fashioned these days! We got Avis away from her husband!'

Flo thought about this. 'You've got to remember you may be going back to live there.'

'I certainly won't be afraid of Paul Kerrow – not now. I've faced him out once. He knows what Sid found. I can go straight to his boss or his boss's landlady. There's no way he dare step too far out of line.'

'But you can't live at the farm by yourself – you couldn't do that. I wouldn't want you there by yourself.'

'John's aunt offered to put me up at the Lodge.'

Ma nodded her solemn approval. 'Sid tells me you promised John to stay at Trewellan, to be there when he comes back.'

'Sid!' she exclaimed, but more gently than she used.

'He worries about people,' Ma defended.

'Like you then.' She glanced at the fading evening light. 'Shouldn't he be in by now?'

'He's gone round to see one of his old mates. I thought he'd fret for that horse more than anything, but he's never said a word.'

'He knows you want to stay home.'

'I should never have left.'

'We didn't have much choice when . . .' Vi began but could not continue and they both dissolved into tears. She wondered how long it would be before they could think of Pa without crying or having to fight back the tears. Years and years, she imagined, perhaps never.

'Oh dear,' Ma sobbed.

'It'll pass, won't it, Ma?' She was unsure herself whether it was question or reassurance.

'They say everything does.' Ma pushed the five-pound note and some silver across to Vi. 'Will you get a postal order. We'll send it to Audrey anyway, then she'll always have her fare and a bit over if she ever needs it.'

'We'll send it care of the Lodge,' Vi decided.

In the next few weeks there was no more news, no more letters. Ma began to put her home to rights, cleaning and polishing, burnishing the range and the brasses. It seemed to Vi that the cleaning was going on too long. Then one day when she returned from shopping and meeting Sid from school – much to his complete disgust – she found her pressing Pa's shirts.

'I can't bear to see them like this. I have to do something, keep busy.' She renewed the pressure of the iron even harder, bending close to make sure there was not the tiniest crease left in the thick working shirts.

'Mrs Moore needs help in the shop,' Sid put in, his voice carrying that over-anxious note that these days usually came before tears. 'She's at 'er wits' end, she ses.'

'Me too,' Ma said suddenly, sitting down, the hot iron still in her hand. Vi rushed forward and took it from her before she did herself any harm.

'You don't need to fetch me from school,' Sid told her accusingly and the unspoken criticism was that she should not have left Ma alone. 'Out of the mouths of babes and infants,' Pa might have said.

Vi had finished rubbing over the shirts so that Ma could lovingly fold them before they were put away – well away Vi planned – when there was a knock on the front door. Vi looked at Sid who was holding an old copy of the *Beano* comic half over his face but was well aware of every move the other two made.

That it was someone he knew was quickly obvious by his shouts for them to come, but before they could move he was back carrying a young child. They both gasped. 'Noelle!' Then Vi dived passed into the hallway. 'Audrey!'

'Audrey!'

The figure still on the doorstep looked defensive, unsure, a refugee burdened down, bags in both hands, a shoulder-bag strap across her chest. Vi wondered how she had managed Noelle as well. 'Come in! Come in!' Taking the bags she pulled her friend inside, kissed her cheek and realised there was something different about her.

'Come and sit down. You both look all in.' Ma swept the shirts from Pa's old chair to the table, took the baby into her arms and ordered Sid to put the kettle on.

Vi was overwhelmed to see her friend. Somehow, her walking into their Brierly Street home contracted time back to their days as schoolgirls, as, unencumbered, they had a proper hug. But Audrey had never looked older than she did now. She could, Vi thought with some alarm, be a middle-aged woman. Then she realised what was so different. 'You've had your hair cut.'

Audrey seemed to freeze under her hands. Alarmed, Vi put her at arms' length to see what had caused the change, study her face. 'Paul did it,' she said.

'Paul?'

Ma gestured with her head to the easy chair. 'She's all in.'

'Yes, I know how those mums felt when we were evacuated, remember?'

They nodded and waited, Ma pulling little Noelle's arms gently from her coat. 'Do you want a drink of milk, m'luv?'

When they were sipping tea and Noelle was asleep on the chair by the attendant Sid, Audrey said, 'It was my hair that was the last straw, I suppose. Before that I really did try to please him, but . . .' She shook her head having to grit her teeth momentarily before she could go on.

'He's never struck me. Grabbed me 'ard a time or two. But he's thrown all the furniture out once or twice and let my washing line down into the dirt. Just because, well, I was looking after baby instead of 'im I think. Of all people it was Cyril Spurrier who brought this on.' She thrust a hand up through the uneven spikes of her hair. 'He came to the cottage to see Paul about some beasts coming from market and he said that you didn't see many women with hair my colour.

'So Paul cut if off when he'd gone, held me down and hacked it off.' She paused her eyes hard, bitter, as she relived the experience. 'Said he wasn't having any man looking at his wife. Then later, when I was putting Noelle to bed, the sun caught a glint of gold in her hair and I wondered if she would have hair my colour, wondered what would happen when she was growing up. I knew then I was going to leave. I was so wrong to marry him. I know now – now it's too late.'

'You're not going back,' Vi stated.

'I wondered if you'd have me back until I can find somewhere?'

'We'll 'ave you back, never mind the rest,' Ma said.

Audrey sank back into the chair, closing her eyes like one who has had an enormous weight lifted from her shoulders. 'With the baby . . . I mean . . . it's a lot for anyone to do, and you're not family.'

'I can be Noelle's uncle,' Sid suggested.

'That's about the smartest thing you've ever said,' Vi told him smiling to reassure him it was a serious not sarcastic comment.

'You don't think he'll follow you.' Ma expressed a sudden anxious thought.

'Does he know where we live?' Vi was startled into asking.

'Nah! He wouldn't come anyway,' Audrey said with a flash of her old self. 'He'd turn into a bleedin' pumpkin if he ever left Cornwall!'

Their laughter was like a blessing to the sad household, just as the little girl was to be to Ma. The sick, constant cleaning stopped as the two took to each other.

Audrey did not take any of their kindness for granted. 'Didn't know which side my bread was buttered until too late,' she stated emphatically. Then, as she saw how little Noelle and Ma got on, her little daughter holding Flo's apron end and carrying a piece of cloth, or the little brush from the hearth, she was quick to accept Mrs Moore's offer of a job in the newly renovated shop. The living part of the property would take longer to repair, but it was being put under way as fast as the War Damage Commission would pay out compensation. Meantime, Mrs Moore had insisted on having a bed in the front room, leaving the main bedroom free for Ma and Vi. Audrey and the baby took Vi's old room and Sid went to the boxroom.

Even in their bereavement, Vi began to see there was a new routine being established – a routine she was beginning to realise did not really need her.

One afternoon, she rather reluctantly agreed to go for a walk in Victoria Park. Ma had recently acquired a pushchair for Noelle from a neighbour, so walking out further was now possible. All the familiar images plagued her and soon they came to the spot where she had parted with John. *Don't look back.* She could hear his voice, and there across the bridge, near the red pavilion, Pa had stood waiting for her. Without conscious thought, she said 'It's time I went back to Trewellan.'

'Yes,' Ma agreed immediately. 'I knew you had it on your mind. I'll be all right now with Sid and this little one to help with.'

Vi swallowed hard, thinking, but not saying, that it gave Ma a role, just like John's aunt, a purpose in life, a useful purpose. Another of life's fairground rides which only make sense in retrospect.

The next morning, as she made plans to leave, a uniformed messenger came from John's uncle asking her to join him at dinner the next evening. He would send a car at seven. 'So are you from the Hyde Park Hotel?' she asked the boy. He nodded and as she hesitated between delaying her return to Cornwall and seeing John's uncle, she suddenly realised he could have news of John and wrote a note of acceptance.

She was shown into a private room when she arrived at the Hyde Park Hotel. The whole place it seemed to her shouted 'discretion and good taste'.

James rose to meet her from a window seat and they shook hands solemnly. Somehow his manner was a little different today. He had a slight headmaster-like air, making her feel not exactly that she had done wrong but that she was not so much approved of today.

His first words after the greetings and enquiries revealed the truth of this.

'Old Annie is getting a bit agitated. I've had her on the telephone almost every night since your friend jumped ship.'

'I planned to go back to Trewellan today but when your note came . . .' she said stiffly, feeling a sense of acute disappointment. So it was not about John.

'Ah! Glad you told me, old thing. Now we can enjoy our dinner.'

'You mean you're not going to tell me off!' She couldn't quite let this go without comment. 'I should not be going to Cornwall at all if I thought for one moment my mother still needed me.'

He looked across the table they had been escorted to and raised his hands as if in surrender. 'Put in my place.'

She waited while he consented to the meal the hotel offered of vegetable soup followed by turkey, then a rhubarb cobbler with cream. It raised a lot of questions in Vi's mind about what rationing meant to some people.

'I thought you'd asked me to come because you had news of John.'

'Ah!' He tutted at her disappointment. 'You'll have had no more news of him, I guess, no more letters? No. Very confused situation.' He finished the last of his soup. 'Not at all bad.'

'The war's confusing, but . . .' She regarded him keenly. There was something in the way he had said the three words that made her believe he had more he could tell. 'Where in particular?'

He waited as their main course was served, then once they were alone again, he said, 'John is a prisoner of war in Italy.'

'Italy! I thought – I imagined he'd be taken to Germany.'

'That might have been worse, according to the few reports we are getting from men that have escaped. The Germans are what you would see as a united force. Italy is a very divided country. The royalist High Command officers were not consulted when the country entered the war on the Fascist side in 1940 and the people, I believe, have no will to fight. Mussolini is unpopular and many prefer King Victor Emmanuel to Il Duce.' He paused and leaned across the table. 'We are about to go on the offensive. Anything can happen!'

'And John?'

'He's a resourceful chap, he'll take any chances that come his way. But I'm not going to make wild guesses, that would do neither of us any good at all.' He wiped his mouth on his napkin and laid it down thoughtfully. 'Look, old thing, the best for us all, Annie in particular, is if you would go back and help, learn a lot about running our house, our way of life, our business interests, think about the Manor House and about making it shipshape again when it's derequisitioned. There's a lot to busy yourself with and it'll free my telephone quite a lot if Annie keeps off it!'

The Commodore sent her home in a car and ordered one to pick her up to take her all the way to Paddington station the next morning. 'I'll try and rustle up something nice for you to take to Annie for me, nothing big – some books probably.'

He held on to her hand as they parted. 'You remind me so much of my girl when she was your age – not in looks of course, but spirit.' She smiled at him. It would be fulsome, she thought, to say how much like John she thought him. He had also said all the same things Pa had told her – so he must definitely be right!

There were two parcels in the car the next morning – obviously books – one with her name on it.

It was not easy saying goodbye. Sid had for once won and not gone to school and it was his request for her to give Major a big pat for him that brought tears. They had all born up well until then. They stood outside to wave her off and she turned and looked at the close group through the back window of the cab. It took her until Paddington to regain some kind of control.

'Never mind, luv,' the driver said as he helped her unload cases and bags and parcels, 'they say worse 'appens at sea.'

On the train she opened her parcel of books. There was a new Raymond Chandler thriller, *Farewell My Lovely*, a *Golden Treasury of English Verse* and *Ornaments for Homes of Taste* which made her raise her eyebrows. There was a note. 'Save the thriller for me to read when I come down. J. M. T.' His initials, she thought, were the same as John's.

Almost in spite of herself, the book that fascinated her most was that containing the ideas for enhancing the beauty of large and gracious mansions. It was more the pictures of the rooms themselves, the furniture and the way it was grouped she found intriguing, than the actual subject matter of the book. She had a lot to learn – and perhaps they had a lot to learn from her too. There was some real snobbish humbug, some 'valued antiquities' which were so ugly she could never imagine them ornamenting anywhere.

She had not really given thought to her arrival, but when she alighted at Penzance she felt a certain 'homecoming' quality, as not only did the porter give her a welcoming salute and a cheery, 'Hello again, m'andsome!' but Sam was there with the trap.

'Good to see you back, Miss. My Alice ses they need you at the Lodge.'

'Nice to see *you* Sam. You keeping all right? Can't see your Alice saying that though.'

'Well . . .' Grinning, self-conscious, he rolled the word around his Cornish tongue. 'She said someone – needs *someone* – *I* reckon that's you.'

They travelled to the Lodge in good-humoured exchanges of sympathy and information. 'It's a bugger this war,' was his comment after hearing how her father had died. For her it somehow took away the raw edge talking to this sympathetic old man, to his back, dabbing her eyes discreetly. She knew there would be others she would need to tell.

255

Neither Sam nor John's uncle had exaggerated Mrs Trewellan's need for help. Not only was the desk piled high with unopened letters and irate anxious notes from tenants about leaky roofs and fences damaged by the army, Annie herself looked in need of attention. Vi wondered if she was drinking. She had that air of vague dishevelment she had seen on women in the East End as circumstances became intolerable and they began to neglect their homes and families in favour of the gin or stout.

The one thing that had most certainty been attended to was her rooms. Mrs Trewellan had allotted her a first-floor bedroom, bathroom and sitting room overlooking the back garden. There was a desk with a clean blotter, ink and pens under the window. 'I thought you could write your diaries there.'

She had quite forgotten she had told John's aunt about those. 'I'll have to go to the farm and collect them – and close it down I suppose.'

'There's no hurry.' Mrs. Trewellan idly realigned the pens on their rest. 'Did Jimmie tell you what he believes?'

'He said he felt John would take advantage of any chances that came his way.'

'He thinks we've not heard again because John may have already escaped.'

'Why should he think that!' Vi demanded. There had seemed a certain 'safeness' in the idea of John being locked away from the war.

'Other people with men in the same regiment, engaged in the same actions in Greece and Crete, are still hearing from their POWs.'

'I didn't realise he mean't escaping.' Vi was startled, thinking aloud rather than conversing. 'Is that good? Perhaps something else . . . I mean. No I don't know what I mean. Do they shoot men who escape?'

'I think if they are not in uniform they leave themselves open to being . . .' Mrs Trewellan broke off and sat down suddenly in the basket chair by Vi's bed. 'I'm so weary of it all.'

But Vi was still thinking of John on the loose behind enemy lines. A bit of a pirate, she remembered someone calling him that, so he probably would escape given half a chance. His uncle was probably right.

He had been right about his wife. The sight of her now slumped so inelegantly in the chair reminded her of the parcel of books. She tore it open like a child, Vi thought, a rather spoilt child. 'Oh, bless him! Books about the theatre and some critiques of old theatre stars! I may be in one of those!' she exclaimed, her spirits and good humour refreshed by her beloved theatre. Rather shyly, Vi showed her books. 'He's a good man, and John's like him. I just wish we had them both here!'

'Me too, but . . .' she nearly added that she wished her father was alive again but knew she was much too tired to fight the trauma of voicing that. 'Your husband said there may be an offensive soon.'

Chapter 30

In September the news of the Allies invasion of Italy came and it was soon rumoured than many Italian soldiers were simply going home. Some fought with German units in the North but it seemed the whole Italian army was very poorly equipped. Vi wondered if the current joke about Italian tanks being the only ones in the world with reverse gears was either true or justified. Not everyone, she realised, had the glimpse of understanding into the background of Italian affairs that James Trewellan had given her.

Vi found escape in the work she and Mrs Trewellan now shared jointly, John's aunt including her in any visits they had to make to tenants. She was becoming better known, in the district, introduced as John's friend, leaving conclusions to others. It made her feel at once more confident yet still her own woman. She was also lonely, missing the company of people her own age and desperately missing John in this part of the world he so loved. One letter, then nothing more – the lack of news began to feel ever more ominous.

She and his aunt seemed to talk of him less, though every time the telephone rang, or a telegram boy was seen – or even Mrs. Stevens cycling dutifully on her rounds – they automatically both held pause to hope – or fear. Vi felt Annie Trewellan was losing heart and interest in the Cornish end of the family affairs. She supposed she could understand this. If John did not come back, then she had wasted a lot of her life living and working in the country when her heart was in London. And if he did come back then he would take over – perhaps with a new wife. It felt a presumptuous dream!

That autumn had many glorious days and it was Alice who on seeing Vi transfixed by the sight of telegraph boy cycling past the end of the drive, surprisingly advised her in a sympathetic manner to, 'Go walk on a beach, look at the sea. It helps. Cuts us and our problems down to size.'

Vi reflected she might a short time ago have suspected Alice's motive but now she accepted it as a breakthrough in their relationship and did as suggested.

She began by cycling up to the farmhouse at Gerrard's Head, leaving the bike there and walking over the cliff paths and the beaches. She found it so true, one's mind was freer outdoors, could soar and plummet more freely, more in keeping with the moods of the sea, the sun, the wind. The yearning was easier to indulge alone, out of doors.

For a time she had been uneasy about encountering Paul, but it was rumoured he had left the district, even left with his wife she had been told by Alice. Vi shared the truth only with Doris and it was Doris who learned the truth of Paul's absence.

After Audrey had left, Paul had disappeared for a time, everything was neglected. Then Cyril Spurrier had found him just lazing about. The butcher had shouted at him and shook his fist. Paul had picked up a length of wood and threatened him. Spurrier had sacked him and registered a new man as his employee. Not long after this Paul was arrested as a draft dodger. Then Doris said there had then been a series of police searches for illegal slaughterhouses but nothing had been found. 'Some villains,' Vi concluded, 'are clever than others.'

She went to the farmhouse which still contained many of their things. Upstairs she carefully unpinned all Sid's maps and sent them to him at his request. Also, a few parcels of clothes. Many of Miss Swanton's that they had not used before were now being transformed into stylish coats and bonnets for Noelle.

The campaign in Italy dragged endlessly on and it was not until June 4th 1944 that US General Mark Clark entered Rome after a bitter struggle while the battle for the rest of Italy went on. That same month news came of a new weapon Hitler was using as pilotless flying bombs began to bring a new terror to London. Vi wrote urgently for them to all come back to the farm, but it was to no use.

'We're sticking it out now,' Ma replied. Then with D Day on June 6th 1944 the country's hopes surged upwards and all Vi could think of was that they should have had news of John by now.

At the Lodge they listened to the excited tones of the BBC announcer, then the field reports of newsmen who had landed with the troops. Annie tried to contact her husband but was told he was not available. For days there seemed to be a kind of communication blackout. Their news came like everyone else's from the wireless. The second front had begun, the Allies were truly on the offensive. And where was John?

The news was electrifying, unsettling, and never had her personal anxieties reached such a pitch. She soon felt all she wanted to do was get away, away from the Lodge kitchen where she, Alice and Mrs Trewellan had been poring over the wireless for every news bulletin because the reception was better there.

She pedalled away from the house to the farm, then walked furiously as far as The Soldier's Field on the top path, then crashed recklessly down to the beach, walking on and on towards Gerrard's Head, to that black looking pirates' hide out of a pub, where Audrey had heard news of Noel's death.

When she reached the point she had finally exhausted herself striding out over the soft sands, deliberately making it hard for herself. She perched on the rocks just watching the sea rolling ever in, breakers crashing over the rocks not much further out. It was rougher than she had thought and now she had stopped she realised how loud the breakers were and how high. The tide had turned. She should walk back. Instead she lingered, remembering a girl who had become pregnant at School and had thrown herself into the Thames from Westminster Bridge. She wondered what it was like to drown, but that would be pretty stupid when the war was on the turn, when still – she felt too mind weary to hope any more that day . . .

Wearily she began to walk back. The sun began to set behind her casting her shadow long before her. Then she had a sudden extra pang of worry as she noticed quite a number of the large herring gulls on the beach in front of her, seeming to graze in the shallow water, their reflections mirror images so they looked doubly locked to earth. 'Why aren't you flying you stupid birds?' she exclaimed and ran at them until they took off in the air, screaming and protesting. As she walked on they landed again behind her. She went back and frightened them again. 'Keep flying. Keep flying! I love him, I love him, you have to understand.'

It was the birds that gave up, flying high over her head, seeming to circle, looking down at the strange being who would not let them land before sweeping up over the cliffs.

She decided she was too exhausted now to climb up the steep path to The Soldier's Field. She'd go instead to the gentler farmhouse path, though this was the one she and Pa had climbed together to find Mrs Trewellan at the top with the news of John being missing.

She walked back so slowly now, wandering back to the lip of the sea, lingering, a pretty unbroken shell catching her eye but she was not moved to pick it up, merely watching the water wash gently up and over its minute serrated mound. Then, turning away, someone on the top of the cliff caught her eye. Local people often walked their dogs on fine evenings. This man was tall and began to wave – and wave. There was something familiar about him. For a moment she thought it was the Commodore. He wasn't due to come from London? Was there news? Then the man came to the edge of the steep path and she knew it was not James for this man hurtled down the path with abandon, waving and shouting.

Before she realised it, she was running towards him, the feeling of disbelief and joy mounting in her so she felt she could fly if only her legs would go a little faster. 'John!' she shouted to the wind like a long lingering cry. 'John!'

They ran with arms spread wide. They ran and held each other, their eyes

259

closed, crying and laughing and disbelieving until they must take time to really look at each other, to see each other properly for the first time.

Through her tears she saw a man who had suffered deprivation, so thin, so gaunt. But John was grinning. 'I couldn't get through. There's an invasion and some kind of communication blackout.'

'Oh!' She could not express aloud how she felt, could only hear Sid's words, 'He's come! He's come! The soldier's come!'

Hot tears came flooding over her cheeks and she found herself mildly beating on his chest. 'Where have you been? Where have you been?'

'In hiding – in Turkey – waiting for a boat – God knows – everywhere!' He caught her hands and held them. They were very still then, looking at each other, feasting each in the sight of the other.

'But I'm home now,' he said and folded her gently close as if never to release her. 'Now I'm home.'

Chapter 31

It was a golden autumn day, the 20th day of October 1945, when Vi sat before her mirror at the Lodge as Alice helped adjust her bridal headdress. Their eyes met in the mirror. 'I was here the night Mr John was born.'

'I know, he told me,' Vi answered gently, 'and I hope you'll be here when his children are born.'

Alice looked for a moment as if she was going to either cry or say thank you but instead gave a brusque nod and readjusted a pearly leaf on the half coronet. Only then did she think it proper that the bride's mother be admitted to the bedroom.

Vi sat looking at herself in the mirror. She did not feel like her reflection that was for sure. The young woman she saw was beautiful, like a plate from a glossy magazine of Society brides. Through the mirror she saw the door open and Ma come and stand equally awestruck just behind her. Neither had to say the words that were uppermost in their minds.

'He'd have been proud, that proud.'

'And you, Ma?'

'It all frightens me to death, but no one's going to guess!'

'Wish me well, Ma?' she asked. It was the closest she could come to asking for a blessing.

A hand fell on her shoulder, lightly so as not to disturb the heavy white satin with its embroidered pearls. 'I wish you all the luck in the world.'

'And keep your Cockney chin up no matter what!' another voice said from the doorway.

'Audrey! What do you think then?' She stood and fanned the train behind herself.

'It's wonderful. Beyond even my wildest dreams!'

There was another tap on the door and Mrs Trewellan came in, resplendent, one might have said theatrically so, in pale blue suit and soft grey fox-fur stole and hat, with plume of blue feathers. She was carrying a small box. 'I thought it was the ladies who had the vapours on their wedding day!' she exclaimed. 'John, has been driving his best man, his uncle and all around frantic because this hadn't arrived.'

She gave Vi the box. 'He wants you to wear it. It's been specially made to go with your wedding dress.'

This jewel box was long and new and every eye was on her as she opened it. Inside was a pendant made from irridescent mother-of-pearl in the form of a flying gull. From the wings to the gold neckchain was a tracery of delicate pearls graded to the finest seed. Everyone exclaimed. It was beautiful. Amazingly so because the jeweller had caught the bird as if in true flight, the tiny thing looked as if it had life.

Vi was too moved to speak. She handed it to her mother and sat down again while it was put around her neck and fastened.

'Seagull summers,' John's aunt murmured, 'it's what we used to say when we came down to Trewellan for the long school holidays. But we must go, m'dear. Jimmie will be here any moment and we must all be in church long before that. Where's your brother?'

There was some consternation as Sid could not be found. Ma and John's aunt had gone in search when Audrey and Vi heard Alice's voice raised outside the window.

'Mr Sid! Mr Sid! Come on now, everyone's waiting!'

'Mr Sid!' Audrey repeated, covering her mouth to smother the laughter.

'That's one for the book! You always did want him called Mr Sid in 'is pram,' Vi said.

'In Viccy Park! Remember, when we tipped him out!'

In the church the organ played softly as Vi arrived on Commodore James Trewellan's arm, while outside the crowd gasped and clapped their appreciation of the splendour of the wonderfully renovated Trewellan gown, the dark navy and gold of the Commodore's uniform a perfect foil.

Vi caught glimpses of familiar faces, Doris and her Derrick returned from the Navy, tenants from farms. Then there was time for no more for as she reached the porch, Jimmie patted her arm and asked quickly, 'All right, old thing? Ready for the launching! Off we go!'

The wedding march thundered, the congregation rose in an upward surge and rustle of expectation. She could see John's head, his dark wing of hair above the mass of people, then she saw his dark blue and gold officer's uniform as he stepped to the centre of the chancel.

There was a radiance about the morning that had nothing to do with sunlight through stained glass but more with the held breaths and the concentrated attention of all present as they watched the two come together.

John held out his hand – though at that moment he should not have done – and as she released the Commodore's arm she took it. It was the heart at the centre of the ceremony, the moment many would always remember. It was the fulfillment of the wish to do so when Vi had first seen him in the kitchen of the Lodge several lost lifetimes ago.

You have been reading a novel published by Piatkus Books. We hope you have enjoyed it and that you would like to read more of our titles. Please ask for them in your local library or bookshop.

If you would like to be put on our mailing list to receive details of new publications, please send a large stamped addressed envelope (UK only) to:

Piatkus Books: 5 Windmill Street
London W1P 1HF

PIATKUS

The sign of a good book